CYBERSP@CE

I0618868

A Novel by

Jeff W. Horton

World Castle Publishing

Jeff W. Horton

Cybersp@ce

World Castle Publishing
Pensacola, Florida

Copyright © Jeff W. Horton 2013
ISBN: 9781938961571
First Edition World Castle Publishing January 1, 2013
http://www.worldcastlepublishing.com

Licensing Notes

Cover: Select-O-Grafix. LLC
Editor: Maxine Bringenberg

Prologue

July 2, 1947-Corona, New Mexico

It was the storm that would forever change the course of human destiny.

A small, curly-haired boy sat frozen in anticipation, watching it from the edge of an old, olive-colored chair. From his seat in front of a large living room window, he peered out into the night, gazing in awe at the fierce, frequent displays of lightning which appeared in stark contrast to the blackness of the dark, western night. Many of the vengeful flashes reached for the ground, while other multi-forked lightning bolts stretched across the sinister sky as far as the eye could see. Henry's parents had long ago abandoned any hope of keeping the curious boy away from the window completely during such storms, so they had struck a compromise...the six-year old would sit in a chair well away from the window, yet close enough that he still maintained a commanding view.

While Henry took in the fabulous fireworks that lit up the night sky outside their home, his parents went about their daily routine, seemingly oblivious to the commotion outside. His father sat back in his recliner and quietly read *War of the Worlds*, while his mother busily worked to finish a sweater she'd been knitting for over a month.

"Wow!" Henry yelled out, pointing towards the window. "That one had like five forks—it was huge!" The boy's eyes lit up, wide with wonder as a thunderous boom reverberated throughout the house. Jake Summers looked at his son and smiled, fondly remembering a time when, many years earlier, he had been the little boy sitting by the window, wondering at the awesome, raw power of nature on display.

The flashes of lightning and the booming thunder continued to intensify as Henry watched the ferocious storm come closer and closer. Two hundred yards away from the house, several trees stood on top of a tall hill. The boy watched closely in anticipation, expecting that the lightning would at any moment strike one of them.

That's when he first saw it; an object, illuminated by the abundant lightning that surrounded it, was floating quietly above the tree line. In the brief seconds during which it was visible, the object had appeared to be a round, metallic craft of some sort. The lightning quickly disappeared however, immediately plunging the sky back into darkness so that he could not be certain what he had seen. He continued looking toward the tree line, hoping to catch another glimpse of the object during the next flash of lightning.

Suddenly, there was another huge flash of light, except this time it wasn't lightning. A loud noise that sounded like a small explosion soon followed the flash. Everyone in the house had heard it, and Jake Summers wasted no time getting to the window, followed closely by his wife. By the time he arrived next to little Henry, however, the darkness had once more enveloped everything.

"Henry, what happened? Did you see anything?"

"Yes, sir! I was watching, waiting to see if the lightning would strike any of the trees on that hill over there, when the lightning lit up the sky all around, and I saw something over the tops of the trees. I was trying to see it better when lightning struck again and hit it! I was—"

A second, much louder explosion suddenly reverberated through the night, interrupting Henry's recounting and violently shaking the house.

"Henry, listen to me, this is important. This 'object' you saw, was it an airplane? If it was, that sound we heard just now could have been the plane crashing; somebody could have been hurt! Was it an airplane, son?"

"No—maybe—I'm not sure, Dad. Whatever it was, it was big, really, really, big! It didn't really look like an airplane though; it looked more like one of those flying saucer things the guy in the newspaper said he saw last week."

"Okay, son, thank you." Jake then turned to his wife. "I've got to go see if anyone's hurt, sweetheart, in case it was a plane. I should be back in a little while."

"Please don't go out there, Jake!" his wife pleaded. "That's a terrible storm out there tonight, one of the worst we've had in years!"

Jake stood next to the window for several moments and looked out, saying nothing for several minutes.

"Look out there now, can you see?" he asked finally. "The storm's already passed over us." Another flash of lightning flashed in the distance, followed several seconds later by distant thunder. "Well, almost. Listen, Liz, I'll be fine. If anyone survived the crash, we need to try to help them."

Elizabeth Summers looked out the window and listened for several moments before replying. "Okay, Jake, I think you might be right. It sounds like the storm's nearly passed."

Jake picked up his keys and walked towards the door with little Henry following close behind.

"Take me with you, Daddy, please! I've never seen an airplane up close before, please!"

"No, Henry. If a plane *has* crashed and people are badly hurt, I don't want you to see it, you're too young."

"Please, Daddy, please!" Jake and Elizabeth exchanged glances, knowing that Jake was right; they had no idea what to expect out there. Yet, the boy was getting older and Jake might need his help. Besides, he wanted to try to find a way to appease the boy's excitement.

"Tell you what, Henry, why don't you and your mother both come with me? If someone is injured out there, maybe her training as a nurse will come in handy. But I insist that, regardless of what we find, *you* stay put in the truck and do exactly what we tell you. Can you do that, Henry?"

"Yes, sir, I will, I promise!" Henry turned to his mother, preparing his most pitiful, pleading face, the one with the really sad eyes. "Can we go Mommy, please?" She looked at her husband with a grimace before looking back at Henry. She let out a sigh and smiled.

"Yeah, okay, Henry. It looks like the lightning's stopped completely now. Let's go check it out. Remember though, you must stay in the truck like your father said, and you will do *exactly* as we tell you, no complaining or whining, understood?"

"Yes, ma'am!" answered Henry, already bouncing toward the door.

The small family had a difficult time finding the spot where the craft had crashed to the Earth. They drove all around the hill with the trees, but it was still dark out, and the rain made visibility poor. They circled the area several times and were about to give up their search when they suddenly spotted a series of flashing, multi-colored lights in the distance, coming from behind another hill. The location was several miles from where Henry had seen something just before it was struck by lightning.

The rain gradually eased up as they made their way toward the lights, the object slowly came into view. Two things soon became evident to Jake Summers. First, whatever the thing was that had crashed near his home, it was enormous, much larger than he had expected. He had thought Henry might be exaggerating, but he could now see that his son had not told the half of it. Second, the craft was definitely *not* an airplane, but more like what Henry had described; similar to one of the flying saucers he had recently read about in the newspaper.

Jake decided to try to find a better vantage point, and to look for survivors. He suspected that the craft could be an experimental military aircraft of some sort. After a few minutes, they finally arrived at a spot that overlooked the large field where the craft had crashed. Jake drove to the edge of the field where they could get the best view. All three of them sat there, speechless. They were surprised to see that not one craft, but two, had crashed in the large field. The larger craft, the one they had seen first, appeared to be out of commission, but still mostly intact. The second, smaller craft had sustained heavy damage and now lay in many pieces. Before them, spread out over the landscape as far as the eye could see, was metallic-looking wreckage. A large section of the smaller, badly damaged craft lay intact in the field a hundred yards from them. Brush was burning in orange flames all around the crash site. About that time the clouds began to part and a full moon revealed itself, bathing the entire scene with enough light that they could now clearly see the reflective, metallic substance which was strewn all over the field.

"We've got to get back to the house and call the army base in Roswell," Jake said, pointing to something on the ground close by. Henry looked down, following his father's finger until he saw it. His eyes widened when he saw, less than twenty-five yards from them, what appeared to be a small child lying lifeless on the ground. What disturbed him the most, however, was the fact that once he'd drawn closer to it, he could clearly see that it wasn't a child after all; nor was it human.

Chapter 1

"The only thing we have to fear is fear itself—nameless, unreasoning, unjustified terror which paralyzes...."
Franklin D. Roosevelt's First Inaugural Address

Present Day-Fort Meade, Maryland

"This is a special Cox News Alert. If you are just now joining us this morning, we have some important, late-breaking news this hour. Last night, Cox News learned from an anonymous source within the U.S. Cyber Command in Fort Meade, Maryland, that two major cyber attacks took place yesterday against the United States. Less than one hour ago, we contacted Cyber Command and they were able to confirm for Cox News that two attacks did indeed occur, although officials there refused to elaborate. Both cyber attacks are strongly suspected to have been state-sponsored attacks.

"According to the source, one of yesterday's assaults was launched against a specific group of computers at the United States Department of Defense. The DOD attack specifically targeted an electronic listing that contained the location of all intercontinental ballistic missile launch sites situated across the United States, along with a listing of all United States Navy ships that regularly carry nuclear armaments. This incursion has already been described by some as the worst breach of military security since the Cold War.

"In the second attack, which occurred at exactly the same time as the first, the attackers broke into a computer system at the U.S. Department of Energy and stole detailed data, plans, and schematics for the facilities and the computer systems at no fewer than fifty nuclear power plants scattered across the country. That means the intruders now have detailed information on nearly half of the hundred or so nuclear power plants built across the United States from Seattle to Florida. With the data they stole, the people or entity responsible for the attack could conceivably shut down nuclear power plants, damage systems, or trigger false alarms. It's remotely possible that they could even cause some or all of the reactors in a plant to melt down.

"While Cyber Command refused to provide any specifics about the attacks, our source told us that yesterday's cyber attacks against the Department of Defense and the Department of Energy were later traced back to locations inside of the People's Republic of China. While the Chinese government vehemently denies having anything to do with yesterday's attacks and offers to do what it can to help bring the perpetrators to justice, it seems clear to everyone at Cyber Command that these are only empty assurances.

"Indeed, yesterday's cyber attacks will be added to a long list of successful incursions against government and civilian agencies within the United States over the last decade that have been attributed to the Chinese. Recent cyber attacks have become increasingly effective, however, and sources within the intelligence community as well as the military have now become very concerned about the possible theft of top secret data on subjects ranging from advanced weapons technologies and military battle plans, to data on the civilian power grid, water systems, and transportation systems.

"To add to the growing concern over yesterday's attacks, there has been a persistent rumor circulating around the Internet for the last few months, a warning to the United States that China's agency for cyber warfare, the Online Blue Army, has been using cyber warfare to steal sensitive, U.S. military data for quite some time. The warning suggests that the theft of military data is in preparation for a massive, preemptive strike against the United States by the Chinese. The Online Blue Army has allegedly been seeking data related to American high tech, cutting-edge weapons technology, like the futuristic rail-gun and a variety of particle beam weapons.

"According to the warning, the Online Blue Army recently began gathering intelligence on the U.S. civilian infrastructure as well, intel that could be used to cripple the U.S. civilian infrastructure. By doing so, the Online Blue Army allegedly believes it would make winning an all out war against America a much simpler task. When asked to speculate about whether the Chinese could actually be preparing to launch such a preemptive strike against the United States as part of an all-out military campaign, two of the analysts we talked to told us that while it might make sense for the Chinese to prepare such a plan, it seems very unlikely that they would ever implement it. The two military analysts pointed out that the economic ties between the United States and the People's Republic of China are simply too strong for war to ever break out. Others refute that assertion, however, stating that whether over the long-running dispute regarding Taiwan, or the struggle for regional and global influence, particularly in the Pacific Rim, the United States and China often find themselves at odds with one another, and that a preemptive attack is *possible*.

"While they might disagree regarding China, there is one thing on which all of the analysts seem to agree…that any future conflicts between nation states will have to be fought on two major fronts, on the battlefield *and* in cyber space.

"This is definitely something we will be keeping our eye on, and we will bring you breaking news as it happens.

"In other news… a tragic story this morning about a teenage boy who was accidentally shot to death last night by his own father. The boy's father, a Vietnamese immigrant, had been living in fear after hearing and reading about the growing violence and mayhem being committed in his neighborhood by street gangs. As a precaution, he had positioned a shotgun next to his bed in the event of a home invasion. His son, who the father did not know had snuck out through a window earlier last night to go see his girlfriend, had decided to re-enter through the front door after the parents had gone to bed. The boy inadvertently triggered the door alarm upon reentering the home. The father, awakened in the middle of the night by the sound of the alarm, heard someone entering the house and, fearing a home invasion, fired at the supposed intruder, instantly killing his son instead…." CLICK.

* * * *

Nick sat down on the bed and, still holding the remote control, continued staring for several moments at the blank television screen. It seemed that the whole world was falling apart, and he had heard enough depressing news to last a lifetime. He shook it off and glanced over at the clock; it was later than he thought. He had to get going immediately or he'd be late. It was going to be a big day for him, and while he still had only a few details about what lay ahead, he suspected he'd be challenged to the utmost. Based on what he'd heard, his new job was likely to take him to places that he never could have expected..

Everyone had been silent as to exactly what the mission of the new task force was going to be. With his extensive background and knowledge of Chinese cyber warfare tactics, however, he reasoned that it must have something to do with the recent string of cyber attacks and the theft of some very sensitive information, because China was the number one suspect.

Nick checked the time again and found that it was already 7:00 A.M. He finished his orange juice and coffee before snatching up his briefcase and heading for the door. The meeting wasn't until 9:00, but he was supposed to meet his new boss, General George Caprella, Commander, U.S. Cyber Command, for breakfast at 8:00.

As he started the thirty-minute drive from Baltimore to Fort Meade, Nick began to wonder what it would be like reporting directly to Caprella. It was somewhat unusual for a civilian contractor to lead a strategic task force. It was even more unusual for the head of such a task force to report directly to the commander. These were unusual times, however, and the stakes had become exceptionally high, so as a result, those in charge wanted the very best and were unwilling to leave anything to chance.

He arrived at the base thirty minutes later and hurried through security before proceeding to the wing where General Caprella's office was located. Nick arrived at the general's office to find an attractive, female Army officer sitting at the receptionist's desk.

"Good morning. I'm Dr. Nick Reynolds, and I'm here to see General Caprella." The woman looked him over for a moment before smiling, seemingly liking what she saw.

"Please wait just a moment, Dr. Reynolds, while I let his aide know that you're here." She smiled again before picking up the receiver and making a call. General Caprella's aide arrived a few minutes later. Like the receptionist, he was in uniform.

"Hello, Dr. Reynolds, I'm so glad to see you were able to make it…welcome aboard. I'm Colonel Mike Carter, General Caprella's aide."

"It's a pleasure to make your acquaintance, Colonel," Reynolds replied, shaking the man's hand.

"Dr. Reynolds, if you'll please come with me, I'll take you to the conference room. You'll find coffee, soft drinks, and water there, and we've had some breakfast brought in, so please sir, help yourself."

"Thank you, Colonel."

Carter led Reynolds to the conference room where he suspected the general would already be waiting. If Caprella was like most generals he would be punctual, and he would not like to be kept waiting. He found Caprella as predicted, drinking a cup of coffee and reading the morning newspaper. Nick glanced at the headlines and noticed that the recent cyber attacks had made the front page.

At 6 feet 3 inches tall, with thick silver hair and a matching mustache, Caprella looked both intimidating and grandfatherly. He rose as Nick entered the conference room. Carter quietly stepped away.

"Nick, my boy, good morning!" said the general before standing up and extending his hand. Caprella was in a good mood, something for which Nick was extremely grateful. He had heard that the general could be a particularly demanding man to work for. Anticipating the demanding challenge that lay ahead of them before their introductory meeting ever even took place, Nick was uncertain what kind of reception he would get.

"Good morning, General Caprella. It's good to meet you, sir," Nick replied, while the two men shook hands.

"It's good to meet you as well, Nick. There's breakfast and coffee over there on the table, son; please help yourself," Caprella pointed to the doughnuts, bagels, and coffee sitting across from where he was standing.

"Thank you, sir." Nick walked over and picked up a bagel. After adding some cream cheese and grabbing a cup of coffee to go with it, he walked over to sit down at the long conference table across from the commander of Cyber Command. The general wasted no time; he opened a file he had been carrying and placed it on the table.

"Nick Reynolds—you graduated ten years ago from M.I.T. with a PhD in Computer Science, with a special emphasis on cyber warfare. Is that about right, son?" he asked, just after Nick took a big bite out of his bagel. Somewhat flustered, Nick hurried to finish and then swallow the bagel.

"Yes, sir," he answered, after washing the food down with a drink of water. "Except you left out the part about me spending the past ten years consulting for the NSA and later, Cyber Command."

"Ah, yes, then there's that."

"And for the last five of those ten years, I've been studying and assessing the PLA's Blue Army, and their capability for launching cyber attacks against the United States for both reconnaissance and offensive purposes."

"Oh yes, of course. Well you certainly seem to have many impressive qualifications, Nick, that's for sure." Caprella cleared the table in front of him except for a single sheet of paper, which he removed from the folder and handed to Nick. It was stamped "Above Top Secret" in large, red letters.

"As you may know, a lot of people believe that the United States has fallen behind other countries like Russia and China for the past several decades in terms of cyber warfare. It's the elephant in the room that no one wants to admit is there; in some ways, perhaps in many ways, we've been caught with our proverbial pants down. This program has been formed to do whatever it takes to level the playing field. We desperately need a game changer, Nick, something that will put us back on top, for *good*."

The general then looked down for a moment as if collecting his thoughts before solemnly turning his attention back to Nick. "I wanted to tell you a little about what we're planning, since you were initially told that you would be running this effort. Look, Nick—I'm sorry to have to tell you this, son, but I've reconsidered this arrangement and frankly, I don't think this task force is the right fit for you. You just don't seem to have what it takes to successfully lead this effort. Our national security is at stake here, so I can't afford to hand this project over to a rookie. I'm sorry, son."

Nick's initial reaction was beyond shock. He felt like a child being scolded by a parent. He had always been a humble man, one who had always believed in following orders and respecting the chain of command. Then he thought back to the countless all-nighters at MIT, however, and the endless research. He recalled the eighty-hour workweeks after graduating, the working weekends, and the non-stop sacrifices he had made first at the NSA and then later at Cyber Command; and when he thought about how he had placed his personal life on hold over the last ten years, he suddenly grew angry.

"Excuse me? With all due respect, General, you've got to be kidding me! There is *no one* more qualified to lead this mission than I am!"

"No, Nick, I'm afraid you're out of the picture now. This project is just too big for you to handle. There's too much riding on it!"

"Now listen to me, General. I know ten times more about the cyber attack and defensive capabilities of the Online Blue Army than any other analyst in the NSA does. Again with all due respect, General, I *should* lead this task force, and frankly I think you know it and you're just afraid to admit it."

The general sat there with a scowl for a moment and studied Nick's face. Nick's heart raced, unsure whether the general would have him tossed out of the building or agree with him. Suddenly, the tight lips turned into a smile.

"Great job, son...bravo!"

"Sir?"

"As I said son, this is an extraordinarily important mission. It's going to require someone with enough moxie and determination to push through the many obstacles that will present themselves. Furthermore, as you so aptly pointed out, you *are* the most qualified individual in the nation to handle this mission."

"You were just *testing* me?"

"Of course I was, son. I'm sorry, Nick, but I had to make certain that you were ready, and that you would be able to see this thing through. Now, are you still interested?"

"Yes, sir, I am."

"Well alright then, welcome to the task force designated as 'Operation Counterpunch.' "Caprella reached down and took another, much larger folder from his briefcase and handed it to Nick. The younger man took the folder, which again was stamped with "Above Top Secret" in bold red letters, and laid it on the table before opening it.

"Nick, this task force was formed with the singular objective of defending the United States against and neutralizing the Chinese cyber threat, permanently. The task force will be given anything and everything it needs to fulfill its mission to stop these attacks, to end the threat, and to ensure that never again will the United States be at the mercy of cyber attacks from China, Russia, or any other state, or individuals, who would seek to harm the United States of America via cyberspace."

"What about the rumors?" asked Nick, this time studying Caprella's reaction and enjoying the reversal. Though he was not a trained NSA field agent himself, after working there for years as a contractor, Nick understood how nuances in a person's body language could speak volumes.

"What rumors are you referring to?" asked the general.

"Oh, you know, the rumors that the Chinese are planning a massive cyber attack against the United States in the very near future." Nick looked for any sign of recognition on the general's face. Either he had no idea what Nick was referring to, or he was really, really good.

"Oh, you mean *those* rumors. So you believe them to be legitimate, Nick?" So there it was; the general was aware of the not-so-veiled warnings. Nick realized the general was still testing him, something that was likely to continue for some time. Apparently Caprella *was* really, really good.

Nick rubbed his head. "You know, General, I've been asking myself that same question since I first learned about them."

"Were you ever able to answer it?" the general asked with a furrowed brow. The same question had apparently been troubling his sleep as well.

"Well, sir, I kept asking myself the same question over and over again—why? Why would the Chinese choose to start an all-out war with us now? It's a well-known fact that they've already hacked into a number of our major infrastructure systems. Despite the growing tensions between our two countries, however, our economies are still so tightly intermingled that an all out conflict would be disastrous for both countries."

"So you believe the warnings to be baseless then?" the general asked, a curious, inquisitive expression on his face.

"No, sir, I believe that the intel comes from too high up in the food chain to be labeled as mere fabrication."

"What then?" the general asked, becoming slightly annoyed.

"General, I don't know, sir. Misinformation fed to the right sources, a word here, an innuendo there…it happens all the time."

"Any idea who would want to see a conflict kick-up between China and the U.S.?"

"Who doesn't like the United States, General? It could be Iran, North Korea, al-Qaeda, Hezbollah, Cuba, Russia, or even a rogue element within the Chinese government. A number of the old communists are pretty miffed right now about Taiwan. They'd like nothing more than to be rid of us."

General Caprella looked across the table at Nick and grinned.

"This is precisely the reason I chose you for this position, Nick. I'm very glad to know that my decision was the right one. I'll have Mike

Carter help you work through all the necessary paperwork to make this happen. Welcome aboard, son!"

Jeff W. Horton

Chapter 2

The frigid, sub-zero temperatures and heavy snow had done little to slow down Nikolai Chervanko as he made his way along the streets of Moscow in his Hummer. Chervanko had a dramatic flair about him, and he appreciated the irony that came with an old-school Soviet communist owning and driving around in an American-made vehicle through the heart of Mother Russia. The Hummer was considerably more reliable than its Russian-made counterpart, and owning an American automobile like the Hummer…or any of the higher-end European or Japanese imports…was also something of a status symbol among many of the elite in Moscow. When he'd purchased the Hummer, he had been busy fundraising for his cause and had understood all too well the importance of appearances at such times.

By the time Chervanko reached the Bolshoy Kamenny Bridge, which would carry him over the Moskva River and past the Kremlin on his way to the Arbat District, doubts about the operation began creeping into his mind. He began to question whether they had missed any critical steps during the planning phase of the operation. Perhaps it was the complexity of the plan, and the endless number of variables that were beyond his control that made him uneasy, or maybe it was just his uncertainty about how the various players would respond. After mulling it over for several minutes Chervanko smiled and forced himself to relax. After all, why should he be worried? The plan they were following had been *his* plan, mostly, and they had painstakingly executed each and every detail of it so far, he'd made certain of it.

It was he, Chervanko, who had first suggested the idea as they all sat around the table together one evening, smoking cigarettes and drinking vodka. The combination had served to not only fend off the cold, it had also helped numb each of them to the melancholy each man felt inside as they reminisced about the "good old days," when Mother Russia was still part of the grand and glorious Soviet Union. The new and inferior Commonwealth of Independent States was nothing but a mere shadow of its predecessor, the U.S.S.R., they had all said. The excessive vodka had emboldened them to talk openly amongst themselves for the first time about something that they would hardly have dared discuss otherwise, something that would have been regarded as a crime against the state by the current weak-kneed politicians, and could easily send all of them to the gulag. Since the reforms following the collapse of the Soviet Union, conditions for hardcore criminals in Russia had become substantially tougher, while criminals convicted of much lesser crimes were often shown a corresponding lenience. What the friends discussed that first evening could easily be construed as treason, and would certainly have been had they been overheard…and treason certainly qualified as a hardcore crime.

As he entered the Arbat District, it suddenly occurred to Chervanko that perhaps they should find some men from among their ranks who would be willing to take the fall should their cause start to go badly. He was confident that some of the soldiers—the younger, true believers, who had only been children when the U.S.S.R. fell—would gladly take their place if the plan was uncovered, so that the cause could go on. If he and the other old guard members were caught, however, the movement would certainly come to an immediate end. He decided he would bring this up to the others at some point, but not tonight.

As he considered the state of their movement the hard truth of it kept coming back; if the FSB, Russia's version of the FBI, learned what he and the others were trying to do, they would all be tracked down, and after a brief trial, they would be imprisoned for life, possibly even executed. Each of them understood they were playing a high-stakes game, and the possibility would always exist that they might get caught. They all knew the risks, but they also knew what the payoff would be if they succeeded, and they all knew it would be worth the sacrifices.

A pair of headlights flashing in the rearview mirror suddenly caught his attention, and snapped him back to the present. *Am I being followed?* He cursed under his breath after realizing how careless he had been. How long had it been since he had last checked for a tail? Surely, it had been, what—fifteen or twenty minutes at least? It had been an unforgivable mistake, of course; something he never would have done back in the old days, when he was younger and much more disciplined, when he would have checked the mirrors every few minutes. He wondered whether he was just getting old, careless, or both. He flipped on his turn signal and made the next right, frequently checking his mirrors without making it obvious. The car behind him followed, making the same turn though keeping plenty of distance.

He glanced back long enough to tell that the car was not marked. By now, Chervanko realized that he could have been made by the FSB. His heart began pounding in his chest like a jackhammer as he tried to calm himself and to recall as much as he could of the past thirty minutes. How long had he been followed—since he left his home? No. There had been no unusual cars parked outside his house when he pulled out. Had he checked his mirrors after first leaving? Yes. After a decade working for the KGB, checking the mirrors had become as reflexive for him as turning the car's ignition. The car must have pulled in behind him only a few minutes earlier. He had to determine for certain whether it was a tail or not. If it was, he would start evasive maneuvers and just hope they had not yet called for backup.

He took the next left, followed by another left. The car kept going straight, and he was clear. Perhaps it had only been a coincidence. Regardless, he would make it a point to be extra cautious going forward; there was far too much at stake to be stopped by such an amateurish oversight. He knew it still could have been an FSB tail that had been following him, who upon realizing that they had been spotted, had elected to drop off to avoid raising suspicions. After taking a much longer route to get to his destination and with no further incidents, Chervanko arrived at a modest home on the edge of the Arbat district.

He knocked on the door in a series of three pre-arranged patterns. Moments later the door opened and a tall, older man in spectacles stood in the doorway.

"Nikolai Chervanko, my friend, welcome!" the tall man said, smiling warmly. He looked around carefully outside before slowly closing the door and locking it.

"Greetings, Comrade Smirnov. I was delayed because I thought I was being followed."

"Were you?" Smirnov asked with hesitation.

"No, Viktor, I was not. Do not worry old friend, I still know how to shake a tail when necessary. But I think it was nothing; I was only being cautious."

"Do you ever regret not joining the FSB yourself, Nikolai, after the collapse of the U.S.S.R.?" asked Smirnov, with some hesitation. Chervanko turned to his old friend with a confused look.

"Regret not joining the FSB?" he asked, pausing in the hallway before starting to laugh. "How was *I* to join the FSB, Viktor, when there was so much work for me to do? No Comrade, I do not regret my decision, not in the least. The very day I left the KGB, I vowed to spend the rest of my life, even sacrifice it if necessary, to rebuild my beloved Soviet Empire!"

Smirnov nodded. "I understand, Nikolai, I felt much the same way," he said, as the two walked into the living area, where two other men stood waiting.

"Ah, Nikolai!" one of them exclaimed.

"Dmitry. Ivan. How have you been?" Chervanko greeted each man warmly before sitting down next to Dmitry Levin, another former KGB agent who had previously served with him for five years, including the time during the collapse of the Soviet Union. The other man, Ivan Kozlov, was ex-Spetsnaz, as was Smirnov. All four men, however, had long been and remained loyal and devout members of the Communist Party.

"Please tell us you have some good news!" said Levin. "Tell us, please, we must know what you have learned!"

"All has been going according to plan, my friends. One of my contacts has assured me that the infiltrations have remained undetected."

"And what of our efforts to advertise the campaign?" asked Kozlov, with a look of intensity which Chervanko had long ago learned was common to the man's face.

"On schedule and proceeding exactly as planned, Ivan. In fact, everything seems to be going perfectly. It seems that no one on either side even suspects any outside involvement, or if they do, they have not yet acted on their suspicions. We have been extraordinarily successful, my friends, at manipulating the fears and distrust of our two greatest enemies, and turning this situation to our advantage. The Americans are now convinced—in fact, they are terrified—that the Chinese are ready to launch a massive attack against their national infrastructure; they fear meltdowns at their nuclear power plants, and the potential loss of their national power grid. The Chinese, meanwhile, fear a unilateral military response by the United States for what appears to be cyber warfare attacks originating in China. Soon, they *will* be at war with one another."

"If that is so, then there is nothing anyone can do to stop us now. Even if either country eventually begins to suspect our involvement, by the time they find us it will be far too late for them to do anything about it," Smirnov said somberly.

"Indeed, it would appear that all of our patience and years of planning will soon pay off, gentlemen," Levin added. "Soon, we *will* see Mother Russia rise to her former glory, with us to help guide and shape her going forward—and we will once again be feared the world over."

"What about Lee?" asked Kozlov. "What should we do with him once his work is finished and his usefulness has come to an end? You know that we cannot afford for him to talk to anyone before this is all over; it could destroy everything we've worked for."

"Don't worry, Ivan," answered Chervanko. "Once the attack has commenced, he will be *retired*," he told Kozlov, before looking distantly into the burning embers of the fireplace before him. "It will not be long now, comrades," he continued in a low, somber voice. "By this time next year, the world will look very different than it does today. Out of the ashes of chaos and destruction a new order will arise, one which *we* will be instrumental in building," he said, allowing his voice to trail off before taking another long swig of vodka, while watching the flames burn and crackle in the fire.

Chapter 3

The man walked into the large, open room with the help of a cane, just as sunlight began peeking in through the windows from behind the horizon of the high desert . The upper level of the S-4 facility, like the floor below it, was located above ground level and therefore had windows, unlike the remaining floors in the facility. The windows were one way glass of course, to guard against prying eyes in the sky, particularly satellites, but they still provided a spectacular view of the landscape. Henry enjoyed working where he could see outside because it made him feel less claustrophobic, especially since he and Kate spent so much of their time working in the lab. Unfortunately, when they weren't working in the lab, they were most often on one of the lower levels deep underground, where the hangar was located. With the silver hair of a man well past retirement age, Dr. Henry Summers was getting around slower than he used to but still enjoyed his work, and he relished his time working with Kate.

Upon arriving at the office area at the back of the lab, Henry found his daughter asleep once again at the desk in her office, her head resting beside her keyboard. She had been pulling a lot of all-nighters recently, something he was going to try to remedy. He placed his hand on her shoulder and gently shook her.

"Kate, honey, wake up." She lifted her head from the desk before slowly opening her eyes. The imprint of the desk on the left side of her face caused him to smile.

"Oh, hi Daddy," she said, still trying to focus her vision.

"Good morning, sweetheart," he answered, setting a steaming cup of coffee on the desk in front of her, next to where her head had been moments earlier. "Kate, honey, you have to stop working so much, it's not healthy. Don't you *want* to have some kind of a social life?" he asked, his forehead wrinkled in concern.

"Come on Dad, give it a rest," she answered, before taking a sip of her coffee. "You of all people know how important my work is! I'll have plenty of time to have a social life once I make the breakthrough. I'm so close now I can taste it!"

"The group has been at this for decades now, Kate; what makes you think you're so close to a breakthrough now?"

"It's largely because of our current level of technology, Dad. It's advanced so rapidly over the last fifty years, especially over the last decade or so, that we finally have the technical know-how and enough computing power that we are close to being able to safely remove and then access the data in that box. Once we have access to the data, it will change the world." She took another long sip of her coffee and looked at the computer monitor on her desk. "I found something last night, Dad. I think it might be the key to creating an interface that we can use to talk with the box. Here, let me show you." Kate began pounding on her keyboard and screen after screen popped up.

Her father reached in front of his daughter and turned off the computer monitor. He then turned his daughter's chair around until she faced him.

"Kate, listen to me. You can show me later, after you get back."

"Back? Back from where?"

"Back from Las Vegas. You're catching the next Janet flight back there today; I want you to get away from here for a few days," her father said sternly. "Since the government is kind enough to offer us these free shuttle flights between Area 51 and the Las Vegas airport, we might as well take advantage of them once in a while, don't you think?"

"What? No—Dad, I can't leave now, not when I'm so close!" He could see the pleading in his daughter's eyes. He could also, however, see how frail she was starting to look, and it worried him.

"Look, Kate, you need some rest. You're starting to look terrible! When was the last time you took some time off, or at least caught a Janet back to your place in Vegas for a weekend?"

Kate sighed and looked down at the floor. "I don't know," she answered after looking back up at him. "I guess it's been a few months."

"It's been over a year now, Kate."

"It doesn't matter, Dad; you know how much I enjoy it here at the base anyway. I have food and a nice apartment here. What do I need to go to Vegas for, anyway?"

This time it was her father who let out a heavy sigh. How many times would they have this same conversation?

"Have you looked in the mirror lately, Kate? You're beginning to look puny. You need some time off to rest, to recharge your batteries. The data you're trying to get your hands on will still be here when you get back."

"But Dad—"

"No buts, little lady. Now I know I'm your father Kate, but I'm also your boss, and I'm ordering you to take some time off from the base and from our work."

"But I—"

He looked at her with the simultaneous concern and determination that only a loving parent can have. "I said no buts. Now get back to your quarters, get cleaned up, and be on the next flight to Vegas."

"What about my breakthrough? I'm almost to the point that I can safely remove the box from the ship and bring it here, where I can interface it to our systems!"

"Kate, I've been trying to reverse-engineer this technology for decades now; the government's been at it for considerably longer. I seriously doubt that another couple of days will make that much difference. Besides, what good are you to the project if you end up collapsing out of exhaustion? Today's Wednesday; I want you to take some time off tomorrow and Friday, along with the weekend. Your work will still be waiting for you when you return on Monday, okay?" He gave her the look, which he knew would convince her that he was resolute in his decision. He cared about her well-being, not only as her father but also as the supervisor of an invaluable and irreplaceable research scientist as well. Recognizing the familiar, stubborn look of determination on her father's face, Kate let out a heavy sigh and came over to Henry.

"Okay, Dad, you win. I'll catch the next Janet to Vegas for some R&R; but I'll be back here the day after tomorrow to pick up where I left off, okay?"

"No, Kate, *Monday*. The next Janet leaves Groom Lake this afternoon and I want you on it. You need a long weekend away from this place, honey; it will chew you up and spit you out if you let it."

She threw her hands up in the air and shrugged before turning to leave.

"Are we still on for dinner on Friday?" he asked hopefully, just as she was about to leave.

Kate was noticeably upset with him, despite the fact that she knew he was right. She turned to face her father and gave him a pseudo-stern look before smiling.

"Of course, Daddy. Just call me tomorrow or Friday morning as a reminder, okay?"

"You've got it honey," he replied, giving her a hug before watching her walk out the door.

* * * *

It had been another long, busy week for Henry Summers. There had been significant progress on a number of the initiatives that made up the Prometheus Project, including Kate's. He was looking forward to her return on the following Monday, and the possibility of finally unlocking some of the mysteries of the device and of the civilization that created it. Some of the best scientists in the country had attempted to learn the true nature of the device and how it integrated with the ship, a prerequisite for moving the box out of the ship and elsewhere on the base.

Regardless of whatever lay ahead for Dr. Kate Summers the scientist on Monday, it was almost time for him to call Kate Summers, the daughter, about dinner. He had not spoken with her since she left the base on Wednesday because he wanted to give her plenty of time to herself, but he was looking forward to some quality personal time with her away from work. He made a mental note to speak with her about spending too much time alone. Based on what he had been able to learn without prying too much, she had met very few people since joining the project, outside of those on the base, and he was growing increasingly concerned.

After approving several requisitions for some new equipment Kate had requested, Henry turned off his computer, grabbed his coat, picked up his phone's receiver, and dialed her number. He glanced at his watch and realized that he had only twenty minutes left until the plane would leave, whether he was on it or not. The phone rang four times before the answering machine picked up and he heard Kate's voice. He was preparing to leave a message when suddenly the voice on the machine changed.

"Hello, Dr. Summers," the voice said. It was a man's voice, deep, and with some kind of accent. "I suppose by now you must realize that we have your beautiful daughter. If you want her to remain beautiful, and alive for that matter, you will come alone to the following address by 9:00 A.M. Saturday. Come alone, Dr. Summers, or don't bother coming. The address is...."

Henry Summers hung up the phone and tried not to panic. Security had briefed him on how to handle a situation like this, but this involved Kate, his daughter. He walked over to the window and stared out into the desert. After considering his options for several moments, he realized he had no choice. If he ever wanted to see his daughter again, he had to follow protocol. It was the best chance for protecting national security, but more importantly, it was the best chance Kate had to stay alive. He walked back over to the phone and punched in a four-digit code.

"Security. Is this Dr. Henry Summers?" This was his last chance if he wanted to change his mind. He decided to stay the course.

"Yes, this is Henry Summers. We have an urgent problem."

Chapter 4

"It just started, Dr. Reynolds," the younger of the two men walking down the hallway said to the other. He looked more like a male model than he did a nerdy computer security analyst. Nick had come to learn, however, that despite his boyish charms and popularity with the ladies, Mike Menders was by far the best security analyst he had ever seen.

"The company's internal IT security team detected it only moments after it began, and they contacted us right away. They also did some lookups and said it appears to be coming from somewhere in China, sir. Our initial investigation so far seems to confirm their findings."

"Who do you think is responsible?" asked Nick. "The Blue Army again?"

"Most likely," Menders replied. "It's too soon to tell for sure, until we look at more of the logs."

"Great." Nick Reynolds ran his hand through his hair, more as a nervous habit than anything else. It was only his second week leading the Counterpunch team, but it already felt like years. "What kind of attack is it?"

"Distributed Denial of Service."

"Another DDOS. You know, Mike, I've been here just over a week now, and we've had how many attacks, a thousand? Trojans, DDOS, worms, phishing…I'm simply astounded at the frequency and the intensity of these attacks."

"As you know, Dr. Reynolds, for the most part these are not just some pimple-faced teenage hackers we're facing."

"I know, Mike, I know. Our real enemies include powerful nation states with a lot of clout, like China and Russia, and terrorist organizations like Al Queada, Hezbollah, and the Taliban. Oh yes, and let's not forget the rogue states like Iran and North Korea. Finally, we have the friendly states who are supposed to be our allies, countries like Israel, France, even Great Britain, who occasionally go fishing for information we've neglected to share with them. Does that about cover it, Mike?" Reynolds asked sarcastically.

"Yes, sir. Assuming you leave out Anonymous, and the myriads of other hacker groups and script kiddies out there; I believe you've about got it covered." The two men arrived at last at a large conference room, where fifteen people were waiting for them. Reynolds sat down at the head of the table and looked back to Menders.

"Okay, so why a small power plant in the Midwest, and what is their objective? A test?"

"Unlikely, Dr. Reynolds…at least, not a small-scale test. The attack was an attempt to pass through the firewalls by appearing to be legitimate traffic, and then overwhelm outward-facing servers. Once they were on the inside of the network, it looks like they were attempting to activate an emergency shutdown function at the facility, resulting in loss of power to one hundred thousand homes."

"Were the power plant IT personnel able to prevent that from happening?" asked Reynolds. One of the junior analysts raised his hand. Reynolds pointed at him and nodded. "Go."

"John Gilmore, sir, junior analyst for the Rural Power Grid Systems group. No, sir, they were not. By the time they detected the breach, the attackers were already searching for the emergency shutdown switch. The power company pulled the plug on their 100MB Internet connection, but not before the switch was activated and the plant shut down. The phone line went down too, but they called us back on a cell phone moments after the shutdown to let us know what happened."

Reynolds tightened his lips and shook his head from side to side.

"Okay. The attack was successful and the plant shut down. Obviously the plant will simply flip the switch back on and the power will be restored—this time."

Reynolds paused for a moment to look around at the faces in the room. Almost half of them were younger than he was, still in their twenties, most graduates from MIT, Berkley, and UCLA. The other group was evenly split between middle-aged and gray-haired members. Curiously, Nick noted that there were slightly more women than men in the room.

"Okay," he began, "let's do some brainstorming. There has been a sharp increase in the number of cyber attacks against our national infrastructure over the past two years, and there seems to be a pattern emerging. Most of these attacks against us appear to be originating from outside of the United States. They started small, shutting down a pump here, a server there, basically just probing and testing the vulnerability of our infrastructure defenses which are, I'm ashamed to say, in poor shape. Okay, what does this all mean and what can we do about it? Thoughts, people. I need ideas." The room was awkwardly silent for several moments until at last, one of the twenty-something women in the room finally spoke up.

"Good morning, Dr. Reynolds, my name is Dr. Sandra Dyson. I just want to say how strongly I feel that what we are facing is not some low-level, casual probing and penetrations into our national infrastructure. We have been witnessing a progressive, systematic attack pattern all over the United States. The increase in the number of successful attacks and the repercussions of these attacks are far beyond anything we've ever experienced. These hackers don't seem to be interested in stealing data, sir; they're interested in doing damage to the United States."

"Okay, please explain," Nick told her, intrigued with where she was going.

"What would happen, Dr. Reynolds, if this had been a power grid in New York City, home to more than eight million people? Worse yet, what if they had been able to shut down enough power plants simultaneously that it created a chain reaction which shut down the entire grid?"

"What if this is all in preparation for a full-blown military attack against the United States?" another twenty-something, a man this time, chimed in.

"Alright. Assuming that another country, let's just say it...China...is behind these attacks; what can we do about it?" asked Reynolds.

"Why don't you tell us what *you* think, Dr. Reynolds?" asked the twenty-something man.

"We have all of the technology we need to defeat the enemy in Cyberspace as well as on the battlefield," answered Reynolds.

"I'm not so sure that we do, Dr. Reynolds," said Dyson. "We have always believed that the Chinese and the Russians were behind us in capability, or at worst at the same level as us. I'm starting to believe, however, that the Chinese may have already quietly surpassed us both, sir. It seems they've been focused on this theater of battle and preparing for it for much longer than we have. If that *is* the case, Dr. Reynolds, then we have a lot of catching-up to do."

"Are you saying, Dr. Dyson, that you believe the Chinese can hack in at their leisure, attack us in Cyberspace with impunity, and that there's nothing we can do about it?"

"Yes, Dr. Reynolds; unfortunately, that's about the size of it," Dyson answered. "Based on the effectiveness of this recent string of attacks, I think we may be so far behind them now that it could take years for us to catch up."

"Dr. Reynolds, I have a question, sir," said the other twenty-something. "What about the rumor that's been circulating lately that a major cyber attack by the Online Blue Army is imminent? It's been all over the Internet, on chat boards, hacker sites, everywhere. Word is that the attack will be coming within weeks or months. How are we going to defend the United States from an attack like that, given the substantial lead held by China…assuming Dr. Dyson is correct, of course?"

Reynolds felt the acid from his stomach backup into his throat, causing it to slowly burn. He took a sip of his water, which cooled the burn but failed to extinguish it, and looked over the entire team.

"Defending the United States is our mission…it's why we're all here; to detect attacks like these and to find ways to stop these extraordinarily dangerous threats to our way of life. We must and we will do everything in our power to ensure that if the rumors are true, and the Chinese do launch a major cyber offensive against the United States, that they will fail. We will stop the attack in its tracks, and we will make them regret ever attacking the United States.

"Listen everyone, defeating a major cyber attack against our critical national infrastructure isn't an option, it's an obligation. This is the continued existence of the United States of America we're talking about, the preservation of our way of life, our very *survival*. If, by the grace of God, I have anything to say about it, stopping them is exactly what we're going to do, by any and whatever means necessary!"

Nick Reynolds nodded his head and smiled as everyone in the room clapped. He had been there for over a week and was now beginning to get a clear picture of where the United States stood in terms of cyber warfare; the country was in trouble. It was then that Reynolds decided to ask for help. It was becoming evident that they had to do whatever it took to face down the deadly threat that loomed before them. He would call the general the first thing the following morning—he had to.

Chapter 5

Snow still covered the ground when Chervanko pulled into the warehouse parking lot. After swiping his badge, the automatic gate slowly began to slide to the right, allowing him to pass. He drove up to the building and found a parking space near the front. After turning off the engine, he climbed out of the Hummer and walked toward the entrance, swiping his badge once more at the door. A knocking sound signaled that the deadbolt had receded; he pulled the door open and walked inside. He continued down the small passageway until he reached a door, which opened into the large open area of the warehouse.

At twenty five thousand square feet, it was small for a warehouse, but ideal for their purposes. In the center of it stood dozens of computer cabinets, each of them filled to capacity with blade servers, rack servers, network switches, routers, and plenty of Ethernet cabling which connected most of the equipment together. Orange fiber-optic cabling also rose out of each cabinet housing the servers and entered multiple cabinets filled with network equipment. A large bundle of fiber-optic cabling rose from the cabinet housing the network switches, continuing up to the ceiling and along the steel girders to each of the four corners of the building, before running down the wall and into conduits which disappeared underground with the fiber-optic cabling inside.

Chervanko enjoyed perusing the abundance of technology operating inside of the warehouse, which had cost them a small fortune to purchase, install, and configure. He and many of the other party members devoted to the cause had prospered during the chaos that followed the collapse of the Soviet Union. In addition to donations from wealthy supporters, their coffers were also filled with the sizeable revenue they had accumulated by selling interested third-parties information and technologies, which they had already stolen from the Americans. Chervanko and the other members of the old guard had long been planning and preparing for the victory that they knew would come one day, when they would lead their beloved country into a brave new future.

While he had not yet learned as much as he would have liked to about the complex computing environment he'd purchased, which had been built by a team of contractors under the careful supervision of the brilliant Dr. David Lee, he had learned enough. One of the provisions for Lee coming on board was that he would teach Chervanko and the others everything they would need to know in order for any of them to operate the Ares System and launch the virus attacks themselves. Much to his detriment, Lee had done an exemplary job designing and then implementing Ares, which he had named after the ancient Greek's pagan deity Ares, the god of war. Lee had done such a thorough job that Chervanko and the others now felt quite confident that with minimal supplemental training, they would be able to operate and maintain everything themselves if necessary, at least long enough to ensure the success of their mission.

Chervanko had developed a keen admiration of Dr. David Lee and his considerable expertise with computer technology. Lee had proven to be a visionary, with groundbreaking work in the area of cyber warfare long before the term even existed. He had anticipated the growth and dependence on the World Wide Web long before most had even learned of its existence. He had unsuccessfully petitioned his government many times for the additional funding needed for his research into the development of a complex system of cyber warfare, which he theorized would one day make it easy to overwhelm an enemy's computer systems. The tools he developed included a suite of unique, targeted viruses including trojans, worms, and phishing programs, which were so complex that they would automatically adapt to circumvent firewalls, intrusion prevention systems, and most any other obstacles and threats. Some would steal data, some would erase data, and still others would perform very specific actions to shut down or activate programmable logic controllers, which had become so prevalent in the national infrastructure of most developed countries.

Beyond the technology, Lee's system included building a vast network of human assets, who would infiltrate a potential target's organization well ahead of an attack, in order to plant some of the viruses from inside the perimeter of the organization's IT infrastructure, often without their knowledge. Ironically, it wasn't a lack of vision or technical expertise that led to his eventual estrangement with his government and the subsequent termination of funding for his program, it was his politics. Lee had become increasingly disenchanted with the Chinese Communist Party and the one-child policy to the point that his outspoken rants could no longer be ignored. His funding was pulled and, fearing arrest, he fled to Russia.

When Chervanko had heard about the disaffected Dr. Lee and approached him ten years earlier with a virtually unlimited budget to fund his research and development, the Chinese dissident had jumped at the opportunity and eventually developed the Ares System for him. Like many men of uncommon brilliance Lee had his own eccentricities, but Chervanko had learned to overlook them, at least for the moment.

"Good morning, Nikolai," Lee said casually in broken English. They had chosen English as the common language when they first met, and had continued the practice throughout their association. It had proven to be the easiest to use, though each had learned some of the other's native language. "Did you bring me some breakfast?" he asked, smiling hopefully. "I'm starving!"

"What do you think I am, Dr. Lee, your personal errand boy?" Chervanko cast a harsh look at the scientist. The sudden attack startled Lee until Chervanko smiled, bringing his hands from behind his back, which held a cup of steaming coffee in one and a sausage biscuit in the other.

"You're such a *zadnitsa,* Chervanko!*"* Lee answered, smiling. "You'd make a fine servant boy." Chervanko managed a tight smile in reply.

"Ah, very good, Lee. I see you're still learning some of the more elegant words in our language, *net*?" Chervanko walked up to Lee and gave him a firm pat on the back.

"I'm working on it, sort of," Lee answered, before starting to wolf down the biscuit and chasing it with coffee.

"Well, now that your mouth is stuffed full of biscuit, how about telling me about your progress. Are we ready to proceed?"

Lee nodded before swallowing down his last bite. "Yes, everything is set. Based on the results of our most recent set of penetrations into various American systems across the United States, we can now take down select power stations, including a number of nuclear power plants.

You will be able to access and shut down portions of their power grid, possibly all of it."

"What about the Pentagon, the CIA, and the NSA?"

"As you know, we've had surprising success hacking into the Americans' military and intelligence agencies, and that has continued to be the case. I would have thought it would have been much more difficult."

"Over-confidence and complacency; these have always been the greatest weaknesses of the West." Chervanko walked over to the main console, where multiple keyboards and computer consoles rested. "The programs for launching and monitoring the attacks; they are now available in the application's menu structure as requested? Remember, this system has to be foolproof. It must be easy to use, untraceable, and impervious."

"But of course!" answered Lee. "Everything has been done exactly to your specifications. With all the money you've given me, I've been able to build an operation that makes GhostNet look like the work of a script kiddy! Here's what I've done to date: I have dozens of Chinese nationals that I have contracted at numerous government and civilian offices in the United States, usually at low-level agencies or nuclear power plants, with some access into critical systems. They have planted viruses and emailed attachments internally throughout the agency they work for. The emails have trojans attached which will perform the assigned task exactly as you requested."

"And these viruses, what will they do?" asked Chervanko.

"Just what you wanted, boss. Some will shut down systems, others will steal data, while still others will sit idle until the specified time, when they will be part of a massive, distributed attack. With our trojans on so many systems, we will bring down or gain access to the targeted system in minutes. All you have to do is select what you want to attack and how, and the viruses will do the rest!"

"Excellent. And any data that is stolen, you are certain that it will be traced back to the Online Blue Army, and not here?"

"Of course, Comrade Chervanko. Everything from the code in the trojans, the many computers participating in the distributed attacks, and the IP addresses of the servers where the stolen data is sent; everything will point to the PLA. I've been able to bribe enough soldiers there that we've got plenty of viruses that will do our work for us."

"What about ease of use?" asked Chervanko. "Remember, I told you that I want any of us to be able to launch these attacks without you. It would be better for you of course, if you were…not here when the attacks commenced; just in case we are ever compromised, of course."

"Yeah, alright, I appreciate that. No, listen, I've made this system so user-friendly that my five year-old nephew could come in here and bring the Pentagon to its knees, steal sensitive data from the DOD, or cause an American nuclear power plant to meltdown! The virus talks to our system, and we tell the virus what to do, it's that simple. Believe me, *moĭ drug*, you will not be disappointed!"

"Is there any way they might be able to trace it back to us?"

"I told you, there's no way they could ever trace it back here," Lee answered indignantly. "I have the system routing traffic through twenty different providers, bouncing off different satellites, and off of systems throughout the PLA, with at least one of our trojans on each one. I'm telling you, with my brains and your money, stealing data from the Americans or shutting down a power plant is like taking candy from a baby."

Chervanko looked at Lee with a cold look that made Lee take an involuntary step backwards.

"You've done well, Lee. Tonight, I will bring my associates here, and you will show us how everything works, *da*?"

"*Da*," Lee answered. As he looked into the dead, lifeless eyes of his employer, a cold chill suddenly ran down his spine, and he began to worry that maybe, just maybe, he had done his job too well.

Chapter 6

He paced back and forth on the sidewalk, repeatedly staring down at some scribbles on a small piece of paper on which he had written the address left by the kidnapper on his daughter's answering machine. It was, by any account, an unlikely meeting spot. The address had brought him to an abandoned house in the middle of an older residential neighborhood, which bordered a large industrial warehouse district. Nearly all of the houses on the street had been worn down by the passage of time, but none more so than the one in front of which he now stood; it was by far the most dilapidated. The taller, two-story house had a mid-twentieth-century look to it. At some point in the distant past, before the yard had become overgrown with weeds and brush, before the many broken windows, the home had likely been quite respectable in appearance; but that time had long since passed.

Henry Summers glanced down at his watch before quickly looking back up at the sound of several vehicles approaching. He sighed when he recognized them to be only transport trucks on their way to either pick up or deliver merchandise at one of the many warehouses nearby. No doubt much of that merchandise would end up either in a lush hotel lobby along the Vegas strip, at a storefront, or perhaps even in someone's home.

After pacing about impatiently for several more minutes, his mind was suddenly flooded with images and memories of Kate as a little girl. His face broke into a large, warm smile when he recalled the joyous day on which she was born, and he chuckled as he relived a moment years later when Kate was six. It was a warm summer's morning and he had just dropped her off at school for the first time; they both had cried. Next, Henry recalled the day, more than a decade later, when Kate proudly wore her cap and gown at her high school graduation. He remembered how proud he had been the day he helped her move into college, and the day years later when she graduated from M.I.T., first as an undergrad, then again with her masters. He smiled proudly as he thought back to the day she received her PhD at Berkley. The smile fled from his face however, when he also recalled the day soon after, when he had convinced her to come and help him with his work at Groom Lake. Now, she had been kidnapped because of *him*; they had used his precious daughter to get to him. Just as his eyes started to water, he looked up again to find a large, black, four-door sedan approaching. It came to a stop some twenty-five yards from where he stood and sat there motionless for several minutes. With its windshield and windows darkened, Henry Summers could not make out who was in the car, and he kept staring at it with uncertainty. After waiting a few minutes, the driver's door opened and a stocky, sharp dressed man climbed out of the car.

"Hello, Dr. Summers." The elderly Summers eyed the younger man briefly before a combination of fear and rage suddenly began building inside him. The realization that this was the same man who had taken his child and threatened her life was nearly too much for him. "I apologize for making you wait like that; I just wanted to be certain we were alone."

"What have you done with her, you monster?"

The stranger smiled. "Now really, Dr. Summers, is that any way to treat the man who's holding your daughter's life in his hands? I'm usually a nice enough guy, but believe me when I say that I am capable of doing some terrible, nasty things to pretty young things like your daughter, particularly when I get perturbed about something."

"No, please don't do anything to hurt her," he said, very apologetically. "Please, just give me my daughter back, safe and sound; I'll do anything to ensure her safety and get her back."

"That's good, Dr. Summers, that's real good. Now, just stand still for a moment while I check for weapons and wires." The man took a brief glance around before patting Summers down.

"Okay, I'm satisfied. Let's go."

"Why, where are we going?" asked Summers.

"We're going to see your daughter, of course. Wouldn't you like to see her, Dr. Summers?"

"Of course! But before I go with you, I want to know that she's still alive!" he said, with tears forming in his eyes.

"Don't worry, Dr. Summers. I tell you what, just so I can show you what a nice fella I am, I'll let you talk with her." He reached into his pocket and withdrew a cell phone, before dialing a number and placing the phone up to his ear.

"Yeah, it's me. Put her on the phone." He waited a few seconds and put the phone on speaker mode.

"Hello?" Summers was able to hear the voice well enough to know it was Kate. The joy of hearing her voice again caused an involuntary smile to appear.

"Hold on." The kidnapper handed the phone to Summers.

"Hello, Kate, is that you?"

"Daddy!" She sounded somewhat calm considering the circumstances, but he could hear the panic in her voice. "Dad, it's you they're after, stay away from here—"

"Hello Dr. Summers." The voice spoke in English, but it was heavily accented, most likely Oriental, possibly Chinese.

"Who are you, and why have you done this?" Henry asked. "I want to talk with my daughter!"

"You will do exactly as I say, Dr. Summers, or I assure you I will kill her with you still on the phone. Do you understand?"

Summers hesitated momentarily, trying to weigh his options, until finally determining he had none. He let out a heavy sigh and nodded his head.

"I understand. What do you want me to do?"

"Wonderful. Just cooperate with us, Dr. Summers, and your daughter will be back in her own bed tonight. Now, if you'll accompany my associate, Mr. Smith, back to his car, he'll bring you to see your daughter. See you soon, Dr. Summers; I'm so looking forward to meeting you!" The phone clicked and the line went dead. Henry handed it back to Smith, who then gestured for the doctor to move to the car, where they both climbed in.

One of the first things that occurred to Henry as the car pulled away from the house was that Smith had not bothered to blindfold him. That meant one of two things; either he was not going to be allowed to leave after they arrived, or they were planning to kill him. Henry knew that if he didn't go with Smith, however, the man on the phone would certainly kill Kate. Either way, the important thing was that he would soon be with his daughter.

The car pulled away from the house and sped toward the industrial warehouses. Ten minutes later, they arrived at a nondescript building with a gate and a guard out front. After being waved through, Smith parked the car and led Henry into the building. Just inside the door was an office area, where the man he knew only as Smith led him. A middle-aged Asian man sat in a high-backed chair behind the desk.

"Ah, Dr. Summers, it's so good to finally meet you. My name is Wu Chow," he said, extending his hand. Summers ignored the hand and stared at Wu Chow incredulously.

"I'd like to see my daughter," he said, in as calm a voice as he could muster.

"But of course, Dr. Summers; please follow me." Chow left the office and walked down a hall and toward a door. As they entered the warehouse, Summers could see his Kate sitting in the middle of the open space, handcuffed to a chair near racks of computer monitors. His heart sank when he realized that, like him, she wore no blindfold. Whatever Chow was up to, it was for keeps. Henry ran over to Kate and wrapped his arms around her.

"Are you okay, Kate?" he asked, embracing her for several moments.

"Oh, Dad, you shouldn't have come; I told you not to come!"

Summers looked at his daughter and smiled warmly. "Now listen to me, Kate Summers. I'm an old man now, but you still have your entire life in front of you." He turned back to face Chow. "She does, doesn't she?"

Chow clapped his hands together and walked toward them both. "Well now, my dear Dr. Summers, I'm afraid that this will be entirely up to you. If you give me what I want to know, I see no reason why she cannot leave and live a long and healthy life!"

"And what exactly is it that you want, Mr. Chow? Why have you brought me and my daughter here, to this place?"

"Come now, Dr. Summers, surely you must know."

"I'm afraid I have no idea," Summers answered, looking back toward the door for a moment before quickly looking back at Chow. His captor followed his glance before dismissively turning back to Summers.

"I've been fascinated with your work at the base, Dr. Summers. I understand that you have been working on the Prometheus Project for three decades now. I can only *imagine* what incredible discoveries you have made during that time. I simply want you to share those discoveries with me, Dr. Summers, that's all. Give me what I want, and you and your daughter can leave here in peace."

"I don't have any idea what you're talking about, Mr. Chow. You must have the wrong man."

Chow's face soon grew flushed with anger. "Come, Dr. Summers. You're beginning to try my patience now. Do you think me a fool? I know all about your precious S-4 base at Groom Lake and the extraterrestrial technology you have there, technology that you and your government so selfishly keep to yourselves."

Summers just stood there, choosing not to address Chow's accusation. "I only want to leave with my daughter, please."

Chow slowly made his way towards and then behind Kate. "Oh, of course, Dr. Summers, I understand. All I need you to do is tell me everything you have learned about the alien technology that you've recovered, and that you have been attempting to reverse-engineer at S-4. I will need a few 'samples' from the ship as well, of course, to take back with me to my country, for *my* people to benefit from."

"What? There's no way I could ever bring you anything, Mr. Chow. The security is far too tight…it's impossible!" It happened so fast he did not even see it happen. Suddenly, he was staring at the long blade of a knife that Chow held to his daughter's throat. He pressed the blade against her throat until a small streak of blood began flowing down her neck.

"You *will* do this, Dr. Summers, or you will watch your daughter die a slow and agonizing death."

Summers shoulders slumped as he faced the fact that, although he had no idea how he would manage it, he had to agree. "I will try, Mr. Chow."

"I advise you to do more than just try, Dr. Summers, for the sake of your beautiful daughter here, and for your own sake as well. Listen carefully to me; if you are caught, she dies. If you fail to return with all I ask for, she dies. If you notify the authorities, she dies. We had no trouble learning about Prometheus, Dr. Summers; we *will* know if the authorities are notified, I promise you."

"I understand. But please tell me something, Mr. Chow. How did you find out about me—about the Prometheus project? It is one of the closest-guarded secrets in the world."

"Come, Dr. Summers. Do you really see us as such a primitive people? Do you not remember that it was my ancestors who first discovered gunpowder and invented rockets? We have nuclear weapons, missiles, and we have launched satellites into space. Moreover, in the area of cyber warfare…well, let's just say that we surpassed your precious United States years ago. We learned about Prometheus, and you and your daughter, of course, from one of our many cyber attacks. Unfortunately, we were unable to gather any details about the technology itself—"

"Because we store all of it offline, onsite at S-4."

"Yes," replied Chow. "That's why we also need you to retrieve that offline data and bring it to me. You can take this storage device; it will hold several hundred terabytes of data. If that is not enough, then you must—"

Chow was interrupted by an explosion from outside and the sound of rapid gunfire. Henry Summers quickly took hold of the chair Kate was sitting in and lowered it to the floor before covering her with his body. As the gunfire grew much louder, he looked up to see Chow, just as several shells entered and then exited his body. The Chinese national dropped to his knees before collapsing facedown, still holding the storage device in his hand. A few moments later several well-dressed men and women appeared, some carrying HK MP7a1 machine guns. One of the men came over to offer them assistance.

"Clear!" he yelled, before helping Henry stand up, and then setting the chair upright once more. "Need keys for the cuffs!" he yelled.

One of the women responded. "Hold on, I'll check the body." After a couple of minutes, she yelled out. "Found them!" She brought the keys and handed them to the man. He worked quickly and within seconds, Kate was free.

"Thanks." She jumped up and hugged her father. "Thanks for coming for me, Dad. It was reckless and dangerous, but I love you for it!" The two embraced for several moments.

"Dr. Summers, we need to get you and your daughter out of here right now; please come with me." The father and daughter were escorted out of the door and into an unmarked suburban.

"My car—" began Henry Summers.

"Don't worry about anything, Dr. Summers. Just hand me the keys and I'll see that it gets back to your apartment. It will be waiting for you the next time you leave the base."

"Thank you," Henry answered as he handed him the keys. "Thank you, I am in your debt."

"No, sir, you're not. We're just doing our job."

Henry nodded as he and Kate began walking toward the front door.

The door closed behind them and moments later, the SUV was driving away from the warehouse and heading towards the highway. Within thirty minutes they were on a Janet flight headed back to Dreamland. For the first time since it all began, the two were finally able to relax.

"Dad, they know about us, they know about Prometheus!"

Henry Summers let out a heavy sigh. "Yes, Kate, they do. They hacked into our systems and now they know. The general's going to love this."

"What happens now?" she asked him, running her hands through her hair.

"I think we will need to re-double our efforts with Ignis, along with the rest of Prometheus."

Father and daughter then sat back and within a few minutes, both were asleep in their seats, where they remained for the duration of their flight back to Area 51.

Chapter 7

Nick Reynolds tapped his fingers impatiently on the table next to his chair, where he had been waiting for nearly half an hour. He had not even seen Caprella yet and already he hated himself for what he was going to do, but what choice did he have? He didn't care so much that his job was on the line; it was the danger that the entire country was in, and the danger to the way of life of each and every American.

"Dr. Reynolds? The general can see you now. Please come this way." The woman was attractive yet also very professional, and she was a most welcome, temporary distraction from the reason for his visit. Based on the eagle on her collar, which he'd noticed this time, he recognized that she was also a full-bird colonel. That was okay with Nick; she was easy on the eyes and after all, he *had* always respected authority.

"Why thank you, Colonel," he said smoothly. She nodded and smiled knowingly back at Reynolds, with a subtle hint of flirtation. She escorted him to the general's office and knocked on the door.

"Come in," came a gruff response from inside. She brushed gently past Nick and cracked open the door. Nick peered around her and could see that the general was just hanging up his phone and waving him in. Nick acknowledged the colonel and smiled one last time at the woman before walking into the office.

"Thanks again, Colonel," he said again, grinning.

"Anytime, sir," she answered, winking at him before closing the door.

"Come in Nick; it's good to see you again, son."

Reynolds walked in, shook Caprella's extended hand, and sat down. "Hello, General. Thank you for seeing me on such short notice, sir."

Caprella sat back in his chair and assessed Reynolds demeanor. "Not a problem, Nick my boy, that's why I'm here. So tell me, what's on your mind? Have you learned any more about this attack supposedly being planned by the Chinese?"

"Nothing specific, General, no. There has been some increased chatter, however, which seems to indicate that some kind of attack is imminent, and that it's getting closer now. I had some back-channel information given to me that was passed to the CIA by the Russians, which seemed to suggest that an attack could come within the next two months."

"Hmm." Caprella grimaced for a moment before focusing back on Nick. "Have there been any other new developments you can share with me Nick, maybe some evidence which can either link the Chinese to these rumored attacks or else prove their innocence?"

"No, nothing that I haven't included in my reports. We're still working on it, sir."

"Very well then, please keep me posted."

"Yes, sir, I will."

General Caprella furrowed his brow and lowered his head. After several moments, he looked back up to see that Reynolds had not moved.

"Was there something else, Nick?" he asked, somewhat surprised to see him still sitting there.

"Yes, sir, I'm afraid there *is* something else. General, Operation Counterpunch was created with the mission to protect America by safeguarding our secrets and data from foreign states. You put me in charge of this task force, General, and I appreciate the trust that you've placed in me. But honestly sir, the United States appears to be so far behind China at the moment that I don't see any possible way that we can catch up to them, at least not in the foreseeable future."

"And in the meantime you're worried that this imminent attack is real; that it will come once they've finished testing their weapons and our defenses, and after they've stolen enough of our secrets and technology...until there's nothing left that they don't already have. Is that it, son?"

"Yes, General, unfortunately, that is the dilemma that we now find ourselves facing. Sir, I don't know how to stop this from happening. I've tried and I've tried to think of something. I've spoken with a wide variety of security experts: white, gray, blue, and even a few black hat hackers, professors at MIT, executives at software and hardware companies from all over the world. There have been a lot of great ideas presented, but no one has had any ideas or technology that would enable us to catch up to the Chinese in time to defend against these cyber attacks. Sir, I'm afraid that I just don't know how to protect the infrastructure of the United States from this imminent attack."

Caprella focused his gaze on Reynolds. "Why do I get the feeling that there's something else you're not telling me, Nick?"

"General, I feel like I'm failing you and our country, sir. I'm resigning from this task force, and I'm resigning from Phoenix Corporation as well."

"What? But why? You're one of the best IT security men I've ever seen, Nick."

"I figured that maybe if I step aside, you'd be able to find someone a lot more capable than I am, someone that can actually do something to stop this threat."

"Nonsense, my boy. I knew what we were facing when I appointed you to lead this task force; that's *why* I chose you. Cyber Command has some of the brightest and most resourceful minds in the world, and you are among the brightest and most resourceful people here. I need you Nick, and your country needs you."

"General, I joined Phoenix and came to work at Cyber Command because I felt like I could make a difference, and I tried my best to do just that. But what can I possibly do to stop what's coming? We're so far behind the curve at this point that our chances of being ready for this imminent cyber attack are next to nil. We just don't have time to catch up to the Chinese in terms of cyber warfare capabilities, whether offensive or defensive. I've done everything I could to come up with something…anything…we might do to find a solution, and I've come up empty. I've already done what I could to start strengthening our defenses within our critical national infrastructure. I've ordered numerous assessment and remediation projects to be expedited which will either add, update, or replace firewalls, intrusion detection/prevention systems, anti-virus, and PKI at all nuclear power plants, all major components of the electrical grid, all major financial institutions, the DOD, the Pentagon, and every other government institution."

"Will it be enough?" asked Caprella.

"No, General, it will not, but we had to try. It's just going to be too little too late, I'm afraid. I'm sorry, sir. If I had five to ten years, maybe.

Shoot, if I had even three years I might be able to do something, but less than three months? Not a chance."

"So what you're telling me, Nick, is that if and when a major cyber attack *is* launched against the United States, we're completely at the mercy of the attacker?"

"Yes, General, that's exactly what I'm telling you. You'll have my resignation on your desk the first thing tomorrow morning."

General Caprella stared out his window for several moments. Nick turned to walk away but was stopped before he made it to the door.

"No, Nick! Stop, please wait."

Reynolds stopped and turned around.

"Yes, General?"

"Please, just come back in here for a moment and sit down, and listen to what I'm about to tell you. If you don't like what I have to say then fine, but please hear me out."

Nick reluctantly complied.

"Listen, son, I've been in the military for a long time now, and I've seen a lot of great leaders come and go; and I've seen a lot of bad ones come and go during that time as well. Can you guess what characteristic I found the most common in almost every great leader I encountered?"

"No, sir."

"None of them really wanted to *be* a great leader, Nick. They just happened to be at the right place and the right time in history where they were desperately needed to do something great, and they answered that call. Each of them understood the weight and the pressure that came with carrying such responsibility on their shoulders. Having the life and death responsibility of other people that comes with command can be quite a burden; I know that from personal experience. And now, Nick my boy, you're carrying such a burden, and your country needs for you to do something great. If you don't Nick, who will? What would have happened if George Washington or Abraham Lincoln had decided to wait for someone else, someone they considered to be more worthy, to come along to fight the British, or to keep a brand new country from tearing itself apart? You're a great leader Nick; you just need to reach down deep and find the strength you need to carry on. You're right here, right now, for a reason, Nick. God doesn't make mistakes."

General Caprella paused to give Nick a few moments to digest what he was saying.

"But what if I fail, General?"

"Failure sometimes comes with the territory, Nick, and we have to accept that fact. But by all that's holy, if we're gonna take a beating, let's go down fighting!"

Nick smiled at the general's eloquence.

"Okay, General Caprella; I surrender, sir. I promise that I'll do everything I can to stop this attack, and keep the country safe."

"That's the spirit!"

Caprella sat in his chair for several moments, looking at Nick but saying nothing. It took a moment for Nick to realize that Caprella was not actually looking *at* him; rather he was looking *through* him, lost in thought. After several moments, he tilted his head to one side and suddenly smiled. He then rose from his chair and walked around to the other side of his desk. He sat down on the corner of it closest to where Nick was sitting.

"Nick, I have an idea. I want you to do something else for me. Pretend for just a moment that you could have anything you desired to bridge the technology gap that we have with the Chinese, and to counter an imminent cyber attack; what would you need? Please, just let your imagination run wild for a few moments."

"About ten years?" Nick answered.

Caprella just frowned. "How about a thousand, son?"

Nick looked at him for a moment, confused by the question, before deciding to ignore it and continuing.

"Sorry. Oh, I don't know, General...I guess I'd like to have plenty of raw computer processing power, execution speed, at least thirty to forty petabytes of storage. Add to that list a number of completely revolutionary and highly advanced anti-virus programs, which could be used in both offensive and defensive capacities, and an artificial intelligence system capable of communicating and coordinating instructions and activity out to and between all virus programs simultaneously. Finally, I'd need an extremely powerful and advanced firewall platform and intrusion protection system, which would be capable of defending against any and all attacks, while also identifying and distinguishing between friendly programs and viruses. Basically sir, we would need a completely new order of cyber intelligence hardware and software in order to catch up to and surpass the Chinese and stop these attacks cold. As you said before, General, we need a real game changer. In other words sir, we would need the impossible to happen. At this point, I believe the only way we can stop this thing from happening is to suddenly have a boatload of advanced technology suddenly fall into our laps."

General George Caprella suddenly and inexplicably smiled broadly.

"Nick, what you just described may not be as impossible as you think."

"Sir?"

"Were you aware Nick, that in addition to Cyber Command, I have overseen a number of black and highly secretive projects, which are also considered of vital importance to national security?"

"No sir, I wasn't; but I'm not surprised to hear that you are, given your years of experience and ability."

"Thank you. So there is another project in particular which I've been overseeing for quite a few years now, which I believe, with some work, might be able to help us out of this jam we're in. After I came to work with the NSA and Cyber Command, I continued my oversight of this particular program because of its strategic value. Tell me something, Nick; how would you like to visit Area 51?"

Chapter 8

Chervanko poured himself another glass of vodka before passing the bottle along to the others. He took a sip and sat back in his chair. The presentation had gone better than he had expected, *much* better than he expected. Not only had Lee done a fabulous job of making the Ares system foolproof and extraordinarily easy to use, he also had built in a significant amount of redundancy, including a hot site in Minsk. It was a ten hour drive from Moscow, but the site and its distance from Moscow would make it an effective secondary base of operations should the Americans prove to be smarter and more resourceful than he thought they were and retaliate with some kind of limited counter-attack against their base of operations in Moscow.

"Everyone, I propose a toast!" Chervanko stood and was soon joined by Levin, Kozlov, and Smirnoff. "To Comrade Lee, the most ingenious, capable, and thorough computer expert I have ever met. *Za zdorovje!* To your health, Dr. Lee!" he said to the Chinese national.

"*Za zdorovje!*" they all repeated.

Chervanko poured another glass of vodka for Lee, who clearly felt confident that his presentation had gone well, especially since everyone seemed to be in high spirits, and in awe of his superior handiwork. When he looked up at Chervanko to thank him for the drink, however, he once again found himself unexpectedly backing away from the much taller Russian. Chervanko's face had suddenly transformed into something cold, impersonal, and hard, as if it had just been carved out of stone.

"Please, Comrade Lee, finish your drink. Once you have finished, there is just one more thing I'd like to go over with you." His voice was cool and steady, his eyes dark.

A confused Lee finished off his vodka. He ignored the sinking feeling he suddenly had as the cold chill of fear raced down his spine.

"What is left to go over, Comrade Chervanko?" he asked shakily. "The system is ready, I have given all of you an overview of how it works, and I have taught you how to use it."

An icy smile appeared on Chervanko's face, which seemed to betray something vile within his heart.

"Why, my dear Dr. Lee, we must test this wonderful system of yours. How else will we know for certain that it works as you have promised?"

"Oh yes...of course...I understand. You wish to steal some data?"

"Oh, no, my dear doctor, we need to do something much more...substantial. We must test the system to ensure it delivers, while also getting the complete attention of our American friends. But first I must know something; can you tell me with absolute certainty that everything we do with Ares will appear to the Americans as if it came from our dear friends in China?"

"Of course, Comrade Chervanko," Lee said with an unsteady, nervous sound in his voice. "Most attacks will appear to come from somewhere near Beijing, the rest from other large cities in China.

"You are absolutely certain of this?" Chervanko asked, edging much closer to Lee until they stood toe-to-toe, and their faces were no more than six inches apart. "Are you willing to stake your life on it?"

Lee stared at him, frozen, and said nothing.

Chervanko asked the question again in a calm, steady voice. "Answer me, Dr. Lee; are you willing to stake your life on it?"

After several moments, Lee, beginning to fear what would happen if he said nothing, finally managed to force a weak and timid response.

"Yes, Comrade Chervanko, I guess so."

Chervanko stepped back, looked at the others, and offered a broad smile.

"Good! Then let's test this electronic marvel that you've created for us."

The ex-KGB agent motioned to Lee, who then followed him into the large open room where he had spent so much time over the last two years. He sat down at the console and logged into the system. A splash screen with the red Chinese flag appeared. Something had been super-imposed on the flag, to the right of the one large star and the four smaller stars. The image was comprised of a different flag, featuring the skull and crossbones of the internationally recognized pirate flag, the Jolly Roger. A few moments later the flag disappeared and an image of Ares, the Greek god of war, filled the screen for several moments, before also disappearing just before a menu screen appeared. The menu selections represented twenty-five categories of attacks. Lee looked up nervously at Chervanko, who was hovering closely over his right shoulder.

"Which category of attacks, Mr. Chervanko? 'Get Data'?"

"No," the Russian answered firmly. "'Infrastructure.'"

Lee tapped a key and another menu appeared. He began running through the menu selections as they appeared on the screen. "'Electric Grid,' 'Water & Sewage'…?"

"'Nuclear Power Plants,'" Chervanko said coldly.

Lee cast a brief glance back at Chervanko, but looked back at the screen to avert his eyes when the Russian looked back.

"Which facility?" asked Lee, now starting to shake slightly.

"Indian Lake in Buchanan, New York."

"'Access floor plans and schematics'?" Lee asked fearfully, afraid he already knew the answer.

"No, 'Nuclear Meltdown,'" Chervanko replied.

Lee turned to protest, but the determined look on the man's face convinced him otherwise.

"Which reactor?"

"Both, Comrade Lee…both."

"Um, you do realize, Comrade Chervanko, that if both reactors melt down, over one hundred thousand people will die within days from the radiation?"

Chervanko didn't bother answering; he continued staring at Lee impatiently. "Now, Mr. Lee. I want the two reactors at the Indian Lake plant to melt down immediately."

Lee hesitated, looking up at Chervanko once more. He prepared to ask again whether he was certain he wanted to murder over one hundred thousand human beings, but the expressionless face, carved in granite, gave him his answer. Lee let out a heavy sigh. After several moments he reached out, selected both of the active reactors at Indian Lake which were depicted on the screen, and reached out to press the red, soft button on the screen which would launch the attack. His hand began to tremble and he withdrew it.

"I…I'm sorry, Mr. Chervanko. I…I can't do it. I…can't kill over a hundred thousand people!"

Chervanko walked over, grabbed Lee, and hurled him to the ground.

"Pathetic. I had hoped you might show yourself a man, Comrade Lee, but instead you have proven you are only a mouse." Chervanko reached over and pressed the red button before closing his eyes and smiling. A progress bar appeared next to a Jolly Roger.

"It's done, gentlemen," Chervanko stated enthusiastically. "Now we will see how the Americans react when they see one hundred thousand citizens of New York dead because of a cyber attack by the Chinese."

"Do you think our plan will work? Will the Americans retaliate against China?" asked Smirnoff.

"If they do not, we will be in great danger I think," said Levin, still sipping on his vodka.

"When the Saudi terrorists attacked the World Trade Center in New York in 2001, the Americans reacted swiftly in Afghanistan. They will attack," Kozlov said, finishing his glass of vodka and pouring another.

"Yes, my dear comrades, the Americans will respond to the massacre of a hundred thousand of its citizens; they will have no choice."

"Then, of course, the Chinese, knowing they had nothing to do with the attack in New York, will respond in kind," Koslov added.

"Yes, my friends…once the war between the United States and China is finally over, our country—and the entire world—will be in complete disarray and chaos. We will convince our brothers and sisters that we must rebuild our great country; that our beloved U.S.S.R. must be reborn to become even greater, stronger, and more glorious than ever before!" said Chervanko, nodding his head with his eyes closed.

"What do we do now, Nikolai?" asked Smirnoff.

"Now we get lunch, and wait," Chervanko answered, walking toward the door wearing a big smile.

* * * *

Several hours passed, and the foursome returned to the warehouse.

"Come! We must turn on the television and watch the news. How else will we know for sure whether the attack worked as planned?" asked Chervanko, as he led the way into the office where a small television sat, and turned it so they could see. He turned it on and flipped through the channels until an image of two nuclear reactors appeared. Underneath was a caption that read, "Nuclear Meltdown Possible At New York Power Plant." The reporter was saying something as Chervanko turned up the volume.

"—and the local sheriff's office informed us only moments ago that they have done all that *they* can do to evacuate the area, given the extremely congested roadways which are already virtually nothing but parking lots. The National Guard is also being deployed, although few believe they will be able to evacuate so many in such a brief period of time. If you've just joined us, we have some very important, late-breaking news. New York City, along with the Department of Homeland Defense, held a joint press conference just fifteen minutes ago, announcing that a serious problem was detected at the Indian Lake nuclear power plant only two hours ago. The problem, which has been closely monitored since, is reported to be a problem with the coolant system at the plant, a problem which could very well lead to a meltdown. While not yet calling such a meltdown imminent, the government has issued an evacuation for anyone living or working within thirty miles of the Indian Lake nuclear power plant, warning of a deadly threat from radiation fallout facing anyone within the evacuation zone. We've invited Dr. Marcella Blanco to join us; she is an expert with the CDC. Welcome, Dr. Blanco, thank you for joining us."

"Thank you for having me."

"Dr. Blanco, if both reactors do somehow melt down, how bad will it be? Will it result in many deaths?"

"Absolutely. Early estimates from a decade ago suggested that at least one hundred thousand people would receive a fatal dose of radiation. That area has seen a significant amount of growth over the past decade, however, so the number has climbed to perhaps as high as one hundred twenty-five thousand people."

The anchor sat silently, looking stunned for a moment. It was one of those rare moments of silence on live television when no one speaks. One of the producers must have yelled at her through her earpiece because she suddenly jolted out of it.

"Excuse me, Dr. Blanco, but you're saying over one hundred twenty-five thousand people are going to die tonight?"

Her face was still pale, white as a sheet.

"Well, if both reactors melt down, as many as one hundred twenty-five thousand people would likely be exposed to a fatal dose of radiation, yes. Depending on their level of exposure, death could take days, weeks, possibly even months to occur."

"If someone cannot get away in time, is there anything they can do?"

"Anyone who is within ten to twenty miles of the plant and is unable to leave should get inside and as far underground as possible. But let me please reiterate that this is a very serious danger to everyone in the area. If at all possible, everyone within a thirty mile radius should evacuate immediately. Please don't wait until it's too late."

"Thank you, Dr. Blanco."

"You're very welcome."

The news anchor turned to face the camera.

"Next up, we have Jason Michaels, a former consultant to the Department of Homeland Security. Welcome Mr. Michaels, it's great to have you with us today."

"Thank you, Michelle; it's great to be here, though I wish it were under better circumstances of course."

"Of course," she repeated. "So Jason, do you have any idea what happened at the plant; was it some kind of equipment failure?"

"From what I'm told, Michelle, at approximately 2:05 p.m. today, the systems at the plant that control the water used for cooling the control rods in both reactors suddenly shut down, but only after sending instructions to the programmable logic controllers to close all valves in the cooling system. At this time the PLCs continue to be unresponsive and all valves remain closed. Once the super-heated water evaporates, the rods will be exposed and the reactors *will* melt down. I'll tell you something else, too…the most disturbing aspect of this disaster is that the shutdown appears to have been done intentionally by someone, remotely."

"So the system was shut down remotely. Why would someone with the power company have done that intentionally, while the plants are still in operation; isn't that dangerous?"

"Very. Apparently the systems were not shut down by anyone at the plant though. Based on all of the information I've been able to gather, everyone associated with the Indian Lake plant denies having anything to do with what's happened. My contacts told me that the system wasn't designed like that anyway. That's why this was, *in my opinion*, an act of terrorism."

"Wow, that is really frightening!" exclaimed the anchor, staring in disbelief. "How could an unauthorized person access the water control system remotely? Why would that even be possible?"

"I asked that same question. It seems that the company installed the remote access capability so they would be able to activate the water control pumps remotely in the event of some kind of accident, in case there was no one able to do it at the plant itself. Unfortunately, with so many systems connected to the Internet these days, it's possible—let me stress possible—that someone hacked in, circumvented the considerable security, and shut them down remotely."

"But wouldn't it require substantial resources to be able to pull something like that off without being caught?"

"Yes, it would. Typically, only nation states have the kind of access to the resources needed to pull something like this off, not to mention the skills. It might be possible that an individual could do this I suppose, but I don't see how."

"Does the DHS have any idea where the attack originated?"

"Well, as you noted earlier, I no longer work at the DHS. A source of mine does still work there, however, and they called me thirty minutes after they learned the systems had been shutdown."

"What did they tell you?"

"They told me that they had traced the IP address of the intruder."

"To where?" asked the anchor.

"China."

* * * *

Chervanko pressed a button on the remote control and the television flickered off. He then looked down at the table for several moments before looking around at his friends.

"Comrades, this is indeed a historical day. Soon, very soon, the two greatest obstacles to the rebirth of the U.S.S.R. will annihilate one another. With these two world powers crippled or destroyed, the world will be ripe for Mother Russia to rise as the *new* U.S.S.R., and it will restore order to a frightened world. We, my friends, will then be forced to step in, of course, to help lead our nation and the world back from the brink!"

Levin stood to offer a toast. "To Mother Russia!" he said, before the others rose to join him.

Lee, who looked terrified at this point, rose and meekly touched his glass to the others. As if a cold chill had just run down his spine, he shivered when Chervanko started walking towards him.

"Mr. Lee, you are looking at the rulers of the new world! Please, come here my friend and let me embrace you, for none of this would be possible were it not for you!"

Lee timidly took a few steps to meet Chervanko, who placed his right arm around Lee's shoulder.

"Gentlemen, another toast to Comrade Lee!" The others looked at Lee and smiled before turning to Chervanko, each wearing the same solemn expression on their faces. Chervanko nodded slightly and set his glass down on the table. He turned to look at Lee and smiled. "We will always be in your debt!" he said. In a fluid movement that he had clearly executed before, he then grabbed the back of Lee's head with his right hand just as he brought up his left hand and placed it on the front of Lee's face. With a quick thrust with the left and a pull with the right, Lee's neck snapped and he fell lifeless to the floor. Chervanko then picked up his glass, turned to the others, and once more raised the glass for a toast. "To Comrade Lee and to Mother Russia!"

"To Comrade Lee, and to Mother Russia," they all repeated, with fierce and determined looks in their eyes.

Chapter 9

Henry Summers walked tentatively into the lab where his daughter was busy looking at a computer monitor. On the screen was an unusual object, which was a pale greenish-gray in color. It bore bizarre symbols that he had seen many times before. He placed a hand on Kate's shoulder, then sat down on a stool beside her. "Hi, Dad," she said, smiling, without turning around. Whatever she was working on she was focused on it intensely.

"How are you doing?" he asked her, looking over his daughter's smooth features. She looked a lot like her mother had when they first met decades earlier. He smiled when the thought occurred to him that she could have been her mother's twin.

"I've been making some real progress, Dad. After all these years, I believe I'm finally ready to try removing Ignis. I've spent the last year trying to verify that Ignis itself is a standalone unit, so I can separate it from the cables and conduit which connect it to the rest of the craft. Do you know what this means, Dad?" She turned to her father, her eyes wide with excitement and anticipation. He looked as if he had not heard a word she had spoken.

"I meant, how are *you*?" He glanced back up at the screen for a moment. "And by the way, why did you name the thing Ignis anyway?" he asked after several moments of silence. Kate looked back at him with a blank expression.

"What? Oh, that. I'm doing okay, Dad...I guess. I'm just glad neither of us was hurt. We've got to be more careful from now on, Dad. Now that it's gotten out about Prometheus, someone may try again. Maybe we should spend less time off of the base."

"Or maybe we should just take Security up on their offer to provide an escort whenever we leave the base. After all, we are working on what's probably the most secret project in the world.

"As to how the Chinese learned about Prometheus, I was talking with General Caprella about that just yesterday. He suspects they came across Prometheus buried in some of the sensitive data they stole from the D.O.D."

His daughter stopped what she was doing for a moment and looked at her father.

"Dad, does he think the Chinese were responsible for what happened in New York yesterday?" She looked worried and fearful. Everyone knew what would happen once the investigation was finished; whoever was responsible was going to pay a very high price for the horrific crime.

"He said that there appears to be evidence pointing to that, yes. I got the feeling he wasn't as certain about it as so many of the pundits and politicians are."

"Well, they have been hacking our systems for a number of years now. I wouldn't be one bit surprised if they're responsible for the meltdowns. Has there been any talk of retaliation yet? I watched the news, but I was curious about what General Caprella said."

"He said that there's a lot of back and forth accusations between Chinese and American diplomats... pretty much what we see on the news. The Chinese are vigorously denying any involvement whatsoever with what happened in New York, despite the evidence presented. They've finally admitted to some of the other hacks into some of our more sensitive systems over the last couple of decades, and they accuse us of doing the same, of course. Regardless, I don't think our government will do anything until the evidence has been laid out and thoroughly examined... unless something else happens, of course. If the government ends up declaring this an act of war by the Chinese and the United States does retaliate, we could be looking at the world's first nuclear war."

Kate looked at her father before looking back at the screen.

"It makes Prometheus seem unimportant, doesn't it?" she asked.

"Nonsense, Kate," Henry answered calmly. "Prometheus could be the key to eventual world peace, if properly handled," he added.

"Oh, and Dad?"

"Yes?"

"You asked me about why I named the device 'Ignis.' I thought that since, in Greek mythology, Prometheus brought fire to mankind, 'Ignis' was a great name, since it means 'fire.' After all, while the ship's propulsion systems may enable us to one day travel to the stars, it may well be Ignis that helps us get there sooner. Not to mention the fact that it could revolutionize our computer and navigation technology."

"Oh yes, fire, of course!" Her father smiled in response.

Kate turned back to the screen and, after moving the joystick slightly, she zoomed the remote camera in at a joint between the strange object and the console where it rested. She looked at her dad before looking back at the screen.

"Look, Dad. Do you see this here?" she asked, pointing with the tip of her well-groomed fingernail. "I'm confident that this is the joint here, below the console, where Ignis is resting. It's barely visible, even when I've been right next to it looking at it under magnification, and it looks like it's part of the device. After studying it for a while, however, I now believe it's a joint. If I gently disconnect the conduits and slowly move them out of the console, I think we can safely remove Ignis. Once we have it here in the lab, I can begin working to fabricate an interface between Ignis and our computer system."

"Take your time, Kate, and do your best to be certain before trying it. Remember, we can't just run down to the local computer store and pick one of these things up when they're on sale."

"Come on, Dad, give me some credit! I've been extraordinarily meticulous about this, and while there's no way to be certain, I'm finally confident enough about the joint and the rest of the considerations that I think I'm finally ready to disconnect it from the ship!"

"I know how meticulous you are, Kate...I'm sorry."

"That's okay, Dad, and rest assured that I know it's the only one we have; that's why I've taken such a long time to study it."

"So do you still think Ignis is some type of on-board navigation system? If so, how can you be so sure?"

"I'm not sure. But I also no longer think that Ignis is *just* a navigational system, Dad...I think it ran the whole ship."

Henry Summers carefully studied where the object rested in some sort of cradle-type structure. If Kate was right, the system was designed to run the entire ship, and to be removable from the rest of the ship if needed as well, something he thought peculiar.

"Fascinating. Well then, you have my authorization to go ahead and remove Ignis from the rest of the ship, Kate. I suppose we can't learn any more about it without further testing and study here in the lab." He turned back to Kate. "That's why I needed the very best and brightest to work on this part of the project, Kate. I needed someone who could find the answers; someone who was every bit as determined and capable as I am."

"I guess it's a good thing that you chose your daughter then, isn't it Dad?" She looked at him and smiled.

"Yes, I suppose it is," he answered. "Okay, so when will you try and detach Ignis from the rest of the ship?"

"Well, if I can get my hands on Tom and Frank, we might be able to get it on a cart with just the three of us. Nothing on that ship seems to have much weight to it."

"Do you want some help with your testing? I'm sure Lou or Dave would be happy to help, maybe one day get their name on the Nobel Prize next to yours."

"Thanks, Dad, but no. You know me, I work faster on my own."

"Okay then, Kate. Well, I'm off to yet another meeting."

"Who is it with this time, the president?"

"No," he chuckled. "General Caprella is supposed to be bringing someone from another project of his in to meet with me. It sounds like he thinks there may be some kind of tie-in between this other project of his and Prometheus."

"Does this guy have high enough clearance to be read in on Prometheus?" she asked her father.

"If he didn't before I suppose he does now," he answered. Henry studied his daughter. Her cheeks were flushed and her jaw was set. A storm was coming.

"Well, I don't want some government stooge from another project to come in here and try to take over. I'll go over Caprella's head if I have to. I'm too close to a breakthrough to let this joker interfere with the fantastic progress I've been making."

"Now just calm yourself, Kate. Let me find out what's going on, then we'll see if there's anything I need to discuss with George, okay?"

"Okay, Dad." She turned back to the computer screen. "If I'm not in here when you get back, I'll be on the ship. Please find me and tell me what's going on, okay?"

"Sure thing, sweetheart, back in a bit."

Chapter 10

Henry Summers left the lab and proceeded to the elevator. He pressed the button for Level 4 and considered Kate's reaction. If Caprella *was* bringing someone in to take over their project, or someone to work with them who could jeopardize the progress they had both been making, he knew Kate would have nothing to do with it. She would do just as she had threatened and go over Caprella's head to the president if necessary. They had been making tremendous strides in their research and she would be able to make a great case against endangering that progress.

The elevator sounded and the doors opened. Summers exited the elevator and walked toward the Relativity meeting room. Some geek had thought it would be clever to name each meeting room after a scientist or scientific term that was somehow related to their work on Prometheus. When he reached the meeting room, he found the door already cracked and heard voices coming from within. Upon entering, he saw Caprella and a much younger man stand up.

"I'm sorry I'm late, gentlemen. We are close to a critical step in one of our projects." He walked over to the younger man and introduced himself. "Good morning, I'm Dr. Henry Summers."

"It's a pleasure to meet you, Dr. Summers," the young man said in a pleasant voice. "I'm Dr. Nick Reynolds. I've worked for General Caprella here for a long time over at Cyber Command, but most recently I've been heading up Operation Counterpunch, a Cyber Command task force."

"Hmm, Cyber Command," he said, slowly rubbing his chin as he sat down. "Now I think I might have an idea why General Caprella has brought you here then, however outlandish his idea might be," he stated flatly, staring at Caprella.

"Take it easy, Henry," Caprella said calmly. "I know it's a long shot, but you need to hear us out on this. There are a lot of lives on the line here and, well, I know how brilliant you and Kate are, so I figured that if anyone would be able to find a way for us to utilize Ignis, it would be the two of you."

"Who's Kate?" asked Nick.

"Dr. Kate Reynolds, Nick...that's his daughter," Caprella informed him. "They work together on the Prometheus Project, along with a staff of other scientists, of course." Caprella turned back to Summers. "Henry, Nick is tasked with finding a means to stop the constant cyber attacks that have been plaguing us over the last few years. I guess you've heard about the meltdown in New York?"

"Yes, of course," Henry answered while shaking his head. "Awful; all those people dead. I just don't understand how anyone could do something so horrific! Have you been able to determine for certain that it was the Chinese?"

"Well, we're still working on that; but for now I just wanted for you understand how important this is. Look, Henry, regardless of who is behind these most recent attacks, we know for certain that the Chinese have been hacking into our systems at the U.S. Department of Defense, NASA, and pretty much every other organization that had any data they wanted and didn't already have, for at least a decade now, maybe more. Like I told you earlier, that's how the Chinese found out about Prometheus." Henry nodded. "Frankly, we've allowed ourselves to fall so far behind *whoever* is behind these recent attacks, whether it's the Chinese or someone else, that we now have very little to no chance of catching them at this point. Even more disconcerting is the considerable chatter over the past year or so about an imminent, massive, and catastrophic cyber attack against the infrastructure of the United States, which is supposed to occur sometime between now and Christmas. Think about it, Henry; something far worse than what just happened in New York is just around the corner."

"By Christmas, that's only three months from now!" replied Summers. He looked down at the table for several moments, contemplating what he had just been told, before looking back up at Caprella. "The meltdown in New York, could *it* have been the rumored attack?"

"No. We believe that Indian Lake was only another test, intended to get our attention, and that the real attack could occur at any moment. "

"Why would someone do this, George, kill so many innocent people?" asked Summers.

"That, Henry is the right question to ask," Caprella replied.

"There could be any number of reasons why China would attack the infrastructure of the United States," offered Nick. "The one that worries us the most, however, is that it could be a precursor to a first-strike."

"A first-strike by China?" asked Summers. "But why? What do they have to gain by declaring an act of war against the United States?"

"Perhaps they see us as the greatest threat to their growing global influence, Dr. Summers. Do you recall their anger about us selling arms to Taiwan?"

Henry nodded.

"But again, we're not 100% convinced that the Chinese *are* behind this," continued Nick. "Certainly they deny any involvement with what happened at Indian Lake, or with the rumored cyber attack that's supposedly imminent. They admit only to the occasional theft of data. Despite these denials, however, it is a fact that the attack appears to have originated in China."

"I see," Summers said quietly, before turning back to the general. "So George, you think that Ignis may be able to help somehow?"

This time Caprella nodded in reply. "Maybe. I hope it can because frankly, I'm getting desperate. What do you think, Henry?"

"You mean, assuming Kate's theories are correct; that she is able to get it to work; that she is able to get it to integrate with our systems; and that it has the capability to do what you want it to do?"

Caprella grinned slightly and raised his eyebrows. "Yeah, I guess that's a lot of assuming, isn't it?" Caprella acknowledged, grinning.

Henry's eyes opened wide as he nodded.

"Look, I know it's a Hail Mary, Henry, but we already have our best people working on more conventional solutions and so far, they've turned up empty. Nick and I have discussed it and we believe there's just not enough time to stop these attacks through any conventional means. If there's a possibility, no matter how far remote, that Ignis *could* help stop the attacks, prevent a nuclear war, and save millions of lives, it's worth a try, isn't it Henry? I need to know that I can count on your support with this."

"I don't know, George; what you're proposing really worries me. You've got to keep in mind that we've spent decades studying this technology, and we still don't understand how it works, or even if it still does—it could turn out to be broken. But even if we were, somehow, able to get it to work, we just don't know the ramifications of activating Ignis and using it to access our alien systems." Summers paused as Caprella sat back and crossed his arms.

"I understand it's a risk, Henry, but remember what we're up against...consider the alternative."

"Global thermonuclear war."

"Exactly," Caprella offered in response.

Henry glanced inconspicuously over at Nick for a moment as he considered it, before eventually letting out a heavy sigh. "Okay, I understand what we're up against, George, and I suppose we have no choice but to try it and see how far we can get. I'll certainly do everything that I can to help get Ignis operational."

"Wonderful! So, Henry, why don't you give Nick here an overview of Prometheus, and then Ignis."

"Okay. What have you told him about it so far, George?"

"Only that you've been working with some *very* advanced technology, and that some of it might help with his mission to leapfrog the enemy's cyber warfare capabilities in order to protect the United States."

"Okay, I guess you'd better get comfortable, Dr. Reynolds, because this will take a while." Summers sighed and took a deep breath before starting. "I was still a young boy living in Corona, New Mexico in 1947, when I saw something crash near there. We thought at first it was a plane, but when we went to check for survivors, we found it wasn't an airplane at all, but something else."

"Oh, no, you've got to be kidding! Are you saying that a spacecraft from another world really did crash near Roswell, New Mexico in 1947?"

"That's precisely what I'm telling you, Dr. Reynolds," Henry answered bluntly. "Except we didn't find just one craft, we found two. One of them had been destroyed; the other was damaged but still intact."

"So all of the stories about Roswell—the conspiracy theories, the alien technology, the reverse-engineering at Area 51—they're all true?"

"Well, not all of them, Nick, but there is a lot of truth in the mix," answered Caprella.

"Misinformation?"

"Of course —well, at least some of it. It's amazing, really. You give people a little nudge and their imagination does the rest." Henry continued. "Soon after the discovery of the craft on the morning following a severe lightning storm, an announcement was prematurely made by Roswell Army Air Field public information officer Walter Haut, that the wreckage of a flying saucer had been found. Now, the last thing the military leadership at the time wanted was for the Russians to learn that we had the most advanced technology on the planet in our possession. Remember, there was never any love lost between communist Russia and the United States, and our possession of such technology would probably have been seen by the Soviets as a provocation of war.

"So, after a second announcement was made by the military contradicting the one made by Haut, Prometheus was handed over to a government agency, which in turn contracted out the project in order to give the U.S. government plausible deniability, though it was very tightly controlled by the agency. The secret intelligence agency, set up in 1947 by Harry Truman after the war, was originally referred to as Majestic 12, or MJ-12, though it was later renamed. This agency was a secret committee comprised of scientists, military leaders, and government officials. The purpose of the committee was to investigate and oversee the recovery of the craft.

"So the craft, the remains of the dead pilots, and the lone survivor, along with all of the pieces of the other ship which were scattered across several square miles, were eventually brought here, to S-4." Henry Summers paused when he saw the stupefied response on Nick's face, because it was the same look he almost always saw on the faces of individuals he had just debriefed about Prometheus for the first time.

"How many ships are here?" asked Reynolds, barely able to contain himself.

"I'm afraid there's just the one," answered Summers, smiling.

"Did you say that one of the aliens survived the crash?"

"Yes, one of them did, but only for a few months. His injuries were too severe and we had no idea how to treat him. Fortunately, our guest was able to share a few things about their technology before he died. What he attempted, however, was much like trying to explain particle physics to a child in kindergarten; we were only able to grasp bits and pieces. Those bits and pieces were enough, however, so that over the decades we were able to develop a very basic understanding of their technology."

"You've been reverse-engineering their technology?"

"Absolutely—well, saying that we've been *trying to* would be more precise," answered Summers. "How do you think the world's been able to come along so far so fast in terms of our technology? Once we finally understood how some the fundamentals of their technology operated, it was only a matter of time. Products like fiber-optic cabling, integrated circuits, many of the other major technological breakthroughs in the 20th and 21st century are all, in part, a result of what we learned from the craft. Mostly what we learned was just enough to push us into trying new ideas, and going in new directions in our research where we might never have gone without what we'd learned here, at Area 51.

"We've had small teams of scientists working on specific parts of the craft since the early 1950s. As George mentioned earlier, my daughter is herself a scientist here and is part of Project Prometheus. Lately she's been leading up a team working to analyze and try to understand what we believe to be an onboard navigational system of sorts. She's been making great progress and had a few breakthroughs recently."

"Incredible."

"Yes, isn't it?" Caprella asked, wearing an uncharacteristic grin on his face. Nick smiled when he noticed the boyish enthusiasm on his face, because he shared it.

"But as fantastic as all of this is, what does any of this have to do with our little 'problem' in cyberspace?" asked Reynolds, impressed but still somewhat perplexed. "Is there something you've learned that can help stop this imminent attack?"

"Go ahead; tell him about Ignis, Henry."

"Ah yes, Ignis. Kate, my daughter, was the first to identify it as a key component of the craft. It was installed apart from the bridge in a different part of the ship, and was so inconspicuous it was overlooked for decades. She thinks Ignis is an extremely advanced computer, far beyond and very unlike anything we've ever seen or even thought of before. We've been unable to test it while it's still installed in the ship, however, because power and some other onboard systems seem to have been damaged by the lightning strike and the subsequent crash. It's possible that Ignis, if it even is a computer as she suggests, was also damaged in the crash. We won't know anything, however, until we separate Ignis from the craft and get it installed in the lab, where we can work with it better." Henry turned to the general.

"Your timing is impeccable, George, as always. Kate will be attempting to remove Ignis and set it up in our lab today, where we can try and get some power to it. We will finally be in a position to start doing some testing…assuming she's right about it, of course."

"That sounds fantastic, Dr. Summers," Nick exclaimed, excited at the prospect. He turned to address Caprella. "So you were thinking that if they *are* able to get Ignis operational, we might be able to find a way to use it to stop the enemy, and help us head-off a war with China?"

"Yep. It's a long shot, Nick, I know, but the future of our country, of the world, may depend on whether Kate's theories are correct, and whether she is able to get Ignis operational."

"I see," Reynolds said at last, following several long moments of contemplation. "So, they've got to get Ignis into the lab, powered up, and operational in time for us to use it as a tool? I would think that it would take quite some time to accomplish all of that, and we need something *today*."

"Like I said, it's a long shot, Nick, I know. Still, it's better than nothing."

"Okay, sir, I understand. So, what would you like for me to do, General?" Reynolds knew they were grasping at straws, but with so much at stake, he also knew they had no choice.

"Is there anyone on Counterpunch that can run things for a while in your absence? I'd like for you to come and setup an office here at S-4. You can still work and meet remotely with the others on your team, but I'd like for you to work with Henry and Kate to see if we can make this thing work, *yesterday*. I want you close in the event Kate is successful. How about it, Nick; will you do this for me, and more importantly, for your country?"

Nick spent several moments trying to think things through and assess the situation and their options. While he would never have admitted it to Caprella or anyone else, in his heart he had already given up on any chance of attaining their objective using conventional means. Developing and implementing defensive countermeasures in the allotted time that were advanced enough to have even a remote chance of stopping the hackers was impossible, much less propagating the protective tool to all critical infrastructure systems across the United States in time, though his team members at Cyber Command were still trying. He knew the cyber attackers would continue to infiltrate the nation's infrastructure systems at will, and if someone did not come up with a solution soon, the imminent attack mentioned in the ominous warning could well end up destroying the country he loved so much, perhaps the world. An attack had already caused the meltdown and the deaths of so many innocent, unsuspecting Americans in New York. Based on what he'd heard, Ignis seemed to Nick to be about as plausible as any other approach. He doubted whether any of them would survive what was coming, but he was determined to go down fighting.

"Sure, General, I'm in," said Nick. "Assuming Dr. Summers is as well." He could not help noticing the scientist's doubtful expressions.

Henry looked first at Reynolds, then at Caprella, saying nothing for the longest time. Eventually he raised his eyebrows and shrugged his shoulders.

"I guess I'm 'in' too. But listen, George, I can't speak for Kate. As you know, she has a mind of her own, and she doesn't work very well with others; sometimes I think she tolerates me only because I'm her father. If we can't get her to buy into this, we're sunk. Ignis is her baby; she's been doing all of the research, developing all of the theories. I can't do it without her."

"Will you please talk with her, Henry? She'll listen to you. Just explain how dire the situation is, and that this is our last and best hope."

Summers nodded slowly before turning to Reynolds.

"I hope you have thick skin and a lot of patience, Dr. Reynolds. My daughter can be a bit…feisty. She's a wonderful young woman, don't get me wrong, but she's somewhat lacking in people skills."

"Don't worry, Dr. Summers. I'm sure we'll get on just fine. I can handle her."

Summers looked at Reynolds and then at Caprella, making a humorous face and raising his eyebrows.

"Did you hear that, George? He said he could 'handle' Kate."

General Caprella and Dr. Henry burst out laughing.

Chapter 11

The man sat at the large, antique desk wearing a troubled expression, carefully studying the assortment of papers and photographs spread out before him. Light filtered in from the window behind him, making the use of the lamp on his desk unnecessary. The man sitting across from him, an Asian man with graying hair, waited patiently.

"How did you say your government came about acquiring this 'information', Mr. Ho?" he asked. The Asian man shrugged slightly and allowed a slight smile to appear.

"I never said, Mr. Andropov. Honestly, I do not know, but even if I did, I'm afraid I would be unable to tell you. My government merely provided me, as our government's diplomat here to your country, with this information and instructed me to bring this to your attention, for you to utilize as you see fit."

"You do realize that you are accusing a highly decorated veteran of the former Soviet army, a man who retired with great distinction from the KGB, *and* a lifetime member of the Communist party, of treason?

"My dear comrade, I'm accusing no one. I'm only doing what I was instructed to do; in an effort to avoid a costly and horrific war, I might add. I assume that you have heard by now what happened in America last week?"

"Are you referring to the accidental meltdown at the nuclear power plant in New York?" asked Andropov.

"The same, only the meltdown was no accident. The U.S. government has, at least for now, only reported it as such, but it was caused when someone hacked into the cooling system at the plant, and remotely shut down the water pumps."

"They suspect that your government might be behind this attack, and your leaders fear the Americans might retaliate for the deaths of so many of their people."

"Precisely. But as you can see, we have recently learned that your former KGB agent was responsible for it, though he made it appear as if it originated from within our country."

"Have you presented any of this information to the Americans yet?"

"We have told them that we are not responsible, but they have not believed us. When we told them of what we know, they responded that they would require 'hard' evidence to convince them of our innocence. They are insisting that they will conduct their own investigations and take appropriate actions once *their* investigations have concluded. My government fears that without sufficient evidence to the contrary, however, the United States will be forced to respond in a manner which could, given my country's innocence in this matter, trigger an all-out war. I believe this is something that your government would prefer to avoid as well, is it not?" Ho glanced at Andropov with a look of hopeful expectation.

"Of course, Mr. Ambassador. A war of that magnitude would wreak the world's economy, not to mention the danger of the conflict spreading, or going nuclear." He took time to read over several of the documents, which listed transactions, biographies of everyone involved, even locations. "Please tell me, Ambassador Ho; why would anyone in their right mind want to start a war like this? You must be mistaken."

"All of the evidence is there in front of you, Mr. Andropov. As to why someone would seek to start this conflict, who can know? I suggest you look into this matter and then ask him yourself. But you must act soon. You have heard the rumors of an imminent cyber attack against the United States?"

Andropov looked up at Ho with a focused intensity. "The attack against their national infrastructure? Yes, from what I understand that is something your government is planning as well, isn't it? I can see why the Americans are so quick to believe this rumor, given the years of cyber attacks by your country."

"And by yours as well, Comrade," Ho was quick to add.

"Hmmph." This time it was Andropov who smiled. "Perhaps this is so." Andropov rose from his desk, followed immediately by Ho.

"You will investigate this matter thoroughly I hope, and soon?" inquired the ambassador.

"I understand what's at stake, Mr. Ambassador. I promise I will let you know what I find as soon as I have anything, *if* I have anything." He extended his hand to the ambassador. "Please thank your government for us for bringing this matter to our attention, Ambassador Ho, instead of foolishly taking matters into their own hands, and by doing so making matters even worse."

"You are most welcome, Colonel Andropov. Please do not give us any reason to regret this course of action, Colonel. I shall be at the embassy, anxiously awaiting your call."

"Thank you, Mr. Ambassador." He walked the ambassador to the door, and after his guest had departed, he returned to his desk.

Andropov sat at his desk for nearly an hour, reading the reports and staring at the photograph of a man who most members of the FSB *still* greatly admired, considering the situation, and trying to determine a proper course of action. He could inform the president, but given the friendship and history between him and Chervanko from the days when the two men had served together in the KGB, he knew that he would likely be reprimanded rather than commended for bringing it to the leader's attention. No, if he were going to bring this to the president, he would need to have rock solid evidence, not just a few sheets of paper and some photographs brought to him by another country's ambassador. Only with real evidence would he be able to convince the president of Chervanko's involvement. Andropov picked up the phone and pushed a button. "Tell Drago, Volkov, and Dudko that I want them in my office in fifteen minutes. I've got something important that I need them to check out immediately; thank you."

* * * *

After a thirty-minute drive, the three FSB agents arrived at the address given to Andropov by the Chinese. Two guards were stationed at the gate that led into the small facility's parking area. Drago grimaced when he noticed that the guards were armed; it wasn't a good sign. The agents pulled up to the gate and one of the guards approached the car.

"Good afternoon, Comrade. This is private property; you'll have to turn around and leave."

Drago pulled out his FSB identification and the startled guard's eyes opened wide.

"Open the gate, now," Drago ordered him.

The man hesitated and looked at his fellow guard briefly, as if asking him what he should do, before turning back to the car. "Please, wait one moment, sir."

The guard walked away from the car and pulled out a cell phone. After dialing a phone number, he began talking with someone. The guard was too far from Drago for the FSB agent to make out what was said. Moments after hanging up the phone, however, the guard returned, pushed a button, and the gate lifted.

"Thank you for waiting, sir. Please, have a nice afternoon."

Drago and the two other agents stared at the guard for a moment before driving past the gate and parking next to a large Hummer. They walked into the office area, where they were immediately met by Chervanko.

"Good afternoon, comrades, I am Nikolai Chervanko." He was smiling, though Drago sensed something sinister under the surface. The men pulled out their badges and presented them to Chervanko.

"We know who you are, Mr. Chervanko. Do you know why we're here?" It was a loaded question, but Chervanko did not bite.

"No, of course not; how could I possibly know why you're here, since you've only just arrived? It's not every day that I'm paid a visit by the FSB. Please, tell me what I can do for you."

Drago began looking around the facility, carefully inspecting and making note of everything he saw.

"Oh yes, of course. I would just like to have a look around, if you don't mind. This is the entrance into the facility?" asked Drago, pointing towards a gray metal door.

"Yes, it is. Please, help yourself and look around for as long as you like. Just let me know if you have any questions." Drago led the way with Volkov and Dudko behind him, while Chervanko pulled up the rear.

"I'm curious; is this an official FSB investigation?" Chervanko asked.

"Perhaps," Drago answered, intending to be vague. He grew interested in all of the computer equipment concentrated in the middle of such a large, empty space.

"So I'm guessing that we don't have to worry about the entire Russian army appearing in our small parking lot anytime soon, do we?"

"No, of course not, it's only us; no one else even knows we're here," Dudko answered absent-mindedly.

Drago turned, preparing to reprimand his subordinate for revealing such a fact to a suspect, but it was too late. He heard the whisper followed by a thumping sound, before watching Dudko collapse in a heap in front of him, followed by Volkov. He recognized within a split-second what had occurred; he immediately leapt behind several large cabinets full of computer equipment just as he heard the muffled sound of several bullets whizzing by his head. The silencer on the PB 9 mm had muffled the sound enough that no one standing outside the building could possibly have heard it fire. Several more shots struck the equipment all around him as he rose to take out his own firearm. Drago pulled his weapon and was preparing to level it when Chervanko suddenly appeared in front of him, and placed the barrel of the PB to the agent's temple.

"Drop it," Chervanko calmly ordered. Drago dropped his own PB to the floor. "You can join us, Comrade Drago, help us restore our Mother Russia to her former glory. The Soviet Empire *will* rise once more, and the world will never be the same again!"

"So, this is what the attacks on America are all about?" Drago asked Chervanko, who was still holding the weapon to his head. "You're going to start a world war in which hundreds of millions of people will die, just so you can chase your personal dreams of glory, chasing after a dream whose time has already come and gone? Those days are behind us now, Mr. Chervanko, they—" He was interrupted by the muted sound of the PB firing another fatal 9mm round. Drago grabbed for his chest before falling to the floor.

"Wrong answer," said Chervanko, before looking around to make sure the area was cleared of agents. Smirnoff, Levin, and the others soon joined him.

"Is he—"

"Is he dead, Comrade Smirnoff? Oh yes, I'd say he is most definitely dead. Did you see any others?"

"No, that was it, Nikolai," Levin replied. "It must have been just the three of them. Why didn't they bring more?"

"I think they were merely acting on a tip, and didn't want to bring anything to President Kireyev until they had more evidence."

"Probably because they knew you served with Kireyev in the KGB," added Levin. Chervanko looked at him and nodded.

Chervanko left Drago's body and walked around to the front of the computer cabinets. Several 9mms had passed through some of the equipment. Sparks appeared just before all of the lights on the equipment flickered and went dark. Nikolai Chervanko cursed his own shortsightedness in retiring Lee too soon.

Chapter 12

All he could do was smile as Henry continued trying to prepare him for his first encounter with Kate Reynolds. It seemed unfair to Nick that carrying the fate of the world on his shoulders wasn't enough; that he was now going to have a prima donna to deal with on a daily basis as well. Although it struck him as odd that her own father had felt compelled to warn him about her, Nick still wasn't particularly concerned. Why should he be? After all, hadn't women always *loved* Nick Reynolds?

As they walked down the hallway to the elevator, Henry continued his warning, alternately describing Kate as extremely headstrong, driven, and unusually territorial. *Just what I need right before the world burns*, Nick thought to himself. *That's okay; I'll just turn on the old Nick Reynolds charm, and then watch her melt.*

"Are you sure you're ready to go in there, Nick?" Dr. Henry Summers asked once more as they exited the elevator, just before walking into the lab area where she worked. Reynolds nodded confidently. "Okay then, here we go."

Nick followed closely behind Henry as they walked into the lab area where Dr. Kate Summers worked. Reynolds was immediately impressed with most of what he saw. There were state of the art electronics everywhere. Desktops, laptops, servers, mobile computers, routers and switches; there was even equipment he'd never seen before.

That's when he saw her. Only then did it occur to him that while they had often described her overbearing behavior, not once had they given a physical description of her. He had expected her to be the stereotypical nerdy scientist; thick glasses, pocket protector, and lab coat. But Dr. Kate Reynolds was no nerdy scientist in appearance; she was a ravishing beauty. With long, dark hair that reached to the small of her back, her face was smooth and her features delicate. Set in a stark contrast to her dark hair and soft features, the fire in her eyes flickered with a beauty and intensity that resembled brilliant blue sapphires. In the midst of trying to save the world, Nick Reynolds had suddenly and quite unexpectedly found himself smitten.

"Hi, sweetheart," Henry said to his daughter. He walked up to her and put his hands on her shoulders. She glanced back and smiled at him for a moment before turning back to something resting on the large table before her.

"Hi, Daddy. Did you meet our new lord and master, yet?" she asked casually. Henry looked over at Nick and offered him an embarrassed smile.

"If you're referring to Dr. Nick Reynolds, then yes, I did. In fact, I brought our new 'lord and master' back with me, honey; he's standing right over there."

Kate suddenly looked up with a start. She turned slowly, trying to appear uninterested and unconcerned. Nick walked over to where the father and daughter were standing.

"Hello, Dr. Summers, it's a pleasure to meet you; your father's told me so much about you!" Nick nearly tripped over himself, still intoxicated with her beauty. If she felt the same way about Nick, however, she certainly had a strange way of showing it. The extended hand was ignored, while she paused to study the intruder who had invaded her world.

"So, *you're* that military stooge, the Phoenix contractor who works over at Cyber Command?"

Nick, taken aback by her ferocity, struggled to answer. She had definitely just thrown a wet blanket on a simmering fire. "Yes...well...that is...I'm the team leader for Operation Counterpunch, a task force within Cyber Command," he answered nervously.

Kate continued looking at him with a look of disdain. "You'll have to forgive me, Dr. Reynolds. I'm afraid I don't much like anyone associated with the military, including your boss, General Caprella."

"What do you have against the military, Miss Summers?"

"Doctor. It's *Doctor* Summers," Kate corrected, with a tone of indignation.

"What about the military men and women at Groom Lake and here at S-4...you don't like them either?"

"No, Dr. Reynolds, I do not."

"Please, call me Nick."

"Please, *don't* call me Kate."

"Okay, fair enough. So what do you have against the military, *Doctor* Summers?" Nick's infatuation was long gone now, replaced by a thorny irritation.

"Their weapons, if you must know...*Nick*. Each and every time there is something they're afraid of, they pick up or build a new, more powerful weapon, something bigger and better than the other guy's, which they then use to kill. It's like this, Nick...it's the fear. You big boys with your big guns and your missiles, you're nothing but scared, irrational little boys. Your lack of trust leads to fear, and the fear leads to violence, which then leads to calamity and death. When people surrender to fear, violence inevitably follows. That's why I don't like the military, Dr. Reynolds."

"Okay...tell me something though; where would you be, little Miss High and Mighty, if you didn't *have* these 'boys with their guns'? You'd be enslaved to the British, the Germans, the Russians, take your pick. These 'boys' bleed and die each and every day to protect your right to belittle them as much as you want."

"Okay, but would it hurt to actually try and talk before blowing each other's heads off? Humanity claims to be an intelligent, sentient species, but sometimes I'm not so sure. We allow our fear to drive us to commit unspeakable acts in the name of security."

"Believe me Ka...Dr. Summers, there's nothing I'd like more than to have peace. Unfortunately, however, given our current situation with the Chinese, we have to act, and quickly, before our infrastructure is attacked again. Based on some back channel chatter, our intelligence agencies have already informed the president that they believe the warning posted on the Internet is legitimate, and that the Chinese are planning another cyber attack like the one at Indian Lake, except this one will be much, much bigger. The number of casualties resulting from such a massive cyber attack would far exceed the hundred thousand who lost their lives in New York. The death toll would be catastrophic, probably in the millions. Listen, our country is extremely vulnerable right now, Dr. Summers, and we need your help. If we can't find a means in your Project Prometheus to stop such an attack, well, I'm afraid we'll have no other choice when the time comes other than to retaliate."

"What? You mean a full-scale war with the Chinese?"

Nick nodded.

"What, are you insane? What if it goes nuclear?"

"Oh, that's a distinct possibility. But what are our options?"

"Have you tried *talking* with the Chinese, moron?" she asked.

"Hey, I'm not the bad guy here! Yes, we have spoken with them, many times in fact, and they have assured us repeatedly that they had nothing to do with the attack in New York."

"So there you go, problem solved."

"Hold on now. I indicated that they 'said' they had nothing to do with it. We have evidence that the attack originated from somewhere inside of China."

"So that sort of thing can't be *faked* then, Dr. Reynolds? What if someone else is trying to start a war between the United States and China for some reason, and they figured this would be a good way to do it? Isn't that a possibility?"

"Why would someone want to start a war between the United States and China?" Nick asked, trying to sound surprised that someone would even suggest such a thing.

"How should I know? I'm just asking if it's possible!"

Nick stood quietly, glaring at her for several moments.

"That's what I thought."

"So what would you have us do, *Doctor* Summers? What if it *is* the Chinese? Should we just let them get away with blowing up more nuclear power plants, murdering a million civilians here or there, whenever they get the urge?"

Kate took a deep breath before letting out a heavy sigh. "Look, you guys have to do your job to protect us; I get it. All I'm asking is, shouldn't we try to calmly and methodically assess the situation, to determine for certain who's behind the attack, before going off with guns blazing? If we, as a species, cannot learn to control our mistrust and fear of one another, I fear for our future."

Her last point stuck with Nick; she was right on that one, of course, he just hated to admit it.   "Agreed, and that's exactly what we're doing. While we strongly suspect that the Chinese are behind this, we realize that we cannot completely rule out another country, or even terrorists like Al Qaeda or Hezbollah either. Hopefully, if your little science project works out, it can help protect our country from these attacks and help identify who's behind them, *before* war breaks out between our two countries."

Henry Summers, who had been intentionally staying out of the way to let this interaction play out, was glad it was finally over. He figured it was inevitable and he'd hoped it would be relatively short-lived, and that it would end without violence. Fortunately, he was right on both counts.

"Well then, Kate, why don't you bring us up to speed on where you are with Ignis, honey?" Henry asked at length.

Kate finally took her eyes off of Nick long enough to turn to her father. That's when Henry first noticed that there was a look in her eyes that he'd never seen before, something mixed in with the annoyance and the irritation; could it be that she liked this young man? Whatever it was, she quickly shook it off.

"Sure, Dad. Well, as you can see," she began, gesturing toward an object resting on the table before her, "I was successful in removing Ignis from the ship. I was just evaluating options for supplying power to it. Based on the work I've done on Prometheus to date, we know that at least parts of the ship seem to utilize electricity. My guess is that the ship uses it much like we do for the secondary systems, though probably not for main propulsion. If we can figure out a way to supply electricity to Ignis, I think it might power up, assuming it wasn't damaged in the crash."

Nick looked at the device sitting on the large table before her. It was about three feet long, one foot wide, and nearly a foot high. Its shape made it look something like a small coffin, except the corners were rounded and smooth. The entire device was an odd metallic, greenish-silver color. There were several small, circular openings on the side of the casing at one end.

"These three holes on the end, Kate…that's where the device was connected to the ship?" Henry asked, after joining his daughter at the table.

"Yes. The connectors are inside the holes on the end. The slightly larger one appeared to be where the power flowed from the ship into the device. The other two are probably some type of conduit for data streams."

"I hope you're right. If not, we could fry Ignis by connecting power to the wrong connector."

"The cabling I disconnected from the smaller two connectors on Ignis looked like the same fiber cabling that we've found throughout the ship, while the other cabling looked like a different type of metallic conduit. I removed enough of each so we could reconnect it here in the lab. I also removed a very small piece of the device itself which we can later send off to the research lab so that they can run a series of tests on it.

"I think that figuring out how to supply power and pass data will be the easy part, however. If we're both right and Ignis *is* some sort of advanced, alien computer, interfacing it with our systems will be the really hard part. Honestly, Dad, it could take us years, or even decades, to make it work, if ever."

"Like, I've always told you, sweetheart, with science you've got to take things—"

"One step at a time. Yeah, I know," she said, smiling and kissing her father on the cheek. Nick couldn't help but notice that she had a beautiful, radiant smile. "Okay then, let's start by figuring out how we're going to get power to this thing. I've got a twelve-volt battery that I ordered; I thought we'd start with that." She took out two insulated copper cables and connected them to the battery. She then took a cable in each hand and laid them next to the conduit she'd removed along with the device. "Now then, where did I set that tool kit?"

"Kate!" Nick had yelled out her name.

"What, I—" Nick never had to answer her, because when she turned to him, she saw that his eyes were looking down at the table beside her. A slight movement to her right just within her peripheral vision caused her to turn. Multiple metallic fibers were inexplicably protruding from the conduit which was connected to the device. The metallic fibers were extending to and intertwining with the insulated copper cables connected to the batteries. The device then began emitting a faint glow from inside.

"Wow! Did you see that?" asked Nick. "I've never seen anything like that in my entire life. That's freaking awesome!"

"It was incredible!" Henry added as he studied his daughter's reaction for several moments. He had noticed that she wasn't nearly as shocked by what had transpired as he and Nick had been. "Kate, you knew about this, didn't you?" She looked at him with a sly grin. "Tell me, how did you know?" Henry asked with a huge smile.

"Let's just say…I considered it a possibility. I guess I figured that any technology that's advanced enough to cross vast interstellar distances might not require needle-nose pliers to do any crimping."

"I wonder what would happen if we connected 110 volts to it?"

Kate and Henry both looked back at Nick with blank expressions. Kate was the first to recover.

"Let's find out!" she answered enthusiastically. She ran and grabbed an electric pencil sharpener. After unplugging it, she cut the cord close to the sharpener, separated the wires slightly, laid it on the table near the device, and plugged it in. The conduit from the device immediately released the battery cable and attached to the 110 cord. The device suddenly started to sizzle slightly and the lights in the lab dimmed momentarily before quickly returning to normal. The Ignis device was now glowing a bright greenish color, while emitting a low, steady hum.

"Alright!" yelled Kate. All of them stood around the table for several minutes, fascinated by the glow and hum of the alien device.

"Do you realize, Kate, that I've been trying for decades to figure out how to get power to the ship, and you figured it out in a day!"

"Well, I've been working on this for years as well, Dad. Honestly, I've suspected this would happen for a while, but until now I was afraid to try it."

"Well, they say that necessity is the mother of invention," Nick remarked casually. Kate turned to him with a frown.

"Oh, is that what they say, Dr. Reynolds?" she replied mockingly.

"What's your problem this time, dragon lady?" asked Nick, perturbed at Kate yet again. "You know something? You may be like, really intelligent, but you're also a real pain in the...neck. You've got the personality of a rattlesnake!" Nick stormed out of the room and back to his office, slamming the door after him.

"You've really got to try and get along with him, honey," he said softly after the flare up. "He's really a very intelligent young man in his own right. If he wasn't, General Caprella never would have given him so much responsibility."

Kate just walked over to a chair and sat down.

"Come on, Dad, what are you and Caprella doing, bringing him here? I can work with *things* all day long just fine, but you both know how well I get along with other human beings."

"We need him here, Kate, to help us find a way to use this device to stop the cyber attacks and prevent a third world war. Now tell me, was this hostility really necessary?"

"Yes...no...I don't know." A few moments later, after her temper had cooled, she added, "I messed things up, didn't I?"

Henry nodded in reply.

"I guess I should go apologize, shouldn't I?"

Henry nodded again.

Jeff W. Horton

Chapter 13

Nick sat in the chair in his office, fuming over his new coworker. In fairness, her father had tried to warn him, though in Nick's opinion and contrary to what he'd thought earlier, the elder Summers had actually undersold how difficult she could be. Kate Summers was already proving to be impossibly difficult to work with, and they had very little time to deal with the threats at hand without the added drama. He was debating whether he should pick up the phone and call Caprella when, through the glass in the door, he saw Kate walk up and knock.

"Come in," he said reluctantly and against his better judgment. Kate sheepishly opened the door and stuck her head in.

"I, um, just wanted to say that I am sorry about my smart mouth, um...Nick? You said I could call you Nick, right?" Nick just threw his hands up in reply. "I've always been pretty lousy around people; that's why I spend so much time around *things* instead."

Nick's face softened when he looked up and saw the genuine look of regret. He looked at her for several moments before speaking.

"Look, I get it. You've been here a long time working with these toys, and then I suddenly show up out of the blue. This is your turf...I understand that...so can we please just move on?" he asked.

Kate smiled. "Yeah, that would be great." She looked at Nick and smiled for a moment before turning back toward the lab. "Well, I guess we should head back to the lab now, okay?"

"Sure," Nick replied. He stood and began walking back towards the lab with Kate. "So what's next?" he asked. His voice still sounded agitated, but his temper had cooled.

"Now, we find a way to talk with Ignis," she said confidently.

When they arrived back at the table, the device was still on, but it was no good to them without being able to interact with it. They found Henry still at the table, studying the alien device. He looked up when he heard them approaching.

"Is everything okay?" he asked both of them.

"Oh yeah, sure," Nick answered.

"Absolutely."

Henry just grinned at the two young people before turning back to Ignis. "Okay, so how do we interface with it? Kate, you said that the other two cables appear to be some type of advanced fiber optic cabling?"

"Yes," she answered enthusiastically. "If that's what they are, perhaps we can find a way to connect it into one of the fiber interfaces on our network."

"Do you have a data switch in the lab that's got connectivity to the Internet?" asked Nick.

"Yes, of course," Kate answered.

"What about fiber optic connections; does it support fiber connections?"

"Yes, I believe so," Kate answered again, slightly annoyed this time.

"Okay, why not try the same thing with a fiber optic cable that we did with the power; connect one end to the send/receive pair to the switch, and the other one to Ignis."

"Okay, great idea, I never would have thought about that if you hadn't mentioned it," she said sarcastically. "So how are we supposed to give it an IP address and a default-gateway, and does it come with the latest Linux OS pre-installed, *Nick*?" asked Kate, a sharp edge to her voice. Nick sighed after recognizing the truce had already ended.

"One step at a time, sweetheart," her father said again. Kate cast a sharp look to her father, who seemed to be siding with Nick. "Where are the fiber cables kept, Kate?" he asked her.

"Okay, okay. Give me a minute and I'll grab a switch and a cable, and then we can try patching Ignis into the rest of the network. I guess it's worth a shot. I'll be right back."

Kate disappeared and returned ten minutes later with a switch and an orange fiber optic cable.

"Okay, here they are, let's see what happens." She took the two ends of the fiber optic cable and laid it next to the two empty ports on the device. Moments later, as before, two conduit cables emerged from the device and intertwined with the fiber, just as it had with the power. They all sat in amazement, staring down at the now fully-connected Ignis device.

"Well it's powered on, it *appears* to be connected to the network; so how do we interface with it?" Kate asked, furrowing her brow. She and her father sat down in their chairs, and began batting around various theories, ranging from keyboards, mice, and audio, to somehow touching the outside of the device. After fifteen or twenty minutes, they had exhausted their ideas and both grew silent. Nick decided to try speaking up again.

"Maybe we're missing something. Was there anything else in the ship connected to the device? Anything that could conceivably be used to communicate with it?" asked Nick.

"Oh, great. G.I. Joe here thinks he's a scientist all of a sudden. If we'd seen anything, Einstein, don't you think it would already be in here on this table?"

Nick decided he'd had enough of the prima donna. "Okay, now listen here, little Miss Fancy Pants, I hold a doctorate as well, remember?"

"That doesn't make you a scientist, soldier boy."

"I'm a civilian contractor, not a soldier; will you give it a rest? Listen, it's not my job to get this thing working, it's *yours*, I was just trying to help out. It's my job to help figure out how to use this thing to stop the attacks *after* it's operational. So I tell you what, I think I'll just go back and wait in my office and put my time to better use getting some work done, until *you* have this all figured out. There's no rush or anything; millions of people could die at any time, and our country could very well be engaged in a thermonuclear war with China at any moment, but please, take your time, and no pressure." Nick walked away from the table and stormed back out of the lab for a second time, furious and exhausted from his effort's in trying to get along with Kate, who watched with her mouth agape as he walked out of the lab once more and back towards the office.

* * * *

"I can't believe the way he just spoke to me. Can you believe that, Dad?" When she turned to her father she was surprised to find him looking at her with such disappointment.

"You don't really have to keep antagonizing him like that, do you, Kate?" Henry asked, with a little more firmness than normal. "After all, we are all on the same team here, aren't we?" She glared at her father for a moment before turning away. "You're acting a little more hostile than usual, even for you, Kate. Is there something wrong?"

"Ugh! People like him—they just get under my skin, Dad! They think they're...they think they're all that!"

"They think they're what, Kate? Good looking? Intelligent? Courageous? Yes, people like that truly are incorrigible, aren't they? I understand completely now." Henry allowed himself to smile. "Just give him a chance, Kate—a *real* chance—and I don't think you'll regret it. By the way, don't think I haven't noticed the way you look at him when he's not watching you, Kate. I'm your father, remember? If you're interested in him, you might want to stop insulting him so much."

"Him? Please! He thinks he can just waltz in here, and suddenly find things that we've been too dim to recognize after all this time...how arrogant!" She stopped suddenly, and grew quiet for a few moments, as if staring beside and beyond her father.

"What is it Kate?" asked her father. "Is something wrong."

"No, it's just something Nick said a moment ago. Um, Dad, do you remember the last time we were in the craft together?"

"Yes, I think so. I seem to recall that we were both in there together just last week."

"Do you remember when we were talking about bringing Ignis back here to the lab, and about how close we were to being able to safely remove it?"

"Yes, I remember."

"Do you remember that small helmet-looking thing in the ship, the one that we've never been able to figure out what it was for? We were talking about it the other day, and I guessed it might be part of a uniform, something indicative of rank like an insignia, do you remember?"

"Yes, that's right," he answered. "Why, do you think the helmet could be the 'something' that we overlooked in the ship? Yes, I suppose it is possible that the helmet could be an interface of some sort that our 'guests' used to interface with Ignis."

"Why not?" she answered. "We found it in the same general area as Ignis, and we *are* talking about extraterrestrials, remember? Anyway, it's late now, and like everything else we do here it's a long shot. I'll go by the ship the first thing in the morning and bring it back here. Who knows, if it *is* the interface, we could be talking with Ignis tomorrow!"

Chapter 14

When his daughter stopped by his office on the way out the door later that same evening, Henry Summers told her he had more work to do before calling it a day so Kate, wanting to be well rested when she tested the helmet the following morning, kissed him on the cheek and told him goodnight. She then began making her way back towards her quarters, leaving her father alone in the lab.

Most of the men and women working at S-4 had small apartments located on the base where they could live and sleep when not working. Many of them, both military and civilian, had families living close by in Las Vegas, so they would commute back and forth on the daily Janet flights between Area 51 and Las Vegas. Kate and her father, however, stayed on the base most nights, since their work would often keep them working late into the evenings. For them, like some of the others working at Dreamland, it was much easier and more convenient for them to stay on the base rather than commute. For the most part, the only time Henry or Kate would bother taking the Janet flights back to Las Vegas was after working for long stretches at Groom Lake. On other occasions such as holidays, and when, from time to time, it began to feel as if the base had started to close in on them, they would also leave the base to enjoy a nice meal or to take in some of the vast array of entertainment available in the city. Of course, the government didn't mind them living on the base at all, since it meant greater productivity and presented considerably less security risk for the extremely valuable scientists.

Thinking back about the confrontations with Nick Reynolds and the way the day had gone, however, Kate was beginning to think that a few days in Las Vegas might not be such a bad idea. Her last visit there had not gone well, so hopefully she would actually be able to relax a little the next time. As she approached Nick's office on her way out, she was surprised to find that the light in his office was still on. She still felt guilty, and she knew she needed to apologize for a second time to the man who'd twice retreated to his office to escape the venom of a woman he'd just met. She hated having to deal with people other than her father; it was one of the reasons she had become a scientist, and probably the main reason she was still single.

She walked up to his office door and saw him busy on his computer. *He's probably checking up on today's cyber attacks, as well as the increasingly heated rhetoric between Beijing and Washington,* she thought.

"Hi, how's it going, Nick?" she asked in a soft, feminine voice. She was surprised it had come out that way; it wasn't the way she intended for it to sound…at least she didn't *think* it was.

"Oh, hello again, Dr. Summers. Are you back for Round 3?" Despite herself, Kate chuckled. Even before his arrival, she had viewed Reynolds's coming to Groom Lake as an annoying and unnecessary presence, one that would likely get in her way and detrimentally affect her work. But despite her earlier outbursts, she was starting to warm to him a little, and she'd already decided she could get used to having Nick Reynolds around for a while.

"No, really I'm not; I don't want to go *any* more rounds with you, Nick, I promise. I'm so sorry about my behavior earlier, both times, please believe me; I was way out of line." Nick stopped what he was doing and looked back up at her. "I think you're going to be a real asset here," she said, "I mean it. You've already made some brilliant observations and I know we'll work together fabulously, if you'll just give me another chance. I'm really sorry things got off on the wrong foot, with *us* I mean. If you'll just try to be patient with me and give me some time to adjust, I think we'll end up working very well together. So what do you say?"

Kate grew nervous when she saw Nick hesitate. Her father had always warned her about her quick temper, and her bad habit of stating out loud exactly whatever she was thinking at any given moment.

"Who knows, maybe we'll even end up being great friends given enough time, right? I suppose anything is possible."

The comment troubled Kate and made her feel awful. She knew she could be difficult at times, but now she seemed to be getting even better at pushing people away from her; she'd just met Nick and he'd already had enough of her.

"Am I really *that* bad?" she asked meekly.

Nick burst out laughing. Kate was startled at first, but soon joined him.

"You know, Dr. Summers," he said after the laughter subsided, "I think we're going to be just fine. Okay, sure, I guess I'm willing to keep doing this if you are. I just hope we can eventually get past this and work together. We've got a lot of work to do and besides, I'm really not such a bad guy once you get to know me."

"Kate."

"Excuse me?"

"Please, call me Kate. It seems only fair after all," she said, wearing a hopeful smile.

"Are you sure?" he asked. "After all, you were pretty adamant earlier about me referring to you as *Doctor* Summers."

"Absolutely."

"Alright then, Kate it is."

"That's great, Nick, thank you. I promise you won't regret it." Nick turned back to what he'd been working on. "So how's everything going at Cyber Command?" she asked, hoping to drum up some small talk. It seemed she was going to be working closely with the single, handsome, intelligent man for a while. Her father had been right; if there was even a remote possibility she might ever be interested in Nick, she not only had to stop antagonizing him, she also had to try and smooth things over.

"It's going okay, I guess, all things considered," he answered. "But if we can't find a way to use Ignis or something else to stop these attacks soon before another major infrastructure attack occurs, I think we're going to be in big trouble. The public has been growing increasingly hostile toward China, and angry that the United States government has yet to hold anyone accountable for the deaths of so many people in New York. China continues vehemently proclaiming their innocence in these attacks. It doesn't help their case any, of course, that Chinese Nationals kidnapped you recently. I fear we're creeping closer and closer to a war with the Chinese."

"Don't worry, Nick, we'll get this thing figured out," she replied. "Just think, we had no way of knowing just this morning whether we'd ever be able to get power to Ignis, but now the device has both power *and* data cabling connected, and more importantly, it appears to be working…we just need to test it."

Nick smiled back at her. It was the first time he'd smiled at her like that, and she liked it.

"Thanks, Kate; I hope you're right."

Kate Summers was starting to think she could learn to like Nick, and she now wanted to get to know him better. It was the first interest she'd had in anyone for at least a year. Her work didn't afford her the opportunity to meet many available men, much less try to form and maintain a meaningful relationship. Yes, she decided she'd have to find a way to learn more about Nick Reynolds.

"So—um, it looks like you were right about us overlooking an item that was still in the craft, Nick. We think we may have found something."

"Can we use what you found to interface with Ignis?" he asked with cautious enthusiasm.

"Yes—well, maybe. We found what appears to be a helmet in the ship a while back, and we've never been able to identify a purpose for it. I'd always thought it might be part of a uniform, or something to do with navigation, but we never could figure it out. We're still not sure whether it has anything to do with Ignis, but I'm planning to stop by the hangar where we keep the ship the first thing tomorrow morning, to pick it up and take it to the lab."

"What are you planning to do with it?" asked Nick.

"Oh, just run some tests," she answered matter-of-factly.

"But *how* will you test it?"

"I'm going to put it on so I can find out whether we can interface with Ignis using the helmet. If it works, it could well be the breakthrough we've been looking for."

"That sounds extraordinarily dangerous, Kate. This is alien technology designed for an alien physiology after all—you have no way of knowing what that thing might do to you. Is your father okay with this plan? What did he say?"

"It doesn't matter, Nick. Like you said earlier, our country is on the verge of war with the Chinese, *and* bracing for a massive cyber attack. Look, I'd love to spend a few months running lengthy tests and accumulating a boatload of data before putting that thing on anyone's head, but we don't have months here, do we?"

"No, I'm afraid we don't."

"Then when I get into the lab tomorrow morning, I will determine what, if anything, I can do with Ignis while I'm wearing the helmet. Who knows, maybe nothing will happen. If it works though, maybe I'll try accessing the Internet; you know, order me some new clothes, that sort of thing, as a test."

"I still think it sounds far too dangerous, Kate. I think *I* should be the one to put it on first." He drew back a bit when he noticed her face tightening for a moment and her cheeks turning rosy again, just like they had earlier.

"What makes you think that it would be any safer for you, Nick Reynolds? Tell me you're not trying to practice some kind of pre-nineteenth century chivalry, because it died out a long time ago."

"No, I'm not trying to be chivalrous, or chauvinistic for that matter. I just don't want anything to happen to you, Kate, that's all; we need you."

"Thanks for your concern then, Nick, I appreciate it. Don't worry though, I think the helmet's safe enough. Besides, I think we need our best man at Cyber Command about now, especially when it's all about to hit the fan!"

"Maybe, but we can't afford to lose such a hot scientist either, especially one who also happens to know more about Ignis than anyone else on the planet!" Nick answered, managing a slight smile in the process.

"Do you mean that?" she asked abruptly.

"Of course, you know more about—"

"No," she said, interrupting. "I was referring to the 'hot scientist' part."

"Oh, that? You bet I meant it. You're the most attractive scientist I've ever met."

Kate Summers just stood and stared at Nick for a moment. "Well, Dr. Reynolds, you certainly are a man full of surprises! Were you just flirting with me?"

"Maybe; is it working?" he asked with some trepidation.

"Definitely," she answered, blushing once more, but this time for what Nick hoped was an entirely different reason altogether. She shook her head slightly as if trying to clear her head, before picking back up where they'd left off. "Okay. So, I'm going to test the helmet tomorrow Nick, I have to, and there's nothing you or anyone else can do to stop me. This was my idea; I'll be the one taking the risk." The look in her eyes conveyed the depth of her conviction to Nick. He could see that it was pointless to argue with her about it.

"Okay, okay. Just promise me something," he asked, peering into her eyes.

"What?" she asked quietly.

"Just promise me you'll think about it, and about what I said. We can't afford to lose you, Kate. The technology in this ship could change the world; we need you."

"And I...I mean *we*...need *you* even more, Nick, to resolve the impasse with the Chinese and to protect millions of lives. What good can the technology do us if there's no one left standing in the nuclear ash to take advantage of it?"

"Still, will you at least consider letting me go instead?"

"Sure, Nick, I'll think about it, but I think you know my mind's already made up." She looked at Nick and saw in his eyes the concern he felt for her safety, despite the fact they had only just met, and the way she'd treated him earlier. *What a remarkable man!* "Well, it's been a long day, and a long week for that matter. Why don't we both try to get some rest, and we'll talk about it some more tomorrow, okay?"

"Sure, Kate, good night."

Kate left Nick's office shaking her head. She smiled when it occurred to her that it was starting to get interesting at Area 51 and for the first time, it had nothing to do with an alien spacecraft. She was beginning to think her father was right; Nick was good looking, intelligent, and courageous. Perhaps they would continue that part of the conversation later but for now, they were both tired, and she believed they would all think more clearly after a good night's rest.

* * * *

The sun was starting to set so the light waning through the window was growing exceedingly dim, but there would be plenty of lighting for what he needed to accomplish. Henry Summers entered the elevator and waited for it to descend the five floors. Within thirty seconds he had arrived at the correct level, and strolled purposefully from the elevator. He walked to a nearby door, scanned his badge, and then leaned down and bent over until his eye was level with the retina scanner. A moment later the light flashed green and the door swung open. Henry walked through the door and found himself once again in the vast hangar, standing in front of the craft which had been built and flown by alien beings from a civilization on an alien planet, most likely many light-years from Earth.

Henry walked over to the ship, climbed several steps on the small, erected stairway, and entered the craft. A moment later he emerged with a small helmet tucked under his arm and returned to the lab.

He had taken this course of action only as a last resort. He knew what Kate was planning, and he was determined that if anyone was going to risk their life testing the alien technology's helmet interface to Ignis, it would be him. He was an old man now, while Kate was still young and vibrant, with most of her life still ahead of her.

As he made his way out of the hangar and back to the elevator, he reflected on his long life. If he had any regrets at all it would have to be that he and his wife had waited so long to have Kate. They had both been scientists who had placed their careers ahead of starting a family. By the time they were ready to start trying, they were already in their forties; Henry was nearly fifty by the time Kate was born. His wife had been diagnosed with an aggressive form of cancer when Kate was still a baby, and had passed away by the time she was two, leaving Henry to raise Kate on his own. No, if anyone was going to risk everything testing the helmet, it would be him.

Once he reached the lab, he began examining the helmet more closely. It loosely resembled a bicycle helmet with openings at the top and the sides. There seemed to be no wiring or other means of directly connecting the two devices, so all communications, if any, between the helmet and Ignis must be via some sort of radio waves. There were a number of small, metallic-looking discs inside the helmet, which he assumed helped to complete the cybernetic interface to Ignis.

The aging scientist walked over to where Ignis rested on the large table in the lab and looked it over. He noticed a blue light on Ignis which he'd not seen before. *It must represent an active link between the cybernetic interface and Ignis itself...interesting.*

Henry walked into his office and returned with a high-backed office chair, a camcorder, and a tripod. After getting the camcorder plugged in and situated on top of the tripod, he rolled the chair next to the table where Ignis sat. He turned the camera on, sat back in the chair, and got comfortable.

"Hello Kate. I'm recording this experiment for you in the event that I am somehow incapacitated during or after the test, so that you will know what happened, and so that you Kate, will not risk your life as well. In the event I survive this experiment, this recording will hopefully capture details that I might otherwise have remained ignorant of. One thing before I get started; I noticed a blue light which seemed to activate on Ignis when the cybernetic interface was in proximity…say within twenty meters or so of it. I'm assuming this represents a successful, active link between the helmet and the Ignis device.

"Okay, I'm going to begin the experiment sitting down. What I anticipate will happen is that I will be presented with some sort of holographic image or something comparable, though it is certainly impossible to predict a specific outcome based on what is currently known about the device. Like you, Kate, I'm amazed and thrilled at the progress we've been able to make bringing Ignis online. I can only hope that our success will lead to an outcome that will enable us to protect lives, and our way of life."

Henry picked up the cybernetic interface helmet and held it in his lap, and stared at it for several moments as he began having some second thoughts about putting it on. After checking the camera once more, however, his jaw tightened in resolve as if he suddenly remembered that if *he* didn't put it on, Kate certainly would the following morning.

With a heavy sigh he picked up the helmet, raised it to his head, and put it on.

Chapter 15

Henry had no idea where he was or what had just happened. The old scientist was extremely disoriented, with nothing but white light visible all around him. He felt the urge to panic, but the feeling soon began to ease as he forced himself to stop, calm down, and assess his situation. Henry knew he was supposed to be doing something, trying to accomplish something, but what was it? He couldn't remember.

Henry looked around and suddenly noticed two doors. Had they been there a moment ago? He didn't think they had, but he was too interested in them at this point to care. One of the two doors was on his left, a plain, black door, with an "EXIT" sign overhead. The second door was to his right, and with the word "OUT" printed on it. Curious, Henry turned to his left and walked towards the door with the "EXIT" sign.

Immediately Henry was sitting back in his lab, sitting next to the Ignis device. He checked his watch and looked back up at the camera.

"Something just happened. I suddenly found myself no longer in the lab; instead I was somewhere else, inside a large, white space. There was nothing there at first, and it was all very disorienting. I looked down for a moment and when I looked back up, I saw two doors which had somehow appeared from nowhere. One said "EXIT" and the other "OUT." I chose the EXIT sign, and I was instantly back in the lab. It felt as if ten or fifteen minutes had passed. When I checked my watch, however, it seemed as if no time had passed at all. I suspect time did pass, it was just so small that I missed it. Perhaps the second hand moved ten to fifteen seconds. We shall have to develop a more accurate test." Henry held up his left wrist and examined his digital watch. He clicked a button which reset his built-in stopwatch.

"Okay, I am setting my stopwatch on my wrist watch here. I will start it once I'm ready to begin. I will stop the watch once I've exited the...virtual world, or whatever it is. I will then deduct a second for the time it takes to put the helmet on after clicking start. A more precise test can be done at some point in the future with someone else assisting, of course, but that will not happen until I'm confident it's safe. Despite Kate's determination, I'm still in charge of Prometheus and therefore Ignis also, and I will not allow her to risk her life until I'm comfortable she can do so safely." He looked down at his watch again. "Okay, I will start the stopwatch and place the helmet back on my head in 3-2-1...."

Henry was instantly back in the large, white, virtual room. He suddenly wondered if he said something in the virtual world whether he would be heard in the outside world.

"Okay, I don't know whether anyone else will be able to hear anything that I'm saying now, but we need to know whether or not we can be heard if we speak in the virtual world, while connected to the Ignis device. My interest in this is far more than just curiosity, for if we cannot interact with Ignis and the outside world at the same time, it could pose real challenges." Suddenly he noticed a table and a small earpiece sitting on it. He placed the earpiece in his ear and continued.

"I don't know why, but a small earpiece has suddenly appeared. I have picked up the earpiece and placed it in my ear. I'm assuming that somehow, Ignis knew I needed an earpiece for contact with the outside world, or perhaps it was my subconscious; I'm not certain yet. Anyway, now that I'm back in here, I plan to try the other door. There is no way I can be certain what I will find, but I do have a suspicion where it will lead."

Henry began walking over toward the door with "OUT" printed on it. After reaching the door, Henry hesitated for just a moment before steeling himself and reaching for the doorknob. He turned the knob and entered the room.

The inside of the room was dark, nearly pitch black. After a moment however, a display appeared on the wall in front of him. The image was about the same size as a screen in a movie theater. On the screen was what appeared to be an Internet browser. Henry was wondering how he was going to access the system when he noticed a small table in front of him, which contained a wireless keyboard and mouse. He then sat down and began using the mouse and keyboard to access the system. He attempted to access the browser and found that he was easily able to access any site through the browser. The aged scientist was extremely impressed with how fast everything seemed to move. Never before had he been able to access sites so rapidly. He continued jumping from site to site using the keyboard and mouse.

After visiting a number of websites something suddenly came to him. *Try it without the mouse and keyboard.* Henry wasn't sure where the suggestion came from…maybe the idea had come from his own mind, maybe it hadn't. He had to remind himself frequently that he was still inside a virtual world. On a whim, he decided to follow the suggestion and try something. Dr. Summers set the mouse and keyboard down on the table. He then pictured a specific website in his mind, and willed the screen to go there. Instantly, with no intermediate steps, he found he was there. Henry had accessed the site in under a second, with none of the time usually required for typing. He then pulled up multiple websites at the same time, popping more and more windows up. It seemed to Summers that the computer was no longer the limitation on how fast the system could operate—he was.

Encouraged by his initial test results and curious about its potential, he decided to try something riskier, something bigger. Dr. Summers then brought up the NSA's outward facing, public site and attempted to login. He had no username and password, of course, so Henry concentrated on trying to get past the username and password. Nothing happened at first; instead, the screen sat there and did nothing. After several seconds, however, when he was ready to give up the foolish notion, something started to happen. Henry wasn't sure *how* it happened, but he suddenly had full access to the system, perusing any and all applications, files, etc. that he desired. The scientist started to appreciate the full potential of Ignis for what they needed. It was the perfect computer system, the perfect means of finding and parsing information. Henry merely concentrated on what he wanted, and Ignis made it happen.

He decided to push the envelope even more. Instead of trying to just get past a login prompt, he began concentrating on finding specific information. He thought about the Chinese Online Blue Army, and he suddenly had access not only to information about the Blue Army, but to what appeared to be Blue Army websites as well. They were mostly in Chinese of course, so he would need an interpreter to understand what they said. Perhaps one of the Chinese-Americans who worked and had the right clearance might be able to help.

Henry then decided to try yet something else. He wanted to test the offensive capability of Ignis, so he willed the Online Blue Army website he had opened to crash. He didn't specify a denial-of-service or any other type of attack; he simply *willed* it to go down and a moment later, down it went. When he tried to access the site again he was unable to.

It began to dawn on him that Ignis was somehow able to capture his *intent*, so that it anticipated what to do instead of having to wait to be told. It was a Google search engine on Superman's steroids, and more. Trying to contain his excitement, Henry focused on wanting to leave. He was instantly back in the white room, with the "EXIT" and the "OUT" doors. He went to the "EXIT" door, opened it, and walked out.

Henry opened his eyes and he was back in the lab. He removed the helmet, stood up, and walked around. It took several moments before he was certain he really was back in the lab. Slowly, a thought began to creep into his mind, something that would trouble him for some time. Ignis was an incredibly powerful device, it's power intoxicating, and it would change everything. While he had no way of knowing how powerful it actually was, he felt certain that he had merely scratched the surface of what it was capable of. In the wrong hands there was no question it could do great harm. It could and probably would change the world in profound ways which he could never even imagine.

Dr. Henry Summers then sat the helmet back down on the table and started walking towards the door. He began thinking up a series of tests that he could develop to try and gauge the device's actual capabilities. As he turned off the lights to the lab and closed the door, he never saw the row of lights on the Ignis device that suddenly lit up and started flashing rapidly.

Chapter 16

"They're back, sir." It was Doris's voice coming over the speaker on the phone.

"Please send them in, Doris."

"Yes, sir." A few seconds later two men appeared in his office. One of them was a middle-aged man in his forties, the other was a younger man, probably thirty.

"Come in gentlemen and please, take a seat."

His two subordinates sat down in chairs across from him.

"Well, what did you find?"

"There was no sign of them, Director Andropov," answered the older agent. "It looks like we just missed them though, sir. By the time we arrived there the place was completely deserted."

"Are you sure that was the correct address?" asked Marat Tipalov, the younger of the two subordinates.

"Of course I'm sure!" answered Andropov with some annoyance, and some doubt. He'd been unable to reach any of the three agents he'd sent to check out the lead from the Chinese ambassador, nor had they called him. *Why did I send them in without plenty of backup?* It was possible that the address the Chinese had given him had been wrong. Of course, it was equally possible that they were wrong about Chervanko altogether, though he seriously doubted it. The Chinese were anything if not thorough and meticulous. They would have been as certain about the address as they had been about the rest of their facts, which probably meant his men were already dead.

"What exactly *did* you find?" he asked.

"The building was locked when we arrived, but we forced the door. Once inside, we found some kind of computer cabling hanging from the ceilings and on the floor, but other than that there wasn't much there," answered the older agent.

"Did you see any signs of a firefight anywhere?" asked Andropov.

"No sir, we saw no shells or fragments. That place is a mess though, sir. It's possible that if they were professionals and were careful to pick up all shells—"

"Then we could've been at the right place...we just got there late. Yeah, I know."

"There were some deep, fresh tire tracks outside as well, sir, which had been made recently. It looked like they might have been made by a tractor trailer."

Andropov sat back in his chair and let out a heavy sigh. "Damn, they've moved. What about Drago and the others?"

"No sign of them sir."

"Try calling them again on their cell phones and their radios," said Andropov. The older man, Georgy Ulitsky, nodded at Tipalov, who then pulled out his cell phone and began dialing.

"Sir," began Ulitsky, "do you think that maybe, well, that Chervanko...."

Andropov had already thought the same thing, but no sense talking about it until something turned up.

"I don't know, maybe. Chervanko's extremely intelligent, *and* dangerous. Anyone who spent as much time as he did as a field agent in the KGB during the Cold War—well, let's just say that you need to be armed and ready when you're hunting a hunter."

"Excuse me, sir," the younger man said. "I tried leaving a message for him, but his voicemail was full."

Andropov grimaced. "Very good, thank you." Andropov sat back in his chair and rested his head in his folded hands. "Okay then, what do we know? We've been handed information from a questionable source which seems to suggest that Chervanko is planning something big. I sent three men to investigate whether the information I was given was true, and it's now been two days and we haven't seen or heard anything from them. I then sent you to the address that I was given, and you found that the warehouse appears to have been recently vacated. What does that tell you?"

"That Drago and the others went to that same address, and that they probably saw and spoke with Chervanko," began the younger FSB agent. "They were probably ambushed at some point and killed. Chervanko, now aware that he has been found out, has been forced to relocate in a hurry."

"Exactly," answered Andropov, impressed with Tipalov's assessment. He decided to continue with him. "Okay, Mr. Tipalov, nice job. So what do you suggest he will do next, and how do we find him now?"

The younger man tightened his lips for a moment. "Well, sir, we know that he's a true believer, so he's not going to stop until he's reached his objective and completed his mission, whatever it may be. I think he's obviously going to start by looking for a new base of operations, assuming of course that he doesn't already have a backup location."

"He was one of the KGB's best operatives," Andropov stated dryly. "Chervanko will have a secondary location already prepared. Please go on."

"So even if he and the equipment made it safely to the secondary location, it's still going to take him some time to get all of his equipment set up and operational again. How long this takes him depends, in part, on how prepared he was. It sounds like you believe he's prepared for this eventuality, which means that he may be able to get operational fairly soon."

"Want to take a guess on how long it might take him?" asked Andropov, smiling. He liked the young man.

"Maybe a few days, a week at the most would be my guess," answered Tipalov.

"So how do we find him?" asked Andropov, who already had a few ideas in mind. He had learned many years earlier in his career that having a young, fresh perspective on things could often be enlightening.

"Well sir, I suggest we check with the telephone company, find out when the order went in for his voice and data circuits. Then we check for other locations that had similar circuits installed the same day. It's a long shot, but it may be our best approach."

Andropov looked at the young agent and smiled, before starting to clap. *The young man has real potential.*

"Very good, Agent Tipalov! That was quite impressive. Alright then, I like your plan." Andropov turned to the older man. "Georgy, why don't you and Marat look through connection orders and try to find one with a requisition which was put in that is similar to and was installed about the same time as the ones at the warehouse. If you find his backup site, be sure to check back with me immediately before taking any further action. I want to make certain that we invite all the right people to our welcoming party for Mr. Nikolai Chervanko, and for any accomplices he may have, understood?"

"Yes, sir," both men answered.

"Good. Now that we have that settled, I have another matter I'd like to discuss. Melat, let's you and I talk a little about computers. Please, tell me what you know about cyber warfare."

Chapter 17

"Good morning, Nick, this is General Caprella; how are you doing this morning, my boy?"

Nick became a little edgy when he realized that Caprella had called him on his cell phone; it was the first time he remembered him ever calling it. He hadn't given Caprella a heads-up that he was leaving Groom Lake to fly back home for a few days, and he wondered if that was the reason for the unusual call. While under normal circumstances he doubted Caprella would object to his leaving Dreamland without notifying him first, given the threat they now faced and the criticality of getting Ignis operational as a cyber defense system everything had changed; Nick suddenly felt guilty about leaving. He resolved that he would be forthcoming with Caprella.

"I'm doing fine, General, thanks. I'm actually back at Cyber Command for a couple of days. I had to fly back to Fort Meade unexpectedly to meet with some members of my team here. I'm sorry about leaving Groom Lake, General; please believe me when I say that I wouldn't have left to come here if it weren't important. Don't worry though, I'm scheduled to fly back tomorrow morning."

"Worried? I'm not worried at all, my boy. In fact, I'm extremely pleased to hear that you're back in town for a few days. To be honest with you, Nick, it's worked out perfectly."

"Really? Okay, that's great then. Well, I should have everything wrapped up here later today and as I said, I was planning to head back to Groom Lake tomorrow."

"I might need you to be a little flexible on that, Nick, okay?"

"What do you mean, sir?"

"Listen son, we really need to meet as soon as possible. How long would it take you to get to the Pentagon from your office?"

"Maybe an hour or two."

"Good enough. I would come there instead, Nick, but there are some other folks that will be in on our meeting. Is there any way you could leave now? I know it's quite an imposition, Nick, but this is very important and it really can't wait."

Nick looked around the table at his Counter Punch teammates. Whatever Caprella wanted, it sounded urgent. The others at the table just shrugged at him or nodded toward the door.

"Yes, sir. I'm on my way."

"Great. Please call me when you get here, alright?"

"Yes, sir." Nick pressed the "End" button to terminate the call. He looked around at the six men and five women seated around the table. He had been in a middle of a staff meeting, discussing the attack in New York, the various proposals for putting a stop to the attacks originating out of China, and the effort to confirm for certain that the attack did, in fact, originate in China. It would be hard to determine remotely, though there were some tricks a couple of folks had in regards to accessing Chinese telcos. It would also be a risky move politically, given the current state of relations with China. But in Nick's opinion, it had to be done. They must find concrete evidence linking the attack to the Chinese in order to confront them, because risky or not, over one hundred thousand American citizens had been murdered; someone had to be held accountable. He would discuss it with Caprella in their meeting.

"I'm sorry everyone, but General Caprella needs me at the Pentagon A.S.A.P. All of you need to stay focused, and remember what happened at Indian Lake; perhaps it will help motivate you to find the dirt bags responsible for the New York meltdown, and help avert a nuclear war with China." The tension in the room was palpable. "No pressure though," he said, smiling, before standing up to leave. A light chuckle reverberated throughout the conference room.

"Dr. Reynolds?" It was one of the fresh recruits from M.I.T. Nick turned to face him.

"Yes?"

"How's it going with your 'off-site' project, sir; any progress yet?"

"Why do you ask?" Nick inquired, curious.

"Because frankly, Dr. Reynolds, we've been trying everything we can think of here, and there's only so much we can do in terms of forensics without having access to more equipment. Everything we've uncovered so far points to zombies in China, that's it. I know I'm still fairly new here, sir, but everyone's been saying pretty much the same thing."

Nick considered for a moment how he should respond. "We're definitely making progress, and I'm cautiously optimistic about our chances for success, but it's still too soon to tell," he answered, exuding as much confidence and excitement as he could muster. During one of those brief intervals of time that exist as spaces or gaps between sentences within a conversation, when Nick was pondering what he would say next, his heart sank. He knew, he'd always known, that Ignis was really nothing more than a wild shot in the dark. If they were going to find what they needed to either convict or acquit the Chinese, it would almost certainly be the old-fashioned way, through hard work and perseverance. But Nick couldn't tell his team that, because when he looked around the room, all he saw was exhaustion; it rested on the faces of everyone in the room. They needed a respite, but he was unable to offer it to them, at least not yet. "But don't worry about that now. Listen, I know you're all tired and you want to go home. Try to remember, however, that if we don't succeed, there might not be a home for you to go back to in a few days. I need all of you to keep working diligently to find a way to stop the bastards who are attacking us, and I need you to tell me with absolute certainty whether the Chinese are behind the Indian Lake attack or not."

"Yes, sir. Good luck with General Caprella," the young man responded, wearing a frown.

"Thank you. Okay everyone, our meeting is adjourned. I'm supposed to fly out of town again tomorrow morning, but I'll be available by cell and email when I'm not in the air. Remember, I need everyone to keep me posted!"

It took Nick the full two hours to get to the Pentagon. Roadwork and a wreck on 295 combined to bring traffic to a crawl for a while, and he was thankful when he finally passed the fender bender and was out of the congestion. He enjoyed his occasional visits to the Pentagon. They often involved a lot of walking, and a lot of the folks who made things happen at Cyber Command could be found there. Nick had come to know many of them on a first name basis.

After moving through security considerably faster than usual, Nick was at the closed door of the general's assigned office within fifteen minutes. He took a deep breath, forced himself to relax, and knocked.

"Come in." Nick opened the door and found the general sitting at his desk, which was covered in stacks of papers and manila folders.

"Good morning, Gen—" Nick stopped when he realized there was someone else already sitting across from Caprella. He was stunned when he recognized the man was none other than Joseph Whitmore, the Secretary of State of the United States. Nick quickly recovered and extended his hand. "Good morning, Mr. Secretary. Please pardon my interruption, I didn't know you were here." Nick turned to walk out.

"Wait!" Caprella jumped out of his chair and ushered Nick back into his office. "He's the reason I called you, Nick."

Whitmore stood up and extended his hand. "You must be Dr. Nick Reynolds, it's such a pleasure to meet you, young man! Please, come in and join us, we both wanted you here for this meeting. Give us just a moment and the general and I will try and explain why we've asked you here."

"Okay, sure, Mr. Secretary." Nick turned to Caprella. "General?" Nick looked to Caprella for direction.

"Yes, Nick, please stay, that's why I asked you here. We have some very important information to share with you.

"Okay, General, what can I do for you?"

"Mr. Secretary?" Caprella nodded toward Whitmore.

"Thank you, George."

Whitmore turned to Nick. "Dr. Reynolds—"

"Please, call me Nick."

"Okay, fine, then you'll have to call me Joe."

"Okay, Joe."

"So, Nick, I believe you're up to speed with the attacks against our national infrastructure and the recent meltdown in New York, which appears to have been an act of aggression by another country."

"Yes, sir."

"I believe your team at Cyber Command is also in the process of confirming that these attacks actually *did* originate in China as all of the evidence seems to suggest?"

"Yes, sir, it is."

"Good. How about your work on that other little 'science project' that General Caprella seems to think might be able to help us?"

"It's looking better every day, Mr. Secretary…Joe…but as to whether it will work out or not, I still have my doubts. There's just so much that we don't know about the technology. Rest assured, however, that we're working as hard as we can to determine what's possible."

"Understood. I hope the technology proves more useful than you seem to think it will, Nick, because we are now at the very brink of war with the Chinese. We have already accused them of numerous cyber hacks into some of our most sensitive government systems, not to mention their tinkering around in our infrastructure."

"Which is absolutely true, sir. We know for certain that they've been hacking our systems for a decade or more," Nick argued.

"But do we know for certain whether the Chinese are behind the meltdown at Indian Lake? We must know the answer to this all-important question, because if it is proven that they are, we will be irrevocably committed to a path which will lead the world where it does not want to go."

"We traced the IP address to China."

"Yes, I'm aware of that. Now, I realize you're much more knowledgeable about these things than I am, but tell me…can't IP addresses be spoofed?"

Nick tightened his lips and looked down. "Yes, sir, they can be. It's also possible that someone planted a virus on the computer in China that has that IP address assigned to it, turning it into something we call a zombie computer. I've been considering the possibility that someone, a rogue state, or a terrorist group, might be trying to cause a major conflict between the United States and China. Certainly killing a hundred thousand people is a good way to do that. The problem is, I've been unable to find any evidence to contradict what we've already found implicating the Chinese."

"You probably don't know this yet, Nick, but there was a resolution which unexpectedly passed in the House of Representatives today, a resolution declaring war on China."

Nick's heart stopped. *There it is.*

"It's not official, of course, until a similar resolution, which is also expected to pass, comes up for a vote in the Senate tomorrow. If we don't act quickly, then by this time tomorrow night, the United States and China will formally be at war."

Nick was quiet for several moments, taking it all in.

"At the moment, Mr. Secretary, all of the evidence seems to point to the Chinese. My gut, however, tells me they are innocent. Maybe my gut is wrong, however...maybe they *are* responsible, I just don't know yet. For what it's worth, Joe, if it turns out the Chinese did murder a hundred thousand innocent American civilians, then I believe they must be held accountable."

"And what if we end up uncovering evidence to the contrary, what then?" asked Caprella.

"Sir, I don't understand why you're asking *me* that question. With all due respect, General, I'm not the president; I'm just a contractor who works for Cyber Command."

"No, Nick, you are much more than that. I recognized your abilities early on while you were still at M.I.T.; that's why I brought you here to the NSA and then to Cyber Command. It's also why I put you on the Prometheus Project. The fate of the world will hinge on what happens tomorrow, Nick." Caprella turned to Whitmore. "Joe?"

The Secretary of State of the United States turned to Nick. "Nick, we were recently presented with information from the Chinese which points to a man named Nikolai Chervanko as the one behind the attack at Indian Lake. Do you know the name?"

"Yes, sir, a little. I've read a bio about him. He was the head of the cyber research division within the KGB for a short time back near the end of the cold war. He was a real hard case KGB agent and a dedicated communist, from what I've read."

"That's about the size of it. Anyway, the Chinese have been telling us for the past week or so that they believe Chervanko was behind the attack. They're also telling us that while they had no qualms about stealing technology and information from us, a nuclear war with the United States is something they most certainly do not want. They continue to deny having any involvement with the meltdown in New York."

"Of course that's what they're saying, sir; it's what I'd expect them to say. Did you believe them?" asked Nick.

"No, as a matter of fact we didn't believe them."

"Then why—"

"We didn't believe the Chinese when they came to us, Nick, but we did believe the Russians."

"What?" Nick was now completely confused.

"The Russians came to us yesterday, Nick," Caprella told him. "The Russians had been caught off guard when the Chinese first came to them several weeks ago, warning them that a group of old-guard communists, led by Nikolai Chervanko, was behind the cyber attacks. The Chinese ambassador to Russia told someone high up in the FSB that China was being setup."

"Did they say why?" Nick asked, intrigued but not stunned by the allegation.

"Apparently Chervanko was even more of a hard-core communist than we realized. It seems he's determined to start a war between China and the United States."

Nick thought about that for a moment. Some of the hard core communists still longed for the glory days of the Soviet Union, lamenting over its eventual collapse. "So...," Nick replied slowly. "Chervanko wanted to create a war between his country's two greatest rivals in order to create a vacuum, one which only his beloved Soviet Union could fill."

"Exactly. Oh, you're quite right about him George, he really is a bright young man."

"So the FSB has him in custody now?" asked Nick. "Can I talk with him?" The other men glanced at each other for a moment until their eyes made contact. Nick understood what that meant. "Okay, so they tried for a grab, but he got away?"

"Killed three of their best men, based on my information," the secretary told him. "So you see our dilemma then, Nick?"

"You can't exactly bring the Russian FSB and the Chinese Online Blue Army into the Senate tomorrow morning to convince them the Chinese are innocent," Nick surmised.

"That's it, Nick. We want you to gather as much detail as you can from our meeting with the Chinese and Russian ambassadors before taking it into a hearing before the subcommittee. We have a meeting scheduled with them for 9:00 A.M. tomorrow. Their vote on the resolution is at 10:00 A.M. This may be our only shot at explaining everything to a hundred furious, vengeful senators, all wanting to send a message to the world that such a massacre of Americans will not go unpunished."

Nick opened his mouth and raised his eyebrows. "Ah, so you want *me* to do the presentation to the Senate tomorrow morning, and try to stop a group of men and women out for blood from starting World War III?"

"Yes, Nick, we do," the secretary answered. "Think about it for just a moment. Are they more likely to listen to me, another politician, or to you? You're the Cyber Command task force leader for Operation Counterpunch; you're the one they're most likely to listen to."

"What about the president?" Nick objected. "Why would they believe me over the president?"

"Because they perceive him to be much more dovish about this. They believe, perhaps rightly so, that this president would tolerate the death of a hundred thousand Americans before he would risk sentencing hundreds of millions of Americans and Chinese to death. It would be better if *you* presented this to the American people, Nick."

"I would need some evidence to present to the senators," Nick warned them.

"No problem," said Joe. "The Russians were able to provide information on various Internet connections Chervanko had operational, an address, and some pictures. The Chinese have evidence that the IP address that was used during the attack was associated with a computer infected with a complex zombie computer virus."

"That's a little weak, Joe. I'm not sure they'll buy it."

"We don't need them to buy it, Nick. We just need them to give us some time to capture or kill Chervanko and collect the hard evidence we need to convince everyone," Caprella told him.

Nick could see Caprella's apprehension. *He's afraid I'll say no.* The general's concern was unfounded, however, because Nick Reynolds had already made up his mind.

"Sure, no problem. My guess is that by now, the FSB is hot on his trail." Nick looked up at both men. "Tell me, gentlemen, what happens if they don't buy it? What if they declare war anyway?"

"If the United States declares war on the People's Republic of China, then sooner or later it *will* go nuclear."

Nick just shook his head. *No pressure, Nick; it's just the fate of the world that hangs in the balance during your testimony tomorrow.*

Chapter 18

Chervanko paid the man at the counter and sipped on his coffee as he walked back to his car. He reflected that there were two things made in Mother Russia that he was particularly fond of—vodka and coffee.

He climbed back into his Volkswagen and started the motor. It had long been a matter of policy for him to leave in the opposite direction of where he was really going, and it was something he did once more upon pulling away from the curb. It was an old trick which still seemed to be surprisingly effective. Perhaps the government didn't train the FSB as well as it had the KGB.

It had been the first time Chervanko had dared venture out since cleaning up at the old warehouse. They had only just pulled out when the new FSB agents had arrived, no doubt looking for Chervanko, the dead FSB agents, and any evidence they could find. Chervanko's biggest regret was that he had been forced to clear out in such a hurry, leaving the large bulks of dangling cables. Certainly the FSB would recognize it had been no ordinary warehouse, based on the amount of fiber optic cable they had purchased. Otherwise, they had successfully shutdown and removed everything from the old warehouse to the secondary location.

Chervanko was suddenly grateful for the foresight he had shown in turning up the secondary site six months after getting the primary site live and operational. He had intentionally spaced them apart, since the secondary site was setup in case the first was compromised. It would take the FSB much longer to find the secondary site, since the data circuits there had been turned up six to nine months after the primary site was installed. It was a cautionary step that he never thought he'd need to rely on, but this time it had paid off.

He pulled into the parking lot of the small office building he'd purchased. It was more space than they actually needed, but the dozens of vacant offices offered a reasonable explanation for the abundance of data bandwidth coming into the building. Chervanko climbed out of the car and after unlocking the front door, walked through a couple of hallways and into the larger office space where they had built the data center. The office was still in disarray, with some of the cabinets and all of the file servers and consoles still in boxes. The other three waited in another office while the two computer experts they had hired worked to get the cabinets together and all of the cables pulled.

"Gentlemen, good morning! How's it going?" he asked after walking in.

"It's going great, sir. We should have all of the cabinets out and set up by the end of the day, and most of the cables pulled by the end of tomorrow." Chervanko frowned. *Why did I have to kill Lee so soon?* He cursed his impatience.

They had thrown the FSB off their trail for the moment, but he was uncertain how long that would last. Even after he and his comrades had Ares back up and running, they would still have to run another test before launching the major cyber offensive that would start World War III. He looked at the men putting the cabinets together. They were moving far too slowly for his liking. "How soon before you have everything connected and operational?" he asked them. The two men walked over to talk with Chervanko.

"Getting the cabinets racked, the cable pulled, and the rack-mount servers installed; that's the easy part. Getting everything connected correctly, and getting your data lines tested and operational, that's another," the man answered.

"How long?" Chervanko asked, a little more forcefully this time.

"At least one week, probably two, possibly even three," he answered, looking over what they had accomplished, and how much they still had in boxes. Chervanko grew flushed at the news. Three weeks was entirely too long a time to wait to launch the attack. The FSB, not to mention the American CIA and the Chinese Ministry of State Security, were surely working overtime to find his lowly band. *If we move quickly we still have a chance to make this work.*

"How much to get it finished in under a week?" asked Levin, who had quietly walked in through another door. He had overheard their discussion, a fact that somewhat worried Chervanko. If Levin grew fearful, the others might follow, causing everything he had worked so long and hard for to suddenly unravel.

"Oh, we might could get everything finished in under a week if we had enough help. If we could add as many as another half-dozen people, we might be able to have you up and operational in three days! But with just the two of us, well—two weeks is really pushing it." Levin looked at Chervanko, who shook his head. Introducing even one other person dramatically increased their chances of being discovered, much less another half-dozen. They had to make do with the two they had. They had conducted background checks on these two. They were both unmarried, needed the money, and could be trusted to keep quiet.

"I'll tell you what," said Chervanko. "We are in a bit of a hurry to get this done on time for our company. Get the work done in under a week, and I'll pay you triple what we hired you for, plus a bonus for each of you!" The older man looked at the younger. They both shrugged and smiled.

"If it can be done, we will do it! Thank you for the very generous offer, sir!"

Chervanko smiled. *You'll not live long enough to spend any of it, so you're welcome!* "As I said, our company is really pressuring us to have this site fully operational in one week. Now you two get busy, and just be thinking about how you're going to spend all that money when you're done, okay?" He grabbed Levin by his arm and began walking him back towards the others.

Levin looked at his friend and smiled. "I don't know, comrade," he whispered as they walked out the door, "Are you certain you want to go through with our plan? I suspect you might prosper in America; perhaps you would even make a fine capitalist!" Levin patted his friend on the back as they neared the office in the adjoining space, far enough away that they need not fear being overheard by the technicians.

"How much longer?" asked Smirnov, as Levin and Chervanko entered the conference room, closed the door, and sat down.

"Another week, maybe two," answered Chervanko grimly.

"Our friend Nikolai here is now a capitalist! He may have just saved us a week or two by offering the workers a substantial financial reward as incentive to finish on time. Oh! Poor Comrade Lenin is rolling over in his grave!" They laughed it up for several moments at Chervanko's expense. It was okay with him; they'd labored hard and nearly had their mission end in disaster. With a new lease on life, the mission would go on.

"Okay, so we had a close-call back at the warehouse. We must be prepared once the two workers have everything back up and operational. As soon as Ares is once again functional, I believe we should move quickly, and more decidedly than we had originally planned," Chervanko announced.

"What do you have in mind, Nikolai?" asked Smirnov.

"Just this—that we launch the campaign immediately following another test; a test which will ensure that the Ares system is once again fully operational. Once the test has been deemed a success, we can launch Phase II of our plan, an all-out offensive. While simultaneously providing overwhelming evidence to the Americans that the Chinese have indeed been behind the recent devastating attack against their country, we will have Ares launch an assault which, once 'proven' to have been launched by the Online Blue Army, will leave the Americans with no alternative other than to declare war on China."

"And the American targets?" asked Kozlov.

"Ten nuclear power plants and much of their power grid, just as we discussed, Ivan." Kozlov nodded his head in affirmation. "The attack will be so painful, the Americans will be forced to lash out; their people will demand it, so great will be their cry. And then, my friends, and then—"

"Our beloved Soviet Union will arise once more," finished Kozlov.

"Yes, Ivan, our beloved U.S.S.R. will rise again."

Chapter 19

By the time Henry Summers stepped foot outside of the elevator, he could already make out commotion coming from the lab. The one-woman storm known as Kate Summers had blown in, and Henry knew at that moment he would have made a fine weatherman. When he walked inside, Kate was kicking at the furniture, knocking things off the table, and using more than a few expletives as she did so. She glanced up when she heard the door open, just long enough to see her father walking in.

"Can you believe this? I walked in this morning, preparing to test our theory, and I found that the cybernetic helmet went missing overnight! If they expect us to figure out how to use and apply this alien technology, they'd better start doing a better job of leaving us alone with it long enough for us to do some testing! Now why would they have taken the helmet and not Ignis?" she asked, pointing to the device still sitting on the table behind her.

"Kate, honey, look here." She had only glanced up at her father when he first walked into the room. She had neglected to notice what he carried with him at his side. In his right hand, Henry Summers carried the Cybernetic interface to the Ignis computer.

"What—Dad, *you* took it? But why?" Her rage had disappeared from her face, replaced with an expression of bewilderment. They had worked together on the Prometheus Project for years, and neither of them had ever taken anything with them back to their quarters on the S-4 base. While it wasn't necessarily forbidden for them to do so, since they were still inside the security perimeter, it was a bit unusual. Normally, they might take some notes back with them, but that was about all.

"I'm sorry, Kate. I did what I did to protect you, sweetheart. I took the helmet because I knew what you were planning to do when you came in this morning. I couldn't allow you to test this thing on yourself, Kate, at least not until I was able to determine that it was safe to do so. We had no idea what would happen."

Kate walked around until she stood directly in front of her father where she could look him in the eye.

"What did you do, Dad?" She started waving her finger in front of her father's face. "You said 'had,' not have. You've done something, haven't you?" Her eyes widened and her jaw dropped. "Dad, you put it on, didn't you?"

Henry reached out and placed one hand on each of Kate's shoulders, allowing a slight grin to escape before nodding.

"I did, Kate, and I have recorded the experience on a disk if you'd like to see it sometime."

She gasped and fell back into a nearby chair. "Wow! Okay, well, tell me…what happened…did it work? If it did, what did you see? Were you able to access anything? Did you try and get on the Internet and if so, how? Did you try and get on any websites? Well say something, Dad, please!" She leaned forward in her chair, impatiently waiting for his reply.

Henry just smiled. "Well, it took a second for it to work. I…." Henry spent a good hour explaining everything he had experienced as clearly and accurately as possible. Kate interrupted him several times despite a sincere effort to allow him to continue through to the end. When he finally finished, she sat back in her chair and ran her hands through her long dark hair.

"Wow. It sounds like we may actually be onto something here, Dad." She stared blankly into space, squinting her eyes as if trying to see something in the distance. "So not only does Ignis respond to our thoughts, it can actually interpret them as well? How's that even possible?"

"I don't know, Kate, yet it is. I merely thought about getting into the system and Ignis did 'all of the heavy lifting,' so to speak. For example, it knew that I wanted to access a system, so it created all the algorithms and code necessary to make it happen with no effort on my part at all."

"So if Ignis is interpreting our intent, the question is how accurate is it in that interpretation? I mean, it could be a bad thing if what I want is to *learn about* all of the nuclear missiles in China but Ignis interprets my intent as wanting to *launch* all of the nuclear missiles in China!"

"It doesn't work that way, Kate, at least I don't think it does. There seemed to be a much finer level of interaction between my mind and Ignis then that. There must certainly be some sort of artificial intelligence built into it. And...." Henry started to say something but let his voice trail off, hoping Kate wouldn't pick up on it.

"And what, Dad? Is there something you haven't told me?"

"I don't really know how to say it, Kate, and I certainly have no rational explanation for why I feel this way. All I can say is that, at times, I didn't quite feel like I was alone in there."

"That's understandable, Dad. Despite all of the years spent studying the ship, and Ignis, we still really know next to nothing about any of it. We can, and we probably will, for that matter, spend another hundred years studying this technology before really understanding what all of the components are, how they are supposed to function, and why." Kate looked out a window and into the desert for several moments.

"I was just thinking about something one of my computer professors said while I was still an undergraduate, Dad. He said that the more user-friendly and flexible a computer program was, the more work and thought had to go into its design and implementation. If Ignis really is so easy to use, the beings who created it must truly be incredibly advanced." Kate turned back to her father. "You know, Dad, you never talk about it much, but I remember once when I was little you said that you saw a UFO just before it was struck by lightning and crashed. Were you talking about this one, about Prometheus?"

Henry smiled and started to laugh. "You were only nine years old or so when I told you that, Kate. What an impressive memory you have!"

"Hey, you know how kids are, Dad; they won't remember a thing they learn in school but they remember every detail about something they're interested in."

"Like alien spacecraft?" he asked, smiling.

"Exactly! Which reminds me, you never answered my question."

"What? Oh...yes, I believe this is the same craft I saw that night. When I started working on Project Prometheus decades ago someone told me they'd heard that it was downed during a severe lightning storm about the same time as the one I saw. We may have more of these, but to the best of my knowledge, it's the only one." They both grew quiet, staring at the Ignis device together in silence for some time. After a few minutes, Henry stood up and walked towards his office.

"What are you doing, Dad?" Kate asked.

"We need to tell Nick what we've discovered. He'll want to know that we've had such a major breakthrough. I'll let him tell General Caprella."

"No! I mean, we can't tell him, Dad, not yet!"

"Why not, for goodness sake? This has been an extraordinary find," her father responded.

"No, Dad, listen. First of all, they're going to end up turning Ignis into an offensive weapon, not just a defensive one. Besides, we still need to do some more testing before we get too carried away. I mean, we need to test something more concrete than just accessing a few systems."

"What do you have in mind? I told you I was able to shutdown a system belonging to the Online Blue Army."

"Yes, but you weren't able to test whether you could detect much less stop a virus, or bring a nuclear power plant back online."

Henry studied his daughter for several moments, until he realized what was happening. *She's scared of losing it.* "Kate, honey, I know that you're probably worried about losing both Ignis and Prometheus, but we have to take that chance. Ignis could be the key to preventing World War III. We don't have the right to keep it to ourselves, especially not now. We must to tell Nick what we've discovered."

"But we're not ready!" complained Kate. "There are still so many questions we have to get answered!"

"Well then, as soon as I've told Nick, we'll get started. Why don't you work up a series of tests that we can use to test Ignis' capabilities while I give him a call?"

"But, Dad!" Since her mother's death decades earlier, Henry Summers had rarely been inflexible with his daughter, preferring rather to do most anything he could to please her. On the few occasions when he had been firm and unmoving, he had always had a peculiar and unmistakable look on his face, at which times Kate had learned that continued pleading had only served to worsen the situation.

"No buts, Kate. The sooner we have a slate of tests to run, the sooner you can put on the helmet, connect to Ignis, and try it out for yourself. Now then, think can you get started on that while I call Nick?"

"Sure, Dad."

After recognizing that offering her a chance to try on the helmet did the trick, Henry stood up and began walking toward the door. "I think it will be good to see Nick Reynolds again, don't you?" he asked.

Kate looked down at her hands and blushed ever so slightly. She never answered her father, choosing instead to continue looking down.

As he reached the door, Henry looked back at his daughter, shook his head, and smiled.

Chapter 20

His palms were sweating and his heart pounded in his chest as he walked into the Senate chambers. Although he was flanked by two other members of his team, he would be sitting alone when he faced the bipartisan committee and a room full of angry senators. Each of them represented a state full of vengeful American citizens who wanted nothing more than to make China pay for what happened at Indian Lake. He knew that it might well be too late to try to reason with anyone about what was happening, but he had to try.

As he neared the front the others peeled off to take their own seats. Once he sat down, the noise in the senate chamber suddenly dissipated to the point that the occasional shuffle of a piece of paper could be heard. It seemed that everyone very much wanted to hear what Nick Reynolds from Cyber Command had to say. Nick noted that Ben Rogers, the senator from North Carolina and the chair of the United States Senate Homeland Security Permanent Subcommittee on Investigations, was preparing to speak.

"Welcome, everyone. I would like to start off this morning by reminding everyone that this hearing is classified, and may not be discussed outside this chamber. I would also like to welcome our guest today, Dr. Nick Reynolds, the head of Operation Counterpunch at Cyber Command, the task force specifically assigned the task of detecting and stopping these devastating cyber attacks. With a PhD in Computer Science from M.I.T. with a special emphasis in cyber warfare, ten years working at the NSA, and five years experience researching Chinese cyber warfare capabilities, I think you'll agree that he is uniquely qualified to provide us with a clearer picture of exactly what we do and do not know. Welcome, Dr. Reynolds."

"Thank you, Senator Rogers." Nick repeatedly shuffled in his seat. He recognized that some of the senators were starting to take notice of it, so he exerted as much effort as he could spare remaining still.

"Have you been sworn-in, Dr. Reynolds?"

"I have, Senator." The senator simply nodded in response.

"Okay, Dr. Reynolds, I understand that you're prepared to debrief us on some of your findings that have come out of your investigations into the cyber attack at Indian Lake, is that correct?"

"Yes, Senator, I am. Before we start, however, I was told that you will be holding a vote in about an hour to discuss a declaration of war against the People's Republic of China."

"Yes, Dr. Reynolds, that's correct."

"Then I'll try to be brief. Well sir, as you know, our job at Cyber Command is to try to prevent, identify, locate, and halt cyber attacks against the United States."

"Yes, I believe all of us here are aware of that, Dr. Reynolds." The senators had already started losing interest, choosing instead to prepare for their upcoming vote unless Reynolds had something substantial to say. It seemed to Nick that most of them had already determined that the United States going to war with China was a foregone conclusion.

"Mr. Chairman, as the head of Operation Counterpunch, I have been tasked with investigating the cyber attack that killed over one hundred thousand people when the reactor at the Indian Lake power plant melted down. Senator Rogers, I'm here before you today to inform you that, based on all of the evidence that is currently at our disposal, I strongly believe that the Chinese are, in fact, *not* behind what happened at Indian Lake." The proclamation got everyone's attention and a brief outburst occurred, until Rogers brought the chamber back to order. Once more all eyes were focused on Nick Reynolds.

"What? But your office said there was evidence that the Chinese have been snooping around our systems for decades, and that the attack which took place at Indian Lake originated in China! Please clarify your remark, Dr. Reynolds."

"That's true sir, the Chinese have been hacking into some of our sensitive, classified systems for decades, and the preliminary evidence we had *did* suggest that the attack originated in China."

"Okay then, so obviously you now believe that someone other than China is responsible for the recent attack at Indian Lake. Who is responsible and what caused you to change your mind?"

"That is an excellent question, Mr. Chairman. As I mentioned, in the beginning of our investigation, the initial evidence, which suggested the attack originated from China, was all we had to go on. I've always had my doubts about the Indian Lake attack, however, because it was out of character for the Chinese to change tactics so dramatically. They've always been more interested in stealing secrets than they were in attacking us.

"Anyway, new evidence has just come to light which points to a rogue Russian element that was once part of the KGB in the former Soviet Union. Apparently this rogue former-KGB agent seems to have developed an elaborate plan, which he and those who follow him hope will pave the way to a devastating war between the United States and China. He anticipates that such a war between our two countries would create a global leadership vacuum, which only the Soviet Union could then fill." The chamber started to buzz as senators on the committee, as well as their aides, began discussing the matter.

"What evidence do you have that this rogue Russian agent is responsible for what happened at Indian Lake?" Senator Rogers asked, before whispering something about the CIA to one of his aides, then focusing his attention back on Reynolds.

"Well, sir, we have corroborating evidence from both the Chinese and the Russians. The Chinese were able to provide information regarding a zombie server found in China, near Beijing, which was the proxy system used to launch the actual attack and cause the Indian Lake meltdown, sir."

Rogers eyes opened wide and his nostrils flared. "Is that what you came here to tell us, Dr. Reynolds? Is that the best you've been able to come up with? That the Chinese are claiming to be innocent, after decades of hacking into American systems and stealing information which is not only highly sensitive, but vital to our national interest? And now, are you seriously expecting us to happily jump on the bandwagon and sing Kumbaya with you, the Russians, and the Chinese? Did you know that the Chinese stole the neutron bomb, not to mention numerous other technologies of mass destruction from the United States?" The senator had become so incensed that he stood up while talking with Reynolds. "Need I remind you, Dr. Reynolds, that over one hundred *thousand* Americans died as a result of this attack from China? The House voted only yesterday on a declaration of war, and we are scheduled to vote in under an hour." The chairman sighed deeply and sat back down; after a few deep breaths he continued. "Look, Dr. Reynolds, no one here wants a war with China, or with anyone else for that matter. But there are over one hundred thousand men, women, and children dead, and someone has to answer for that. An investigation has already been done, and the report concluded that the Indian Lake attack was the work of the Chinese." Rogers was raising the gavel to end the hearing when Reynolds stood up.

"Please, Mr. Chairman, don't do this. Give us some more time to gather the additional evidence we need. The Russian's FSB attempted to capture or kill the leader of the rogue KGB agents, Nikolai Chervanko, just a few days ago, but they missed him. My team is working day and night on this, and we may be close to a break through that will put an end to the attacks. Please, just give us another week to bring you some indisputable evidence, Senator. A war with China is exactly what Chervanko wants, and would result in millions of deaths. By declaring war on the Chinese, you would be playing right into his hands."

Rogers began slowly shaking his head. "I'd like to give you more time, Dr. Reynolds, but I'm afraid I can't. The American people are out there screaming for justice for all of the victims in New York; they want blood, son."

Nick thought about that for a moment. "Will adding millions, possibly even hundreds of millions, of dead to that number satisfy their bloodlust, Senator?" Rogers was on the ropes now, so Nick moved in for the kill. "Won't you give me just one more week, Senator, to spare the world from a global catastrophe?"

The chairman surveyed those seated to his right and to his left. It was a mixed bag; some of them wanted to delay, a few did not. After an informal vote, they decided.

"Okay, Dr. Reynolds, you've convinced us to wait one more week before re-convening this committee. Make it count, Dr. Reynolds, because if you fail, we *will* be at war with the Peoples Republic of China."

"Yes, sir. Thank you Mr. Chairman; I promise I'll do my best to make sure that doesn't happen."

Senator Rogers then announced, "The vote for the declaration of war will be re-scheduled for exactly one week from today, at 10:00 A.M., while Cyber Command looks for evidence to corroborate the scenario put forth by the governments of the People's Republic of China and the Russian Confederation. Until then, this meeting is adjourned."

Nick was stopped more than once on his way out of the Senate chambers. He felt overwhelmed, fielding questions about their findings, about Chervanko, and about what they were doing to address the threat of cyber attacks to prevent another Indian Lake.

By the time Nick climbed back into his Honda Accord, he was exhausted. He started the engine and began making his way back to Ft. Meade. His thoughts drifted back to the hearing, to the cries for justice, and to the tremendous suffering and death the world would face should he and the others fail. He wondered how Kate and her father were making out with the Ignis device, a piece of technology recovered from an alien spacecraft. His mind raced as he picked up the John Hanson Highway; what were they doing—the fate of the planet resting on some weird alien technology? It was risky, crazy even, but it might be their best shot at avoiding a global thermonuclear war.

Nick hurried back to his apartment to change before catching the next flight back to McCarran International Airport in Las Vegas, where he would then pick up a Janet flight back to S-4. If there was anything he could do to help Henry and Kate with Ignis, he'd do it. He also decided that once he was back at S-4, he would also touch base with some colleagues in China and Russia. Perhaps if they cooperated fully and agreed to pull out all stops to find and kill Chervanko, the three nations might succeed in finding a way to stop his mad scheme. If they couldn't find the evidence they needed to prove China's innocence in one week, the world, as he'd known it, would change forever.

Chapter 21

The young man with the unkempt hair sat at a desk at the Hat Creek Radio Observatory, 290 miles northeast of San Francisco, California. Wearing headphones, he sat quietly at the desk and listened intently to the music of the cosmos. It was Mark Goddard's turn to get some quality radio time on the Allen Telescope Array, so he had come prepared with drinks, a late dinner, and some spare time. A graduate student at Berkeley, Goddard was thrilled when he learned he was going to have an opportunity to fill in for someone at the observatory for a while. He knew it was the opportunity of a lifetime, and had already added it to his resume.

Having taken cosmology courses for most of his college career, all he'd needed was a small amount of supplemental training, and after sitting with someone else for a few weeks, he was now running solo. Mark Goddard, graduate student, was now on the hunt for extra-terrestrials. He munched on a fish sandwich he'd picked up on his way to the observatory and washed it down with a few swallows from his soft drink. He thoroughly enjoyed listening to the sounds of the cosmos. One day someone—he could only hope it would be him—would be the first to detect the signal from another civilization, from a non-human intelligence, the first to interact in a meaningful way with humanity.

He soon finished his sandwich and went to work on an apple pie while checking his list of the systems he would be scanning. He would be starting with Beta Canum Venaticorum, a Sun-like star about twenty six light years away from Earth in the constellation Canes Venatici. It had been included on a list drawn up by astronomer Margaret Turnbull over a decade earlier, which included ten stellar systems, also called habstars. The ten systems on the list were the ones considered to be the most likely to include planets capable of supporting life. It was also one of the exoplanet candidates recently discovered by NASA's Kepler space telescope. After spending his childhood dreaming about alien civilizations, he was now living the dream in his effort to find one.

Goddard set the array to begin scanning the Beta Canum Venaticorum system, and left to make a much needed trip to the break room for a cup of coffee. He was pulling the graveyard shift again, after burning the midnight oil all week preparing his dissertation on celestial mechanics. If he were going to pull another all-nighter on the array, he would need the strong stuff. After the long walk down the hallway, he finally arrived at the break room, where he grabbed a porcelain cup, rinsed it clean, and placed it in the machine. He searched for and found a packet of his favorite blend of coffee, Sumatran, and placed it in the machine. He loved the blend because it gave him the most caffeine of any blend in the coffee machine. After pressing the button he watched as the elixir slowly began to pour into his cup below. The smell alone was enough to perk him up, despite his substantial sleep deficit. He waited while the cup filled, and began planning out his evening.

He would grade undergrad papers for the class he helped teach while he listened for signals. It was just one more of the many great things he enjoyed about working at S.E.T.I., or Search for Extraterrestrial Intelligence. With any luck and some additional private or government funding, he would be able to return to work fulltime at SETI once he finished his PhD program at Berkeley.

The coffee had eventually finished draining so he mixed in some creamer and artificial sweetener. He was starting to leave when he noticed a large cheese danish in the snack machine. He thought about getting back, but he knew he'd be busy grading papers for hours. He decided that finishing off his meal with the coffee and danish was an ideal way to start the evening, so he inserted a couple of dollar bills into the vending machine, which, after he pressed a button, rewarded him with Big Mike's Cheese Danish. The morning's paper lay on the table, left there by someone from the day shift. After flipping to the sports page, he took his time eating the danish and washing it down with his Sumatran. After all, the array would still be busy at work when he returned.

After finishing the danish Goddard returned to the desk where he would be stationed for the remainder of the evening. He then picked up his book bag, unzipped it, and retrieved the stack of undergrad papers.

With his pen in hand, he glanced up at the monitor for a moment, expecting to see the results from the scans of the Beta Canum Venaticorum system up to that point. After a quick glimpse, he looked down at the first paper and started to read the first paragraph. He had only read a few sentences when it hit him; there was something wrong with the data on the monitor. He set the stack of papers down on the desk and took a second look at it.

What he found made no sense. Based on the data, the array was no longer pointed towards the Beta Canum Venaticorum system. It was now pointing towards a completely different part of the sky, towards 18 Sco: a near-identical twin of our own star, located in the constellation Scorpio.

Unbelievable! Goddard cursed under his breath. Whether he had accidentally keyed in the wrong sequence, or whether there had been a glitch, he was going to have to reset the array so it pointed at the right part of the sky. How could he have been so careless? It wasn't an unforgivable sin after all; mistakes happened all the time, even by people brilliant enough to be part of SETI, but he had lost at least an hour. It was going to be obvious when the day-shift arrived the following morning that an hour's worth of data was from the wrong star system, and it was something he would have preferred to avoid.

When he had finished his mini-tirade, Goddard settled down and looked up the settings for the Beta Canum Venaticorum system once more. Once he had them in hand he happened to glance once more at the monitor, noticing something this time that *would* likely have been considered an unforgiveable sin. He stared at the screen in complete disbelief. If what he found was correct, it would be a first for the array, perhaps the first time this had ever occurred on Earth before.

He looked around for a laminated piece of paper. After a minute searching around the cluttered desk, he finally found it. He grabbed the phone, dialed a number he had located on the paper, and waited for it to ring. His heart was pounding in his chest. *Why did this have to happen on my watch?*

"Hello?" The voice on the other end was female. He recognized that the voice was indeed Dr. Linda Zimmerman.

"Hello, Dr. Zimmerman? I'm so sorry to disturb you this late!"

"I'm sorry, who is this?"

It sounded like she had been asleep. He felt badly, but he knew he'd done the right thing; he'd followed protocol.

"Dr. Zimmerman, this is Mark Goddard, at the Hat Creek Radio Observatory. I never would have called you this late but it seemed important, and it was never discussed in any of the training I received."

"What is it Mark, what's wrong?"

"Well, I set the array to start scanning the Beta Canum Venaticorum system when I first arrived. After making certain that it was scanning the right star system, I went to grab a cup of coffee. I didn't mean to stay gone so long!" he said nervously.

"That's okay Mark, that's okay. Tell me what happened."

"Well, I came back and found that the array was pointed to the wrong part of the sky, towards 18 Sco, which is in Scorpio!"

"Don't worry about it, Mark. Just point the array back toward Beta Canum Venaticorum and watch it for a bit. Perhaps it was just a glitch, or maybe you accidentally set it up incorrectly. Either way, don't worry about it."

"But that's not everything, Dr. Zimmerman; the fact that it was pointing at the wrong system is only part of the problem."

"What else happened?"

"The strangest thing happened after I was back at the station, before I was able to change where the dish was pointing to. Just as I was about to enter in the correct coordinates, the array began *broadcasting* transmissions to 18 Sco, instead of receiving them!

"It looks like SETI's systems were hacked tonight!"

Chapter 22

Kate awoke to the buzzing of her alarm clock. It was such an annoying sound that there could be little doubt as to why they were so effective at rousing people from their slumber. After staying up late again the night before, putting the final touches on the suite of tests they would run with Ignis, her hand instinctively went to the snooze button; it took a last minute burst of willpower to fight the urge to press it. Kate withdrew her hand and reluctantly began climbing out from under the covers before sitting up on the side of her bed. After a few moments, once she was convinced that she was awake enough, she turned off the alarm and walked over to the linen closet, where she retrieved some towels and a washcloth for a shower. She decided that no matter what happened during the testing, they would have to find time to get more rest. The scientist knew she was running a serious sleep deficit and it was starting to take its toll. She desperately wanted to spend as much time as possible developing and then executing the tests, but the scientist in her knew she needed to keep her mind clear and sharp if they were ever going to find a way to use Ignis in time to save the planet.

Kate decided to start a fresh pot of coffee brewing, which was finished draining by the time she emerged from the shower fifteen minutes later. After dressing, she poured herself a cup of coffee before adding some French vanilla creamer and an artificial sweetener to it. She then placed a sausage, egg, & cheese omelet in the microwave, and two minutes later, sat down at the breakfast table to enjoy it.

While she ate, she allowed her mind to wander, something she frequently did in order to help free-up her mind's creativity. She thought about the escalating conflict between the United States and China, two of the most powerful economies, and militaries, in the world. With the deaths of so many still fresh in America's psyche, Kate shared Nick's fear that the situation could easily spiral out of control. Even worse was the fact that so many more Americans could die if there was another cyber attack, especially if the attack was as enormous as the warnings seemed to suggest it would be. Ignis might prove to be the only thing standing in the way of genocide, and World War III. She began to feel the weight of the world on her shoulders; it was up to her, Nick, and her father to find a way to use Ignis to counter the threat. Fortunately, based on what her father had told her, Ignis might just be up to the task. He'd been able to easily hack the NSA and the Chinese Online Blue Army sites merely by focusing his thoughts on them. That meant that the device had generated code on the fly complex enough that it was easily able to bypass the vast defenses put in place by both countries to stop such a thing from happening. *Could it be that hacking the world's greatest security was mere child's play to Ignis?* After all, the device must have been able to perform numerous calculations in order to navigate the galaxy. Perhaps bypassing security on some of the Earth's most secure and sophisticated computers *was* a ridiculously simple task for a device as advanced as Ignis. Her thoughts were suddenly interrupted by the phone ringing from across the breakfast table.

"Hello?"

"Oh, hi, Kate, good morning! Are you excited about working with Ignis this morning? Oh, I just noticed what time it is. I'm sorry if I'm calling too early, sweetheart." He was, but Kate knew that if her father was calling this early, there was a good reason why.

"Um, no Dad, it's fine. I was just finishing my breakfast. What's up?"

"Well, Nick's back this morning, and he's got some interesting news for us. We will be accelerating our timetable for testing Ignis. It looks like we have less than a week to prove it works, and to locate and stop the cyber attackers." Her father paused to give her a chance to say something, but Kate found herself unable to say anything in response. "Don't worry about it now sweetheart, we can discuss it when you get here. See you in a while."

"Okay, bye, Dad." *Okay, that was a bit disturbing.* They'd already been under a compressed schedule in an effort to find a way to stop the attacks and cripple the operations of the attackers. But a week? She picked up her papers and reviewed her notes regarding the suite of tests. She felt good about the plan, but she couldn't help but feel she might be missing something important, though not necessarily relevant to cyber warfare.

They would begin the tests by determining Ignis' ability to penetrate enemy defenses. They had to be careful not to strike at the enemy systems until they were confident about a successful outcome. No need to tip off the enemy, since even if Ignis was able to penetrate all of their defenses, they could always turn off the remote system, or disconnect it from the Internet entirely, severing Ignis' connection. Kate pondered for a moment, wondering whether Ignis might be able to penetrate another way, even if the Chinese *did* pull their Internet connection. Most systems would have some sort of internal connectivity between their remote sites as well, whether it was an Internet VPN, a frame-relay WAN link, or satellite. It was possible that Ignis would be able to identify the means of connectivity the remote sites were using and exploit it. She made herself a note.

She glanced down at the remaining list of tests that she wanted to run, including the ability to detect any incoming cyber attacks, the ability to proactively protect American sites, and the ability to quickly trace an attack back to its origin, despite how many times the attackers had routed the attack. Perhaps when Ignis encountered a zombie, it would still be able to trace the remote controlling system back to its source as well. Kate thought about that and made an additional note. She also remembered she had wanted to evaluate the ability of Ignis to detect internal attacks. Many times internal systems had been compromised by human agency, someone on the inside who had installed a virus or downloaded unauthorized information to a USB storage device. Kate allowed herself to smile at that one. If Ignis was even a fraction as advanced as she suspected it was, it would be able to do everything she wanted, and more.

She glanced down at her watch and decided she should get to the lab, where her father, Nick, and Ignis would be waiting. She needed to run everything by her father first anyway for his approval, before they could pull together a lab of equipment to test with. It occurred to her that with less than a week, they really didn't have the time or resources readily available to do the kind of testing she wanted to do, and that posed a real challenge. She sat back down in a chair in the living room for a moment to ponder how to get the needed equipment in time.

She was about to get up to leave when the solution to the problem suddenly came to her; Cyber Command. According to Nick, they had been apportioned a generous budget, and they would already have such penetration labs built. She would have to play nice with Nick Reynolds today if she wanted his cooperation. Certainly Nick would have some motivation to go along anyway since he had been tasked to stop the Chinese threat, but she doubted he would readily open his lab up to tests with an alien device with unknown capabilities. As far as she knew, granting Ignis access to Cyber Command could open the world up to an alien invasion of some sort. She started laughing, surprised that the ridiculous thought had ever occurred to her. As a scientist, she knew very well that any civilization capable of developing such advanced technology would likely find humanity to be of little or no threat to it from either a technological or military point of view. Still, if she were going to persuade Nick, perhaps she should take some extra steps to help win him over.

Despite her initial animosity towards Nick, Kate had sensed a connection with Nick from their first meeting, and she could tell that he was attracted to her. Ordinarily she would never stoop to such levels just to try to win someone over to her way of thinking, but truth be known, she had discovered that she was somewhat attracted to Nick as well. He was a handsome enough man, fit and muscular, yet not so much so as to appear brutish. In addition, while he was not a scientist, he was rather intelligent, and well-educated. Doubtless he would never have been placed in charge of Operation Counterpunch at Cyber Command at such a young age were he not among the nation's best and brightest.

She walked into the bathroom and opened a drawer, where she kept her makeup. It had been a while since she'd used it last, since there was little need for it during the daily activities at the lab. Not that she required any makeup at all, because most men found her beautiful without it. But when she made an effort to look her best, well, men had always seemed to take extra notice. She felt that the additional attention to her looks, the correct choice in clothing, and her solid argument for using the facilities at Cyber Command would be enough to win Nick over, perhaps in more ways than one. It suddenly occurred to Kate that she wasn't really sure whether she wanted to impress Nick so she could use his lab at Cyber Command, or whether she just wanted to impress Nick. Either way, she was looking forward to finding out how he reacted. As she began applying her foundation, she suddenly realized that it was the first time she had been so interested in a man since she'd been in college; it was long overdue.

Chapter 23

Nick left the small apartment and closed the door behind him. It was smaller than his apartment back in Maryland, but it was still large enough to make him feel comfortable; more like an apartment than a hotel room. He walked down the corridor to the elevator, which then took him down two floors to the mezzanine area. A few small restaurants and coffee shops were set up all around, scattered among the many small stores which had been built near where the underground tram system connected the main base at Groom Lake to several interconnecting facilities, including the S-4 base.

As had been his custom since first arriving at the Area 51 facility, he stopped by one of the small shops that carried the Wall Street Journal, along with books, magazines, and several dozen miscellaneous other items. After paying for a copy of the paper, he walked over to his favorite restaurant, where he decided to enjoy a hot breakfast for a change, rather than the cold cereal and fruit which so often made up his first meal of the day. After taking his order, the waitress returned moments later with a pitcher of ice water in one hand and a carafe of freshly brewed coffee in the other. She then poured him a glass of water and a cup of coffee before disappearing through a small door which led to the kitchen.

Nick sipped on his coffee as he opened the paper to the front page. There on page one, as had been the case for weeks, was more speculation on what the motive for the Chinese attacks on New York had been, and why they would risk World War III and certain destruction by killing one hundred thousand Americans with a crippled nuclear power plant. When he glanced down the page, he found another small article, which purported that startling new evidence had been presented to a Senate subcommittee, prompting the committee chair to postpone the Senate vote on a war resolution. *Blasted leaks.* He continued sipping his coffee, wondering whether it had been a senator or a staff member that had leaked the information. Thankfully they'd only passed along a small portion of what had been discussed to the press, not enough that it was going to tip off Chervanko.

The waitress arrived a few minutes later with a glass of orange juice, followed moments later by a plate full of crispy bacon, fried eggs, and a piece of toast. Nick thanked the waitress, and after bowing his head to give thanks—a practice he'd continued since childhood—he attacked the meal with a vengeance; apparently the long trip from Maryland the night before had left him with an appetite. He had just shoveled a spoonful of eggs into his mouth when his cell phone rang. *Timing is everything.* After a few rings and a swallow of orange juice, Nick picked up his cell phone.

"Hello?"

"Nick? General Caprella here." He wasn't wasting any time. Nick had only flown out to Nevada the night before. Even with the time difference it was still late by the time he arrived at the base.

"Hello, General."

"Good morning. I trust you had a nice flight and were able to get good night's rest last night, because you're going to need it."

"Yes, General, I did; thank you."

"Good. Have you had a chance to brief them yet?"

"No sir, not yet, but I'm supposed to meet with them in less than an hour."

"That's good. Listen, Nick, I know I've had to place a lot on your shoulders and I'm really sorry about that. You've done an incredible job, though, and for what it's worth, I'm proud of you. You're one of the best we have when it comes to cyber warfare; I can't think of anyone better suited or more qualified to deal with the threat we're facing."

"If it were the Chinese, General, maybe I'd agree with you, if only because I've spent years trying to keep up with what they've been doing in cyber space. But Chervanko isn't Chinese, he's Russian."

"True. But remember, he's trying to make this *look* like a Chinese attack, so in a sense, you are still working against a Chinese threat...at least in a manner of speaking."

"Yes, sir," Nick answered, aware that trying to argue with a general was a lost cause from the beginning. "Hopefully, Henry and Kate have found a way to use Ignis to help us track down Chervanko and the other animals responsible for what happened in New York, before this thing turns into a full-scale nuclear war."

"From your lips to God's ears, son. By the way, let me say again what a fine job you did yesterday in front of that Senate committee. It was a fine piece of negotiation; very impressive. They were ready to issue a formal declaration yesterday, Nick, and you talked them down and bought us some time. Thank you."

"Yeah, well, they seemed a little too anxious to pull the trigger, if you ask me," replied Nick. "Don't they realize what will happen if they declare war on the Chinese? The Chinese are aware that they're no match for us militarily, so they will throw everything they've got at us in a first-strike. They know they can't afford to sit back and wait for us to attack, because by then it will be too late. This thing will escalate five minutes after they declare war."

"I *am* a general, Nick, remember?"

"Of course. Sorry, General."

"But you're probably right, Nick. Only someone who's never fought in a war ever goes looking for one, and unfortunately, most of them have never seen one. Chervanko and his band of merry men are the only ones insane enough to try and predict the outcome of a global thermonuclear war. The fallout and subsequent nuclear winter would probably wreak as much havoc on Russia as it does China and the United States." There was a brief pause on the line before Caprella continued. "We have to try and keep in mind, however, that the American people *are* pressuring their representatives, Nick, and the military is merely an extension of the civilian government. You *must* convey to Dr. Summers and his daughter, Kate, what's at stake here. Work around the clock if you have to. Shoot, we can send a whole battalion of computer scientists your way if you need them to help head this thing off; all you have to do is ask."

"What about the secrecy, General?"

"Who cares? It won't matter much if there's no world left, now will it?"

"No sir, General, I suppose it won't."

"Alright, Nick, I'm going to get off this phone so you can get going and save the world. Do what you have to do Nick, but get it done, for all of our sakes. Also, I meant what I said; if you need people, I'll get you people. If you need equipment, let me know and I'll get it on a flight out the same day, and you'll have it that night or the following morning, if not before. Call me anytime, day or night; you know how to reach me.

You just find and stop this S.O.B., and then let me know where he is. I'm confident that between us, the Russians, and the Chinese, Comrade Chervanko won't be a problem much longer."

"I hope you're right about that, General."

"So do I, son. Oh, there's something I needed to tell you, I nearly forgot."

"Yes, sir?"

"I had a surprise call late last night. It seems that S.E.T.I. was hacked the day before yesterday. That's something you don't see every day."

"It's a first, General, to the best of my knowledge. What did they get, sir?"

"Well, that's the really peculiar thing about the hack, and the most disturbing. There was no data theft at all from what they could tell. Oh, and that's not all, something else happened out there during the hack; the array *sent* a signal, instead of receiving one."

"That's interesting," Nick said after several moments. "I didn't even know that was possible. I thought they could only receive."

"So did I. Any thoughts about what the hackers might have been up to?"

"Well sir, unless it was E.T. phoning home, I can't imagine what reason a hacker could have had for using the array to send a signal. Perhaps they were trying to send a signal toward a satellite, bounce a signal off of the moon, or maybe it was just some bright kid trying to see if he could do it."

"Well, the moon wasn't in that part of the sky, nor was a satellite in its path. You're probably right, it was most likely just a kid having some fun. Alright, Nick, please let me know if you come up with anything at the lab."

"Okay, General, I'll keep you posted. Have a good day, sir."

"You too, my boy, and God speed."

"Thank you, sir."

* * * *

Nick's mind was filled with many thoughts and emotions which were battling for dominance in his conscious mind. He was scared, terrified really. But he'd been in the game long enough to understand that problems are rarely solved with panic. If they were going to survive the ordeal it was going to require level heads and an abundance of brain power and focus. By the time he reached the lab and opened the door, he was as solemn as a judge, determined to find answers no matter what they faced.

When he looked up and saw Dr. Kate Summers, however, everything suddenly flew out the window. For one of the very few times in his life, Nick Reynolds was at a complete loss for words. She stood at the table next to Ignis, examining the device. She wasn't wearing her lab coat, instead she looked...*was she wearing make-up?* Her clothes looked nothing like what she'd worn every other time he'd seen her. She was dressed in slacks and a blouse, looking more like a hot date than she did a scientist. Without her lab coat on Nick was able to see that she had a surprisingly athletic build, though it was slight enough that it enhanced rather than detracted from her more feminine attributes.

"Are you going to stand there in the doorway like a statue all morning Nick, or are you going to come in and say hello?" She wore a genuine, mischievous smile. Nick suddenly realized that he'd been staring at her like an amorous, forlorn schoolboy. *How long was I standing here before she noticed me?*

"Oh, hi Kate, good morning," he answered, trying to sound casual as he started walking awkwardly into the lab and toward his office. It required all of his willpower not to look back at her, fearing that if he did, he'd end up making a complete fool of himself by once more gawking at his coworker. He had no idea how long he'd stood in the doorway taking in the sights before she said something. *I'm an idiot.*

"So how was your trip, Nick?" She'd followed him to his office. Unable to bear it any longer, he looked up at her and noticed, for the first time, how stunning her blue eyes were against her long, dark, silky hair. At that moment he realized that she was the most beautiful woman he'd ever seen.

"It...um...went great I guess, Kate, thanks."

"Are you okay, Nick?" she asked with a mixture of concern and mischief.

Nick looked up at her, confused. He'd thought her to be attractive before but now, she was stunning. After his last serious relationship had turned sour three years earlier, he'd dealt with it by immersing himself in his work, and had kept any women he'd dated at arm's length emotionally. He'd not had a real relationship since.

"Sure...I'm...um, fine! So how have things been going here?" he asked, starting to regain his footing after being so unbalanced. She started talking about some tests she had been working on, and about various sets of data she'd been able to glean from the test results. None of it registered with Nick, however, because all he could think about was her. He found himself wondering whether the difference in her appearance the same day he returned was intentional, or whether it was just a coincidence. *Is she flirting with me?*

"Because I found that when I interfaced with Ignis I—"

"What?" Nick interrupted her, suddenly jolted back to reality.

"I was saying that when I interfaced with Ignis, I found I was able to easily access any system I wanted in the blink of an eye, as long as it was somehow connected. It was amazing, absolutely incredible!"

"Wait a minute, Kate. Are you saying that you did it, that you found a way to interface with Ignis?"

"Haven't you been listening, Nick? Yes, we did! Now all we need is access to the right test bed of equipment to verify my hypothesis, and I believe we will be ready."

"Ready for what?" asked Nick, once more finding himself off-balance.

"I think we can stop Chervanko now, Nick. More than that, I think we will be able to use Ignis to stop his next attack, *and* trace the attack through the zombie computer and back to wherever he is. Just imagine, Nick, within a few days this could all be over!"

Chapter 24

Nick could hardly believe it. He had only been connected a few minutes, yet he was already able to access any system, anywhere, that was somehow directly or indirectly connected to the Internet. He tried accessing a system at Cyber Command which he knew to be heavily secured. The system was designed so that it required a retina scanner, a palm-scanner, and a randomly-generated key code entered in order to access it. Nick concentrated and the screen before him morphed as he was able to progress past all the security measures without any difficulty at all. He was suddenly looking at secure directories and files stored on the vast storage area network sitting across the country at Cyber Command in Fort Meade, Maryland. He opened a file sent to him by General Caprella, which had been certified as Sensitive Compartmented Information (SCI) with a codeword. Once again Ignis was able to open the file and display the content on the screen with no effort whatsoever, overcoming every security hurdle along the way. It then occurred to Nick that they would need to be able to somehow capture and store sufficient quantities of important data, which had been retrieved from an enemy system; perhaps a type of localized SAN system, for dissemination and access by those with proper clearance. The possibilities were endless from an offensive posture; but what about a defensive posture? In order to answer that question and determine defensive capabilities, they would have to test that capability in a lab, just as Kate had said. Nick couldn't wait to share what he'd learned with General Caprella, whose idea to explore the alien technology as a potential countermeasure against the imminent, deadly cyber attack had just been vindicated. Ignis could very well be the answer to fending off the potentially devastating cyber attack, and to preventing the deaths of hundreds of millions of people. They were also going to find Chervanko, along with the evidence they needed to prove that *he* was behind the attack, and not the Chinese. Time was running out, however. They now had less than a week before the Senate voted on the declaration of war.

After spending another thirty minutes using Ignis to explore cyberspace from a truly unique perspective, he decided it was time to take the next step.

Nick exited the interface with Ignis and opened his eyes, only to find Kate staring at him with what looked like a mixture of expectation and excitement. Henry wore a similar expression on his face, before taking another puff on his pipe. Nick caught a whiff of pipe tobacco before climbing off of the table and sitting in a chair. It occurred to him that the no-smoking rule seemed to have little meaning at S-4. Kate walked over until she stood in front of him. Nick smiled warmly at her and she returned the gesture.

"So how did it go, Nick? Are you convinced now that what we said about Ignis is true?"

Nick looked up at her and smiled, his eyes still opened wide in wonder. "It was the most unusual and amazing experience of my life!" He jumped up and placed a hand on each of Kate's shoulders. He felt her pull away from him slightly, before settling into his touch, and smiling back at him with a warm, tender expression. Nick continued, overflowing with excitement, much like a child with a new toy at Christmas. "I was able to access systems I should never have been able to access—some weren't even directly connected to the Internet!"

"So will you give us permission to access the computer testing facility at Cyber Command?" asked Dr. Henry Summers?

"Absolutely! I suggest we start immediately. We must begin testing the *defensive* capabilities of Ignis." Nick turned back to face Kate for a moment, a question burning in his mind. Instead, his mind blanked out for a moment, and he found himself staring into her eyes, feeling, just for a moment, as if he might lose himself in them. Whatever feelings he was developing for Dr. Kate Summers, he was thankful that they seemed, at least at the moment, to be mutual. There was a world to be saved, however, so whatever they might or might not want to do about it would have to wait. "Kate, do you think we can duplicate Ignis?" Kate's face suddenly went from flushed to all-business.

"Well, I don't really know yet, Nick. This technology is so far beyond where we are today. I suppose that eventually, given enough time, people, and resources, we *might* be able to recreate Ignis or at least some of its components. Once all of this is over, I certainly would like to try. What do we do for now, though?"

"Now, we find out what Ignis can really do, and how it can help us save millions of lives. I'll give General Caprella a quick call; let him know what's going on and why."

* * * *

"They're making great progress, Nikolai. They say they should be finished in another day or two," Smirnov told his friend. Both men sat out on the porch of their safe house, where they had stayed since the close call a week earlier. Chervanko had been taking a break from planning the mission, taking a moment to enjoy watching the sunset. They had positioned the secondary location and the safe house within only a few miles of each other in the city of Reutov, a city about thirty miles east of Moscow. He loved his beloved Moscow, but he found the landscape in Reutov to be more tranquil than the hustle and bustle of the capital city. "At this rate, we should be back in business in a couple more days." Chervanko turned and nodded his head for a moment but said nothing. Smirnov watched his friend for a moment.

"Is everything okay, Nikolai? I hope you're not having second thoughts now, old friend. We've come too far now to turn back. Besides, in all likelihood, every intelligence agency in the world now knows who we are, and are out looking for us; there is no going back."

Chervanko turned back to Smirnov and stared at him for a moment, looking very solemnly and intently at his comrade, before breaking into laughter.

"Back out? You must be joking, Viktor! I'd sooner cut off my right arm, followed by my left, before swallowing hot coals, rather than turn back!" he said emphatically. "Turn back? My dear Viktor, this is exactly what we have dreamt of, worked for, slaved for, for so many years now. No, comrade, I am having no doubts whatsoever; rather, I am thinking about how glorious it will be when once again our beloved Mother Russia, the New Soviet Union, will have her boot on the neck of the American dog. Then, dear Viktor, *we* will be the only great superpower left in the world!" He paused, taking a moment to look up at the night sky. A half moon hung overhead and stars filled the sky, which seemed much clearer in Reutov than it had in Moscow. He noticed Orion's belt amidst the stars, and was reminded of something. "What of our friends in the United States—do they continue to blame our friends to the south?"

"They do. I just learned this afternoon that the United States has raised their threat level from DEFCON 4 to DEFCON 3. All indications are that their senate will soon vote to declare war on our Chinese brothers over the incident in New York."

"If they don't before, they most certainly will after our next attack. The death toll will be too catastrophic to ignore. Soon, very soon, it will all be over, my friend, one way or the other."

Chapter 25

Kate laughed as she took the edge of the napkin and used it to wipe away some of the mustard at the corner of his mouth. She had grown to enjoy his company more and more during the time they'd spent together. Despite the tremendous pressure they were all under to stop the attacks and prevent a nuclear war, she had somehow managed it so she and Nick were alone together with increasing frequency. They had been taking meals together in the cafeteria while her father ate in the lab.

It seemed to Kate that her father was encouraging the budding relationship between her and Nick. He'd been pressuring her to find someone for the last few years, fearing his eventual death would leave her all alone, and that was something he couldn't bear the thought of. She was beginning to think perhaps she had found someone in Nick, and had come to learn that they had quite a bit in common.

"So tell me more about what you were like growing up, Dr. Reynolds," she asked. "Wait, let me guess; I bet you were the captain of your football team, the president of your class, and the one voted 'Most Likely to Succeed'!"

"Hah! Far from it," he said, laughing. "No, I was the ultimate 'lone wolf.' I was more likely to tell my classmates to get lost than I was to ask for their vote when running for a school office. I did play some sports for a while, mostly baseball, but I was never all that good. So what about you? Were you a cheerleader, the prom queen, and Little Miss Popular in high school?"

She smiled at him as she sipped on her soft drink. "Would it surprise you if I said I was guilty on all three counts, or did you think I was a nerd all through school?"

Nick looked into her eyes and said, "Actually, Dr. Summers, it wouldn't surprise me one little bit if you were a cheerleader, the prom queen, Little Miss Popular, Miss USA, Miss Universe, a Nobel Prize winner, and the one who finally found a cure for cancer, all rolled into one. I think you are a very beautiful and very intelligent woman, Dr. Kate Summers."

Kate just stared at him for a moment, saying nothing. She wasn't accustomed to men talking to her that way. Most often men were jealous or intimidated by the fact that she was a brilliant scientist who also was physically attractive. After several moments, she smiled tentatively and rose to leave the table.

"Um, thank you." Kate started to blush. "Well, I guess that we'd better get back to the lab and start that testing; Dad should be finished going over all of the planned tests by now. Are we able to access the lab at Fort Meade now?"

"You bet. Everything's ready and waiting for us to start our testing." Nick looked at her, trying to find the right words to express what he wanted to say. "Um, Kate, you know, I'd like to…we should.…"

Kate took his hands in hers, nodded, and smiled. "I think so too, Nick. But after this is all over, okay?"

Nick nodded, and smiled. Kate Summers then stood up and began walking towards the cafeteria exit, wanting to ensure that she liked where things were going with Nick Reynolds. By the time they'd made it to the elevator, she'd decided that indeed, she very much liked where things were going with the man she now adored.

They arrived back at the lab to find Dr. Henry Summers finishing up his own lunch. He stood up as soon as they entered the lab.

"Hi, Dad. So, how did the latest set of tests look? Do you think I covered everything?"

"Hi, sweetheart. Actually, Kate, I think you might have been a little *too* thorough." He handed over a white clipboard with a dozen sheets of paper on it. Many lines had been marked over, though there a couple of new entries scattered throughout all twelve pages.

"Why did you scratch out so many, Dad? We need to run a lot of tests with Ignis; after all, we know next to nothing about how it works!"

Henry sighed and walked over to a nearby chair and collapsed into it. Kate noticed he looked exhausted.

"Kate, we have only days now until the Congress of the United States of America officially declares war on the People's Republic of China. We don't have time to learn every detail about how Ignis operates before then, as much as I wish we did. I realize it's a risky proposition, relying on an alien technology to stop a devastating world war, but we have no choice. Bring that over here, Kate."

She obeyed, walking over to her father and handing him the battery of tests.

"Dad, you look exhausted. Maybe you should go back to your apartment and get some rest. Nick and I can handle things here for a while."

"Do you remember what Benjamin Franklin said in 'The Way to Wealth' in *Poor Richard's Almanack*, sweetheart? 'How much more than is necessary do we spend in sleep! Forgetting that the sleeping fox catches no poultry, and that there will be sleeping enough in the grave.' If we don't catch Mr. Chervanko and prove that he has been the one launching these attacks, there may be sleep enough for us all in the grave."

Kate just stared at him for a moment, her resentment quickly fading as the cold hard reality began to sink in. He was right; they had to focus on stopping the attacks and proving that Chervanko was behind what happened at Indian Lake; it was the only way. There would be time enough after the crisis had passed to study Ignis. Kate began nodding her head while looking up at her father.

"You're right, Dad. We'll just focus on the minimal amount of testing that's necessary for us to determine how to protect our infrastructure and find the ones responsible."

Kate turned to Nick. "Want to go ahead and let them know we're getting ready to start, Nick?" He had been watching uncomfortably while the father and daughter went back and forth. "Nick?" she repeated.

"Oh, sorry, Kate," he answered, jolted from his passive observations. "Yeah, I'll give them a call to let them know." He walked over to a phone in the corner of the lab and called Cyber Command.

"So Dad, the first thing you want to test is what Ignis can do to defend a very hardened system, correct?"

"Yes, Kate. I suggest we start with some of Nick's penetration attacks, so we can then use Ignis to ensure all of our critical systems are protected. If we find that Ignis is able to protect our most critical systems, I think we should then try the test for assessing Ignis' ability to trace a hack in spite of how difficult the hackers attempt to make it to trace."

"The test Nick and I developed includes tracing the attack beyond the zombie computer and back to the controlling system as well. Based on what I've seen of Ignis, that shouldn't be a problem at all. As to the defensive capability, I want to try and get Ignis to write code that will recognize and instantly destroy any malicious code that tries to circumvent security. Ignis seems to have the ability to generate code on the fly, apparently with very little effort."

"As you know, Kate, it's important that Ignis not only stop the attacks but that it can also rapidly find who and where the attackers are, so that the authorities can find evidence before the attackers have a chance to destroy all of it."

"Don't worry about it, Dad, I'll take care of it."

"I'd like to drive if it's all the same to you."

A startled Kate and Henry turned to look at Nick.

"What? What are you talking about, Nick? I'm going in to do the testing." Kate looked betrayed.

"It needs to be me, Kate."

"No way! I've been working on the Prometheus Project for years now...my father's worked on it for decades. What makes you think *you'll* be the one to interface with Ignis? This is my project, I'm going in."

"And you've done a tremendous job too, Kate, really. But it *has* to be me."

Kate started growing increasingly incensed, doubly so since she and Nick had been growing so close and spending so much time together. It was the added feeling of duplicity which helped fuel her anger.

"Listen here, *Doctor* Reynolds, the only way you're going in to do this is over my dead body."

Nick had been sitting at the far end of the table from Kate. Given her animosity, she could see him hesitate as he stood up and began walking towards her. She bristled as he drew nearer.

"Kate...."

She jerked back and recoiled away from him. "Get away from me...jerk! I thought you and I...." She turned to her father, still fuming. "Dad, you have to say something! He's trying to cut me out here!" She looked imploringly at her father, who only grimaced and gently shook his head.

"I'm afraid that I can't, sweetheart. Nick is right, it needs to be him. I believe he's better suited for the mission."

"What? Ugghh! I simply can't believe it! Even my own father is on your side!"

"Kate, please listen to me," implored Nick. "There are no *sides* here. You'll have years and years to work with Ignis, testing and measuring its capabilities, trying to determine and map its limitations. But right now, this very minute, the world is hanging in the balance, and I know the Chinese cyber attack strategy better than anyone else on the planet. I'm also much more informed about Chervanko and his men, how they operate, where they might go if they get into trouble. The science is all yours, Kate; just leave the cyber warfare to me...it's *my* area of expertise. You know what's at stake here. We have to stop any further attacks, find Chervanko, and collect enough evidence that he was purposefully impersonating a Chinese cyber attack and not just working for them, and we have to accomplish all of this in only three days. That leaves us only one day to present the evidence to the United States Senate, and stop a war.

"Please...let me do this, Kate. I need you, I need both of you, if we are going to pull this off. Besides, I've been pretty useless on this project since I got here. Isn't it about time for me to carry my weight? Prometheus is your project, Ignis is *your* baby; just let me stop this attack and save the world, and I'll get out of your hair; well...out of the lab at least." The whole time he'd been looking apologetically into her eyes, trying to convey to her how much he cared for her, and that he was in no way attempting to undermine her. The redness in Kate's cheeks slowly began to fade and the look in her eyes began to cool. She believed him; Nick only wanted to stop a war that a madman had been trying to start.

"I want to have the ability to monitor all local and remote systems involved during the test, and I want the same when it's all happening for real. I also want assurances from you and from General Caprella that Dad and I will have full control over Prometheus and Ignis once more after the danger has passed. Can you live with that, Nick?" This time her demeanor was much more agreeable.

"Absolutely," Nick answered, before letting out a heavy sigh of relief.

Jeff W. Horton

Chapter 26

Linda Zimmerman sipped on her coffee, adjusted her headphones, and sat back down to sift through some of the data. The array was pumping out data so much faster and more efficiently than Project Phoenix that she wondered how long it would be until they finally detected radio signals created by an extraterrestrial civilization. She had little doubt that it was just a matter of time.

Zimmerman reached over and picked up another document laying on her desk, a work order left by the big-dollar security consultants S.E.T.I. had hired to install a pair of new firewalls on their outward facing network. The consultant, who also did work with the N.S.A., had vouched that the firewalls were the same make and model commonly used in organizations like the N.S.A. She was glad to see that, as she had requested, the vendor had added a paragraph assuring S.E.T.I. that they would receive a full refund, and could keep the firewalls as well, should hackers once again penetrate the security. After feeling a twinge of guilt at having pressured the vendor as she had on the paragraph, she took another swallow of coffee and got back to the data.

Zimmerman was always excited when they were examining a section of space which had never before been surveyed. Tonight was going to be one of those times. If they were ever able to get the funding to complete the ATA, the 350 dishes and ever-increasing computing power would give S.E.T.I. an exponentially greater capability to scan the sky for alien signals. She was certain that if Earth was ever contacted by an alien civilization, they would know about it.

She was looking out the window at a beautiful sunset when some unexpected movement suddenly caught her eye. She was startled when she looked down to find that the dishes in the array were starting to slowly turn. She glanced back at the monitor for confirmation and found that the dishes were indeed realigning to a point in the sky they had surveyed some time ago. It had been one of the systems on the list which had been long thought to be a system that could support life. She quickly checked her notes and found it to be the same system the array had turned and pointed toward when Mark Goddard had called her several days earlier—18 Sco. Zimmerman was looking forward to getting her refund.

She was reaching for the phone to contact Cyber Command and report the intrusion, when her scientific curiosity abruptly got the better of her, and she decided to put on her headphones instead and wait to see what happened. The array stopped once it locked on to 18 Sco. She sat there waiting while nothing happened for several minutes. She checked and was able to determine that the array was indeed listening, and not transmitting as it had with Goddard. After another few minutes of silence, her curiosity abated somewhat and she picked up the phone and started to dial the number she had for Cyber Command. She continued listening in one ear with the phone in the other.

"Hello?"

"Good evening. I'm sorry to bother you, but this is Dr. Zimmerman at S.E.T.I. We called a few days ago and reported that someone had hacked into our system. We had new firewalls installed, which the company reps guaranteed would stop the hackers. Well, they didn't; we were just hacked again. I was hoping that I might speak with General Caprella. Okay, thanks, I'll hold."

Suddenly the array began picking up a signal, one unlike anything she'd ever heard before. It was a high pitched series of tones and clicks, more like an insect than a radio signal. A few moments later, the signal suddenly grew much stronger; no…it sounded like the same signal, but it wasn't the same one. This was a different, much more powerful signal; in fact it was a surprisingly powerful signal. Zimmerman surmised that the source of the new signal had to be in the neighborhood. Panic suddenly gripped her when she realized she'd forgotten to make certain the historical signal was being recorded. In her excitement and her haste, she had neglected to check. Dr. Linda Zimmerman let out a huge sigh of relief when she found that indeed, the event was mercifully being recorded. She was confident that no one outside of S.E.T.I. would have believed what had happened without at least a recording to back her up. Suddenly the phone came alive again and she heard a voice.

"Hello? This is General Caprella."

"General, this is Dr. Zimmerman at S.E.T.I. Please forgive me, but I'm going to have to call you back. Something extraordinary is happening here now and I have to make another phone call."

"Understood, Dr. Zimmerman. Just call us back when you can, and if you would, please ask for me again. You've now aroused my curiosity, so I hope that you'll be so kind as to fill me in later."

"Certainly, General, and thank you." She hung up the phone, and after looking up a couple of phone numbers, she commenced to dialing the observatory in Australia. A different, distinct male voice suddenly came over the handset.

"Hello, this is Dr. Stevens."

"Hello, Alistair, this is Linda Zimmerman at S.E.T.I. I've got the granddaddy of all signals. There are two coming from the same quadrant of space. They're definitely not ours, but guess what? One of them's in the neighborhood!"

"What? Please tell me where they are!"

Linda provided the location and waited several moments while the observatory on the other side of the planet pointed its own radio telescope to the same patch of sky. A short time later the voice came back through the phone.

"Hey, Linda, listen to this!" Linda could hear the same signal coming across the phone line that she was continuing to listen to through the Allen Telescope Array. "Linda, I've got to make a few quick phone calls, do you mind?"

"No, of course not, Alistair. I'd better make a few more my own as well, or I'll be skinned alive. It's incredible, isn't it?" She suddenly felt as giddy as a schoolgirl. She'd waited her whole life for a moment like this.

"You bet it is, Linda! Okay, I've got to go now. Congratulations!"

"Thanks! We'll talk soon!" She ended the call and busily set about dialing a list of phone numbers. A series of brief conversations followed, which were, for the most part, very similar to the one she'd just had with a colleague a half-a-world away. Fifteen minutes after it had begun, both signals suddenly ceased. That was okay though, because Dr. Linda Zimmerman had more than enough data to analyze. Further, thanks to her hacker friend, she'd just picked up transmissions unlike any signals ever heard, much less recorded, by anyone on the Earth. If General Caprella ever caught the son-of-a-gun who'd hacked into S.E.T.I.'s systems, probably for the second time, she'd have to give him a big wet kiss.

* * * *

Kate Summers had stayed late at the lab, at least two hours after Nick and her father had left to get some dinner together. Her father had tried to drag her away, insisting that despite everything happening she still needed to eat and get some rest. Without it, they knew she'd be of little value to anyone. With the final tests scheduled for the following day, however, she'd insisted on staying late so she could finish making all of the changes they'd decided on throughout the day. Besides, Nick was going to do all of the heavy lifting, and her father was going to be doing the lion's share of the monitoring. Nick had finally convinced her that her most important contribution at the moment was to ensure they tested everything necessary to prepare for the next major cyber attack, and to catch the men responsible for taking the world to the brink of war.

Kate's head began to bob and she was having an increasingly difficult time staying awake. She'd finally hit a wall, and decided it was time for her to go home; well, back to her quarters on the base at least. After logging off of the computer and shoving her written notes into a filing drawer, she then locked the desk. Flicking off the lights, she then turned to close the door, unaware of the flashing illuminations on the lab table in the lab behind her, where Ignis had been quietly active for the past fifteen minutes. By the time she walked out into the lab area, however, the activity had suddenly stopped. As Kate turned around to leave the room, she glanced back at the table in the lab where Ignis sat, and found the device looking much as it did the day she'd first noticed it in the ship. She casually walked toward the door, turned off the light in the lab, and walked away. She wasn't even halfway to the elevator when Ignis suddenly re-activated.

Chapter 27

"It has been nearly a week since the postponement of the scheduled discussion in the United States Senate to consider a formal declaration of war against the government of the Peoples Republic of China. Unsubstantiated leaks and a wide range of theories have surrounded the committee hearing, which was supposed to be followed by a formal recommendation to the full Senate. Let's go now to Washington, DC, where Brian James is standing just outside of the Capitol building."

The man stood outside in a raincoat and an umbrella, with the Capitol Building in the background. Was there some reason American reporters did this; standing outside in the rain unnecessarily, to discuss something totally unrelated to the weather going on inside the building? *It's amazing they won the Cold War.*

"What are some of the most predominant rumors, Brian?"

"Well Susan, one of the strangest, yet seemingly also the most credible rumors, is that there is supposedly new evidence, which even now is still being gathered, which will prove China's innocence in these cyber attacks. According to our source, who wishes to remain anonymous, this evidence will clearly point to a rogue group of foreign agents as the ones responsible for the attack on the Indian Lake nuclear power plant. Our source tells us that they have been attempting to frame the Chinese for at least a year now, and that Indian Lake was only the most significant attack yet."

"Well, Brian, if these terrorists are trying to provoke a world war between the United States and the Chinese, it seems to be working. The President of the United States and the Secretary of Defense, through the Chairman of the Joint Chiefs of Staff, have already set the readiness level at Defcon-3, and it's been suggested that they could be planning to take it to Defcon-2 as soon as tomorrow morning."

"Exactly. Now you understand the danger, Susan. But wait, there's more. There is supposedly another attack yet to come, one which will make Indian Lake look like a walk in the park. Now whether these unsubstantiated rumors are accurate or not I can't say, but one thing I do know; if there is another attack appearing to originate from China, and if it is indeed worse than the attack at the Indian Lake station, where over one hundred thousand Americans died, it is pretty much a certainty that the United States of America will declare war on the People's Republic of China. Suffice it to say it is theoretically possible that when we wake up in the morning, Susan, we could find ourselves in the middle of World War III."

The female anchor's face drained of color on international television. She sat there dumbfounded for several moments, until the sound of a voice in her earpiece jolted her out of it.

"Oh...wow...okay, you can bet that *I'll* be in church this evening, and on my knees at home after that, folks. Thanks for the update, Brian. Next in the news today...." CLICK.

After clicking the power button on the remote, Yuri Andropov, Director of the Russian FSB, collapsed into his chair and sighed deeply. He'd been working for Russian intelligence agencies for decades, having been a promising young KGB agent before the collapse of the Soviet Union. The East and the West had been at war for a half-century without either side deploying a single nuclear weapon against the other. Now the Americans and the Chinese were about to destroy the world; and it was all because of Nikolai Chervanko. The intercom on the phone suddenly emitted a familiar tone before projecting the voice of his assistant.

"Director Andropov, Ambassador Lee Ho from the Chinese Embassy is here to see you." *Great.*

"Okay, send him in." A few moments later he was once again standing in front of the Chinese ambassador. "Good morning, Mr. Ambassador," he said, cordially extending his hand toward his guest, who then took it into his own. The grip was firm and determined, much like the look on his face.

"Good morning, Director Andropov, I hope that you are well this morning."

"I am, thank you." With the obligatory greetings behind them, both men sat down.

"Please forgive my abruptness," Ho began, "but you no doubt know now of the urgency of our predicament. The United States Senate is scheduled to convene the day after tomorrow, when they are expected to join with the American House of Representatives to declare war on my country." The relaxed, friendly, diplomatic air was gone. In its place there was a look of resignation, combined with a desperate intensity. "You know who is really responsible for these acts of terror against the Americans. If something isn't done soon, it will be too late, Director Andropov."

The director smiled weakly. "I understand, Mr. Ambassador, and I want to assure you that we fully appreciate the gravity of your predicament, and that we are doing everything we can to locate and eliminate this threat to world peace. The Americans recently informed us that they may have a means of locating him and stopping further attacks, though it's only a possibility and by no means certain. They've asked us to have a rapid deployment team ready to take out Chervanko and his crew, which we will gladly do of course, once we have a fix on his location."

"You believe him to still be in Moscow?" asked the diplomat.

"We do not know, Mr. Ambassador. We think it is likely that he left Moscow after we nearly apprehended him last week."

Ho eyed Andropov with considerable scrutiny. "You think he is on the run then?" Ho asked with raised eyebrows.

Andropov was beginning to tire of the interrogation by the Chinese diplomat. He had work to do, and he knew he wasn't going to find Chervanko babysitting the Chinese ambassador.

"Mr. Ambassador, please forgive my forthrightness in this matter, it is one of my qualities which most people either appreciate or detest. I understand that your government has been falsely accused of committing the cyber attack against the American nuclear power plant in New York. Perhaps, if your government had refrained from conducting so many cyber attacks against them in the past, however, stealing everything from data on weapons and technologies to military tactics and the like, the Americans would be more inclined to believe you in this instance."

Ho's face reddened, flushed mostly with embarrassment, along with a touch of feigned rage. "Mr. Andropov, how dare you accuse my government of stealing sensitive information from anyone, especially the Americans, given what is happening today?!"

Andropov smiled for a moment, pleased that he had successfully taken some of the wind out of the ambassador's sails. "Relax, Mr. Ambassador, please. I am well aware that my own government is not beneath using such tactics to obtain information from other sovereign nations which it considers in the best interest of our own national security. Though I have no specific knowledge of it, I suspect that the American government has conducted its own fair share of cyber espionage against other countries, such as the mysterious Stuxnet Virus, which impacted the Iranian nuclear program a while back." Andropov pushed away from his desk and stood, looking out the window behind his desk, which looked out over Moscow. "It is regrettable, isn't it Mr. Ho, that our countries, our peoples, cannot trust one another any more than we do? One country fears and keeps secrets from the other because we know we may one day be at war with another, and we feel compelled to steal those same secrets from other nations for the selfsame reason! Our fear of one another then fuels violence, which of course, causes even more fear, which in turn brings us closer to war, thus seemingly legitimizing our original fear! What a world we live in, Mr. Ambassador."

The Chinese diplomat sighed deeply as he sat back and sank into the comfortable chair. "Yes, Director Andropov, I agree it is most regrettable. It seems that people can be reasonable, even when nations cannot." Ho then brought up his briefcase and set it in his lap. He opened it and took out a manila folder, from which he removed a number of photographs. "One of our contacts here was able to snap these the other day at a grocery store. It seems that Mr. Chervanko is quite adept in spy craft, Mr. Andropov." He laid the photographs on Andropov's desk and spread them out. "We were told that Chervanko and the others appear to be picking up and bringing supplies to their new facility. We suspect that they are careful not to frequent the same establishments twice, which increases our odds of spotting them—"

"But it makes it considerably more difficult to apprehend or eliminate them, because they're never together in the same place again in public," said Andropov, finishing the ambassador's sentence. Ho nodded in agreement. Andropov examined the photographs. "It looks like they started to follow him; I guess they lost him in traffic?"

"So it would seem," answered Ho. "Chervanko was spotted in the southern part of the city, just before rush hour traffic. Soon after being spotted and trailed for a few kilometers, he suddenly disappeared in the traffic. It seems he knew he was being followed."

Andropov walked over to a large map of the city, which hung on a wall in his office. He reached down, and after looking at a couple of pictures, he placed a red peg in the southeastern edge of Moscow.

"This is useful intelligence, Mr. Ambassador. Thank you for sharing it with me. We've had only two sightings ourselves since they abandoned their old command center. One of those sightings was just east of the city, the other northeast. Now assuming that Chervanko and the others have chosen to setup their secondary site close to Moscow, which they would almost certainly do in order to arouse the least suspicion, they would likely be traveling north and south on this highway, looking for supplies. We also suspect that they need to be relatively close to the city for their post-war plans, yet most likely they remain outside of the city limits. Of course, they could also be in one of the smaller cities surrounding Moscow." Andropov began carefully examining the map. Ho stood up and joined Andropov at the map, unwilling to pass on the opportunity to learn more about where the rogue Russians could be. Whereas the Russians might fail to find and assassinate Chervanko, the Chinese would not.

Andropov began moving his finger around the map while he tried to correlate all of the data that had been coming in. After a minute of internal debate, his finger came to and stopped on a point on the map just east of Moscow. He turned to Ho, nodded his head, and said, "Reutov."

Chapter 28

"One of my contacts in the FSB phoned me this morning. He said that the FSB was somehow able to narrow their search based on several sightings over the last week. They know, Nikolai, somehow they know where we are."

"They do not *know*, Viktor, they only suspect. Apparently they have more men than I thought they would looking for us; perhaps intelligence agents from other countries as well, but they do not know where we are, Comrade, not yet anyway."

"Why do you say that; how can you be so sure?"

Chervanko turned, looked at Smirnov, and smiled. The thin smile hid the slight disdain and contempt he sometimes had for all ex-Spetsnaz in general, and Smirnov in particular. Most of the Spetsnaz lacked the shrewdness, discipline, and patience to plan and execute complex strategies, but for Smirnov this was doubly so. What he lacked in wits, however, Smirnov more than made up for in fierce loyalty and devotion to the communist party, and to their operation. It was because of his loyalty and devotion that Chervanko had trusted Smirnov enough to invite him to join his cause.

"I know this because if they knew where we were, Comrade, we would all now be in custody, or dead." Chervanko stood up from where he had been sitting at the table reading a newspaper, just before Smirnov had walked into the room in a panic. He looked at Smirnov with a vacant stare for several seconds before continuing. "You might be right, however, in growing concerned about them finding us. I suspect that they are closing in on us, considerably faster than I had anticipated. It appears our leaders no longer have the stomach for what needs to be done. It is a good thing that we do, eh, Viktor?" He sat back down in his chair and stared blankly at a wall for a moment, before standing up once more and leaving the room.

Chervanko walked down the hallway and to the large open office area, where racks of computer equipment stood, cabling feeding into and leaving out of the tops of the cabinets. The two technicians busied themselves pulling and wrapping cables together. He walked over to the lead engineer, who had just left the cabling and was now logging onto one of the workstations.

"How much longer until you are finished?" Chervanko asked bluntly.

"We should be done by late this evening, Mr. Chervanko."

"What is the reason for the delay?" He spoke slowly and his voice was low and controlled. He burned with a cold rage upon learning that they still had more to do. Chervanko wanted so badly to "retire" the technician in charge and to make him an example, but he knew that the shock and the fear of his own death would probably just slow down the work of the remaining man, resulting in even longer delays.

"The carrier was late delivering the Ethernet connections out to the Internet yesterday, so we just started testing the modified BGP configurations with them this morning. We also have to finish reconfiguring the firewalls and the intrusion-detection systems as well."

Chervanko just nodded slightly. He didn't know a lot about technology, but he was able to follow what the computer engineer was talking about enough that he understood. He considered the delay and weighed his options for addressing it.

"I tell you what; I will pay you a twenty-five percent bonus if you have the work finished before dinner. Deal?"

"But, Mr. Chervanko," the lead engineer protested, "we have so much—"

"Fifty-percent! That's all I can do." *It's not, of course, but it's all I'm willing to pretend I'll pay you idiots.* The lead engineer considered it for a minute before looking to the other tech, who had been listening to the exchange. After whispering with the other man for several moments, the lead finally returned.

"Mr. Chervanko, we'll find a way to have everything ready by 6:00. Any problem with paying the fifty-percent to us directly?"

Chervanko smiled.

"None at all. Just be sure to have it finished by 6:00, as agreed." A cold, steel look flashed in his eyes, both as motivation, and as a warning to the engineers. Chervanko then turned and left, feeling the workers were now sufficiently motivated, and threatened, to get the Ares system fully operational on time. He walked over to the office area and locked the door behind him. He then grabbed a clean glass, walked to the refrigerator, and took a few ice cubes from the freezer. From the counter beside the refrigerator, he picked up a bottle of vodka and poured it over the ice before joining the others, who were relaxing in the makeshift living area. Two sofas, several chairs, and three end tables sectioned a portion of the otherwise largely vacant office space. A large flat-screen television sat against the back wall.

"How did it go, Nikolai?" asked Levin, his former KGB colleague.

"They will be done by 6:00 today."

"What then, Nikolai?" asked Ivan Kozlov.

"Then, we test the device once more, to make sure everything works as it did before we moved."

"We should test a power grid this time, Nikolai. Perhaps something small, which will impact a few cities or a single state."

Chervanko nodded in agreement. "That sounds like a good idea, Dmitry."

"And if the test is successful?" asked Smirnov.

"Then we wait," Chervanko answered simply.

"Wait for what?"

"Simple, Viktor….we wait for tomorrow morning, when we bring the Americans and the Chinese to their knees, paving the way for the rise of the New U.S.S.R." Nikolai Chervanko answered coldly, while he stared at the television screen with disdain, his thoughts only on revenge, and on glory.

Chapter 29

While he couldn't be certain, Nick believed the phone had probably been ringing for a while. Only the combination of his alarm coupled with the phone had been sufficient to rouse him. As he reached to turn off the alarm clock Nick knew he could hardly be blamed for it; they'd been working long hours trying to prepare. Nick grabbed the phone, which incredibly was still ringing, and answered it.

"Hello?"

"Nick? This is General Caprella."

"Oh, hello General." The phone call from Caprella so early in the morning for the second time in a week could hardly be good news. Nick felt the cobwebs in his head rapidly clearing.

"Nick, something's happened. I need you to wake everyone on the Prometheus team and have them convene in the main conference room at 0900 hours your time. I'll give you all a rundown as to where we are, and what you need to do."

"What happened, sir?"

"I'd rather tell you all at the same time, if that's okay with you Nick."

"Okay, General; sure, no problem. We'll be there." Nick hung up with Caprella, and called Henry and Kate.

* * * *

The three of them sat together in the conference room, each with a fresh, steaming cup of coffee sitting in front of them. The state-of-the-art projector, which hung from the ceiling in the conference room, displayed the image of General Caprella on the large screen which had descended from the ceiling. The sound would come from the speakers scattered throughout the room, while their voices were picked up by discreetly placed microphones.

"I apologize for taking all of you away from your work. I understand that you've been working tirelessly with the Ignis device to find a way out of our current predicament. On behalf of our government and the people of the United States of America, I want to commend you for your efforts and thank you for your sacrifice."

"Um, General, what's going on?" asked Nick, more than a little confused.

"At 11:03 Eastern Standard Time last night, an HVDC Converter station in the Los Angeles area was shutdown, knocking power out to nearly a million people. The government, various businesses, traffic lights, transportations systems; all have been impacted by the unexpected outages. There have been at least a hundred deaths and thousands of casualties attributed to the unexpected outage, and that's just what we know of so far."

"Don't tell me, General, let me guess. The outage was caused by another cyber attack originating from somewhere in China, and with the same method of operation?"

"You nailed it, son. Everyone, from the city councilmen, the governor of California, Congress, even the president now...all of them are publicly denouncing the Chinese for yet another attack. The Senate held an emergency meeting early this morning; I regret to inform you that as of 9:45 EST this morning, the United States of America has been at war with the People's Republic of China."

Silence fell amongst the three in the conference room as Caprella gave the full significance of the moment a chance to sink in. Nick was the first to respond.

"What's happened since the announcement, General?"

"For starters, for the first time in the history of the United States, we are now at Defcon-1. All bases, ships, planes, and missiles are being prepared for launch. The Chinese protest, of course, continuing to proclaim their innocence. They've also made public their accusation that a rogue, former KGB element in Russia is behind the recent attacks against the United States. Despite these protestations, they have raised their military readiness to their highest levels as well. Thank God that they haven't launched a first strike, despite the many calls for it within the Chinese military."

"What happens next?" asked Nick.

"Who knows?" answered Caprella. "I suppose that decision is being discussed among the president and his staff, and the Joint Chiefs. I've been ordered to attend a meeting with the Joint Chiefs myself a couple of hours from now. I just wanted to give you three a heads-up."

"What do you think we're looking at, George? Do you expect to see an all-out conventional assault, a nuclear launch, or what?" asked Henry Summers.

"I can't say for certain, Henry, because I just don't know. Anyone who says they know where a war is going to lead once started is a liar or a fool. I believe, however, that we will seek to find a way to punish them through conventional means first."

"How can we do that?" asked Kate.

"One thing we can do, something I think is very likely, is to move aircraft carriers into position to launch airstrikes against key command centers for the Online Blue Army. We'll want to diminish their capability without necessarily going nuclear."

"Do you think that's really possible, George?" asked Henry. "After the way the Chinese have upgraded their military capabilities over the last few decades, is it likely they'll stand by and let us launch attacks without a response?"

There were several uncomfortable moments of silence before Caprella responded. "I'll be straight with you, Henry. It is my opinion that once we launch what the Chinese consider to be an unprovoked attack against their sovereign territory, they will respond with any and all means they feel necessary."

"It's my opinion that Chervanko will not stop his attacks either," Nick told the general. "Last night was probably just another test, something he felt necessary after moving to his new location."

"That's just great. So now we're going to be fighting against the Chinese *and* the Russians!" Caprella growled.

"General, I believe that we're ready to activate the Ignis Protocol, assuming the president gives us the green light, of course."

Caprella stared into the camera, speechless for a moment. "Really, Nick? You've made that much progress already?"

"Yes, sir, we have. The Ignis device is incredibly advanced, and the neural interface remarkably effective. We've already tested deploying code created by Ignis to systems in the lab and they were able to stop everything we threw at it. We're ready."

"That's great news, Nick! What about Chervanko?"

"If he launches another attack, I strongly believe that Ignis will be able to provide a location for Chervanko in less than one minute."

"Fantastic! I'll alert the president immediately. Please stand by while I get approval to initiate the Ignis Protocol."

While Caprella contacted the president, Kate and Henry looked across the table at Nick.

"Nick?" asked Kate, looking hurt and confused.

"It's nothing, Kate. It's just putting into practice what we've been testing in the lab. We came up with the Ignis Protocol in the event we were actually successful in finding a way to use Ignis to protect the United States against a major cyber attack. Since it's now unlikely that Chervanko will stop his attacks until the United States and China are fully engaged in a nuclear conflict, now seems like the right time."

"But what does the protocol do, Nick?"

"It's a series of steps for coordinating with various governmental agencies ranging from the Department of Homeland Defense to the Congress, the Department of Energy, the military, and every other major governmental agency, as well as the many private institutions that have been declared to be critical."

"Financial institutions like banks, nuclear power plants, large civilian contractors, and the like?" asked Henry.

"Exactly," Nick replied. "Should the president decide to proceed, Ignis will push code out to systems which each organization has deemed to be critical for the continued operation of that organization."

"Wow, that must be a lot of systems!" Kate observed.

"It is," Nick acknowledged. "There are over ten thousand organizations and around ten times as many systems."

"One hundred thousand systems. I wonder how long it will take Ignis to push code out to that many systems?" Henry asked, looking at Nick then Kate.

"Based on the tests, and the numbers Kate passed along to me, I'd estimate about ten minutes," Nick replied, with a smile.

"That's incredible!" Henry exclaimed.

"Oh, that's nothing, Dad," Kate interjected. "Ignis could do it in seconds, were it not for the limited connectivity to the Internet."

Caprella's image suddenly re-appeared on the screen. "Team, I just spoke with the President of the United States. He has given us the green light to proceed with initiating the Ignis Protocol; repeat, we are go for the Ignis Protocol."

"Alright!" Kate yelled out, until her father cast a stern look in her direction.

"That's great news, General, we'll get started immediately," Nick replied.

"Very good. Please remember, Nick, we need to know immediately if there is another attack. I'll do everything I can to slow down the hawks in Washington. Maybe I can even buy you some more time, convince them not to do anything stupid. But if there's another attack...."

"Yes, sir, I understand. Ignis will be writing code which will instantly notify us should there be another attack which matches the signature of the previous ones."

"Very good. Please let me know as soon as it's done so I can let the president know, okay?" He turned away for a moment, and just before Nick terminated the call, he turned back to face the camera. "By the way, I'm curious. Which of you will be interfacing with Ignis to deploy the necessary code?"

"I will, General," Nick replied, trying hard not to sound like a braggart in any way. The last thing he wanted to do was to get Kate worked up again over it. The general let a thin smile appear, before nodding.

"Very good. Alright then Nick, good luck and God speed!"

"Thank you, General Caprella." The image of Caprella disappeared and the lights came back on.

Henry stood up and started to leave the room as Kate reached across the table and took Nick's hands into hers.

"Be careful in there, Nick. Remember what I said about after this is all over," she said, as the look of concern vanished and a mischievous smile appeared. Nick smiled back and nodded.

Before Dr. Henry Summers left the conference room, he looked back at the two young people holding hands as they sat across the table from one another, and a smile of deep satisfaction and approval crossed his face.

"Okay Nick, you heard the general. Are you ready to make this happen?" he asked without looking back.

"You bet I am, Dr. Summers," he answered, before releasing Kate's hands and following Henry out of the room.

"Do you think there's a chance we might be able to catch this Chervanko character, and put an end to this war before things get out of hand, Nick?" asked Henry.

"I certainly hope so, Dr. Summers," Nick answered. "What about you?"

"Frankly Nick, I'm just not as confident as you are that he will even strike again. Surely he watches the news and knows that we are already at war with China. Why should he risk getting caught when things will take care of themselves?"

"You could be right, of course, Dr. Summers. It would seem logical that he would stop the attacks now that the war has started. But from what I know of the man, he's anything *but* logical. He's an ideologue, a patriot, and he's a megalomaniac. I doubt he will stop the attacks until the Soviet Union rises from the nuclear ash, or until he's dead, whichever happens first."

"Well, it's best not to take any chances at this point I suppose, just in case you're right about him, Nick."

"Believe me, I am. Okay, so the president's given us approval to go ahead, so I guess we should finish our testing today as scheduled, and initiate the Ignis Protocol the first thing tomorrow morning. Is that okay with you, Dr. Summers?"

"Of course, Nick."

"Kate?"

"Sure, Nick. Sounds good to me too."

"Okay then, let's get busy."

Chapter 30

"Well?" Chervanko was growing increasingly annoyed, uneasy that the FSB might find them before events had completely unfolded and before they had successfully completed their mission.

"Don't worry, Nikolai!" Smirnov reassured him, as he ensured the door was locked after closing behind him. "We now have another dozen men inside and a dozen men outside, each of them armed with a PP-19 Bizons. With all of that firepower protecting this facility, nothing can get in or out of here without our permission."

"Good. You were right, they're closing in on us, Viktor, just when we are so close to achieving our goal—nothing can be allowed to stop us now, nothing!"

"Do not worry, my friend, nothing *can* stop us now. When will we execute the final phase of the plan?" Smirnov asked.

"The Chinese and the Americans are officially at war. Now it is just a matter of timing. We must not strike too quickly, or it may work against us. We will give them another day or two. Our test was successful, so Ares still works as well as before."

"The engineers have nearly finished their work here and will leave once they are done with a few loose ends."

"No loose ends...my sentiments exactly," he said, staring firmly at Smirnov. "For Mother Russia," he added, carefully studying his friend. He had caught Smirnov off-guard. Clearly, he'd planned on letting the men go since the engineers were not Chinese this time, but Russian. Desperate times required desperate measures, however, and sacrifices had to be made. Chervanko knew that his old friend understood this. After a few moments the other man nodded in agreement.

"For Mother Russia," Smirnov repeated, before turning to leave the room.

* * * *

"How long until everyone is in position?" asked Andropov, his eyes never leaving the monitors. A number of them lined the right wall on the inside of the van, near the ceiling. Each screen pictured a different entrance or exit to the building. Armed guards walked back and forth, at least two men to each entrance.

"Another fifteen minutes or so, sir," answered Ulitsky. "Do you really think we need so many men?"

"Absolutely. I count at least twelve men on the outside, heavily armed with what look to be PP-19 Bizons. I can pretty much guarantee you that there are at least as many men inside, similarly armed I would imagine. Besides, we need to take them by surprise if at all possible."

"Director Andropov, may I make a suggestion, sir?" asked Ulitsky.

"Of course, Georgy, what is it?" he asked.

"Should we contact the Americans, and possibly even the Chinese, to let them know that we've found Chervanko, before we go in?"

"Who would I call? I could try going through back channels, I suppose, but the American president seems pretty convinced that the Chinese are behind the attacks; much of the American Congress shares his sentiment. Hmm, it's a good idea though, Georgy." He rubbed his chin for several moments. Then it came to him.

* * * *

"What? Are you sure?" asked Chervanko, looking outside the front office window. "I don't see anything!" he said, continuing to peer outside.

"Well sir, all I can tell you is that there's a van parked down the road and around the corner, and I've seen a number of cars driving by today, more than usual." Chervanko didn't know the man, but he'd been told by Smirnov that he was a loyal and committed communist. His family had been killed by the Russian mafia, and as a result he'd become a devoted and steadfast Marxist.

"Keep an eye out, and let me know if you see anything else unusual," Chervanko instructed, before turning to head back inside and into the open space where the Ares system now resided.

"Yes, sir," the guard responded, before heading back outside.

Chervanko found the others inside, relaxing on the sofas in front of the television. They had it on the American news channel, where a banner read, "America At War!"

"And as has been the case for days now, several American aircraft carriers continue making their way toward the Eastern China Sea. Speculation has been rampant as to what will happen once the American ships arrive there, but there can be little doubt that the Chinese military is keeping a very close watch on the situation. In response to the movement of the American carriers, a number of People's Liberation Army Navy destroyers are lining up to block entry into both the South and the Eastern China Sea. With both fleets due to face-off as soon as tomorrow, the world waits to see where the conflict will go next...." CLICK

Chervanko sat the remote control down on the table beside him.

"One of the guards reported seeing some unusual activity outside," he said, staring coldly at each of his comrades. "The time has come, comrades, for us to make some hard decisions."

"You think they've found us, already?" asked Levin, shifting uncomfortably in his seat, before mustering the courage to face the moment. He'd been a fierce soldier and afterwards an exceptional KGB agent. But all of them, including Chervanko, had grown older following the demise of the great Soviet Union. Despite their age, however, they were still serving a cause greater than themselves...they were building a new world order for their children, and their children's children.

"I believe they have, Dmitry," he answered. "And if they are here, they will be making a run at us sooner rather than later."

"What should we do now, Nikolai? There's no time to move everything again," said Smirnov plainly.

"We need to get out of here," said Levin. "We can always rebuild and start over. If we're caught, then the dream is over."

"That's true, brother," said Chervanko. "We can leave, and we can try again in a few years, or we can finish what we've started here."

"What do you have in mind, Nikolai?" he asked.

"I believe we should proceed with our contingency plan to activate Ares now. Let's launch the attack that will ensure our plan's success, even if it costs us our lives. I know what we agreed to earlier, comrades, but I am still willing to exchange places with one of you should you so choose." Chervanko gave them a few moments to consider the offer he had just made to them. They looked at one another several times, yet said nothing. After several moments of silence, Levin finally spoke up.

"No, Comrade Chervanko, this privilege should be *yours*! Let me add that it has been my great honor to serve with you, Nikolai my friend, the most noble and mighty warrior of us all!" He extended his hand to Chervanko, who took it and clasped it with the other as well.

"The honor has been all mine, Comrade Levin," he replied solemnly.

Each man in turn said likewise to Chervanko. When they'd finished, Levin began chanting. "For Mother Russia! For Mother Russia!" One by one the others joined in the chant, each of them fondly recalling the glorious times they remembered as children, when the powerful Soviet Union stared down the heady America.

The sound of gunfire suddenly erupted, and the sound of glass shattering came from the front entrance. Chervanko stood up and began walking towards the control room, as the sound of yelling and gunfire grew louder. The others knew what to do. They took up positions outside of the control room and took out their weapons. As he reached the door, Chervanko turned to face each of them one last time, nodding his head to each, before entering into the control room and locking the door behind him.

He walked over to the console for the Ares system and began typing at the keyboard. He chose the option on the menu on the screen in front of him which read, "All." Despite the sound of gunfire suddenly exploding just outside the room, he continued watching the screen to make certain the Ares system was completing its assigned task. Once he was satisfied the deed was done, he pressed a small button underneath the desk before grabbing a small gasmask from a compartment next to it. The outside room suddenly began filling with a smoky gas and after a few seconds, he could hear everyone collapsing on the floor. Chervanko opened the door and walked out into the open space. He looked around at the mass of bodies lying on the floor. He soon found Levin, Smirnov, and Kozlov, all either dead or nearly so. With the exception of one of the guards, who had apparently gone above and beyond the call of duty trying to defend his comrades, the rest were FSB. Chervanko nearly killed the FSB who were not dead but merely unconscious from the gas. He changed his mind at the last minute, deciding that they had been misled by the weak-minded leaders who now ruled the country. He would help them see the truth once he was in a position of power.

After looking over the bodies of his fallen comrades one last time with a faint twinge of regret, Chervanko began making his way through a door which opened to stairs and descended into the basement. Upon reaching the bottom of the stairs, the Russian walked over to a door which opened into a hallway. Seeing no FSB agents, Chervanko walked down the long passageway and into the adjoining building. The former KGB agent quietly ascended the stairs with his weapon raised. An abundance of caution had kept him alive throughout his career in the KGB, and he knew it would help do so now. When he reached the top of the stairs, he slowly turned the knob counter-clockwise, before pushing the door slightly, peering through the crack for any FSB or military personnel. After seeing none, he lowered his weapon and tucked it into his jacket. He emerged from the stairwell and into a vacant office, which they had also leased for this very purpose. *My comrades! It should have been me!* He had wanted to stay and fight should they be faced with the scenario which had come to be, but they all felt that he should be the one to survive, because he would be the one most likely to succeed, for the good of Mother Russia.

He made his way to the exit nearest the rear of the building, where they had all parked. He saw a lone FSB agent standing outside, about fifteen meters from the door. After quietly opening the door just enough to get his hand out, a single shot from the silencer was enough to terminate the target and clear his way. Chervanko then exited the building and walked calmly to his car without looking suspicious. If he was seen and approached he would deal with it then, but he wasn't. He climbed smoothly and quickly into his car and drove off, in the direction opposite the commotion. He was relieved to find that the FSB had not yet setup a roadblock in the direction he was heading. The building from which he had exited was on the opposite corner of the lot where the command center was located, so it made sense it would be the last one they closed.

Chervanko was now a few miles from the command center and getting on the highway, heading away from Moscow and towards a more friendly city. He would drive to the safe house they had setup in the city of Minsk in Belarus, where he would stay to see how events would unfold. The Russian had already made all of the necessary preparations ahead of time. He still had many like-minded friends in Parliament who knew of his loyalty to the Communist party, and his service in the KGB, and they had committed to back him when the time came. All he had to do was wait for the proper time to emerge on the world stage, which he would do once the smoke began to clear, and the United States and China were no longer the threats they had been for so long. As he made his way toward Minsk, his mind filled with the many changes that President

Chervanko, the defacto leader of the New Communist Party, would implement in the name of the working class.

* * * *

"He's in here, sir!" The lower-ranking FSB agent led the way into the room outside of the command center. Bodies were strewn all over the floor; some were dead and some were still unconscious from the gas, while the rest were just starting to wake up. One of those starting to sit-up up next to the wall was Yuri Andropov, Director of the FSB.

"Director, are you alright?" asked Ulitsky, as he helped his boss up off of the floor. "What happened, sir?"

Andropov shook his head back and forth in an effort to help the cobwebs clear faster; it didn't help. "I, um...we were...we had just fought our way into the room here. We were...um...about to take the command center there, when something—I guess it was gas—suddenly started coming out of the vents. We were out in seconds. Where is Chervanko?"

Ulitsky lowered his head and shook it back and forth. "I'm sorry, Director, he got out somehow. We found an underground passageway leading to the building across the parking lot. We think he slipped out after hitting you with the gas, made it to the other building, and drove off before we'd blocked off the surrounding streets. I'm sorry, sir, I had no idea...."

Andropov, whose mind was finally starting to sharpen, read his subordinate's expression of guilt. "Nonsense, don't worry about it, Georgy. I have a feeling he'll turn up. Make sure we beef up the checkpoints however, in case he tries to flee the country. But for now, I need a team of techs in here immediately. We need to collect any and all evidence we can that will prove beyond any doubt that Chervanko was behind this whole operation and that he was trying to frame the Chinese. Also, call Ambassador Ho immediately; let him know that we have found Chervanko's base of operations."

"Yes, sir."

Andropov didn't care for the way his friend and associate was behaving. "What's wrong, Georgy? You should be thrilled! We may have just stopped World War III!"

"That's just it, sir. There's something else I need to show you." Ulitsky began walking toward and then into the command center, with Andropov following just behind. He stopped when they reached a monitor sitting on the top shelf of the console. On the screen, in large flashing red letters, a single message flashed over and over; "All attacks against the United States of America have been successfully executed. Long-live Mother Russia!"

Chapter 31

"Nick, it's General Caprella, it sounds urgent."

Nick looked at Kate briefly and met Henry halfway. "Thanks, Dr. Summers."

The elder Summers smiled, handed him the phone, and walked back towards his office.

"Yes, General?" *What is it this time! I'll be glad when things get back to normal!*

"Nick, execute Ignis Protocol, now!"

"General, what? Why?"

"Not now, Nick! Listen, I just received a call from someone I know within the Russian FSB. He called me a few minutes ago to warn me that they're preparing to raid Chervanko's office building. They're only giving us a thirty-minute warning before they go in. You must do it now, Nick. If they go in, Chervanko will instantly initiate whatever attack he has planned."

"What about the evidence to stop the war, General?"

"I'll worry about that Nick, now please, get moving! Millions of lives are at stake here!"

"Yes, sir. We'll initiate the Ignis Protocol immediately. I'll let you know as soon as I'm finished."

"Go Nick, and may God go with you." Nick hung up the phone and alerted Kate and Henry.

"Dr. Summers, Kate, we've got to initiate the Ignis Protocol immediately. They're getting ready to raid Chervanko's building."

"What, now?" asked Kate, confused by the sudden change of plans. Her father however, moved quickly.

"Come on Nick, let's get you into the chair." He walked over to the chair they used when interfacing with Ignis. "Okay, Nick. Now, you remember what we talked about, everything we did in the labs, right?"

"Yes, Dr. Summers, of course."

Henry smiled. "Sorry, Nick, I have to ask."

"I understand, no problem."

"Remember, Nick," Kate began. "You've reviewed the list of all the systems, their IPv4 or IPv6 addresses, DNS names, even their Mac addresses, and we also have it stored on a computer sitting on our network. Ignis should be able to pull those addresses from your memory even when your conscious mind never could. If for some reason that doesn't work, Ignis can just as easily pull the addresses from the list stored on the computer."

"No problem, Kate. We've done this before in the lab, remember?"

Kate came over and placed one hand on each shoulder. "Listen, Nick, this is the same but it's different. You need to try and relax your mind, then focus everything you can on protecting all of the systems on the list. Once you're certain all of them have the Ignis-generated code to protect them from this cyber attack, see if you can get Ignis to locate and destroy all instances of this virus on any systems it can access. And Nick?"

"Yes, Kate."

"Please, be careful, and take care of yourself! We don't know what this might do to you." She leaned into him and he met her halfway, pulling her closer in, embracing her as they kissed.

"Don't worry, Kate," he said, after what seemed a blissful eternity. "I'll be alright, and this will all be over soon."

"Just come back to me, okay?" she asked.

The concern on her face affected Nick deeply...what a passionate woman she was.

"You bet."

Henry walked over, and once Nick was seated, held the helmet just above his head. "Okay, Nick, are you ready?"

"Ready as I'll ever be, Dr. Summers."

"Okay then, here we go. God speed!"

The world around Nick suddenly disappeared and he found himself back in the white room. He quickly chose "Out" and found himself in a strange, dark place, which simultaneously had the feel of a large room inside a large building and the vast expanse of space. It was dark as night, with the only light emanating from an endless wall array of computer monitors, which had suddenly appeared in the darkness and stretched before him as far as he could see. He recognized that what he was looking at was a vast number of computer systems, all of the systems on the list for the Ignis Protocol. Ignis would need to develop, download, and deploy programs to each of the over one hundred thousand systems. The Ignis-generated programs would need to protect the systems, rendering them impenetrable by Chervanko's virus.

Nick forced himself to relax and cleared his mind before carefully formulating his thoughts. Just as during the tests, he began slowly focusing on protecting each and every system on the list. He pictured the long list in his mind, and he thought about the lab computer and the name of the file that contained the list. Moments later, blue bolts of flashing light began emanating from the blackness behind him. The light shot forth and began bathing each of the seemingly endless array of computers in an eerie, glowing blue light. This continued for several minutes, until finally the bolts of light disappeared, leaving the computer systems glowing blue. It seemed Ignis had correctly interpreted his objective.

Next, as in the lab, he picked one of the systems and launched an attack that simulated one of Chervanko's attacks. The attack would have worked before Ignis had protected the system, but now it did not. It would take some time to verify the results of course, but it seemed to Nick that the defense Ignis had installed on the system was successful.

Nick then instructed Ignis to erase the screen and begin searching worldwide for any trace of viruses related to the Ares system, based on the known Ares attacks, like the one which had attacked the Indian Lake station. If the same programmer or team of programmers had developed all of the viruses, which was a near certainty, then there would be lines or even modules of code which would be very similar. Ignis could look for certain markers, file names, code sequences, etc. in its search for comparison.

Nick had Ignis start at the Blue Army headquarters before working its way out from there. Ignis complied, and Nick saw a *different* set of computer systems bathed in a red light. Once more bolts of light erupted from behind him and targeted the systems bathed in the red light. As the systems were purged of the virus, the light surrounding each system would eventually change to green. This continued for a while, until a few minutes later, Ignis presented a globe of the Earth, itself bathed in a green glow. Ignis had searched and all trace of the Ares viruses had been eliminated worldwide.

Now, it was time to find the Ares system itself. Nick concentrated, trying to focus on the one system from which all of the other systems had received instructions. In his mind he pictured a map, and then Russia. Within moments, a single cluster of systems, larger than the rest and bathed in a deep red light, appeared, surrounded by hundreds, perhaps thousands of other systems bathed in the green light because they were no longer infected. Nick knew this was Ignis' representation of Chervanko's Ares system. He then focused on completely erasing all contents, flashing the bios, and shutting down all computers that comprised the Ares system, permanently.

Nick then, for good measure, decided to try one more thing, though he was uncertain whether it would work. He tried to envision a power overload over the power circuit on which all components of the Ares system had been connected. Hopefully Ignis had understood and had completely destroyed the sensitive circuit boards in the computers which together, made up the Ares system.

There was one last precaution. Nick focused on instructing Ignis to write code that would be installed on every system on the Ignis Protocol list, as well as the systems in the Cyber Command Lab, and the S-4 lab. The code would be a search and destroy menu-driven program which could be executed outside of Ignis by a human being to detect and destroy any Ares-related code. After a few moments, Ignis flashed another image of the systems on the lists, but this time the systems in the Cyber Command lab were depicted in a separate, but smaller image, as was the systems in the S-4 lab. When they all glowed green, Nick knew it was finished.

Content that Ignis had completed the tasks requested of it, Nick suddenly felt very tired, and sat down to catch his breath.

After resting a few moments, he then stood up, returned to the white room, and exited the interface.

"Look, he's opened his eyes! Nick, are you okay? I was so worried about you!" Kate was looking down on him from above. She reached down and snatched the helmet off his head before wrapping her arms around him, tightly embracing, and then kissing him. When she pulled away, he saw she had been crying.

"Kate, what's wrong?"

She didn't answer. Instead, she sat down beside him and busied herself with a flashlight, which she then flashed in and out of his eyes, apparently checking the pupil dilation.

"What are you doing, Kate? You don't need to worry about me, I'm fine. I've done this several times now, remember?"

Kate moved over and sat down across from Nick and next to her father. Nick looked around, confused. He saw Kate and Henry look at one another, then back at him. It was only then that Nick noticed that General Caprella was there as well. How had he gotten to Nevada so quickly?

"Hey, General Caprella! What are you doing out here, sir? I would have thought you'd be in Washington with everything that's going on."

"Hello, Nick, welcome back."

"I think everything went well in there, General. First, I instructed Ignis to protect the systems on the Ignis Protocol list. Then, I attempted to have it eliminate the virus on systems worldwide. Finally, I instructed Ignis to create code that could search and destroy any Ares virus, even without Ignis' interaction. This should keep anyone Chervanko may have been working with from being able to access and control an Ares zombie system again. So tell me, have we heard anything yet; do we know if it worked yet?"

"Yes, Nick, it worked like a charm. You did a great job in there, I'm very proud of you, son!" Caprella then looked at Henry and then Kate, before looking back down at Nick. "Um, tell me something though, son, how long were you in there; how long did it take you to accomplish your mission?"

"I'd say I was only in there for maybe thirty minutes or so, General."

Their eyes opened wide before Caprella and the others dropped their heads. Henry walked over to him and placed a hand on Nick's shoulder.

"Nick, son, you've been in there for over two days now," Henry told him. "We've been worried sick about you. I don't know if Kate here's left your side for more than thirty minutes the entire time."

"We were afraid to move you, Nick," Kate said quietly. "We had no way of knowing what would happen if the helmet came off your head while you were still in there; in fact we still don't." Nick noticed Kate's hands were trembling slightly. *Is that because of me?* He turned back to Henry.

"Two days? No way, that's not possible! I was only in there for thirty-minutes, forty-five at the most. You're joking with me, aren't you, Dr. Summers?" He looked around the room at all of the worried faces. "Uh-oh. I guess not. Two days? How is that even possible?"

"We've been asking ourselves that same question, Nick," said Kate. "We couldn't understand what was different this time."

He looked down to find she was now holding his hand, something that caused Nick to smile. "Well, we're all still here, so I guess it worked?" he asked.

"It did!" Caprella answered, patting Nick on the back. "The Ignis Protocol worked beyond our greatest expectations, Nick! We know that because around the same time you went in, I received another phone call from my 'acquaintance' in Moscow. It seems after they stormed Chervanko's compound outside of Moscow, they found his command center. He told me that Chervanko had executed the all-out attack against our infrastructure that we've been so worried about. We immediately started spot-checking systems on the list and found, thankfully, that not one of them had anything unusual happen all day. What's more, the Chinese told us that all remnants of the zombie virus had 'mysteriously disappeared' from all of the systems they knew or suspected to have been infected."

"What about the Ares system, General?"

"That's an even more incredible story, Nick. It seems the circuits feeding power to the Ares system mysteriously overloaded, frying not just the one computer, but the entire cluster, the SAN, everything! I don't suppose you and Ignis had anything to do with that, did you?"

"Maybe." Nick smiled.

"I thought as much. Well done, Nick!"

"What about the United States and China, are we still at war?" Caprella shook his head.

"No, I'm very glad to say that we are no longer at war with the Chinese. The Russian FSB was able to provide sufficient evidence that Chervanko and his associates had been the ones behind the recent attacks. We flew an FBI investigative team to Moscow to assist the FSB in their investigation, as did the Chinese. After reviewing all of the evidence, they all came to the same conclusion as the Russians." Caprella began laughing. "The Chinese ambassador to the United States was hopping mad, demanding that we apologize to them for falsely accusing them of cyber terrorism, and for declaring war on his country.

Our president did apologize for the declaration of war, but not for accusing them of cyber crimes. He told the diplomat, 'I'm afraid I can't, in good conscience, sir, deny that your country has committed cyber warfare crimes, because I'm no liar.' He then told the Chinese president to his face, 'Perhaps, if your country would refrain from using cyber warfare to steal data from the United States so often, and then afterwards pleading your innocence, it might be a little easier for us to believe you the next time you deny it.' They weren't too happy with the back-handed apology, but like us, they were just glad to have averted a full-scale war. They finally did acknowledge how their prior cyber crimes had enabled Chervanko's plan to nearly succeed, and publicly accepted America's apology for incorrectly blaming them for the crisis. Then just yesterday, to his credit, the Chinese president committed to purchase a plot of land and erect a memorial 'for the one hundred thousand American citizens who died, that one hundred million might live.'"

"Wow, that's great. I'm just glad it worked, General."

"Me too, son."

"I'm more worried about you now, my boy," Henry Summers said with sincerity. "You were in there for two whole days. What were you doing all that time?"

"I guess I don't know," he answered honestly. "All I remember is instructing Ignis to stop Ares. Then afterwards, I suddenly felt really tired and sat down for a few moments to rest. After a couple of minutes, I got up and exited the system. Other than that, there's nothing. I'm really glad it worked, though. It certainly sounds as if things are considerably better out there now than they were when I went in."

"Do you need anything?" asked Kate. "Are you hungry?"

"Yeah, now that you mention it, I am. I feel like I haven't eaten in days!"

Kate smacked him on the arm. "Very funny! It's your hydration I'm more worried about. Here." She shoved a bottled water in his direction. "Start off slowly at first. You need to drink at least sixty-four ounces of water a day for the next week, okay?"

"Yes, Doctor." Kate smiled at his play on words.

"It's a good thing you came out of it when you did, Nick," Henry told him. "We were making arrangements for transferring you to the infirmary to get you hooked up to an I.V. just so you could get some fluids, and there was talk about removing the helmet. If you don't mind, I'd still like to have the infirmary run some more tests on you, to see if we can determine what happened while you were in there, and so they can make sure you're okay."

"Come on, Dad! Nick's not a lab rat!"

"Sure, Dr. Summers, it's okay, no problem," Nick answered. "I don't mind, Kate, really. I'd like to know what happened as well."

"General, do you mind if we hang on to Nick for a little while longer?"

"You mean so you can run some more tests?"

"Well, not just for the tests. I was thinking we could use him here for a while longer, assuming it's okay with the two of you, of course. We've only just begun to scratch the surface of what Ignis can do, and who knows? Maybe it's the key to understanding *all* of the alien technology."

"Well, while we certainly need him back at Cyber Command, it sounds to me like he might be of considerably more use to our government right here, then. After all, Nick, Ignis has proven its worth by saving our country, our world even. How about it, are you up for it? The decision is all yours, son."

"Of course, General," he answered, looking at Kate. "I wouldn't mind staying on here for a while."

"Good! It's settled then. Nick will stay here to help discover what all we can learn about this Ignis device, and the rest of the ship as well for that matter. I, for one, would like to know more about how it operates," Caprella told them.

"We'll have a set of blueprints and instructions typed up for you by next week, General," Nick offered with a grin.

"I like the sound of that, son," Caprella replied, before walking towards the door, nodding, and leaving the room.

Chapter 32

The safe house in Minsk was older, like most of the other houses in the city. One of the younger, more devout members in Chervanko's New Communist Party had volunteered to live at the house indefinitely. His presence at the house served several purposes for Chervanko. For one, the house always appeared to be lived-in. The young man regularly collected the newspapers and the mail, which Chervanko had arranged to be regularly delivered there, and kept the overall appearance of the house presentable. To an outsider, there would be nothing whatsoever that would stand out about the house; there was nothing remarkable about it whatsoever, and that was just the way Chervanko had wanted it.

When he finally arrived at the house two days following the FSB raid, he gave the house a quick perusal and was pleased to see that the young man, Aleksandr Reuka, had done a fine job at keeping the small house up just as he'd instructed; he'd even mown the lawn recently. Reuka was originally from Belarus, so when the time came to find someone to stay at the safe house, he'd been the perfect choice. He was young and still quite naïve about the ways of the world, but Reuka had demonstrated his fervent loyalty to the party and, more importantly, to their cause. His family had once been well-respected across the Soviet Union. Reuka's father had once been the distinguished captain of a Typhoon class ballistic missile submarine, until he retired early into obscurity after the end of the Cold War. The captain had become very disheartened about his own uselessness and the decline of the once great Soviet navy, and he began to drink heavily soon after returning home to Belarus. He died a few years later of cancer while still in his fifties, when Reuka was still only nine years old. Though it had most likely been long-term exposure to radiation that had killed him, Reuka blamed the United States and its allies. His hatred for the Americans and his desire for a new Soviet empire made him a most reliable asset to Chervanko, one that he would hold on to for as long as he could, at least as long as circumstance or recklessness did not force Chervanko to do otherwise.

"Comrade Chervanko, it is so good to see you, sir!" Reuka exclaimed, upon answering the knock on the door and finding his boss on the porch. "Please, sir, come inside and rest." He looked uneasy to Chervanko, something he couldn't account for.

"Hello Alex. It looks like you've been doing a fine job here," he said truthfully.

"Thank you, sir." Reuka sat down in a chair across from where Chervanko sat on the sofa, never holding the older man's eyes for more than a split second. "So, how did it go with the Ares System? Were there any problems?" he asked expectantly. Something was troubling Reuka, and the former KGB agent was determined to find out what it was.

"Why, Alex? Why do you ask this?" A cold chill ran down his spine when he saw the nervous look in the younger man's eyes.

"Well, because nothing's happened sir, not since the power outage in Los Angeles, anyway. Perhaps I am mistaken sir, and the Ares system will strike sometime later, while you're far away, *da*?"

Chervanko's expression changed from one of curiosity to one of deadly intensity. "What are you talking about, Alex? Everything went as planned. With the exception of our being interrupted and the unfortunate demise of our friends and comrades, everything in the operation was nearly flawless. Are you telling me that no American nuclear power plants have gone offline and melted down? No American power grids have shut down? There's been nothing at all?!" He took off his coat and threw it across the room, knocking a ceramic vase over which had been on the hearth, sending it crashing on the stone fireplace below into a hundred pieces.

"No, sir. If anything has happened, it has not been in the news. China and America *were* at war for a few days, and it looked like they would each soon be launching nuclear missiles."

"So what happened, Alex? That's exactly what they were supposed to do!"

"Well, sir, from what the news reporter said, it appears that when the building you were in was raided by the FSB, they were able to find some important evidence, which they then shared with the Americans and the Chinese, clearly implicating your business in this affair."

"The traitors! I knew I should have killed all of them while they were still knocked out by the gas. Go on."

"So after the evidence was presented, each country then gradually began lowering their respective readiness levels, and will soon begin talks on how to keep this from happening again. I just assumed this was part of your plan, sir."

"But I activated the Ares system; I know it worked, I saw it!"

Reuka's eyes opened wide at this.

"But all of the testing, it went so well! I read in the papers and saw on the television about the failure of the system at their Indian Lake nuclear power plant, and I saw on the news about the power going out in Los Angeles when the system crashed. What happened?"

"That's exactly what I intend to find out." Chervanko said nothing else. After a few moments he got up from the sofa and walked into the kitchen. "You have been keeping vodka here I hope, Alex," Chervanko said in a low, deep voice. The tension in his words was palpable. He was not a happy man, and Alex's terrified expression reflected his awareness that he needed to tread very carefully.

"I have, Comrade Chervanko. It is in the cabinet above the sink." Chervanko reached up and took the bottle down from the cabinet before pouring it into a glass filled with ice cubes.

"Come, Alex, have a drink with me, please."

The younger man made his way uneasily over to where Chervanko now sat on a stool in the kitchen. Reuka fixed himself a drink and joined Chervanko at the small, white, square table. Each of them sat quietly for a couple of minutes, taking some time to let the vodka do its work, allowing it to take the edge off of some very troubling news.

"So you have been monitoring the news, day and night, as I instructed?"

"I have."

"And there has been no mention of a massive cyber attack against the United States by the Chinese?"

"The Americans and the Chinese issued a joint statement yesterday afternoon, formally calling for the military on both sides to stand down. The American president explained that there had been a grave misunderstanding; he said that the attack at Indian Lake was only made to appear as if it came from China. He also said that he could confirm the rumors that a major cyber assault had been launched against many U.S. installations, both military and civilian. He said only that the United

States Cyber Command dealt with and eliminated the threat. They said that the attack, as well as the one at Indian Lake, was actually the work of terrorists, not another country."

"Terrorists?" Chervanko threw his glass across the room, where it struck the fireplace and shattered, leaving pieces of razor-sharp chards lying near the remains of the porcelain bowl. "Terrorists!" he yelled again, kicking at two of the chairs at the table. "They have the audacity to call *me* a terrorist? I am no terrorist, I am a patriot! How dare they compare me to some fanatic terrorist! Am I setting bombs to explode in busy airports or markets? Am I the one hijacking planes or kidnapping and then executing innocent civilians? What I do is for the good of my country, Mother Russia. Those weaklings in Washington and Beijing, they have never had nor will they every have the same raw strength and courage our former Soviet leaders had." He looked at Reuka and after fixing and downing another drink, he said to him, "They called me a lousy, stinking terrorist! Okay then, we'll have to prove them wrong."

Chervanko drained the glass and poured himself another drink before walking into one of the extra bedrooms, where he kept the business and personal belongings that he'd stored there. The spy turned on the light, opened the closet door, and knelt down on his knees. He then took a small Swiss army knife out of his pocket and pulled out the small screwdriver, which he then put to work on a board in the closet. After twenty seconds the board loosened and he was able to grab it with his right hand. Chervanko pulled hard and the board gave way, enabling him to remove a small metal box out from under the board. He opened the box and dumped its contents out onto the bed. A dozen passports, each with a different name and identity, along with stacks of currency from around the world, lay strewn across the comforter. Reuka, who had followed him, gasped in awe. Chervanko looked up at him and grinned.

"Look at me, Alex, do I still look like a young man to you?"

As if his heart had stopped Reuka's face went pale. "Um, yes sir, of course!"

Chervanko gave him a cold stare. "Do you really think I have the time or the luxury to care about how I appear to a boy?

"But you—"

"My point is that I didn't stay alive this long in my line of work by being careless; or worse, reckless. You always need to maintain a set of documents—like these: passports, driver's licenses, the works. You'll also need cash, which you will certainly need wherever you go." He turned and looked back at Reuka. "Do you understand?"

"Yes, sir, I do. So what now?" he asked Chervanko, who by now held a folder which contained a number of papers. He didn't share with Reuka that the papers made up a list of deep cover agents in the United States, all of whom had been active at one time. Since the demise of the Soviet Union, he was uncertain which were still active Russian spies working for the Foreign Intelligence Service, and which ones were no longer active assets. All he needed to know was what was next.

"Somehow, the American's were able to counter the Ares system. The problem is, that should have been impossible." He took several more swallows from his drink, then refilled it. "Lee had that system designed so that it was foolproof. Sure, given enough time they would eventually have found a way to counter the attacks, but not until long after the damage was already done. Whatever the cost, no matter how long it takes, I must know how this was accomplished, how they thwarted our plans."

"Will you travel to America, Comrade Chervanko?"

"Yes. And I will not return until I learn how the Americans did it. Then…then I will make them pay."

Chapter 33

Nick and Kate caught Janet Flight CT-43A from Groom Lake to McCarran Airport in Las Vegas late on the Friday afternoon following Nick's two-day interface with Ignis. After everything they had been through over the course of the past several weeks, they needed a serious break, and some quality time alone. Both of them had tried to convince Henry to come along as well, but he had adamantly refused, claiming that he'd rest much better at his residence on the base. Although he'd suggested he might end up joining them at some point over the weekend, it seemed unlikely to both of them that he ever would. Nick suspected that Henry had seen the sparks fly between him and Kate, and that he was doing everything he could to fan the flames. Nick didn't mind it though; he was actually very appreciative.

It was a Friday so the flight was packed full of Groom Lake commuters anxious to get back home so they could enjoy time with their families, before heading back to Groom Lake on Monday's return flight. Nick wanted to talk with Kate about everything that had occurred, but she and Henry had been quite adamant that they could not talk about anything on the flight, that it would have to wait until they were alone; or better still, until they were back at S-4 on Monday. Not all of the many civilian contractors who worked at Dreamland had the same security clearance. In fact, what they did was often highly compartmentalized, so that any one group usually had no idea what the other groups were working on. The approach had proven to be quite effective in keeping the bigger picture from all but a few. That, and the threat of life in prison should they ever discuss what they did at the base with any unauthorized personnel, helped maintain the tight secrecy.

It was a fairly short flight so Kate passed the time thumbing through some science journals. Nick had brought a spy novel along which he'd been meaning to finish for months, but had never been able to find the time. They traveled silently together for some time, until Kate finally grew tired of the technical magazine and decided to get a head start on some quality time with Nick.

"So, tall, dark, and handsome, how about telling me something about yourself?"

Nick smiled. "What would you like to know, beautiful?" he asked, interested in sharing anything and everything with the woman he had once loathed. "My life's an open book."

Kate eyed him suspiciously after the last statement. "I doubt that, mister." She sat back in her seat and ran her hands through her hair, something she'd done frequently when she was younger. "Okay, so let's see…where did you grow up, and how did you end up here?"

"I grew up in a small town in North Carolina. I wanted to join the Air Force after I graduated from high school but I was unable to due to a heart murmur. I had been a straight-A student in school, so since I couldn't join the Air Force and become a soldier, I decided to attend M.I.T. and become a geek instead. I started off by taking a lot of computer science courses. I'd always been a bit of a hacker, so as a sophomore I found that I had a knack for computer security. I enjoyed it enough that I decided to major in computer science. I later went on to get a masters and later a PhD in computer science with an emphasis on security. I was recruited right out of college by Phoenix Corporation. The man who recruited me into Phoenix promised me I would be able to do some great things for my country, far more working for them than I ever could have in the Air Force. I'm not sure about the last part, but it turns out that I have been able to accomplish a few things, not the least of which is meeting you." He looked over at Kate, ashamed that he'd spent so much time talking about himself. He was surprised to find her smiling warmly at him, interested in every word he'd spoken. "What about you, *Doctor* Summers?"

"Stop it," she protested. "Don't you ever call me that again."

"Then what should I call you?"

"Oh, I don't know, how about 'beautiful,' 'gorgeous,' 'ravenous,' 'ma'am,' or maybe even, '*Your Highness*'?" she asked, playfully.

He didn't say so, but Nick was glad to see her happy. "I think I could manage that," he said to her, now with a serious expression on his face. He looked deeply into her eyes, which seemed so welcoming, and at the beautiful smile she wore. Now that the crisis was over, he had finally giving himself permission to relax a little. Their rocky introduction now only a fading memory, Kate Summers had been growing on him, and he now longed to spend more time in her company. After gazing into one another's eyes like young lovers for several moments, the two leaned in for a long, passionate kiss. Kate, who was seated next to the window, opened her eyes just long enough to notice a woman in the seat across the aisle from Nick smiling at them. She gently pushed Nick away long enough to nod in the direction of his neighbor. They both smiled and sat back up in their seats.

"So, do you think our 'crisis' is over?" she asked, changing the subject as she smiled at the woman across the aisle. Nick smiled at the woman as well before turning back to Kate and answering.

"Yeah, I suppose it is, at least for now." Nick spent a few moments thinking about that some more. Chances were there would be many more attacks, most of which would be to steal data, not kill people. Nick had to wonder for a moment whether many international terrorists would seize upon the success they'd witnessed and try to emulate Chervanko's success.

"What about our 'friend,' Nick? From what I understand he got away."

"Yeah, but I doubt we'll ever hear from him again. He's on the radar now so everyone will be looking for him. If he so much as peeks his head out from whatever rock he's hiding under, you can bet that the first jarhead, grunt, or Navy Seal that sees it will make it their mission to remove it from his shoulders. Besides, he's not getting any younger. My guess is he's living it up on some beach somewhere, holding a beer in his blood-stained hands."

"I hope so, Nick, because it was getting very scary, really intense."

"I know, Kate." This time it was Nick's turn to change the subject. "So...*Your Highness*...would you like to take in a show tonight?"

Kate looked warmly at him, before gently shaking her head. "Not tonight, Nick, but I'll take a rain check." She turned and looked back absent-mindedly at her journal.

"How about a candlelight dinner and some very pleasant conversation then?"

Kate looked up and smiled, placing her hand on his. "Now *that* sounds more like it," she answered, turning to look out the window. They were both quiet for several moments, the kind of silence that can be felt; a good silence, a time for warm feelings to pass between two people while nothing is said. "I've not been on a date for a very long time, Nick," she offered, still looking out the window. "I guess I've pretty much kept myself wrapped up in my work, ever since I started working on the Prometheus Project."

The female flight attendant came around with a refreshment. Kate asked for water, as did Nick.

"You never told me about yourself, Kate; I want to hear about *you* now," he said gently. "Where did you grow up?" he asked, sincerely ignorant about the past of the woman he'd just saved the world with. Kate turned back from the window to look at Nick.

"Do you really want to know?"

"Of course I do," Nick answered. "I want to learn everything I can about you this weekend. I want to know everything from who was at your first birthday party, how old you were when you said your first word, when you kissed your first boy, and when you first decided to become a scientist. Most importantly, however, I want to know at what moment you finally realized that you were falling for me." The flirting was turned up to maximum now, but neither of them seemed to care.

"What makes you think I'm falling for you?"

If he wasn't sure before, he was now; she was definitely into him.

"I have four reasons why I *know* that you're falling for me. First, because you didn't hit me with your journal just now when I said it. Second, because you didn't just call the flight attendant so you could be assigned another seat. Third, because you're still talking with me and fourth, because you haven't denied it...yet," he added, with a slight cringe.

"I haven't, huh? Well, should I?"

"Only if you mean it, Kate."

She closed her mouth, turned away, and smiled as she returned to her journal. *Alright!*

Fifteen minutes later the plane landed at McCarran Airport in Las Vegas. After waiting impatiently for several minutes the crowd of people on the small plane began to move towards the doorway as others began descending the stairs toward the terminal. Nick stretched as soon as his feet hit the tarmac. He was exhausted, but he was so excited about spending some quality time alone with Kate that he barely noticed it. After retrieving their luggage, they began making their way to where their cars were parked.

"Listen Kate, I hope this doesn't sound too chauvinistic, but I'd be happy to drive us to the apartments if you'd like, and you can leave your car parked here; unless of course you'd planned to run a lot of errands while we're here."

Kate walked closer to where Nick was standing at the edge of the parking lot. She sat her luggage down and took his hands in hers.

"I have two things planned for this weekend, Nick; get some rest, and spend a romantic weekend alone, with *you*." She smiled, but this time there was also a seriousness in her voice as well. It sounded to him like the start of a beautiful weekend.

Chapter 34

Chervanko was now growing impatient. His contact was late for their scheduled rendezvous and the Russian knew that the longer he stood exposed and out in the open, the greater his chances were of being spotted and picked up by someone in the FSB. The lakefront was their appointed rendezvous spot, the location chosen by his contact. To make matters worse, it was unseasonably cool outside as the summer transitioned into autumn, and a cold, brisk wind blowing off of the water served only to amplify the chill. Standing by the lake in short pants and a short sleeved shirt he soon found himself shivering, and regretting that he'd not checked the weather forecast before leaving the hotel.

Chervanko knew it would be worth the wait and the substantial expense, *if* his information was as valuable as he'd been told. It would have been extremely difficult, if not impossible, to obtain the sort of information his contact had access to from anywhere else. The former KGB agent was determined that no matter the effort or how much money it required, he *would* learn America's secret, the weapon they'd used to stop Ares…it was inevitable.

Before he traveled to America, however, he had to know where he was going. Had they stopped Ares at each targeted system, and if so, how did they know the targets? Had one of his trusted comrades betrayed him? That possibility troubled him, but he dismissed the thought the moment after it had occurred. He'd left them lying face down at the command center; surely the FSB would have spared a traitor. No, his friends had died as martyrs to the cause, loyal to the end.

During the Cold War, the Soviet Union had placed a substantial number of deep cover sleeper agents in civilian and governmental institutions throughout America. These inactive agents woke up every morning knowing that they could be called upon at any moment to answer the call of duty to the homeland. Thankfully, many had remained active and loyal throughout despite the so-called collapse of the Soviet Empire.

His contact had been one of the agents on a list he'd retrieved from the safe house. The agent, who now worked for the Russian Foreign Intelligence Service, lacked Chervanko's commitment to the cause, though he was sympathetic enough that for the right price, he would provide the necessary information.

Boris Petrov had once been a committed and loyal communist. When the empire began to crumble, however, he grew disheartened and bitter towards the government in particular, and politics in general. As the Foreign Intelligence Service's handler for a particularly valuable deep cover agent, now integrated into some of the American's blackest operations, Petrov was in a unique position, and Chervanko's best option for learning how the government had stopped the attack. The asset's access to Cyber Command alone made the agent, and thus Petrov as well, invaluable to Chervanko; he must gain access to him at all costs.

At last, after waiting for almost an hour, Boris Petrov slowly came into view, walking along the granite path that surrounded the lake. Like Chervanko, he also was a very careful man, using nearly every opportunity at his disposal to subtly shield his face. To be fair, the sun was bright and it was a beautiful day, so it was not unreasonable to wear both a ball cap and sunglasses. He smiled and felt a flush of personal pride in the fact that he wore neither, daring to expose his face to the world despite knowing that so many people were now after him. He had once been a master spy, and knew well that he was much more likely to draw attention to himself if he were conspicuously dressed.

"Excuse me sir, do you have the time?" Petrov asked, after walking up to Chervanko. Petrov was asking him to confirm his identity only as an extra precaution. They had met once years earlier in Moscow, when Chervanko was still in the KGB, but they had only met face to face once since the collapse of the Soviet Union. Nearly all of their subsequent communication had been over the telephone or via email.

Chervanko played along. He considered it all a boring, useless waste of time; unless it put Boris at ease, in which case it was an absolutely necessity. He wanted as much information as he could get and like it or not, Petrov was likely the only Russian who could provide it.

"Now is the time for all good men to come to the aid of the party," he answered in a friendly manner.

Chervanko was patient; he knew that Petrov could be tried and executed for handing such vital secrets over to someone like him. The Russian government knew the heavy price they would pay should Chervanko be linked to the Russian government when it came to the Ares Project, particularly since the concept had originally been conceived in the Kremlin.

"Thank you for meeting me, Boris," Chervanko said, much quieter this time. "I trust all has been well with you?"

"That depends; do you have the money?"

"Of course," he answered, handing a briefcase to Petrov, who then knelt down on the ground to inspect its contents.

"You know, I must be crazy doing this; they'll kill me if they ever find out," he told Chervanko.

"Who are you referring to, Boris, the Russians or the Americans?" Chervanko soon regretted antagonizing the skittish Petrov, who started to turn to leave. "Come now, Comrade, I was only joking, of course!" Chervanko spoke smoothly and in a calming voice. "Neither the Russian or American governments will ever know you assisted in any way, my friend, you have my word. I have already planted evidence suggesting that another agency leaked information about the American activity on the base; this misinformation is certain to clear you. Besides, remember the great service you will be doing for Mother Russia! You and I together can change the world, restore order, and fulfill the grand vision that Comrade Vladimir Lenin had for the working class." Chervanko watched Petrov, who seemed to still be teetering on the edge of changing his mind. "What will happen to our country if we do not do this thing? Perhaps she will slip into obscurity just as so many other great empires have, like the Babylonian Empire, the Roman Empire, and the British Empire. We must do this Boris, and we cannot do it without your help!" After watching and waiting for several moments, he knew that the dramatic close had done the trick when Petrov nodded his head in resolve.

"You are right, Nikolai. Very well." He reached out to shake Chervanko's hand, carefully passing a folded piece of paper, before then turning to look out on the lake. Chervanko slid his hand, and the folded piece of paper, into his right front pocket. "There are two important pieces of information in that paper, Nikolai. The first is the contact information for our comrade in America. He will be able to provide detailed information about the base and some of its personnel, and he will help you with everything you'll need for your cover identity. He'll provide you with an appropriate ID, and everything else you will need, including the fake fingers for fingerprints and the eye contacts you will need to get through security on the base. Your new identity will be that of Joseph Collins, a brilliant scientist in the field of aerospace engineering, with a specialization in theoretical propulsion systems. In terms of impersonation, you already have the same general build as the real Collins. The eye contacts you will receive will also serve to change your eye color from blue to brown. You will require a neat hair cut to match his and will need to color your hair brown. Add some matching glasses to the mix and the base security will not even second guess you, as long as you make it through the biometric scanner."

"What about biographical information on Collins?" asked Chervanko, who suddenly felt as if he were once again in the KGB, receiving a mission briefing.

"Wrapped inside the piece of paper I gave you is a small USB drive. On this disk is the second piece of information. It will provide you with some high-level background information on your man. You will want to have every detail memorized by the time your flight to America lands."

Chervanko studied Petrov for several moments, uncomfortable trusting his life to someone he'd only had a passing acquaintance with. He'd thought of Petrov during the early stages of planning the attacks, considering him to be a man who would likely be sympathetic to their cause. He'd come very highly-recommended, however, by some former KGB agents whom Chervanko *had* known and trusted; so it would have to do.

"Thank you, Boris." Petrov started to walk away in the opposite direction until he stopped and looked back at Chervanko.

"You do realize what you're trying to do here is impossible, don't you?"

"It will be difficult, yes, but it will not be impossible. I will succeed because it is what I was trained to do, and because failure is not an option.

Chapter 35

By the time the plane landed in Los Angeles the following day, Chervanko was grateful to finally exit the cramped aircraft. Using one of the many aliases that had proven so useful to him during his time with the KGB, he'd flown from Belarus to Frankfurt, and then from Tokyo to Alaska, before finally landing in LA. Once he was through customs, Chervanko had gone to Ground Transportation, picked up a rental car, and after asking for directions, drove directly to a nearby electronic store. Once at the store he purchased a disposable phone, which he would later use to call his contact. After getting plenty of minutes loaded onto the phone, he climbed back into the car, bought lunch at a nearby drive-thru restaurant, and began the four-hour drive to Las Vegas. It was a good thing that he'd picked up a car with a GPS, since so many of the roads and landmarks had changed considerably since his last visit, and he had a lot to accomplish before leaving America.

Once on the highway and headed in the right direction, he allowed himself to relax somewhat, before taking out and eating his lunch. While driving down the long road through some of the more scenic and rural areas of California and later Nevada, it occurred to the spy that it had been almost a decade since his last trip to the United States. He marveled at the beauty and grandeur of the desert as he neared Vegas, and suddenly felt a slight twinge of regret, mindful of the wasteland it would soon become. What a shame it was that so much of such a beautiful country would be destroyed soon after he had accomplished his mission; he'd always appreciated the many spectacular landscapes scattered across the United States. But Chervanko was not American, he was Russian. If America had to die in order for his beloved Soviet Union to live, then so be it.

Chervanko was exhausted when he finally arrived at the Grand Flamingo Hotel in Las Vegas. He looked forward to spending the night catching up on his rest, and sleeping off the jetlag which inevitably accompanied such a long flight.

He checked into the hotel, where a non-descript, brown box was waiting for him at the front desk. Chervanko took the package and went directly to his room. After bringing everything inside the room and closing the door, he sat down at the small table and opened the package. Inside were all the items Petrov had told him he would need: an appropriate ID for base access, fake fingers for fingerprints, eye contacts to get through security on the base, and photographs of the real Collins, who he imagined was now lying in a shallow grave somewhere in the Nevada desert.

He ordered room service, unpacked the rest of the box while he waited, and soon had everything out and ready to go. Taking out a small plastic bag, which included a pair of barber scissors and clippers, he went to work. It was something he'd done many times over the years, yet another part of the considerable KGB training he'd received. After working at it for thirty minutes he stopped to look in the mirror and considered his handiwork. He was relatively pleased with the results; his hair now looked to be about the right length and appearance, based on recent photographs of Collins.

About that time there was a knock on the door. Chervanko answered, and after tipping the hotel worker, took the tray of food and sat down to eat his dinner. It took him only a few minutes to eat the generous portions of food they'd given him. He cursed under his breath at the airlines and the way they skimped on the food they'd served, or worse yet, when they had served none at all, just to save a few pennies. Capitalist greed; that was just one of the thousands of reasons a worldwide revolution was needed. He and many others like him feared that governments and the citizens they ruled would never change unless they were forced to change. He comforted himself in the knowledge that everything would be different soon, and the working class would rise up and become the rulers instead of the ruled.

It was a noble cause for which he labored. Many would die of course, but their deaths would not be in vain; they would help usher in a new world, full of fairness and plenty for all. He would re-build the Ares system if he had to; perhaps this time he would setup in another country, where law enforcement was not quite as efficient as the FSB. But first, he would find the weapon the Americans had used to stop him, and he would do everything possible to ensure that they could never use it again.

He went back to work immediately after finishing the brief meal. With his hair now the right length, it needed to be the right color. After putting on a pair of gloves, Chervanko walked over to the sink, took out the two bottles in the box and, after mixing them together, he began changing his blonde hair to dark brown. He spent fifteen minutes coloring his hair, meticulously checking to ensure he'd not accidentally splattered any of the staining dye anywhere on his skin. Thirty minutes later he was finished; he was now a brunette instead of a blonde.

After taking a quick shower, he searched in the plastic bag until he found one of the pair of contacts he'd been given. The contacts would serve a dual purpose; they had been imprinted with the retina pattern of the real Collins. Furthermore, because his eyes were blue while Collins's had been brown, the contacts would change his eye color as well. Chervanko put the contacts in and walked up to the mirror. The Russian took a long look at the complete package staring back from the mirror, assessing his handiwork, and he was quite pleased with what he saw. He walked over to where his briefcase sat on the table, opened it, and took out a recent picture of Collins, which he supposed must have been taken not long before Collins had been retired by another of Petrov's agents. Chervanko held the picture up while he looked at himself in the mirror. After brushing his hair back a little, he extended his hand and said to his reflection, in perfect English, "Hello, Mr. Collins. It's a pleasure to finally meet you."

Satisfied he was ready, Chervanko picked up the laptop case and took out his laptop, turned it on, and inserted the USB drive. He'd reviewed what he'd been able to on the plane, but the fact that all but one of his flights had been full had made it too risky to try to read much of it beforehand. He browsed the files on the USB drive, stopping when he found the document he'd been looking for. He opened it, and after finding the information he needed, he picked up the disposable cell phone and began dialing. Moments later, a man's voice came through the receiver.

"Hello?"

Chervanko looked at the phrase next to the man's name. The activation phrase was different for each sleeper agent. "The red star rises for a new day." There were several moments of awkward silence, perhaps born of hesitation, before the man finally responded.

"I understand. And we will face the day with great hope for the people," came the correct counter phrase. "Would you like to meet?"

"Yes," Chervanko answered. "Tomorrow at 9:00 A.M., at the coffee shop on the corner of Smith and Miller...do you know it?"

"I know it," came the reply.

"I will be wearing a red shirt and a Dodgers hat."

"Understood. Good night."

Chervanko hung up the phone and laid back on the bed, suddenly realizing just how tired he was. The long trip had left him exhausted. He partially closed the computer screen, but left it open enough that he could quickly find and review the background information for his new identity the following morning. The former spy realized he would be putting that knowledge to use very soon. It could be the following day, or it might not be for several weeks; either way, everything would hinge on the meeting with his contact the following morning. Chervanko decided to get ready for bed and get some rest. He fell asleep soon after his head touched the pillow, and dreamt about his KGB days in the Soviet Union, and of a glorious future.

The following morning Chervanko arrived for the meeting a few minutes early. The coffee he ordered was refreshing, and served to help revitalize him. He took another sip and looked over a menu, contemplating getting some breakfast as well. The table he had chosen was in the far corner of the coffee shop, too far away from everything for anyone to eavesdrop on their conversation, and isolated enough that they would have plenty of time to change the subject of their discussion should someone approach. Chervanko glanced up from the menu just as he was joined by a man he'd never seen before, who sat down across from him.

"The red star rises for a new day," Chervanko said, repeating the passphrase.

"And we will face the day with great hope for the people," replied the stranger, once again offering the counter-phrase. "I must say, Mr. Collins, that I'm quite impressed with your appearance, but are you quite certain that you wish to discuss this matter *here*?" the man asked uncertainly.

"Absolutely," Chervanko replied. "Over the years some of my most productive discussions have taken place in such an establishment."

"As you wish. So what exactly can I do for you? You obviously have the package I left for you."

"Yes I do, thank you. I must know how they were able to stop the attack," Chervanko told him.

"Perhaps their defensive capabilities are greater than we originally thought," the man offered.

"Doubtful," Chervanko replied. "We did considerable research into their defensive capacity, not to mention the detailed capabilities listed in your own reports. They have developed something new, a different software program, a new device, a new strategy, something; they were able to stop our attack in its tracks, an attack which they should have been unable to defend against, and I must know how. Once I know that, I will take whatever it is back home with me. Do you have any idea what it could be?"

"I was only able to determine that there does seem to be some kind of new, powerful, and highly experimental device that Cyber Command has been testing recently for cyber warfare. As I told our mutual 'friend' two days ago, whatever *it* is, the device is here, in Nevada, at the base they call Area 51. Whatever this device is, the project is classified 'Above Top-Secret,' so it must be considered extremely important to national security. It is most-likely something highly-experimental. My guess is it that they're keeping it at the S-4 location, not at the main base."

"Can you get me onto the base?"

"I've already arranged for you to be on a Janet flight to the base tomorrow morning; the plane leaves at 5:15 a.m. Your cover will be that you're there to do some propulsion testing, which is what Collins was originally contracted to do. Do you have any background in this area?" asked the man.

"I was a fighter pilot in the Soviet Air Force before joining KGB," Chervanko answered.

"Good. Any background you have in aircraft propulsion systems could come in useful." The man looked around to find someone heading towards them. A waitress came over and filled their cups with coffee before heading back to where she was busy with the busier section of the restaurant. Once they were alone once more, the sleeper continued. "Hopefully, after arriving at the base, you will be taken to the S-4 facility, where most of the propulsion work is done. If you are not taken to S-4, it will be up to you to find the device's location and if necessary, gain entry into the S-4 facility."

"Do you have maps, floor plans, anything that will help me find my way around?"

"What we have you will find on the USB drive that was given to you," the other agent told him.

Chervanko nodded. "How do I find where the device is located?"

"If there is anything really strange or unusual going on at the facility, it is likely that a man named Dr. Henry Summers will know about it. He works at the S-4 facility. He is your best bet for finding this device, whatever it is. I suggest you start with him. Be warned, however, that he is extremely important to what happens at S-4, so he will be closely watched and guarded. There was also a failed kidnapping attempt recently by the Chinese, so security around him will be even tighter than normal. There will probably always be at least one guard posted nearby."

"Anything else?" asked Chervanko.

"Just be sure to be in Collin's apartment tonight when the call comes for the trip to the airport, and pack the large suitcase you will find there, which should last you for the week. There is a hidden compartment in your suitcase, which is large enough to store something small. They conduct very thorough searches of all baggage before allowing you to board the return flight, but this should be undetectable."

"I understand. Thank you for your help, I know the risk you are taking helping me."

"Good luck," the man answered as he stood up and began walking towards the door.

Chervanko took another sip of his coffee as he watched Colonel Mike Carter walk out the door, climb into his car, and drive away.

Chapter 36

Mark Goddard arrived for his shift a few minutes late. Ever since the unusual contact he'd had weeks earlier, he'd re-doubled his effort to arrive early for his shifts at the array. If E.T. had been responsible for the signals, he didn't want to miss the opportunity to be part of history.

The folks at Cyber Command had correctly pointed out that wherever the hack had originated from it had definitely been terrestrial in origin. Goddard and the others at S.E.T.I. had countered, however, that while the sender of the transmitted signal may have been terrestrial in origin, the sender of the received signal most certainly had not. This had, of course, generated no small amount of excitement in the cosmological community. What a shame it had been that the close-call with China had dominated every news cycle for the past several weeks, overshadowing what could be one of the most important events in human history; the first communication from another intelligent species of life. It had been the reason why Goddard had decided to pursue cosmology as a career instead of finance in the first place, and it was the reason he spent so much of his free time at the observatory.

Goddard got comfortable and settled in for his shift. He put on the headset before going to work on a peanut-butter-and-jelly sandwich, which he ate while reading a novel about first contact. He had a lot to do later, gathering data for detecting the gravity-wave background from coalescing massive black holes through pulsar timing, which he'd start just after finishing his dinner. By the time he finished reading two chapters from his novel, he'd finished his sandwich and had already made his second cup of coffee.

Goddard closed his novel, turned around in his chair to face the keyboard and monitors facing him on the table, and got to work. He began typing in the commands to move the array to point to the part of the sky where he would begin his search. Before he was able to execute the command, however, the array once more began moving on its own accord, as it had done once before when he was on duty. His heart started racing as he quickly picked up the phone and called Zimmerman.

"Hello?"

"Hello, Dr. Zimmerman?"

"Yes?"

"It's Mark Goddard. I'm sorry for disturbing you this evening, but I thought you'd want to know; it's happening again!"

"What—the array? It's moving on its own again?" Goddard thought she sounded both irritated and filled with excitement at the same time. "When did it start, and is it sending or receiving signals?"

"I don't know yet, it just began moving a minute ago, Dr. Zimmerman. I called you as soon as it started."

"Okay, very good. Please make sure that we're recording everything. Also, go to the Rolodex on my desk and find the number for Cyber Command. They wanted us to let them know as soon as it happened again so they could trace the signal. They might be able to do something to help us figure out what in the world's going on here."

"Yes, Doctor."

"And Mark?"

"Yes, Dr. Zimmerman?"

"If there turns out to be an incoming signal, please remember to call Dr. Stevens at the observatory in Australia for an independent confirmation. This is important, Mark, so we have to play this by the books."

"Understood. Are you coming in?"

220

"Yes. I'll be there in about thirty minutes."

"Okay, see you then." He hung up the phone and checked the screen once more, only to find that the array was once again transmitting a signal. He raced to Zimmerman's office, nearly tripping over a chair as he made his way to her office. Upon reaching it, he hurried inside and found her Rolodex sitting on top of her desk. He began thumbing through it until he located the number for Cyber Command.

"Hello?" The voice on the line was female.

"Hello, this is Mark Goddard at the Allen Telescope Array, at the Hat Creek Radio Observatory, 290 miles northeast of San Francisco."

"Yes, Mr. Goddard, what can we do for you?" she asked in a very level, nearly monotone voice.

"We were told to contact you if it happened again."

"If what happened again, Mr. Goddard?"

"If the array was hacked again. It started moving by itself just a few minutes ago. I checked it again just before I called and I found that it was transmitting a signal again, just like it did before."

"Understood. We'll start a trace, Mr. Goddard, and we'll let you know if we get anything. Is there a number where we can reach you if we need to talk with you or if we have any questions?" He gave them a couple of different phone numbers, including his personal cell phone number.

"Okay, thanks."

Goddard hung up the phone and left the office to go and monitor the array.

The signal stopped transmitting about the time he arrived back at the console. Disappointed, he tried to figure out what to do next. He began studying the complex signal again and, like before, found himself scratching his head, completely baffled by what he saw. The only thing he'd seen that was even remotely similar to what he was now looking at was a radio signal from a wireless network. The structure appeared to be digital data of some sort. He was pondering this when suddenly, new activity appeared on the screen. This time, there was an *incoming* signal. *What in the world's going on here—a return signal? If it is, what's happening—a conversation?* If it was a conversation, Goddard knew what it meant. In order for there to be a conversation with such a small interval of time between transmission and reception, it meant that both the sender and the receiver had to be in the same galactic neighborhood. Whoever or whatever had just sent the return signal was close. Based on the time, he surmised they were in the Earth's own solar system.

Goddard suddenly realized he'd forgotten to ask for the confirmation. He quickly located the phone number for the Australian laboratory and made the call.

"Hello, this is Dr. Stevens."

"Hello, Dr. Stevens, this is Mark Goddard, with S.E.T.I. I'm at the ATA and I need you to please confirm a signal for me."

"I'd be happy to, mate! Okay, where's it coming from?" Goddard supplied the coordinates and a few minutes later, Stevens was back on the phone.

" Well 'stone the bloody crows' cobber...I never expected to ever see that again so soon! But wait a minute, it's from a slightly different location in the sky, and it's a strong signal too! I think it may even be in the neighborhood."

Goddard contemplated sharing what had just happened with Stevens before deciding against it. Sharing the discovery of the signal was one thing. Announcing to the world that the array had been hacked, and that it was apparently engaged with an E.T. in the same neighborhood was something altogether. Chances were that Zimmerman would make an announcement, but it was her call, not his.

"Yes, Dr. Stevens, that's what it looked like to me as well."

"This is big news, Mark, you must be excited! Does Dr. Zimmerman know yet?"

"No, not yet. She should be here any second."

"Please ask her to call me when she has a moment, will you please? I'd love to discuss this with her!"

"I'll do that, Dr. Stevens. Well, thanks for the confirmation."

"No problem. Congratulations, *again!*"

Goddard hung up the phone and turned back to the screen. Moments later the signal stopped, and the array returned to its previous position. Goddard's thoughts turned to the impact of the news of the hack, and the fact that the unprecedented conversation had taken place before his very eyes. Not only had they captured a signal, they had captured a *conversation*, and they had been the instrument through which someone, either human or E.T., had used for communicating with someone from another civilization.

Jeff W. Horton

Chapter 37

It was not all that unusual for General George Caprella to be woken in the middle of the night by an urgent matter; it was the job, so he really didn't mind it—but that didn't mean he enjoyed it.

"Hello?"

"General, this is Nick Reynolds."

"What is it Nick? Is there something wrong?"

"Well, that's just it, General, I don't know for sure. I debated about calling you at this hour, sir, because I just don't know how important it is."

"That's okay, son, don't worry about it. I know you wouldn't call unless you felt it was necessary. So what's going on?"

"S.E.T.I. was hacked again this evening, sir."

"Didn't we help them strengthen their defenses?"

"Yes, sir, we did."

"Do you think Chervanko is active again?"

"I don't think so, sir, but to be honest, I can't be certain. We assumed after the last time that some kid was probably just messing around and sending a message by hacking the array. It really didn't make any sense, but then hackers often don't."

"I couldn't agree more. Is there anything else you can tell me? Do you know what they were after?"

"Well, General, there is something else kind of odd about what happened. The array sir, it…um…appeared to be communicating with someone, or something."

"What? You did say S.E.T.I., didn't you, Nick?"

"Yes, sir."

"How exactly is it possible that someone was using the ATA to communicate with someone else? Could it have been communicating with a satellite in orbit?"

"I asked the folks at S.E.T.I. that same question, General Caprella. They assured me it couldn't possibly have come from orbit."

"Then where *did* it come from?"

"That, General, is the other odd thing about what happened out there. They told me that the incoming signal originated from somewhere in our solar system, but they don't know exactly where or from what."

"Maybe it was one of the probes NASA's launched over the last few years?" Caprella asked, growing slightly frustrated.

"No, sir. They were certain that it could not possibly be anything of ours."

"Maybe something from another country, maybe Russia or the European Space Agency?"

"Well sir, if it is it's like nothing any of our experts have ever seen before, and we've spent the last few hours analyzing all available data. I think we can rule out about all of the major countries. Oh yeah, the folks at S.E.T.I. told me one more thing, General. They said that the signal matches exactly with the pattern of those sent and received over the last few weeks, including the one that originated from another star system."

There was silence for several moments, so long in fact that Nick began to think they'd been disconnected.

"General?"

"I'm still here, Nick. I was just thinking we deserved a break. We just avoided a nuclear holocaust and World War III, and now this."

"Um, General, there's another reason why I called you about this."

"Go on," the general said.

"After they contacted us the last time they were hacked, we installed a probe on their network so we could capture some more information, and trace the origin of the hack. The trace was interrupted soon after it started. The best we were able to do was trace the call to somewhere from the western United States...." Nick allowed the rest of the sentence to trail off, waiting to see whether Caprella came to the same conclusion he had, no matter how fantastic it might be. It was quite a coincidence, and Nick didn't believe very much in coincidence.

"Nick, could it be that somehow...I mean...is it possible...?"

"That Ignis could somehow be involved?"

"Yes." There it was, laid out on the table. Nick had a gnawing feeling in his gut the moment he'd learned about the first ATA hack from Caprella. Now, the evidence seemed to be more and more obvious. Somehow, Ignis was involved in the hacks. Who else could possibly be communicating with an alien civilization?

"I've been wondering exactly the same thing, General. I don't know how or why, but I think we need to consider the possibility that somehow, Ignis could be trying to call home."

* * * *

Dr. Henry Summers made his way from his office and back to his lab. *Is it possible?* He had to admit that Ignis was the most advanced piece of technology on the planet, with the exception of the ship itself, of course. He was also aware that the hacks at S.E.T.I. had not started until they had removed Ignis from the ship and connected it to the network, when they had been so busy scrambling to determine how they might be able to utilize Ignis to help with the cyber attacks.

He found Kate at the table, leaning over and studying the Ignis device, inspecting the connection it had made with the fiber optic cabling as well as the power cable.

"Kate, do you have a moment?" he asked his daughter, before walking up to her and kissing her on the forehead.

"Sure, Dad," she answered, giving him a strange look.

"Let's go to my office; I'd like to get another coffee along the way." Henry began walking toward his office without offering any explanation. Kate watched him for a moment and shrugged her shoulders before following him out of the lab. They walked down the hallway without saying a word. She walked into her father's office and sat down while Henry stopped by the coffee machine in the hallway and poured himself a cup of coffee. Placing the machine there had been his idea. As an avid coffee drinker, locating it there served as the logical location between the office and the lab, where he divided his time.

"What's going on, Dad, what's with the mystery?" she asked, after he joined her in his office and sat down. He recounted what Nick had told him about his conversation with General Caprella, and the hack at the Allen Telescope Array. Her eyes widened when he got to the part about the timing of the hacks, and about their suspicions.

"That doesn't make sense, Dad! Ignis is a computer navigational system. We've all interfaced with it...you, me, and Nick. We never noticed anything odd that would suggest it intended any harm or mischief. How could it have done this on its own?"

"I think that more important than how is *why* it would have done this," Henry answered. "Why would a device which lay dormant for more than sixty-five years suddenly call home, if indeed that's what it was doing?"

Kate considered that for several moments. "Well, some computer manufacturers design systems to call back to an office or location whenever there is a failure or an issue. Perhaps Ignis is doing this as well, simply calling home to notify someone or something that there's been a problem."

"And the only reason it's done so now and not before is that it's the first time Ignis has had power since the crash in 1947. That's definitely a possibility. The device is obviously extremely advanced, capable of making decisions independently without being given detailed instructions. Once connected to the Internet, it learned about the array, and decided it would be its best option for calling home."

"Dad, didn't you say that the array not only sent signals, but that it received them as well?" she asked abruptly.

"Indeed, I did say that, Kate."

"And that some of the signals were relatively close, somewhere within our own solar system?" The fear in her voice was now apparent to Henry, and he suddenly realized why it was there.

"Yes, I did say that also," he answered. "So you're suggesting that if the entity that received the call responded, then—"

"Ignis didn't make the call home just to let someone know that it was functional, it made the call home as a distress call, and it's been answered. Since someone's apparently received the call, then they're probably on their way here right now to retrieve Ignis!"

Chapter 38

Chervanko had already made it through the first security checkpoint and safely into the Janet terminal, where he waited in line to pass through the second checkpoint. Within a couple of minutes he was through the second checkpoint as well and boarded the aircraft without incident. He breathed easier now that he was on the plane, and since there was no one sitting immediately beside or behind him, he busied himself studying the biography of the dead man he was now impersonating. He had placed the printed biographical information inside a copy of Popular magazine, along with what little classified background information his sources had been able to provide him on the American military base at Groom lake. Like most everyone else on the planet, he'd heard of the infamous Area 51, as well as some of the fantastic, fabricated stories about the place; now he was about to find out how true these stories were. Hopefully, if his information was accurate, he'd come out of it with whatever it was that the Americans had used to stop the cyber attack, which he'd spent nearly a decade out of his life planning.

Collins had been an aeronautical engineer for twenty-five years, with at least ten of those years specializing in propulsion systems, like those on the Lockheed Martin F-22 Raptor, a fifth-generation jet fighter. He'd also worked with NASA on experimental propulsion systems, including efforts to create an artificial gravitational field around a rotating superconductor. The guy had been on the cutting edge of science. Chervanko suddenly felt another twinge of regret that they'd had to "retire" a man as valuable as Collins, though the feeling quickly passed. He reminded himself that great sacrifices often had to be made in the name of progress, and the brilliant scientist had been no exception. Chervanko knew that if he was able to steal the device the Americans had used, it was possible that it could be of far more use to him than Ares ever had been.

The pilot announced over the intercom that they would soon be landing. Chervanko closed the magazine and placed it back in his briefcase, along with the biographical information on the man he was now impersonating. He placed the briefcase under the seat in front of him and sat back in the seat, trying to relax. He replayed events in his mind once more as he recounted the information he'd read and what he'd been told by his contact.

Collins had never been to Area 51 before and as a result, would have to go through an orientation process. He would likely be met immediately upon disembarking the aircraft. To the best of his contact's knowledge, Collins had never met any of the personnel at Area 51 or any of the other scientists he'd be working with there. The assumption was that Collins would have no idea whether he'd be working at the main base at Groom Lake or whether he'd work at S-4 or one of the other facilities nearby. Chervanko only had to avoid getting into any deep technical conversations with the other scientists and he should be fine. The problem was, however, that deep discussions with other scientists was precisely what had generated the interest in him to begin with.

Chervanko knew that he'd have to work quickly to accomplish what he'd come to do. He had to find the device, and if possible, steal it. If he couldn't steal it for any reason, he would learn as much about it as he possibly could and destroy it. He had only sketchy details as to what to expect in terms of security at the base, so he had no idea how or even if he would be able to smuggle the device off of the base; one thing was certain, however…he would do his best.

The plane landed a few minutes later and Chervanko began making his way to the aircraft's exit. The sole flight attendant on the flight made an announcement that for those new to the base, they could pick up their luggage at the bottom of the ramp within just a few minutes. He would be there all week, so Chervanko had brought with him a larger than necessary suitcase, which he would use, if possible, to help smuggle out the American's secret weapon. Just before reaching the exit, the question came to mind whether there was a better way than the Janet flight to get off of the base. He recalled the desolation of the landscape all around the base which would make him much easier to find, and quickly concluded that leaving by any means other than a Janet flight would have to be a last resort, and would definitely require transportation.

He finally reached the exit and proceeded down the ramp of stairs which had been pushed up to the aircraft. He was met at the bottom of the stairs by a beautiful young woman dressed in an American Air Force uniform. It had been a while since he'd seen such an attractive woman.

"Excuse me, are you Dr. Collins? I'm Lieutenant Janet Smythe, no relation to the plane of course." She smiled flirtatiously with Chervanko. A thought crossed his mind for a moment before being summarily discarded. *Stay on task, Chervanko.*

"Yes, I'm Collins," the Russian answered, having regained his composure. He suddenly realized that he'd have to do a lot better than that if he was going to pull off his objective. He'd made it this far, but time was not his ally. Chervanko reminded himself that being patient and keeping a cool head were of paramount importance in order for his mission to succeed.

"Please follow me, Dr. Collins. I'll take you to On Boarding, where you'll be assigned a living quarters, cafeteria information, who to call, that sort of thing."

"Thank you," Chervanko replied as they made their way from the plane and into the closer of the nearby large buildings. He noticed after going inside that there was a significant drop in the ambient air temperature. Only once inside the air conditioned building did he realize how hot it had been outside.

"How will I get around here?" he asked innocently. "I have no car and there do not appear to be any taxis," he added, smiling at her as he did so.

"Oh, don't worry about how to get around, Dr. Collins. We have underground corridors between most buildings. For some of the longer stretches, we have underground shuttles. Wait a minute, I'll take a look at something." She took out a sheet of paper that seemed to have information about him. "Yes," she said a moment later. "It looks like you will be working mostly at our S-4 facility. You'll be taking a shuttle to get there." She must have noticed the look of concern on his face at this news. "Oh don't worry, Dr. Collins, they'll be covering all of this for you in the briefing you'll be attending in about twenty minutes. This is Area 51; believe me when I say that you and everyone else will know exactly where you're supposed to be at all times." Chervanko just smiled.

He carefully evaluated the base environment on their way to the On Boarding session, and the smile slowly morphed into a grimace. He was beginning to realize that his mission was going to be considerably more difficult than he'd already thought. Stationed throughout the facility were teams of Air Force Combat Controllers, one of the Air Force's three special operations teams, armed with M-4 carbine automatic rifles. It was becoming clearer to him by the minute that he would achieve his objective only through great stealth and subtlety.

While the lieutenant carried on about some trivia about the Groom Lake facility and the Nevada atomic tests of the 1940s, Chervanko went to work memorizing what he saw of the layout of the facility, something he'd been trained to do as a spy. He also began forming a plan as to what to do next. He would have to find a way of broaching the topic of computers with someone, as a means of discovering who was responsible for the Ares debacle. He would need to proceed very carefully in his inquiries, however, in a place where questions in general were frowned upon. If he aroused too much suspicion, it would not take long for someone to realize that there was something unusual about Dr. Joseph Collins, and that he was in fact neither a scientist or Joseph Collins. If he were discovered, he had little doubt what would happen to him next. When the Americans learned that the intruder was the individual responsible for the recent murder of over one hundred thousand Americans *and* the attempt to start a nuclear war with China, they'd be filled with rage to the point of madness. If he was lucky, the Americans would kill him themselves. If not, he would be sent back to Russia, where he would either be put to death, or sent to serve out a life sentence in the gulag. Perhaps—

"If it hadn't been for them testing the atomic bomb during World War II, who knows where the world would have ended up? Maybe we'd all be speaking Japanese!" She smiled at Chervanko again and this time he quickly smiled warmly back at her. It seemed she fancied him, and being the consummate spook that he was, he would leverage that for everything he could get out of it.

"Well that is fascinating information, Lieutenant Smythe. I'd love to hear more about it sometime," he said, turning on his charm in a manner he hadn't done in years. *It feels good to be back in the game!*

"Sure, *anytime*, Dr. Collins," she answered. "I'd be happy to tell you anything I can; which unfortunately isn't very much, actually, since so much is classified."

"Well then, why don't you tell me what you can over a friendly dinner this evening, after orientation is over and I've settled into my quarters. I'm assuming there is some sort of restaurant here?"

"Oh yes Dr. Collins, there are a few, actually."
"Please," he said slowly, holding her hand in his. "Call me Joseph."

Chapter 39

"Wow." Kate smiled and her eyes widened. "I mean, think about it; we were all interfaced with Ignis, and we had no idea! If it *is* behind what's been going on at the Allen Telescope Array, then it means that at the very least its artificial intelligence is powerful enough to allow it to independently find and manipulate the array to call home. I guess I shouldn't be surprised, considering everything it's already demonstrated it could do. Can you imagine what Ignis could be capable of that we haven't seen yet?"

A couple walked over and sat down at the table next to them. Nick took a bite from his meatloaf and lowered his voice before speaking again.

"Oh, it's behind the hacks, Kate…it has to be. I completed the trace *and* I checked the firewall logs here. The S.E.T.I. hacks took place after hours, after all of us had left the lab. Unless someone snuck into the lab after we left and decided to hack into their network, which is no easy task by the way, then Ignis is the only reasonable explanation. Think about it, Kate—Ignis was able to stop Chervanko and the cyber attacks merely by us putting on the neural interface helmet and thinking about it. Anything that can do what it did is so far beyond anything that we have today it's ridiculous. It's like comparing today's grid computers with the abacus. I've been thinking about something, Kate. Do you suppose Ignis could be something more than just some new kind of artificial intelligence? Given our experience with it so far, I've been questioning whether it could actually be some sort of artificial life."

"What? Don't be ridiculous, Nick. This is science we're talking about, not science fiction. I *am* a scientist, remember?"

"I know, but I always thought the Roswell crash and the flying saucer at Area 51 were science fiction too, yet here I am at Area 51, working with a flying saucer recovered from the Roswell crash."

"You mean here *we* are," she corrected, holding his hands.

"Exactly," he answered, before leaning in to kiss her. His heart raced for a moment, as it often did when he was thinking about her. Their relationship had continued to blossom the week following the showdown with the Ares system. Kate scooted her chair around until she was sitting close beside Nick, instead of across from him, then wrapped her arm around him and they kissed again.

"You know, Nick, as sappy as it sounds, I must admit that if it took us coming to the brink of a world war for me to find you, it was worth it to me; I'm so glad I met you."

Nick reached over and took her hand in his. "I feel the same way," he responded, squeezing her hand as he did so. They both leaned in again, this time in a hot, passionate kiss instead of a peck. Kate pushed away.

"Okay, I think that better be all for now, Mr. Reynolds," she said, smiling.

Nick smiled back and went to work on his meat loaf and mashed potatoes. He pondered the significance of what Ignis appeared to be doing. At the very least it meant they should accelerate the testing they were doing with Ignis' before its friends from out of town arrived. If it turned out that the visitors were unfriendly, they might have averted a global conflict only to find themselves with a new, interstellar enemy; the implications were staggering.

"You know Kate," he began soon after finishing his meatloaf. "We should probably do whatever testing we're going to do sooner rather than later. We have no idea how long it will take Ignis's friends to get here."

"I was just thinking the same thing, Nick. From what the folks at S.E.T.I. told us, it sounds like they could already be in our solar system."

"I just hope I have my digital camera ready. I'd love to post pictures of E.T. on the Internet."

Both Kate and Nick grew quiet as they became lost in the solitude of their own thoughts, each of them eating dessert in silence.

"You know, Dad's really been vindicated by this whole thing with Ignis," Kate said at last.

"What do you mean?" asked Nick, puzzled by the odd remark.

"I guess Dad has—that is, we both have—been ridiculed at times over our work on the Prometheus Project. Dad's spent decades studying the ship, and I've spent years on it, mostly studying Ignis while it was still in the ship." She paused for a few moments to take another bite of her cake. "I guess the government's spent a lot of money on this project over the years with only limited results to show for it. When the project was first started, they believed we'd be making ships just like it within just a few years." Kate laughed. "Needless to say, we haven't had quite as much success in the reverse-engineering arena as we'd hoped."

"That may be, but Kate, it just kept the planet from going over the edge. I'd say it was well worth the money."

"Exactly. Anyway, I'm just glad. But if they come—"

"If they come, I think we should say thank you and let them have it," Nick told her emphatically. "It belongs to them, Kate, the whole ship does."

"I know, but just think of what we could do with it given some time, Nick; the things it could teach us!" Nick sat there quietly, saying nothing. Instead he just kept looking at her thoughtfully. "What?" She looked at him crossly for several moments, before finally looking down. "I know you're right, Nick. It's just that—well, we could learn so much from it!"

"I know."

"Alright, so what do you think we should do, leave it at the gates to Area 51 with a sign for them saying 'Thanks for loaning us your super-advanced alien computer'?"

"I don't know, Kate; I suspect that when the time comes, we'll know what to do."

They finished their dessert, and as they rose to leave, Nick had an idea. "Say Kate, I picked up a movie I was planning to watch in my quarters tonight…care to join me?"

Kate Summers responded by wrapping her arms around his neck. "I can't think of any place I'd rather be than with you tonight, sir," she said, before pulling him closer and kissing him.

"There's nothing like young love." The man who'd been sitting at the table next to theirs smiled up at them. "You two look like you belong together; you make a wonderful couple."

"Thank you, Mister—"

"The name's Collins, Joseph Collins, my dear. I'm new here, just arrived on the plane. That's where I met my wonderful date here, Jan."

"Oh, hi, Jan," Kate said. "I didn't you were sitting next to us!"

"Hi Kate," she said. "Who's this handsome fellow with you, Kate?"

"Hands off, Jan, he's taken!" Kate said, smiling, but Nick could tell there was a serious tone to her voice as well.

"Hi Jan, Joseph, I'm Nick Reynolds. I'm fairly new here myself, having only been here a month or so."

Kate walked over to where Collins/Chervanko stood. "Did you say your name was Joseph Collins?" she asked him with a surprised expression.

"Yes, indeed I did," answered Collins/Chervanko calmly, successfully hiding his uneasiness. "I'm here to…well, I guess I'm not to say what I'm doing here, or that's what they tell me anyway.

"What wonderful news! We've been waiting months for you to get here. My father thinks he's on the verge of a breakthrough on reverse-engineering the craft's propulsion system. We understand you've already been briefed, so you know what I'm talking about, err—haven't you?" she asked sheepishly.

"Yes, of course," he answered smoothly. "But we, um—probably shouldn't be talking about this now, should we?" he asked quietly, looking back at Jan, who had been talking with Nick.

"No, you're right. Will you be coming to S-4 tomorrow then? I can't wait to tell my father, Dr. Henry Summers, that you're here."

"Yes, of course. I was planning to be there first thing in the morning."

"Wonderful!" Kate exclaimed, walking over to Nick on her way to rescue him from Jan. She wrapped her arm around his, and said, "Ready to go, lover?"

Nick looked at her and grinned. "You bet I am."

"I'll see you in the morning, Dr. Collins!" she said, pulling Nick along with her. "See *you* on Friday, Jan," she said cooly.

"Good night!" Collins/Chervanko told her, wearing a large, sincere smile, still overwhelmed at his good fortune.

Chapter 40

Andropov picked up the report and began thumbing through it. Twice he'd narrowly missed Chervanko, and now he had completely vanished. They'd heard a rumor that he might be planning to leave the country, and that he might have been meeting with someone either in the FSB or the FIS, trying to gather some intelligence on an America military installation, but the rumor could not be confirmed.

The director of the FSB had been ordered to find Chervanko at all costs, so that the Russian Federation could demonstrate to the world that the rogue, former KGB operative, who had murdered one hundred thousand Americans and nearly caused the deaths of hundreds of millions worldwide, had been brought to justice. Chervanko would be tried and convicted for his crimes against humanity, and he would be executed in accordance to those crimes.

The pressure on the Russian Federation to find Chervanko had been steadily building, and Andropov only expected it to get worse, but first he had to find him. *How do you find someone who has spent his entire life disappearing and reappearing at will; how do you bring a ghost to justice?* Andropov was pondering what to do next when the phone suddenly rang.

"Andropov. Yes, I have been and I still am. Why are you telling me this? Very well—I understand. Thank you." Andropov hung up the phone and dialed another number. "Sir, we may have just had a break in the Chervanko case. Yes, sir, I'll be there in five minutes." Andropov brushed off his jacket and walked out of his office for his debriefing with the head of the Ministry of Justice.

* * * *

General George Caprella, Commander, U.S. Cyber Command, was enjoying a lunch outing at the driving range when the cell phone of his assistant, Mike Carter, rang. Caprella had been consistently practicing with his driver over the past several months, and was finally being rewarded with a number of impressive swings. Caprella had the gnawing feeling that Carter was going to interrupt once again during one of his near-spiritual moments with the golf balls. Caprella was preparing to start another run of swings when, right on schedule, Carter came over to him, cell phone in hand.

"General, I have a priority call for you, sir. It is from Yuri Andropov, sir, Director of the Russian FSB. He claims to have some valuable information."

"Okay, I'll take the call." Carter handed him the phone and walked away. Caprella gave him a strange look, noticing the sweat on his forehead and the tension in his voice.

"Hello?"

"Hello once again, General Caprella, Yuri Andropov here. I have some news for you about Nikolai Chervanko. I have been authorized by my government to share what I know with you, as a matter of courtesy, and in the interest of both our countries.

"Apparently he paid one of his former colleagues for information about a top secret military base in America. He was also put in touch with one of our old sleeper agents who is still active from the Cold War. We believe Chervanko is either trying to or has already infiltrated this base looking for something important to him."

"Do you know which base he's trying to break into?" asked Caprella.

"We're not certain, but we believe he plans to try and get into your Area 51; you know, General, the base with the flying saucers, which doesn't exist." Andropov couldn't resist a chuckle.

"Any idea what he might be looking for?" asked Caprella.

" I do not know for certain, General, but at this point I doubt he would risk capture by your government just to gain information about one of your experimental fighter jets. You must understand, General Caprella, that Nikolai Chervanko considers his 'mission,' his grand scheme to re-create the Soviet Union in his image, to be far more important than his own life. I do believe, however, that he would attempt to infiltrate even a top-secret American base like your Area 51, if he felt the payoff would be worth it—say, if you had something or someone there that he believed was responsible for his failed cyber attack. He has to be quite livid that you thwarted his plans for world domination, you know. Perhaps you have some of that fascinating alien technology that I hear so much about on television!"

Andropov laughed for several moments, while a chill ran down Caprella's spine. He suddenly had an image of the Ignis device in the hands of a megalomaniac like Nikolai Chervanko; the prospects were too terrifying to even consider.

"Thank you, Director Andropov, I will be certain to alert the security personnel at our base to be on the lookout for Chervanko, just on the off-chance that he does come here as your intelligence suggests. On behalf of the government of the United States of America, you have our appreciation, sir. I will make it a point to ensure that our president and *yours* is aware of all of the assistance which you and your country have provided to us in regards to Chervanko."

"You are most welcome, General Caprella. I very much regret that this madman is one of ours, and I want to do everything that I can to help you destroy this evil man. You have my number; please do not hesitate to contact me if there is any way I can be of further assistance. Goodbye."

"Goodbye, Director Andropov." Caprella hung up the phone. Considering the implications of the intelligence information he'd just received, he knew there was no way the Russians would have shared it with him unless they felt certain the information was legitimate. Furthermore, Caprella had seen Chervanko's file. He knew all too well that only someone who'd had the training and the skills of a Nikolai Chervanko could ever hope to successfully infiltrate a military installation as secure as Area 51. It would be very risky, but it might be possible, especially by a motivated ideologue.

After flipping through his Rolodex and finding a number, Caprella got on the phone and called the director of base security at Groom Lake.

"Colonel Frost, General Caprella, Cyber Command."

"Oh, hi George; what can I do for you, General?"

"Hi, Bill. Listen, I'm afraid we have a serious problem. I've just received some *very* credible intelligence from the Russians that a former Soviet spy, a KGB officer named Nikolai Chervanko, has plans to infiltrate Area 51."

"You think he's looking for something to do with Prometheus?" As head of base security, it was Frost's duty to know about everything that went on at the base.

"Yes, I do; and based on the intelligence I just received, I'm convinced he'll make an attempt soon, Bill. This is the same upstanding citizen who murdered one hundred thousand people a few weeks ago in New York."

"This is the guy behind the cyber attacks?"

"Yep, the same."

"Well, sir, it would be an honor and a privilege to grease this one, sir."

"Bill, I don't have to tell you what a madman like Chervanko would do with something like Ignis under his control, do I? If he's here, he will find it eventually."

"Understood, General. If we do find him, I'll tell him he needs to be real careful not to accidentally jump in the way of a cartridge from an M-4 carbine automatic rifle. Who knows, it might accidentally hit him right between the eyes or something."

"Yeah well, first we've got to find him. I'll send over the most recent photo of him that I've got. Be certain to circulate it around the base, taking into account that this guy's a master spy. He's almost certainly made changes to his appearance that have to be accounted for. Have security focus on height, weight, build, etc. instead of hair color, facial hair, and such. Also, make sure they're suspicious of anyone new on the base."

"Don't worry, General, I've been at this a long time, sir."

"Sorry, Bill. It's just that with this guy, it's a little personal."

"With all due respect, General, with this guy it's personal to over three hundred million Americans, after what he did in New York."

Caprella smiled at this. He'd always liked Bill Foster.

"Very good then. You'll keep me posted?"

"Roger that, sir. I'll let you know immediately if the S.O.B. shows his face around here."

"Thanks." Caprella hung up the phone, questioning whether the call he'd just made was enough. It was getting late, but since Chervanko would be going after Ignis, he decided he'd better let the Prometheus project members know what was going on so they could be prepared. A new urgency suddenly hit him. *What if he's already there?*

Chapter 41

"This is incredible; it's unbelievable!" Chervanko struggled to maintain his American accent in the midst of being so overwhelmed by the alien ship he was looking at. "Can you imagine flying something like this?" he asked, walking around it.

"Did you fly in the military, Dr. Collins?" Nick asked, walking around the ship with them. It was Nick's first time seeing the craft as well, though he'd spent plenty of time in the lab where Ignis was kept.

"Oh, yes, but never anything like this," Chervanko answered truthfully. "The propulsion system must be extraordinary," he said off-handedly. "What have you learned about it so far?" he asked Henry, more out of curiosity as a former pilot than as a presumed scientist.

"Well, we believe that there's something more than just electro-magnetism involved. We don't think it negates gravity so much as it counteracts or counter-balances it. To be honest, some of the complex theoretical physics associated with Einstein's General Theory of Relativity still continue to elude me somewhat. As I'm sure you know, Dr. Collins, some quantum physicists have suggested the existence of certain massless, elementary particles called gravitons. If they really do exist, it's possible the ship uses gravitons to somehow counteract gravity. The problem has been, of course, that the ship has never been operational, so we haven't been able to study an operational engine. It is our hope that you may be able to help us get the engines online, so that we can finally reverse-engineer them."

"Get the ship's engines online? How is that even possible?" Chervanko asked, in a momentary lapse of discipline. It suddenly dawned on him that he'd allowed himself to slip.

"How? Doctor, we sent you information about that in the secure emails, don't you remember?" asked Kate, confused by his question and now slightly suspicious.

Chervanko took a few seconds to calm himself and to collect his thoughts. He'd seen too many missions blown in the past by less experienced agents who panicked the first time they were thrown a curveball or tripped over themselves. Chervanko was a disciplined, trained, veteran spy, who'd had to deal with worse, much worse, on many occasions.

"Oh, yes, of course, please forgive me. It's just seeing it in person for the first time, it's just so overwhelming!"

"I felt the same way when I first saw it, Dr. Collins," Henry offered sympathetically. "It truly is quite a feat of engineering. We intended to see if we could get her powered up before now, particularly after what we learned about how Ignis powered up, but to be honest we've been so busy, we haven't even had a chance to try it yet."

"Oh yes, I heard about that. You were helping the government defend against the recent cyber attacks; fantastic job by the way!" It was risky, but Chervanko figured he had little to lose at this point.

"How did you know about that?" asked Nick suspiciously. "That information has been limited to only a very select few!" Nick now had a furrowed brow and a concerned look on his face as well.

Chervanko's eyes darted about his surroundings for a few moments. He instantly realized that he was too exposed where they were in the hangar. Several guards stood close by, members of the Air Force's special operations team. No, he would wait to make his move.

"Oh, um, I was told just before I came out here by General, um, Caprella?"

"You spoke with Caprella?" he asked. *What's going on here?*

"Oh yes. He said it wasn't standard practice for him to speak with civilians who were new here, but that he was making an exception in my case, because of what I came here to do," lied Chervanko. "He was very excited about your recent success with some kind of device here, which he said you used to stop the cyber attacks, and he hoped we would have the same kind of success with getting the ship operational. Is that okay?" he asked Nick sheepishly, playing up the hapless, nerdy scientist. Nick just shook his head and shrugged, uncertain how to process the information.

"Yeah, sure, I guess so," he grudgingly replied.

"Would you like to see the device, Dr. Collins?" Henry asked, gesturing towards the lab area. "We call it Ignis. It's really quite remarkable. We thought it was just a navigational system at first, but it has proven to be much more than we ever realized."

"Oh yes, I would very much like to see it, thank you," Chervanko answered, excited beyond measure at his good fortune in being led directly to the device by the hapless American scientists. As he followed Henry into the lab, he felt a slight chill in the air when he walked past the still-suspicious Nick. Once he'd gone on ahead, Nick and Kate stood and stared at one another for several seconds, before both of them turned to follow her father and the master spy inside.

Chervanko followed Summers into the lab. When Henry Summers walked over to the lab table where something about the size of a breadbox sat, the Russian looked at Henry in confusion and disbelief.

"This is it? This little thing controlled the propulsion and navigational systems of an interstellar spacecraft?"

"Oh yes," Henry answered. "I assure you, Dr. Collins, that Ignis is without question the most powerful computer on our planet many times over; it's really quite extraordinary."

"Fascinating," Chervanko said, while inspecting the device as thoroughly as possible from the outside.

"Yes. As you pointed out a moment ago, Ignis was very instrumental in stopping the vicious major cyber attack, which if not countered, would have resulted in the deaths of millions of people and would undoubtedly have triggered a thermonuclear war with the People's Republic of China."

"I understand that a cyber attack was also what caused that nuclear power plant in New York to meltdown."

"Indeed," Summers answered. "It's a shame that we weren't ready in time to use it to stop that attack as well."

"How true," Chervanko said, feigning despondency. He looked at how the cables coming out of the device were intertwined seamlessly with the fiber optic cables and the copper power cables alike. "How were you able to connect the device to the cables so seamlessly?" he asked.

"Dr. Collins, we told you in our last email. Did you forget that as well?" asked Kate, now more suspicious than ever. "You *are* Dr. Collins, aren't you? You're not really like any aeronautical engineer I've ever met."

"Of course I'm Dr. Collins; don't be silly, Dr. Summers. Now please, tell me, how do you interface with it?"

"If you are Dr. Collins," Kate began, "recount and explain to me the scientific equations supporting the artificial gravitational field around a rotating superconductor. That should be easy enough for someone with your background."

"No problem, Dr. Summers." He walked over to her as if he were going to draw on a nearby whiteboard. Once he was beside her, he suddenly grabbed her arm with his left hand as he pulled a steak knife out of his pocket, which he then held at Kate's throat. "You Americans, you think you're so *very* clever," he said, no longer bothering to hide his thick Russian accent. "Now, seal the exits, or I will kill her here while you watch!"

Henry complied, walking over to a nearby wall where a flashing green button was mounted. He pressed the button, which then stopped flashing, remaining a solid green.

"Now, you will tell me how you were able to power Ignis, how you were able to connect it to your network, and lastly, how you interfaced with it. You will do this, or you will watch poor Dr. Summers here die a slow and painful death."

Nick watched him for a moment, while slowly edging closer and closer to the intruder.

"Please don't even try, Dr. Reynolds. I saw you with Dr. Summers here last night, and I know you don't want to watch your pretty girlfriend here bleed to death."

Nick was looking directly into the icy eyes of the imposter, looking for something, anything he could do to save Kate. Suddenly, he realized the horrible truth.

"Chervanko; you're Nikolai Chervanko."

"Very good, Dr. Reynolds. I'm quite impressed. I suppose you are the one I was told worked for Cyber Command?"

Nick said nothing.

"No matter. I must confess that I was quite puzzled, and extremely disappointed when I learned that you'd stopped Ares in its tracks."

"Ares?"

"Why, Ares is the name of the god of war in Greek mythology, Dr. Reynolds, I thought you would have known that."

"I know who Ares is."

"Of course you do. The Ares I was referring to, of course, was my Ares System; the advanced cyber warfare system that I used to launch the cyber attacks against the United States."

"The same one that murdered over a hundred thousand innocent men, women, and children?" Kate asked defiantly.

"Oohh, I see why you like her, Dr. Reynolds, she has lots of spirit. Not many women would be so brazen with a stone-cold killer like me holding a knife to her throat. Yes, Dr. Summers, *I* caused the meltdown in New York, which killed over one hundred thousand Americans. It was unfortunate, but it had to be done in order for me to complete my mission."

"What mission is that, your insane plan to create the perfect geopolitical climate for the rebirth of your beloved Soviet Empire, once the United States and China have destroyed one another? And who would lead this glorious new world order, Comrade Chervanko, you?"

"Why yes, Dr. Reynolds, you're quite correct. I suppose you've been talking with some of my country's pathetically weak leaders. Like the great phoenix, a new and glorious Soviet Empire will emerge from the ashes of the old, and I will lead the world on a path of prosperity and peace for everyone."

"The nuclear fallout from such a war would leave much of the world uninhabitable, not to mention the nuclear winter that would follow. Millions, perhaps billions of people would die. You're insane, Chervanko, you must be."

"You are a pathetic, weak, American, Dr. Reynolds. For anything great to be accomplished in life, there must be great sacrifice. But you do not understand this, nor would I ever expect you to. No matter. Now you will tell me what I want to know. How do I connect the Ignis device?" He looked at Nick, then at Henry Summers. Neither man said anything until he pressed the knife against Kate's neck and a small stream of blood began trickling down her neck.

"Please, Chervanko, don't do it. I don't know anything about the device; I'm not a scientist," Nick said truthfully.

"Exactly what is your area of expertise, Dr. Reynolds?"

"Computer security."

"Ah, then you *are* with Cyber Command. My congratulations to you then, Dr. Reynolds. Using this device to delay my plan was a stroke of genius, there's no way you could have stopped me otherwise. I said 'delay' because now I will use Ignis instead of the Ares system to accomplish my objective. Now, I am an impatient man, so tell me what I wish to know or I will kill her where she stands!"

Henry quickly stepped out in front of him. "No, please, don't harm her, Mr. Chervanko. I will tell you whatever you want to know."

"A father's love for his daughter, how touching. Please, continue Dr. Summers."

"Dad—you can't do it, you can't! Please, Dad, I don't want to die with the blood of so many people on my hands!" Tears now flowed freely down her cheeks as considered what Chervanko would do with Ignis. Henry ignored her plea, staying focused on Chervanko instead.

"We did not have to do anything to connect the device," he told Chervanko. "Once we placed cables close to the device it somehow extended its connectors to intertwine with the power and the fiber optic cables."

"And the interface?" Chervanko asked with anticipation. He saw Henry hesitate and held the blade closer to Kate's neck. "Doctor?"

"No! Stop! Okay, okay. It's sitting there, in that chair." He nodded toward the helmet sitting in the chair.

"What? That helmet, it is the interface? You've got to be kidding!"

Henry shook his head.

"That is the interface. Now please, let my daughter go."

"Oh, of course, Dr. Summers. After all, I have no need to kill her. But first, I want you to take some of that cabling over there on that spool, and kindly tie-up Dr. Reynolds here, then your daughter."

Henry nodded and walked over to a spool of Ethernet cabling sitting in the far corner of the lab. He went to work, cutting off enough cable to do as Chervanko instructed.

"Okay, Dr. Reynolds, please take a seat in that chair, so Dr. Summers can tie you up. Any sudden moves and the woman you love will die."

Nick walked over and reluctantly sat down in the chair. Henry began tying his hands.

"Tie his hands together, then his feet. Be sure to do a good job, Dr. Summers, I will know if you are not. After you're done with that, I want you to tie his hands *to* his feet. Make them all secure, Dr. Summers. I'd hate for Dr. Reynolds to get loose and do something rash. Who knows what might happen to your beautiful daughter in the ensuing struggle?"

Henry nodded toward Chervanko before facing Nick. "I'm so sorry, Nick, but I have no choice."

"I understand, Henry, and you're doing the right thing. He's a cold-blooded killer. From what I know of him, he would kill her without hesitation."

"Now, Dr. Reynolds, is that any way to describe a future head of state? But you're quite right, of course. I've had to kill many people over the course of my life."

"Like the hundred thousand people you murdered in New York?"

"Collateral damage, Dr. Reynolds, as I've already said. You work at Cyber Command, you understand what that means. I had to convince Americans that China was out to destroy the United States. It wasn't so hard to do, really. Both countries were so full of mistrust and fear already, that all they needed was a slight nudge to push them both over the edge. Only then could I force the hand of the United States government to attack the Chinese, triggering a nuclear war that would devastate both countries. The explosive animosity between your two countries was already there; I just lit the match, so to speak."

"So you planned to use fear to start a war," said Nick, as Henry continued tying him securely to the chair.

"Oh, yes, and it nearly worked, too. Fear and mistrust are powerful weapons, Dr. Reynolds, they should never be underestimated. They almost always lead to violence."

"I suppose you're right about that, Chervanko. The dictators in your precious Soviet Union used fear and mistrust very effectively for decades to keep populations under control, didn't they? They used them to force family members to betray one another to the KGB, just so they could watch as their loved ones were executed, or worse, sent off to the gulag."

Chervanko just looked at Nick and smiled. "How true!"

A few minutes later Nick was tied securely.

"Okay, Dr. Summers, now your daughter." Chervanko walked Kate over to a chair and sat her down. He kept the knife at her throat while her father tied her hands and her feet.

"Are you okay, Kate?" he asked her gently, while he wrapped the cable around her feet. She just nodded slightly in reply.

"I'm okay, Dad," she said bitterly, looking up at Chervanko, who just smiled at her. Within a few minutes, Kate was securely tied into the chair.

"Now then, Dr. Summers," began Chervanko, looking at Henry. "You said the helmet *is* the interface? How does it work?"

"You just place the helmet on your head, and you instantly enter into a virtual world. You will find yourself in a room with two exits, either back here, or to cyber space."

"How do I tell Ignis what to do?" Henry just shrugged.

"You just think about it, and it happens. Ignis can interpret your thoughts and translate them into action."

"Fantastic! I cannot wait to try it!" Chervanko picked up a role of duct tape sitting on a shelf in the corner of the lab, and pulled off two strips before pressing them over the mouths of Nick and Kate. He then grabbed another chair and some cable. "Okay Doctor, your turn. Sit here and I will tie you in; there's no need for any of you to die today."

Henry started moving toward Chervanko, then stopped.

"Why are you doing this?" he asked. "What do you want with Ignis? You are wanted all over the world; by the United States, by China...even your own government is looking for you. What are you hoping to accomplish?"

Chervanko smiled and slowly walked toward Henry, the only one of the three not already bound to a chair. Chervanko simply leaned back against a counter.

"What am I hoping to accomplish, Dr. Summers? The Ares system was designed for a variety of conventional cyber attacks, which, with the help of code installed inside a facility's network, had been largely successful. But from what you've told me about this Ignis device of yours, this *alien* technology, it's far beyond the defensive capability of any country on the planet."

"But you must know that getting the Ignis device out of here is next to impossible. Even I would not be allowed to take Ignis out of this facility without proper authorization."

"Don't you see, Dr. Summers? I don't have to take Ignis anywhere! You've already proven the device is capable of doing exactly what I need it to do without ever having to leave this facility. I'm going to interface with the computer, then I'm going to finish what I started, but on a much bigger scale. Once I'm inside, I can use Ignis to order the launches of each country's nuclear arsenal in just a matter of seconds. I can now do much more to ensure that each country is completely devastated and defenseless. When I'm done, the United States, China, and their allies will be nothing more than nuclear ash. Oh, don't worry, I don't want a nuclear winter any more than the next guy, it would be somewhat counter-productive. I'll use just enough nuclear warheads to get the job done; or perhaps I'll use the Neutron Bombs, or some even newer tech for taking each side out. I understand the United States has been experimenting with Rail Guns and various space-based weapons; oh, that would be fun! As per my original plan, the world will be in dire need of leadership. Once I am done here later today, I will return to my beloved Mother Russia, and I will once again consolidate power under the Communist Party banner…with *me* at its head, of course."

"Oh, of course," Summers echoed in reply, dumbfounded by what was about to happen. "Mr. Chervanko, I must appeal to your humanity, sir! Please don't launch those missiles! What of the hundreds of millions, perhaps even billions, of innocent people who would die as a consequence of your actions? They're not politicians, or soldiers, or spies! They're the working class, Mr. Chervanko; they wake up each morning, go to work, and raise their children. How will you be able to live with yourself, knowing what you've done?"

"Dr. Summers, I've been a spy for decades now. I've already done many terrible, awful things that I'm not very proud of. Believe me, however, when I say that I still sleep like a baby. Look, I don't like it very much either; I even find the mass genocide a bit distasteful. If it's what it takes, however, to usher in the peace and security of the new world order that I've always dreamed of, so be it."

"What is it that you're so afraid of, Mr. Chervanko?"

"What? I'm not afraid! What are you talking about, old man?" the spy asked him incredulously.

"You pretty much said it yourself, Mr. Chervanko. As human beings we don't trust those we don't understand, we fear those we don't trust, and we use violence against those whom we fear. You seem to be willing to commit unspeakable acts of violence, Mr. Chervanko. I just assumed that you must be terribly afraid of something or someone; perhaps it's the new government in Russia you fear, so you're planning to replace it? Maybe you're afraid of Russia's diminishing influence in world affairs, or your own loss of influence as you near the twilight of your life; is that what this is all about?"

"Thank you for the free psychoanalysis session, but I'm not afraid of any man, Dr. Summers, or any country. It is true that previous attempts to recreate the Soviet Empire have failed, but that's why I decided to try something different this time.

"Now, if you'll forgive me, I have an appointment to keep. None of you need to worry about the fallout, Dr. Summers. I won't have Ignis launch any missiles that will strike around here. After all, I have to get back home alive, don't I?"

Chervanko smiled, something Henry just did not understand.

"Please, for the love of God, man, don't do this, Mr. Chervanko!"

"Oh but I'm an old-guard Communist, Dr. Summers, we're atheists; we don't believe in God, remember?"

"But they'll kill you, surely you know that."

"Oh, I know they'll try, Dr. Summers. After the missiles have launched, however, they're going to have bigger fish to fry than to worry about me. If they do kill me, however, I will take comfort knowing that a number of my comrades in Russia are ready to step up to fill-in for me, if necessary. The Soviet Union will rise again, Dr. Summers, but this time the spread of her ideology and her control over the entire planet will be fully realized."

Henry shook his head, despondent as he slowly began walking toward the chair which Chervanko had sat before him. Henry looked over at Kate and Nick and saw that they were safe, at least for the moment. He struggled over what to do next, however. How could he allow Chervanko to interface with Ignis, just so he could turn around and kill a billion human beings? He looked around the immediate area where they were standing. Nick sat in a chair to his far left; to Nick's right sat Kate. The third chair, and Chervanko, were slightly off to his right. To his far right was a counter where there was a lamp, and a *phone*.

He looked at Chervanko before glancing back at the phone. He began slowly walking towards Chervanko, with the phone still in his peripheral vision. Chervanko, who had seen what Henry was up to, shook his head slightly as a warning. Henry ignored it however, and leapt for the phone. He'd barely lifted it from the hook, preparing to press eight for security, when Chervanko was suddenly upon him, burying the knife into Henry's chest. The elderly Summers collapsed on the floor while Kate and Nick looked on, struggling violently against their bonds.

Chervanko watched them for a moment until he was confident their bonds were sufficient to hold them. He then walked over to the door to the lab and made sure it was securely locked before damaging the badge entry system and placing a chair against the door and the doorknob. Finally satisfied he would be uninterrupted long enough to achieve his objective, he walked over to the chair next to where Ignis sat on the table. After checking to ensure Nick and Kate were still securely tied to their chairs, and seeing Henry lying on the floor dying, he placed the helmet on his head, ignoring Kate's muffled screams.

Chapter 42

When he opened his eyes it was just as Summers had described it. He found himself in a room filled with blinding white light. To his left he saw a door marked "Exit," and to the right he saw a door marked "Out." His initial disorientation lasted for thirty seconds, before finally starting to wane. He wasted no time, immediately walking towards the "Out" sign.

Chervanko had already decided to use Ignis to hack into the Chinese system first. He would do some searching to discover what missiles the Chinese had at their disposal before triggering a launch against the United States. Next, before initiating a launch by the Chinese, he would then hack into the American system. Once he had full access into the launch systems of both countries, he would initiate a simultaneous launch. This should ensure that maximum damage was inflicted on both sides. He planned to use the minimum amount of nukes necessary to accomplish his objective, to completely destabilize the two governments. After initiating the launches, he would then seek out Air Force One and its Chinese equivalent, and destroy them both, followed by the White House and the Capital Building in Washington, DC. Lastly, he would target the Zhongnanhai complex, in Beijing, the home of the Chinese Communist Party.

Chervanko felt nearly as giddy as a schoolboy. His decades of waiting and planning were about to pay off. He'd ended up taking a slight detour in the execution of his planning, but the results would be even more impressive, and more efficient at achieving his objective, than he ever could have hoped for. He reached out for the door, and passed under the sign.

He immediately found himself surrounded by complete darkness. It was unlike anything he'd ever experienced before, and was even more

255

disorienting than the white room had been. Instead of it just being dark, however, there was a complete absence of light. It felt cold and *unearthly* at first. Something about his being there just didn't feel right, and for the first time he felt something he hadn't felt in a very long time; *fear*.

When the disorientation began to fade, he suddenly realized he had a pervasive feeling that he was not alone. He kept peering into the darkness, hoping to see something, anything. He tried concentrating on the launch systems in the United States and China, hoping that something would appear, but nothing happened. There was only the pervasive feeling that someone, or something, was there with him. The strange, uncomfortable sensation continued to intensify to the point that he could no longer ignore it.

"Is someone there? Who are you and how did you get here?" Chervanko suddenly became aware that there was someone behind him. When he turned to see who or what it was, he saw something for which all of his KGB training had never prepared him, and he screamed.

* * * *

Nick kept working at his bonds, trying to get free. He looked down at where Henry lay on the floor, still bleeding from his wound. His movements were becoming much weaker and more infrequent, and Nick knew that if Henry didn't receive help soon, he would die. Nick felt his bonds starting to give a little, and he began to hope. He then looked over at Kate, who was struggling so much to get free that her wrists began to bleed. A small stream of blood was flowing down her arm, causing a pool of blood to form on the floor. Blood still trickled lightly down her neck from the knife cut as well, though the trickle was insignificant when compared to the tears that continually streamed down her face, as they had since Chervanko had stabbed her father. She just sat there staring at her father as she struggled, almost as if waiting for him to stand up.

Nick continued struggling against his bonds, feeling them loosen even more. He would be free within several minutes, but would it be soon enough? Questions about Chervanko flooded his mind as he struggled to get free. Should they kill Chervanko while he was still interfaced with Ignis? How long would it take him to launch both countries' missiles? When they removed the helmet from his head, would it instantly sever the connection? Would Ignis execute the commands to fire the missiles even after Chervanko was disconnected? It dawned on Nick that they still knew so little about Ignis and how it operated. He was thinking about all of this when he suddenly realized he wasn't making progress quickly enough in getting free from the cabling Chervanko had used to tie them up.

A sudden movement from in front of them caught the attention of both Nick and Kate. Henry had moved a little, though he was still bleeding profusely from the injury. The devoted father glanced up to find Kate and Nick still tied to their chairs, and he saw that Chervanko now had the neural interface helmet on. Henry mustered what strength he could and pushed himself up off of the floor, and moments later, stood wobbly on two feet. The knife Chervanko had used to stab him lay on the table next to the Ignis device. Henry stumbled to the table and picked it up. He kept one hand on the wound, trying to slow the bleeding, and he used the other to carry the knife and for steadying himself. He managed a few more steps to Nick's chair. Henry went to work cutting Nick's feet and then his hands free. Nick reached up immediately and removed the tape from his mouth.

"Henry, just lay down on the floor. I'll help Kate!" Nick helped the elder Summers to the floor before rushing over to cut Kate's bonds, all while keeping an eye on Chervanko's motionless form, which was still seated, and apparently oblivious to everything going on around him. Nick was surprised to see his facial muscles twitching and writhing; he'd not seen anything like it on Kate when she'd been interfaced with Ignis.

The moment Kate was free she removed the tape from her mouth and turned to her father, who lay on the floor beside her, exhausted from the effort he'd expended. After removing her lab coat she raised his head up slightly and placed it underneath, so he could use the coat as a pillow.

Nick reached the phone and immediately began dialing.

"Security," came the response.

"This is Nick Reynolds. We're here in Lab S-5. We need lots of security in here immediately. Be aware that you'll need to manually override the door's security. We've had a major security breach, and there's been a stabbing. We need a medical team here A.S.A.P; this is a Priority 1."

"Understood, sir. Wait one moment." Nick heard some brief conversation and scuffling before the man returned moments later. "On the way, sir. ETA is thirty-seconds."

"Thank you." Nick looked up to find Chervanko still immobile under the helmet and Henry still lying on the floor. Kate kept looking up at him before looking back at her father.

Nick debated what to do next; whether he should pull the helmet and hopefully break Chervanko's connection with Ignis, or attend to Kate and Henry while giving security time to arrive and surround Chervanko. Breaking the connection before security arrived might give Chervanko a chance to escape, this time with Ignis, but Nick decided to risk it...he couldn't wait until security arrived. He snatched the helmet off of Chervanko's head, and ran towards Henry and Kate. When he looked back, Chervanko still hadn't moved. Nick hurried over to Kate and Henry and knelt beside them, though he continued glancing back at Chervanko to watch for movement. He could see that Henry was nearly unconscious again from loss of blood.

"Henry, help will be here any second, you've got to hang in there."

Henry looked up at each of them and shook his head.

"No, Nick, I think my time here is up. I've had a great life, son; I've got no complaints." He looked over at Kate. "You know sweetheart, your mother and I had you late in life, do you know why?"

She smiled and shook her head at her father as her tears grew larger. "No, Daddy, I don't."

He smiled and his eyes suddenly sparkled. "Because we were scared honey, scared of the responsibility for bringing another life into such a crazy and dangerous world." He paused for a moment to catch his breath. "But when you were born Kate, any doubts or fears we'd ever had melted away into nothingness. You were and always have been such a wonderful daughter, and such a beautiful girl...my girl. I'm so proud of you, Kate, so very proud!"

He coughed, and his eyes began to blink rapidly as time suddenly seemed to slow down. Security burst into the room with weapons locked and loaded, flocked by a team of medics, and headed in their direction.

Kate looked down at her father, and smiled back. "And I have been so very proud of you as well, Dad. I never could have asked for a better father, or mother, than what I had."

"I have to go to God now, Kate," he said weakly, "and to your mother."

Kate buried her face in her hands for several moments before looking back at him and smiling through her tears.

"Please tell them both I said hello, Daddy," she told him, sobbing heavily now.

Henry looked over at Nick. "Take good care of her, son, she's worth it."

Nick looked over at Kate. "I know she is, Henry, and I will, I promise."

Henry gasped for air several more times, until at last he stopped breathing altogether. Kate reached down and pulled his lifeless body up to her, weeping bitterly. Nick placed his arm around Kate for several moments before turning back to the chair where Chervanko was seated, and to the security team. The medics arrived and gently moved Kate to one side so they could examine her father, who was already gone. With Henry gone, Nick's attention turned back to the danger at hand.

"Security, surround that man immediately!"

The guards, who had been standing between Chervanko and Nick, stepped aside. Nick could now see Chervanko clearly, and wondered why he hadn't moved. He sat in the chair, motionless, expressionless, staring off into space. The team of Air Force Combat Controllers immediately pointed their M-4s toward Chervanko's head, but he didn't flinch, or even blink. They repeatedly asked questions and barked out orders, even striking Chervanko with the butt of their rifles, assuming he was being uncooperative. They finally threw him to the floor where he landed with a thud, and tied his hands tightly together. As he lay on the floor on his stomach, Nick caught a glimpse of Chervanko's eyes. Peering into the eyes of the master spy, Nick Reynolds found nothing; his entire form now seemed a lifeless husk. Nikolai Chervanko's mind was gone.

Chapter 43

It had been pouring rain at the cemetery of Our Savior's Church in Las Vegas. Nick stood next to Kate holding a large golf umbrella. Despite the weather, it had been a beautiful funeral service. The church's pastor was finishing the sermon.

"Now a reading from Psalm 23.

"The LORD is my shepherd; I shall not want.

He maketh me to lie down in green pastures:

He leadeth me beside the still waters.

He restoreth my soul: He leadeth me in the paths of righteousness for His name's sake.

Yea, though I walk through the valley of the shadow of death, I will fear no evil: for Thou art with me.

Thy rod and Thy staff they comfort me.

Thou preparest a table before me in the presence of mine enemies:

Thou anointest my head with oil; my cup runneth over.

Surely goodness and mercy shall follow me all the days of my life: and I will dwell in the house of the Lord forever.

"Rest in peace with the Lord you loved so much, Henry Summers, my dear friend. Now, let us finish with a benediction.

"The Lord bless you, and keep you:

The Lord make his face shine upon you, and be gracious to you:

The Lord lift up his countenance upon you, and give you peace."

Kate stood at the gravesite beside Nick as friends, family, and acquaintances stopped by to pay their respects. Among them was General George Caprella. He came by and presented the flag to her personally.

"Kate, I want you to know how deeply I feel your loss. Henry was not only a great scientist, he was also an outstanding man, and one of my dearest friends. I hope you will call on me if you ever need to talk; I'm a very good listener."

Kate smiled politely. "Thank you, General," she answered. "I will."

"By the way, I had a chance to debrief with Nick while you were busy making arrangements. I'm sure he would be happy to bring you up to date on everything that's been happening whenever you're ready, if that's okay with you."

"Of course, General," she answered.

Caprella simply nodded, stared down at the ground for a moment with a grimace, and continued down the line.

By the time the last man came through, she was exhausted and ready to go home. The man was average height, but he carried himself in a way that made him appear much taller.

"You are Dr. Kate Summers?" he asked in a thick Russian accent.

"Yes, I am," she answered awkwardly.

"My most sincere condolences to you then, Dr. Summers. I'm afraid this all could have been avoided, had I been able to stop it earlier. I am truly very sorry. I hope that you will find it in your heart one day to forgive me." He now had Kate and Nick's full attention.

"I'm sorry, I didn't catch your name; what is it again?" Nick asked, both surprised and momentarily fearful. The man just smiled.

"Because I didn't give it, Doctor Reynolds. I must apologize, old habits die hard. My name is Yuri Andropov, and I am the Director of the FSB, Russia's 'FBI' if you will. We were very close to capturing the madman Chervanko, but alas, he slipped through our fingers twice. I called your General Caprella to warn him about Chervanko, but I'm afraid it was too late. I am truly sorry that your father was among the many people murdered by my countryman. I hope you will not have the same disdain for all Russians as what you surely must have for that *creature*." The loathing he held for Chervanko was clearly evident in his voice and words.

"I understand, Mr. Andropov, and I'm very grateful that you flew all this way just to pay your respects to my father."

"I understand he was a great man, and a brilliant scientist, Dr. Summers."

"Thank you, Mr. Andropov; he was, on both counts."

Andropov turned to leave, when Kate grabbed his arm.

"Will you be taking *him* back with you Mr. Andropov?" she asked, with a hint of hatred for the man who'd murdered her father in cold blood.

"I regret to say that there doesn't appear to be very much of the man left. It seems that his mind is...how do I say it...*gone?* I had hoped to question him before his public and very long imprisonment, so that I might arrest all of his associates. In addition to the genocide he had planned, he also murdered several of my men back in Russia, my friends. Unfortunately, my government abolished the death penalty some time ago. As to whether I will take him back with me, that is something I will be discussing with General Caprella shortly, among other things.

"By the way, Dr. Summers, I was curious whether you could tell me what happened to the man's mind?" he asked, watching her expressions for truthfulness.

"I can honestly say, Director Andropov, that I have no idea what happened to him. After what he did to my father, however, I can also say that it couldn't have happened to a nicer guy."

Andropov smiled, nodded, and began walking toward his car.

* * * *

Kate sat in the car next to Nick, saying nothing for the first few minutes upon leaving the cemetery. She felt a great emptiness in her heart with the loss of her father, despite knowing that her father had led a full life. She thought back to the words of the minister during the sermon, and at the grave site. She had not felt such grief for as long as she could remember.

"Nick, do you believe in an afterlife, or in God?" she asked suddenly, looking outside the window at the puddles left behind by the sudden rain. Caught off-guard by the question, he paused to consider his own thoughts on the matter, while trying to be sensitive to what she was going through.

"Yeah, I do, Kate, I think there has to be an afterlife; the law of the conservation of energy holds that energy cannot be created or destroyed, it just changes form. I think maybe that's what happens when we die.

"I do believe in God as well, since you asked. The universe is such a wonderful, mysterious place, with everything working together so perfectly, that I concluded long ago that it must have been designed by *someone*. I just can't imagine that everything is the universe is the way it is by pure chance. I think it's kind of like finding a wristwatch, and trying to decide whether it just came together on its own or whether someone designed it. That's just my opinion though. How about you, Kate?"

"Yes. No. I guess I'm not sure, Nick. Like you, my dad always said that there is simply too much order in the universe for it to be explained by the theory of evolution. He'd once been agnostic, until he'd been a scientist for ten or fifteen years." Kate chuckled for a moment. "I guess you could say that he eventually found God through science."

Fifteen minutes later, they pulled into the gated apartment complex where they both stayed, along with others who worked at Groom Lake. As an extra security precaution, the government now owned the entire complex, and unlike other gated apartment communities, these guards carried M-4s.

Their apartments were next door, so they walked together to the top of the stairs.

"Would you like to come over, Nick?" she asked, once they'd reached their apartment doors. "I really don't want to be alone tonight, and I'd like to talk about what happened, if it's alright with you."

"Sure, Kate, of course." The two walked inside her apartment.

"Would you like something to drink?" she asked Nick, while walking towards the kitchen.

"Sure, whatever you want to fix; thanks, Kate." Kate fumbled around the kitchen before joining Nick in the living room.

"What do you think happened in there, Nick? Chervanko's efforts at hacking into the military computers here and in China, to launch missiles using Ignis, he must have failed somehow, right? I haven't heard any air raid sirens, seen any bright flashes in the sky, and my hair hasn't started falling out—yet," she said with a slight smile. Nick smiled back, with a growing confidence that she was going to be okay.

"Well, I don't know exactly. I checked with the folks at Cyber Command and there hasn't been any evidence of any cyber attacks or penetrations at N.O.R.A.D. or any other military installations. General Caprella checked with the Chinese, and from what little they've said, there were no new cyber attacks that had anything to do with missile launch capability."

"So it sounds like, for some reason, Chervanko never used Ignis to initiate the launches. Now isn't that odd, after everything he went through to get to Ignis?"

"Maybe Ignis refused to do it, Kate."

"What? Ignis is just a computer, Nick…a very powerful computer, but still just a computer."

"Remember what we were saying after the S.E.T.I. systems were compromised, and the radio signals they received and transmitted?"

Just then the phone rang, and Kate walked over to answer it.

"Hello?"

"I would like to speak with Nick Reynolds, please," came the voice on the other end. She made a strange, peculiar face, soon after answering.

"Um, Nick, it's for you." She handed Nick the phone, mouthing the words, "Who could it be?"

"Hello?" Nick asked, shrugging his shoulders at Kate.

"Nick Reynolds, it is almost time for me to leave. Would you please return to the lab at S-4 as soon as possible? You must have questions, and the time I have left to answer them grows short."

"Wait a minute, who is this?"

"I believe you call me, 'Ignis.'"

Jeff W. Horton

Chapter 44

"I'm telling you, Kate, I *wasn't* imagining things." He looked out of the window of Kate's apartment and up at the gray sky. The rain had finally stopped. They could catch the afternoon flight back to Groom Lake if they left soon.

"I never said that I thought you were imagining things, Nick. But a phone call from Ignis, really?" Nick could tell she was doing all she could not to laugh.

"Come on, Kate. We have no idea what Ignis is capable of."

"So what are you going to do when we get back to the lab, Nick? Are you going to call it and have a conversation with it over the telephone? Do we just call the number in the lab?" Kate burst out laughing.

"Go ahead and have your fun, Kate. Meanwhile, I'll start making a list of the questions I have for Ignis." He cast an angry look at Kate and she stopped laughing. She could tell he was serious.

"Oh, I'm sorry, Nick. Look, you're right. Ignis has already demonstrated a tremendous technological capability and a capacity to reason that we can only guess at. With the level of artificial intelligence it possesses, hacking into a database with our phone numbers would be child's play, as would accessing a voice synthesizer."

"Thank you. Look, I agree it's incredible, but like you've said, we've probably only scratched the surface of what Ignis is capable of doing. The question is, why did it wait until now to try and establish contact with us? It said its time to answer my questions was growing short; could that be the reason? Do you suppose its friends are here?"

"Well, it certainly appears that whatever sent the last signal to the Allen Telescope Array must have been close by. It makes sense that his ride home might already be here. Dad always thought someone might

267

come back one day for the ship, and for Ignis. He told me recently that he was starting to suspect that Ignis had a level of intelligence that rivals sentient life...maybe he was right." Kate stopped talking and looked at Nick, just before she began to tear up. Nick took her in his arms and held her tight.

"Thinking about your Dad again?" She nodded.

"How can I go back to work in the lab without him, Nick?" She laid her head on his shoulder as the tears continued to flow. Nick searched for the words that would soothe and comfort her, but they never came. Instead of saying anything, he just took her hand and kissed it gently on the back. She looked up at Nick for a moment, placing her hand behind his head, and kissed him for the longest time before embracing him.

"Nick," she began softly, "you said General Caprella gave you the choice of going back to Cyber Command to continue leading Operation Counterpunch, or to stay here at Groom Lake indefinitely to help me with the Prometheus project?"

"Yeah, that's right," Nick answered. Kate gently pushed him back so she could look at him.

"What did you decide?" she asked apprehensively. Nick could see she was worried.

"Well, I guess I haven't really had much time to think about it. What do *you* think I should do?"

Kate's fiery eyes widened. "I'm in love with you, stupid! What do you *think* I want you to do?" She turned away from him and stared out the window.

"You're in love with me? Kate, I thought I was the only one who...well, you never said anything."

"Why should I have to, Nick?! Hasn't it been obvious how I feel about you?"

"Well, yes...I mean no, not really."

"Men!" She sat down on the sofa and stared out the window, saying nothing else. Nick thought about what she'd said, and about how tired she looked. He studied the delicate features on her face for some time, even after she drifted off to sleep. He decided Ignis would have to wait until the morning.

* * * *

The flight back to Groom Lake was less crowded, uneventful, and routine. With the immediate threat of another World War behind them, everyone was able to get back to their routines. For the Prometheus group, that meant the study of the alien technology of course, along with the reverse-engineering efforts that were so important to the United States, and to humanity. Nick, for one, was happy to see things quiet down for a while. By the time the Janet flight landed, he was ready to get to the lab, and to converse with Ignis.

"No, Nick, you can't do it...it's too dangerous!" Her eyes were piercing and determined.

"Don't worry, Kate, I've done it before, remember?" He walked over to the table where Ignis still sat, and picked up the helmet.

"Oh, that's right. You mean the last time, when you thought you were in there for thirty minutes when you'd actually been in there for over two days!"

"Come on, Kate, don't do this!"

"You listen to me, Nick Reynolds. Have you already forgotten what happened to Chervanko? His mind is *gone*, Nick; do you want that to happen to you? Like we both said, we just don't know enough about this device. Your brain could come out scrambled like his!" Nick set the helmet down and walked over to her.

"Kate, there's something I need to tell you. You told me in your apartment that you're in love with me. Well, I've been in love with you from the very first moment I laid eyes on you. I promise that I'll come back to you no matter what happens; you've got to trust me here, please!"

"I do trust *you*, Nick, it's Ignis I don't trust."

"Kate, I can't tell you how I know this, but Ignis has no intentions of harming us. He invited me, remember? We need to learn to not be afraid of everything, Kate. It's our fear of one another that leads to violence and war. Somehow, I know deep down inside my gut that if I don't interface with Ignis this one last time, the whole world's going to regret it."

"But—"

Nick put his index finger on her lips to silence her, then replaced his finger with his lips as he kissed her passionately for several minutes.

"I love you, Kate" he said, when they finished.

"I love you too, Nick; please, come back to me."

"I will, I promise."

Nick walked over to the chair and sat down. He took several deep breaths, and after Kate kissed and embraced him once more, he placed the helmet on his head.

Nick found himself back in the white room, with the same doors on either side. As before, Nick proceeded to the one marked, "OUT", and after going inside everything went black. He looked around and gradually found that he was now in a large room, with only a single light illuminating around a hundred feet or so of floor space. He heard a set of footsteps approaching, distant at first but drawing closer with each step. A few moments later a figure emerged from the darkness. Nick stood speechless, as the form of Dr. Henry Summers walked over and stood before him.

Chapter 45

The man before Nick *was* Henry Summers, down to the most minute details. The two stood for several moments staring at one another, neither of them saying anything. Eventually the form of Henry Summers spoke.

"Hello, Nick Reynolds."

Nick just stared back at him. "Ignis? Why did you choose this form? Surely you must know Henry Summers is dead."

"Yes, I am aware that he is dead," Ignis replied, looking down as he said so. "And I very much regret that *I* was the ultimate cause of his demise, Nick Reynolds. I chose this form to honor him, and because I thought you would find it more comfortable conversing with me this way." Ignis paused for a moment as if for effect. "I touched his mind, Nick Reynolds. He was a good...man. I am very sorry for your loss."

"That's very considerate of you, Ignis, thank you."

Ignis nodded. "You must have questions, Nick. What can I answer for you?"

Wow. It has duplicated Henry's most subtle mannerisms. I'm glad I'm the one in here and not Kate.

"Who and what are you exactly? Are you a computer, or a sentient life form?"

"You would be unable to pronounce my name, so Ignis will suffice. In a sense, I guess I am what you might call a computer, but I'm actually quite a bit more than that. I'm also a sentient, biological life form as well. My people—we are called the Entelli by some—often provide services to other races in a variety of functions, almost always in a symbiotic relationship. We sometimes serve as navigational computers, sometimes as communications interfaces, universal translators between species, etc. My interaction with the ship, for example, was a symbiotic one. The ship served as a source of power which nourished me, kept me alive, but it also provided a way for me to interact with other species. Most of the advanced races prefer working with an Entelli over using non-biological computers in their spacecraft."

"Do all Entelli share in such a symbiotic relationship with other species?"

"No, not all. Some of my people prefer their independence, and their mobility, which they achieve via interaction through a wide variety of cybernetic vehicles that we interface with; some have their own ships, others have synthetic bodies, the variety is nearly endless. Many are connected to a global neural network on our home world of Ente. We are a very social species, Nick Reynolds, so we very much prefer interaction with our own kind, or with other sentient life forms, over solitude. Many Entelli, like me, enjoy traveling the stars."

"How did you end up on Earth to begin with?"

"We were passing through this sector of space when we detected nuclear explosions on your world, so we came here to investigate. Whenever any sentient species first splits the atom, the interstellar races of the galaxy will often investigate, and then share what they find with the other races. It indicates that a level of civilization and a progression of technological prowess has been reached which, if the species survives long enough, will eventually lead to interstellar space travel and therefore, eventual interaction with the other races.

"Did your ship crash?"

"Yes. Our two ships were caught in a particularly strong electrical storm, something we normally try to avoid. The captain took a chance with the storm, and he paid a high price for his recklessness. A lightning strike during the storm destroyed our power grid and our communications, and interfered with the electro-magnetic system the ship used to counteract the force of gravity. Soon afterwards we collided with the other, smaller ship, which I recently learned was completely destroyed. Both ships crashed outside of a small town called Corona in the state of New Mexico. It is the area best known to humans as Roswell."

"Why didn't you make contact with humanity after the ship crashed?"

"The power and communication systems were both damaged during the accident. When my power levels dropped low enough, I entered a state that you might refer to as suspended animation, until I awoke to find myself here."

"We've interfaced with you several times before now, Ignis. Why didn't you make yourself known to us earlier?"

"My systems don't all come online at the same time. At first, only my lower-level systems were activated. Once my higher-functioning systems *did* come online, I decided it would be wise not to make myself known right away, since I had no idea at first where I was or who you were. Thankfully the neural interface was compatible with your species, so I was able to interact with you, as well as connect to your 'Internet.' I wanted to learn more about you and your kind before making myself known to you, but I was hesitant to do a deep scan on any of you, that is until—"

"Until the last time *I* interfaced with you," Nick answered for him. Ignis nodded. "So that's why I was in here for such a long time."

"Among other reasons, yes. Your species is different than any others I have interfaced with before, but still compatible."

"And if we hadn't been?"

"The interface simply would not have worked," Ignis answered plainly. "The fact that it did work, however, bodes well for your species, Nick Reynolds. Your race has potential."

Nick hesitated to ask another, more specific question that crossed his mind, because he wasn't sure whether he wanted to know the answer. Ignis picked upon it.

"You have a question but you hesitate to ask it?" Ignis asked him..

"Yes. What happened to the man we refer to as Nikolai Chervanko? He was interfaced with you a few days ago, but he came out *different* than the rest of us; he was damaged."

"Your premise is incorrect, Nick Reynolds. The human Nikolai Chervanko was already damaged when he interfaced with me. He was the epitome of your race's greatest weakness; senseless violence. It is the primary reason your species has not yet been approached more openly by the other races."

"What do you mean?" Nick asked, his curiosity now piqued.

"Like most uncivilized life forms in the universe, what you do not understand you automatically fear, and that fear often leads to violence."

"Is this not the way of the universe?" asked Nick.

"Most sentient life forms tend to learn this lesson earlier; that they must first try to understand, then to trust, and finally resolve their differences peacefully, in a manner that is fair to all. This eliminates the mistrust and fear of one another, so violence is very rarely necessary, and even then only as a last resort."

"You never really said what happened to Chervanko."

"You might say that I showed him the error of his ways. I opened his eyes, helped him to understand, and to feel, the impact his actions have had on his many human victims and their families."

"What do you mean?"

"Nikolai Chervanko lacked empathy, what you might call 'compassion,' the ability to value life, and to relate to and understand the suffering in others. I helped him to feel, and to understand, the suffering so many human beings had endured as a result of his vicious attacks, and the tremendous suffering that billions of human beings would have endured had his plan of genocide succeeded: great pain, agony, suffering, loneliness, despair, and death. It was the first time he had truly felt anything for others.

"The man, Nikolai Chervanko, wanted to bring about tremendous devastation on your world, Nick Reynolds. He was not like you, or Kate Summers, or Henry Summers. He was going to launch your world's most powerful nuclear weapons to murder billions of sentient human beings, just to satisfy his own unfulfilled ambition. I could not allow myself to be used in such a manner. It is against everything I value and believe. When he finally felt and understood the tremendous pain and suffering he had inflicted on so many; well, somewhere along the way his mind seems to have snapped, and our connection was broken."

"You saved our world by not helping him, Ignis, and the lives of billions of people. On behalf of humanity, I'd like to offer you our most sincere thanks."

"It is what any civilized, sentient being would have done, Nick Reynolds."

"You mentioned beliefs earlier, Ignis; what is it that you believe in?"

"Our beliefs are not so different than yours, Nick Reynolds. You have things which you believe in, do you not? You have a moral code of sorts, a higher being or god, whom you believe in?"

"You know about God?" he asked, genuinely surprised.

"Of course. Surely you did not think yours was the only sentient species in the universe to interact with him, and to see his handiwork?

"And life after death?"

"Oh yes. Many of us believe that when we die our energy, our life-force, continues on, though in a different form. We believe it goes back to the Supreme Being, the one who gave it to us in the first place. Again, much as it is on your world, all of my people do believe the same things. You will find that individuals and races often have different belief systems, and some don't believe at all."

"Our people have long debated the topic of intelligent life in the universe, Ignis. Now that we know you exist, we would very much like to interact with other benign, sentient species like yours. We would like to exchange ideas, wisdom, and knowledge. I'm not sure what we can offer you in terms of technology, however, since yours is so much more advanced, but perhaps you'd be willing to share your technology with us anyway?

"You saved our world with it, Ignis. You stopped Chervanko's attacks against our infrastructure, and his plan to murder millions indirectly with his Ares system, then you stopped him from launching nuclear missiles. If we had access to technology like yours, there are so many wonderful things we could accomplish here!"

"Yes, Nick Reynolds, that is true. Unfortunately, however, you would also be tempted to use that same technology to destroy yourselves, or worse yet, to destroy other, more peaceful species. We must proceed carefully, Nick. The period in a civilization's history when first contact is made and a species first learns of other sentient life in the universe, it's a very delicate time. I'm certain that at some point, however, perhaps very soon, one of the interstellar races, perhaps my own, will make an official first contact with your world, Nick. But in the meantime, your people *must* learn to overcome your primal fear of what you do not understand, because believe me, there is much in the universe that you will not understand for some time."

"I'm curious about where you're from, Ignis. Can you show me an image of what your home world looks like?"

"Certainly." Suddenly Nick found himself surrounded by numerous large, magnificent cities, filled with strange beings and vehicles of various sizes and shapes. Two suns and three moons, one of them with a ring system, were visible in the sky. It was an awe-inspiring, and beautiful sight. Then, just as suddenly as the image had appeared, it vanished, leaving Nick alone with Ignis.

"What happened?"

"They are here for me, Nick. It is time for me to leave your world and to return home, back to where I belong."

"I don't know how to ever thank you for everything you've done for us, Ignis. We will be forever in your debt."

"You are a good man, Nick Reynolds, for a human being," he said, smiling for the first time. "And you are very welcome. I expect good things for humanity going forward, Nick; perhaps you will have a role in that."

"Thank you, Ignis. You are a good man…er, Entelli, as well."

Ignis/Henry smiled again.

"Will we ever see you again, Ignis?" Nick asked as he began walking towards the exit.

"It is possible, Nick, perhaps even *likely,* that we will meet again. I 'left' something for you during the two days when we were interfaced."

"What are you talking about, Ignis?" Nick asked.

"You must leave now, Nick, they're here and I must go. Don't worry, you will understand more when the proper time comes, and when you are ready. Please tell Kate Summers that I'm very sorry for the loss of her father, and that both she and her father give me great hope for the future of your species, as do you."

"Thank you, Ignis, for everything, and goodbye for now." Nick shook hands with Ignis, before turning and walking towards the door.

"Goodbye, Nick Reynolds. Perhaps I *will* see you again," he said, as Nick passed through the door and into the white room.

Nick then moved quickly to the "EXIT" door, just before waking in the lab.

Chapter 46

"Nick, wake-up! They're here! Nick, wake up!" Kate was frantically yelling at him when he opened his eyes. He quickly took off the helmet, stood up, and backed away from Ignis.

"Hi, Kate!" Nick said to her, before pulling her close, embracing and kissing her once more. Kate took a step back and smacked him on the arm.

"Don't you ever scare me like that again, Nick Reynolds! I had no idea whether you were going to come out of it in time, or whether you'd end up going back with Ignis!"

Nick suddenly became aware that the building all around him was shaking.

"What's going on?" he asked. Kate walked over to the window and pointed up.

"Just take a look. It looks like Ignis' friends from out of town have come to take him back home after sixty-five years," she said, smiling, happy to have Nick back. She jumped back into his arms once more before standing next to him with her arm around his waist, alternately looking out the window and back at Ignis.

"Wow," was all Nick said, as he watched the huge alien spacecraft stop when it arrived over their location at S-4. It was beautiful, a circular, saucer-shaped craft. It had considerably more detail than anything he'd ever seen before. There were numerous, square shaped portals all around the craft, and there was a center ring underneath, which rotated in the opposite direction from the larger outer ring. The immense craft from another world filled the sky above them.

"Okay, so I wonder what happens next?" asked Kate. "Will they send a ship down to collect Ignis?" Nick shook his head.

"I don't think so," he answered. "Somehow, I don't think they'll need to." They were watching Ignis when suddenly a bright blue light materialized all around the lab table. The light grew brighter and brighter until a moment later, a brilliant white light appeared in the midst of the blue one. When both lights suddenly disappeared, the Ignis device had disappeared. Moments later, the rattling stopped. When they looked out the window, they found that the ship had already vanished.

"Wow, isn't that something! I guess you don't see that every day," Nick said, smiling at Kate. The two continued looking out the window for a moment, as if the ship, and Ignis, were suddenly going to return. All they could see now, however, was the orange and blue western sky, just as the sun was preparing to set. They walked over to some chairs in the lab next to the table.

"What happened in there, Nick?" Kate asked. "Did you actually talk with Ignis?"

"Yeah, I did," he said, laughing. "Kate! It was incredible!" Nick looked at Kate and just smiled. It earned him another slap on the arm.

"Stop that! Now tell me everything!"

"Okay...okay...take it easy. He wanted me to let you how sorry he was about your father, and that he wanted for you to know that people like you, and your father, give him great hope for the human race. He said that we must learn to overcome our fear and mistrust of others and the unknown, and that once that happens, well, we might be ready to join them."

"You mean...out there?" she asked, pointing to the sky.

"Yeah!" Nick said, picking up Kate and twirling her around the lab. He said nothing about what Ignis had said about "leaving" him something.

"It's too bad we had to lose the technology, and Ignis as well," lamented Kate. "What an incredible piece of technology! It may be centuries, or longer, before we have anything even remotely like it. Why aren't they willing to share it with us?"

Nick walked back over to the window and looked out, staring in wonder as if the ship were still hovering there.

"They might, Kate, one day," he said, hoping that it was true. "But hey, Ignis helped us save the world, and the bad guy is locked away for the rest of his life, right? Who knows what tomorrow will bring? Maybe we'll even invent a ship like theirs one day."

Kate's eyes suddenly opened wide.

"Nick, the ship! Do you know whether they were going to take the ship as well? Maybe it's still here!"

"No, I don't know, Ignis never said. Want to go and find out?"

"Absolutely!"

The pair ran down the hallway and took the elevator down to the hangar floor. Their hearts started to sink at the thought of losing Ignis *and* the ship. The door opened and each of them let out a collective sigh of relief upon seeing that the was craft still there.

"Wow—they actually left it here! I wonder why?" Nick asked absentmindedly. "Who would have thought it?"

They walked up to the ship and began looking it over carefully. Nick studied the symbols which covered the outside of the ship. Satisfied everything looked okay on the outside, they walked inside. Nick had only been in the ship the one time, when they'd shown it to Chervanko, so he'd not had a chance to examine it closely. He noticed that the inside of the craft seemed to be covered in symbols just like the outside had been. There was something different about the craft this time though...something different. He looked up at Kate, who he found smiling back at him.

"Notice anything different?" she asked him. He looked around and noticed that he could suddenly see much better; but why?

"The lights, they're the lights of the ship! You found a way to power the ship? Kate, that's fantastic!"

"I know! I was going to tell you, but everything...with Dad...I guess I forgot."

Nick ran over to her and held her close.

"Do you know what this means, Kate?" His smile and enthusiasm were contagious.

"No, I guess I don't; what?"

"I guess Ignis meant what he said. They're letting us keep the ship, Kate, so we can learn more about it, and one day build our own!"

"Nick, we have power, but we still aren't that much farther along. We still don't understand what most of the things do. No one's ever been able to decipher the writing, the language, and with Ignis gone...." Her face saddened, expecting Nick's to do so as well. "I'm sorry, Nick. I know how excited you were, but until we can understand what all of these strange symbols mean...without Ignis' help, we may *never* figure them out."

Nick was still smiling when he pointed to one of the screens which, now that the ship was powered, had lit up.

"You mean symbols like this one, which means 'Main Console'?" Nick pressed the button and a new screen appeared. "Or this symbol, which means 'Engine Status'?"

Kate stared at him in disbelief. "Nick, are you saying that you can read and understand what these symbols mean?"

Nick held her head in his hands. "Yes, Kate, I can! I guess it must be a gift from Ignis. Maybe they think we're more ready than they let on!"

Kate's face became serious for a moment. "Nick, do you know what this means?"

"What?"

"It means we're going to change the world, forever, and in a very big way! We'll now be able to reverse-engineer this ship in no time!" She then jumped into his arms and wrapped her legs around his waist. "Nick Reynolds, I'm just crazy about you!"

The couple stood there, wrapped up in a warm, gentle, lover's embrace for a long time, standing inside a ship built by beings from another world, out of town visitors who had saved them from certain destruction, and new friends who had just handed them an invitation to join them in the stars.

Epilogue

It seemed as if the traffic light was never going to change. Nick tapped his foot nervously on the floorboard of the car, doing everything he could to resist pulling around the car in front of him and running the red light. After waiting a few seconds longer, Nick was just preparing to jerk the wheel when the light suddenly changed to green. He raced behind the car and soon pulled around and passed it. After traveling another block, Nick arrived at the hospital. He pulled into the "Visitors" parking deck and moments later was jogging through the parking lot of Mountain View Hospital. Once inside, he hit the "Up" arrow and took the elevator to the Women's Center. As he exited the elevator, he suddenly realized he'd forgotten to pick up roses for Kate—no matter, he could pick them up later. The last thing he and Kate would want was for him to miss this event. He was about to pass the nurses' station when he was stopped by a stern, feminine voice.

"Excuse me sir, can I help you?"

"Yes, I'm looking for Kate Reynolds, I'm her husband."

"Oh, she was wondering if you were going to make it, Dr. Reynolds. She's in room 651."

"Thank you," he said, after he'd turned his back to her on his way to the room.

Kate was alone and already in a bed when he walked into the room. The baby heart monitor beeped regularly, providing valuable feedback as to the health of the unborn child. Kate looked tired, but she smiled when Nick walked into the room, and she kissed her husband when he leaned over.

"Hi honey, how are you? Are you doing okay?"

Kate narrowed her gaze for a moment. "Where have you been, mister? You knew I could only wait so long for you to get here!"

"I'm really sorry, Kate. How are the contractions?"

"They're getting more frequent. The baby should be here any moment. How did the meeting go?" Nick shook his head.

"No, Kate. We can talk about that later."

"I want to know now, Nick, tell me!" she stated firmly.

"Well—"

"Nick!"

"They approved the plans, sweetheart. We start work on building the prototype in two weeks!" Nick drew closer and his wife wrapped her arms around him and kissed him.

"That's fantastic news, honey! I can't believe it!"

"I know! Oh, Kate, I'm so glad I came here to work with you, your father, and Ignis. I feel so blessed to be here right now, with you, and our baby on the way."

The two embraced once more, before it was interrupted by constant contractions. Just ten minutes later, Henry Ignis Reynolds was born into the world; it would never be the same again.

About the Author

Jeff Horton was born in North Dakota, the youngest son of a career Air Force Master sergeant, where he spent the first four years of his life before moving to North Carolina. A somewhat voracious reader growing up, he read everything from comic books to The Bible, including stories by many popular authors such as Sir Arthur Conan Doyle, H. G. Wells, Jules Verne, Edgar Rice Burroughs, Michael Crichton, Tom Clancy, C. S. Lewis, and J. R. R. Tolkien.

Jeff Horton's novel, The Great Collapse, a story about the coming of the pulse and the end of civilization, was published in 2010. He is a member of the North Carolina Writers Network.

When he's not penning his next novel, he enjoys reading, going to church, and spending time with his family.
http://www.hortonlibrary.com/